FOOL
MOON

ALSO BY JIM BUTCHER

THE DRESDEN FILES

STORM FRONT
GRAVE PERIL
SUMMER KNIGHT
DEATH MASKS
BLOOD RITES
DEAD BEAT
PROVEN GUILTY
WHITE NIGHT
SMALL FAVOR

THE CODEX ALERA

FURIES OF CALDERON
ACADEM'S FURY
CURSOR'S FURY
CAPTAIN'S FURY

JIM BUTCHER

FOOL MOON

A NOVEL OF THE DRESDEN FILES

A ROC BOOK

294 3274

ROC
Published by New American Library, a division of
Penguin Group (USA) Inc., 375 Hudson Street,
New York, New York 10014, USA
Penguin Group (Canada), 90 Eglinton Avenue East, Suite 700, Toronto,
Ontario M4P 2Y3, Canada (a division of Pearson Penguin Canada Inc.)
Penguin Books Ltd., 80 Strand, London WC2R 0RL, England
Penguin Ireland, 25 St. Stephen's Green, Dublin 2,
Ireland (a division of Penguin Books Ltd.)
Penguin Group (Australia), 250 Camberwell Road, Camberwell, Victoria 3124,
Australia (a division of Pearson Australia Group Pty. Ltd.)
Penguin Books India Pvt. Ltd., 11 Community Centre, Panchsheel Park,
New Delhi - 110 017, India
Penguin Group (NZ), 67 Apollo Drive, Rosedale, North Shore 0632,
New Zealand (a division of Pearson New Zealand Ltd.)
Penguin Books (South Africa) (Pty.) Ltd., 24 Sturdee Avenue,
Rosebank, Johannesburg 2196, South Africa

Penguin Books Ltd., Registered Offices:
80 Strand, London WC2R 0RL, England

Published by Roc, an imprint of New American Library, a division of
Penguin Group (USA) Inc. Previously published in a Roc mass market edition.

First Roc Hardcover Printing, July 2008
10 9 8 7 6 5 4 3 2 1

Copyright © Jim Butcher, 2001
All rights reserved

RoC REGISTERED TRADEMARK—MARCA REGISTRADA

Set in Janson text
Designed by Alissa Amell

Printed in the United States of America

Chapter One

I never used to keep close track of the phases of the moon. So I didn't know that it was one night shy of being full when a young woman sat down across from me in McAnally's pub and asked me to tell her all about something that could get her killed.

"No," I said. "Absolutely not." I folded the piece of paper, with its drawings of three concentric rings of spidery symbols, and slid it back over the polished oak-wood table.

Kim Delaney frowned at me, and brushed some of her dark, shining hair back from her forehead. She was a tall woman, buxom and lovely in an old-world way, with pale, pretty skin and round cheeks well used to smiling. She wasn't smiling now.

"Oh, come on, Harry," she told me. "You're Chicago's only practicing professional wizard, and you're the only one who can help me." She leaned across the table toward me, her eyes intent. "I can't find the references for all of these symbols. No one in local circles recognizes them either. You're the only real wizard I've ever even heard of, much less know. I just want to know what these others are."

"No," I told her. "You don't want to know. You're better off forgetting this circle and concentrating on something else."

"But—"

Mac caught my attention from behind the bar by waving a hand at me, and slid a couple of plates of steaming food onto the polished surface of the crooked oak bar. He added a couple of bottles of his homemade brown ale, and my mouth started watering.

My stomach made an unhappy noise. It was almost as empty as my wallet. I would never have been able to afford dinner tonight, except that Kim had offered to buy, if I'd talk to her about something during the meal. A steak dinner was less than my usual rate, but she was pleasant company, and a sometime apprentice of mine. I knew she didn't have much money, and I had even less.

Despite my rumbling stomach, I didn't rise immediately to pick up the food. (In McAnally's pub and grill, there aren't any service people. According to Mac, if you can't get up and walk over to pick up your own order, you don't need to be there at all.) I looked around the room for a moment, with its annoying combination of low ceilings and lazily spinning fans, its thirteen carved wooden columns and its thirteen windows, plus thirteen tables arranged haphazardly to defray and scatter the residual magical effects that sometimes surrounded hungry (in other words, angry) wizards. McAnally's was a haven in a town where no one believed in magic. A lot of the crowd ate there.

"Look, Harry," Kim said. "I'm not using this for anything serious, I promise. I'm not trying any summoning or binding. It's an academic interest only. Something that's been bothering me for a while." She leaned forward and put her hand over mine, looking me in the face without looking me in the eyes, a trick that few nonpractitioners of the Art could master. She grinned and showed me the deep dimples in her cheeks.

My stomach growled again, and I glanced over at the food on the bar, waiting for me. "You're sure?" I asked her. "This is just you trying to scratch an itch? You're not using it for anything?"

"Cross my heart," she said, doing so.

I frowned. "I don't know . . ."

She laughed at me. "Oh, come *on*, Harry. It's no big deal. Look, if you don't want to tell me, never mind. I'll buy you dinner anyway. I know you're tight for money lately. Since that thing last spring, I mean."

I glowered, but not at Kim. It wasn't her fault that my main employer, Karrin Murphy, the director of Special Investigations at the Chicago Police Department, hadn't called me in for consulting work in more than a month. Most of my living for the past few years had come from serving as a special consultant to SI, but after a fracas last spring involving a dark wizard fighting a gang war for control of Chicago's drug trade, work with SI had slowly tapered off—and with it, my income.

I didn't know why Murphy hadn't been calling me in as often. I had my suspicions, but I hadn't gotten the chance to confront her about them yet. Maybe it wasn't anything I'd done. Maybe the monsters had gone on strike. Yeah, right.

The bottom line was I was strapped for cash. I'd been eating ramen noodles and soup for too many weeks. The steaks Mac had prepared smelled like heaven, even from across the room. My belly protested again, growling its neolithic craving for charred meat.

But I couldn't just go and eat the dinner without giving Kim the information she wanted. It's not that I've never welshed on a deal, but I've never done it with anyone human—and definitely not with someone who looked up to me.

Sometimes I hate having a conscience, and a stupidly thorough sense of honor.

"All right, all right," I sighed. "Let me get the dinner and I'll tell you what I know."

Kim's round cheeks dimpled again. "Thanks, Harry. This means a lot to me."

"Yeah, yeah," I told her, and got up to weave my way toward the bar, through columns and tables and so on. McAnally's had more people than usual tonight, and though Mac rarely smiled, there was a contentment to his manner that indicated that he was happy with the crowd. I snatched up the plates and bottles with a somewhat petulant attitude. It's hard to take much joy in a friend's prosperity when your own business is about to go under.

I took the food, steaks and potatoes and green beans, back to the table and sat down again, placing Kim's plate in front of her. We ate for a while, myself in sullen silence and she in hearty hunger.

"So," Kim said, finally. "What can you tell me about that?" She gestured toward the piece of paper with her fork.

I swallowed my food, took a sip of the rich ale, and picked up the paper again. "All right. This is a figure of High magic. Three of them, really, one inside the other, like layered walls. Remember what I told you about magical circles?"

Kim nodded. "They either hold something out or keep it in. Most work on magic energies or creatures of the Nevernever, but mortal creatures can cross the circles and break them."

"Right," I said. "That's what this outermost circle of symbols is. It's a barrier against creatures of spirit and magical forces. These symbols here, here, here, are the key ones." I pointed out the squiggles in question.

Kim nodded eagerly. "I got the outer one. What's the next?"

"The second circle is more of a spell barrier to *mortal* flesh. It wouldn't work if all you used was a ring of symbols. You'd need something else, stones or gems or something, spaced between the drawings." I took another bite of steak.

Kim frowned at the paper, and then at me. "And then what would that do?"

"Invisible wall," I told her. "Like bricks. Spirits, magic, could go right through it, but mortal flesh couldn't. Neither could a thrown rock, bullets, anything purely physical."

"I see," she said, excited. "Sort of a force field."

I nodded. "Something like that."

Her cheeks glowed with excitement, and her eyes shone. "I *knew* it. And what's this last one?"

I squinted at the innermost ring of symbols, frowning. "A mistake."

"What do you mean?"

"I mean that it's just gobbledygook. It doesn't mean anything useful. Are you sure you copied this correctly?"

Kim's mouth twisted into a frown. "I'm sure, I'm sure. I was careful."

I studied her face for a moment. "If I read the symbols correctly, it's a third wall. Built to withhold creatures of flesh *and* spirit. Neither mortal nor spirit but somewhere in between."

She frowned. "What kind of creatures are like that?"

I shrugged. "None," I said, and officially, it was true. The White Council of wizards did not allow the discussion of demons that could be called to earth, beings of spirit that could gather flesh to themselves. Usually, a spirit-circle was enough to stop all but the most powerful demons or Elder Things of the outer reaches of the Nevernever. But this third circle was built to stop things that could transcend those kinds of boundaries. It was a cage for demonic demigods and archangels.

Kim wasn't buying my answer. "I don't see why anyone would make a circle like this to contain nothing, Harry."

I shrugged. "People don't always do reasonable, sensible things. They're like that."

She rolled her eyes at me. "Come on, Harry. I'm not a baby. You don't have to shelter me."

"And you," I told her, "don't need to know what kind of thing that third circle was built to contain. You don't want to know. Trust me."

She glowered at me for a long moment, then sipped at her ale and shrugged. "All right. Circles have to be empowered, right? You have to know how to switch them on, like lights?"

"Something like that. Sure."

"How would a person turn this one on?"

I stared at her for a long time.

"Harry?" she asked.

"You don't need to know that, either. Not for an academic interest. I don't know what you've got in mind, Kim, but leave it alone. Forget it. Walk away, before you get hurt."

"Harry, I am not—"

"Save it," I told her. "You're sitting on a tiger cage, Kim." I thumped a finger on the paper for emphasis. "And you wouldn't need it if you weren't planning on trying to stick a tiger in there."

Her eyes glittered, and she lifted her chin. "You don't think I'm strong enough."

"Your strength's got nothing to do with it," I said. "You don't have the training. You don't have the knowledge. I wouldn't expect a kid in grade school to be able to sit down and figure out college calculus. And I don't expect it of you, either." I leaned forward. "You don't know enough yet to be toying with this sort of thing, Kim. And even if you did, even if you did manage to become a full-fledged wizard, I'd still tell you not to do it. You mess this up and you could get a lot of people hurt."

"*If* I was planning to do that, it's my business, Harry." Her eyes were bright with anger. "You don't have the right to choose for me."

"No," I told her. "I've got the responsibility to help you make the right choice." I curled the paper in my fingers and crushed it, then tossed it aside, to the floor. She stabbed her fork into a cut of steak, a sharp, vicious gesture. "Look, Kim," I said. "Give it some time. When you're older, when you've had more experience . . ."

"You aren't so much older than me," Kim said.

I shifted uncomfortably in my seat. "I've had a lot of training. And I started young." My own ability with magic, far in excess of my years and education, wasn't a subject I wanted to explore. So I tried to shift the direction of the conversation. "How is this fall's fund-raiser going?"

"It's not," she said. She leaned back wearily in her seat. "I'm tired of trying to pry money out of people to save the planet they're poisoning or the animals they're killing. I'm tired of writing letters and doing marches for causes no one believes in anymore." She rubbed at her eyes. "I'm just tired."

"Look, Kim. Try to get some rest. And please, please don't play with that circle. Promise me."

She tossed her napkin down, left a few bills on the table, and stood up. "Enjoy your meal, Harry," she said. "And thanks for nothing."

I stood up as well. "Kim," I said. "Wait a minute."

But she ignored me. She stalked off toward the door, her skirt swaying along with her long hair. She cut an impressive, statuesque figure. I could feel the anger bubbling off her. One of the ceiling fans shuddered and let out a puff of smoke as she walked under it, then whirled down to a halt. She raced up the short flight of stairs and exited the bar, banging the door shut behind her. People watched her leave, then glanced back to me, speculation on their faces.

I sat back down, frustrated. Dammit. Kim was one of several people I had coached through the difficult period surrounding the discovery of their innate magical talents. It made me feel like crap to withhold information from her, but she had been playing with fire. I couldn't let her do that. It was my responsibility to help protect her from such things, until she knew enough to realize how dangerous they were.

To say nothing of what the White Council would think of a nonwizard toying with major summoning circles. The White Council didn't take chances with things like that. They just acted, decisively, and they weren't always particular about people's lives and safety when they did it.

I had done the right thing. Keeping that kind of information out of Kim's hands had been the right decision. I had been protecting her from danger she didn't, couldn't, fully appreciate.

I had done the right thing—even if she had trusted me to provide answers for her, as I had in the past, when teaching her to contain and control her modest magical talents. Even if she had trusted me to show her the answers she needed, to be her guide through the darkness.

I'd done the right thing.

Dammit.

My stomach was soured. I didn't want any more of Mac's delicious meal, steak or no steak. I didn't feel like I'd earned it.

I was sipping ale and thinking dark thoughts when the door opened again. I didn't look up, occupied as I was with brooding, a famous pastime of wizards everywhere. And then a shadow fell over me.

"Sitting here pouting," Murphy said. She bent over and absently picked up the wadded scrap of paper I had tossed aside earlier, tucking it tidily into her coat pocket rather than letting it lie about as clutter on the floor. "That's not much like you, Harry."

I glanced up at Murphy. I didn't have far to look. Karrin Murphy wasn't much more than five feet tall. She'd gotten her golden hair cut, from shoulder length to something far shorter, and a little longer in front than in back. It was a punky sort of look, and very appealing with her blue eyes and upturned nose. She was dressed for the weather in what must have been her at-home clothes: dark jeans, a flannel shirt, hiking boots, and a heavy woodsman's jacket. She was wearing her badge on her belt.

Murphy was extremely cute, for a grown adult who also held a black belt in aikido, and had several marksmanship awards from Chicago PD. She was a real professional, one who had fought and clawed her way up the ranks to become full lieutenant. She'd made enemies along the way, and one of them had seen to it that she was put in charge of Special Investigations soon after.

"Hello there, Murphy," I told her. I took a swig of ale and said, "Long time, no see." I tried to keep my voice even, but I'm pretty sure she heard the anger in it.

"Look, Harry—"

"Did you read the editorial in the *Tribune*? The one criticizing you for wasting the city's money hiring a 'charlatan psychic named Harry Dresden'? I guess you must have, since I haven't heard from you since it came out."

She rubbed at the bridge of her nose. "I don't have time for this."

I ignored her. "Not that I blame you. I mean, not many of the good taxpayers of Chicago believe in magic, or wizards. Of course, not many of them have seen what you and I have. You know. When we worked together. Or when I was saving your life."

Her eyes tightened at the edges. "I need you. We've got a situation."

"You need me? We haven't talked for more than a month, and you need me all of a sudden? I've got an office and a telephone and everything, Lieutenant. You don't need to track me down here while I'm having dinner."

"I'll tell the killer to be sure to operate during business hours next time," Murphy said. "But I need you to help me find him."

I straightened in my chair, frowning. "There's been a murder? Something in my field?"

Murphy flashed a hard smile at me. "I hope you didn't have anything more important to do."

I felt my jaw grow tense. "No. I'm ready." I stood up.

"Well then," she said, turning and walking away. "Shall we go?"

Chapter Two

Murphy declined to ride in the Blue Beetle, my old Volkswagen bug.

The Beetle wasn't really blue, not anymore. One of the doors had been replaced with a green duplicate, the other one with white, when something with claws had shredded the originals. The hood had been slagged by fire, and my mechanic, Mike, had replaced it with the hood from a red vehicle. The important thing is that the Beetle runs, even if it doesn't do it very fast, and I'm comfortable with the car. Mike has declared that the VW bug is the easiest car in the world to repair, and so that's what I drive. He keeps it running eight or nine days in ten. That's phenomenal.

Technology tends to foul up around wizards—flip on a light switch, and it'll be the time the bulb burns out. Drive past a streetlight, and it'll pick just then to flicker and die. Whatever can go wrong will, automobiles included.

I didn't think it made much sense for Murphy to risk her vehicle when she could have taken mine, but she said she'd take her chances.

She didn't speak as she drove her Saturn down the JFK, out toward Rosemont. I watched her, uncomfortable, as we went. She was in a hurry, taking a few too many chances cutting in and out of traffic, and I put on my seat belt. At least we weren't on her motorcycle.

"Murph," I asked her, "where's the fire?"

She glanced aside at me. "I want you out there before some other people show up."

"Press?" I couldn't quite keep a nasty slur out of the word.

She shrugged. "Whoever."

I frowned at her, but she didn't say anything else—which seemed typical. Murphy didn't speak much to me anymore. We rode the rest of the way in silence, exited the JFK, and pulled into the parking lot of a half-completed little strip mall. We got out of the car.

A jet came in, low, heading for O'Hare International Airport, only a few miles to the west. I squinted at it for a moment, and then frowned at Murphy as a uniformed officer led us toward a building surrounded by police tape. There was an abundance of light, the moon overhead bright silver and almost a completely round circle. I cast an enormous, gangly shadow as I walked, my duster flapping around my legs. It towered beside Murphy's far smaller shadow ahead of me.

"Murphy?" I said. "Aren't we outside Chicago city limits?"

"Yeah," Murphy said shortly.

"Uh. Then aren't we out of your jurisdiction, technically?"

"People need help wherever they can get it, Dresden. And the last several killings happened in Chicago, so we want to look at this firsthand. I already worked things out with the local force. It's not really an issue."

"Several killings?" I said. "Several? As in more than one? Murphy, slow down."

But she didn't. Instead, she led me into a roomy building that proved to be under construction, though all the exterior work was finished. Some of the windows were still covered with board. I didn't see the sign on the building's front doors until I got close.

"The Varsity?" I said, reading it. "I thought Marcone burned it down last spring."

"Mmm-hmm," Murphy said, glancing at me over her shoulder. "Relocated and rebuilding."

Chicago's resident crime lord, Gentleman Johnny Marcone, was the robber baron of the mean streets. He kept all the rough business inside the city proper, leaving his legitimate interests out in the suburbs, like here in Rosemont. Last spring, when I had confronted him in his club, a previous incarnation of the Varsity, about a deadly new drug on the streets, the place had wound up burning to the ground.

After the whole mess was over, word got out that the drug dealer I'd taken out had been Marcone's enemy, and that I had nuked him at the crime lord's request. I hadn't refuted the rumor. It was easier to let people talk than to force Marcone to make an issue of things.

Inside the building, the floors were rough, unfinished. Someone had turned on a couple of halogen work lights, and they cast the interior into brilliant, clear white light. There was drywall dust everywhere. There were a few card tables set up, with workmen's tools left out on them in places. Plastic buckets of paint, tarps, and a sack of new paintbrushes waited for use off to one side. I didn't notice the blood until Murphy put her arm out in front of me to keep me from walking into it.

"Wake up, Dresden," she said. Her voice was grim.

I stopped, and looked down. Blood. A lot of blood. It began near my feet, where a long splatter had reached out like an arm from a drowning man, staining the dusty floor with scarlet. My eyes followed the path of the long bloodstain back to a pool, maybe an eighth of an inch deep, surrounding a mound of ripped cloth and torn meat that must have been the corpse.

My stomach quailed, threatening to eject the bites of steak I'd taken earlier that evening, but I forced it down. I walked in a circle around the body, keeping my distance. The corpse was, I guessed, that of a male in his thirties. He had been a large man, with a short, spiky haircut. He had fallen onto his side, facing away from me, his arms curled up toward his head, his legs up toward his vitals. A weapon, a little automatic pistol, lay seven or eight feet away, uselessly out of the victim's reach.

I walked around the corpse until I could see the face.

Whatever had killed him, it hadn't been human. His face

was gone, simply torn away. Something had ripped his lips off. I could see his bloodstained teeth. His nose had been torn all the way up one side, and part of it dangled toward the floor. His head was misshapen, as though some enormous pressure had been put upon his temples, warping his skull in.

His eyes were gone. Torn out of his head. Bitten out. There were the ragged slash marks of fangs all around the edges of the sockets.

I closed my eyes, tightly. I took a deep breath. Another. A third. That didn't help. The body stank, a sickly sewer-smell that rose up from the torn innards. My stomach wanted to roll up my throat, out my mouth, and onto the floor.

I could remember the other details, even with my eyes closed, and catalogued them neatly for later reference. The victim's jacket and shirt had been torn to bloody ribbons along his forearms, in defensive wounds. His hands and arms were a mass of pulped, ripped meat, the palms and fingers slashed to ragged lumps. The curl of his body hid his abdomen from me, but that was where the blood was pooling from, spreading out like ink from a spilled bottle. The stench only confirmed that he had been eviscerated.

I turned away from the corpse and opened my eyes, staring down at the floor.

"Harry?" Murphy said, from the far side of the body. The note of hardness that had been in her voice all evening was absent. She hadn't moved while I had done my cursory examination.

"I recognize him," I said. "At least, I think I do. You'll need to check dental records or something, to be sure."

I could hear her frown in her words. "Yeah? Who was he?"

"I don't know his name. I always called him Spike. For the haircut. He was one of Johnny Marcone's bodyguards."

Murphy was quiet for a moment, then said, succinctly, "Shit."

"What, Murph?" I looked back at her, without looking down at Spike's mangled remains.

Murphy's face was set in concern, for me, her blue eyes gentle. I saw her wipe the expression away, as quickly as a shadow crosses the floor, a smoothing of lines that left her features neutral. I guess she hadn't expected me to turn to her. "Take a look around a little more," she said. "Then we'll talk."

"What am I looking for?" I asked her.

"You'll know it," she said. Then added, in a whisper that I think she didn't intend me to hear, "I hope."

I turned back to my work, and looked around the room. Off to one side, one of the windows was broken. Near it was a table, lying askew on the floor, its legs warped and bent. I walked over to it.

Broken glass littered the ground around the collapsed table. Since the glass was on the inside of the building, something must have come in through the window. There was blood on several of the broken pieces of glass. I picked up one of the larger ones and frowned at it. The blood was dark red, and not yet wholly dried. I took a white handkerchief from my pocket, folded the shard of glass into it, and then slipped it into the pocket of my duster.

I rose and paced over the floor, my eyes downcast, studying the dust. In one spot, it was rubbed almost clean off the floor, as though a struggle had taken place there without blood being spilled. In another spot, where the halogen lamps didn't quite reach, there was a pool of silver moonlight below a window. I knelt down beside it.

In the center of the pool was a paw print, in the dust, a paw print almost as big as my spread hand. Canine. Dots at the tips of the paw spoke of heavy nails, almost claws.

I looked up through the window at the rounded silver shape of the almost-full moon.

"Oh, hell," I breathed. "Oh, hell."

Murphy came toward me and watched me silently for a moment, waiting. I licked my lips, stood up, and turned to her. "You've got problems."

"No kidding. Talk to me, Dresden."

I nodded, then pointed at the window. "The attacker probably came in there. He went after the victim, attacked him, got the gun away from him, and killed him. It's the attacker's blood on the window. They struggled a while, over there by that clean spot, maybe, and Spike made a break for the door. He didn't make it there. He got torn to pieces first."

I turned toward Murphy, looking down at her solemnly. "You've had other murders happen in the same way. Probably about four weeks ago, when the moon was last full. Those were the other killings you were talking about."

Murphy glanced at my face for a moment, keeping her eyes off mine, and nodded her head. "Yeah. Four weeks ago, almost exactly. But no one else picked up the full moon angle. Just me."

"Uh-huh. Then you should see this, too," I said. I led her over to the window and showed her the paw print in the dust beneath it. She regarded it in silence.

"Harry," she said after a minute. "Are there such things as werewolves?" She brushed a strand of hair back from her cheek, a small and oddly vulnerable gesture. She folded her arms over her stomach, as though she were cold.

I nodded. "Yeah. Not like you see in the movies, but yeah. I figure that's what you got going here."

She drew in a deep breath. "All right, then. All right. What can you tell me? What do I need to know?"

I opened my mouth to speak, but I didn't get a chance to say anything. There was a brief bout of shouting outside, and then the front doors of the building banged open. Murphy tensed, and I saw her mouth set in a hard little line. Her back straightened, and she stopped hugging herself, putting her fists on her hips.

"Goddammit," she said. "How do those assholes get everywhere so fast?"

I stepped forward, so that I could see. A quartet of people in suits came through the door, fanned out in an almost military diamond formation. The man in front was not quite as tall as me, but still very tall, six feet and three or four inches. His hair was jet black, as were his eyebrows, while his eyes were a shade of grey as pale as wood smoke. His dark blue suit fit him well, and I had the impression that it concealed an athletic build, in spite of the fact that he had obviously seen more than four decades. A blue identification badge reading "FBI" in huge, obnoxious letters dangled from one lapel.

"Secure the scene," he said, his voice deep, tense. "Lieutenant Murphy, what the hell are you doing on a crime scene out of your jurisdiction?"

"Nice to see you, too, Agent Denton," Murphy said in a flat tone. "You get around fast."

"I told you that you weren't welcome on this investigation," Denton said, his words crisp. His grey eyes flashed, and I saw a vein bulge rhythmically on his forehead. His gaze shifted to me. "Who is this?"

"Har—" I started to say, but Murphy's snort cut over my words.

"No one," she said. She flashed me a look that said, very clearly, to shut up. That annoyed the hell out of me.

"Harry Dresden," I said, making the words loud and clear. Murphy and I exchanged a glare.

"Ah," Denton said. "The charlatan. I've read about you in the *Tribune*." His clear, tense gaze returned to Murphy. "You and your psychic friend might want to step out of the way. There's police work being done here. The real kind, where we worry about fingerprints, fibers, genetic matches—silly things like that."

Murphy's eyes narrowed, along with mine, but if the twin glares affected Denton, it didn't show in his face. Murphy and Denton had a brief staring match, her fury against his steely intensity.

"Agent Benn!" Denton called.

A woman, not quite into her thirties, with a shoulder-length mane of hair gone prematurely grey, turned toward us from her intent contemplation of the corpse. She had olive skin, deep, green eyes, and a thin, severe mouth. She walked toward us with a sort of hard-muscled sensuality, moving like someone who is capable of being fast and dangerous when necessary. Of the four FBI agents who had entered the room, she was the only one obviously sporting a weapon. Her jacket was unbuttoned, and I could see the straps of her shoulder rig against the white of her shirt.

"Yes, sir," Benn said. Her voice was very quiet. Her eyes took up a position midway between Murphy and me, looking at neither of us while watching us both.

"Please escort these two *civilians*," Denton stressed the word, "from the crime scene."

Benn nodded once, but didn't say anything in reply. Just waited. I gathered myself to go, but paused. Murphy planted her feet and lowered her arms casually to her sides. I recognized the stubborn out-thrust angle of her jaw. She had that look she got when she was behind on points in one of her martial-arts tournaments. Murphy was ready to fight. Damn. I had to get her cooled off before we could accomplish anything.

"Murphy," I said, quietly. "Can we talk outside?"

"Like hell," Murphy said. "Whoever this killer is, he's knocked off half a dozen people in the last month. I'm here, and I'm after this man. The Rosemont department has given their consent for me to be here." Murphy glared up at Benn. The FBI agent had her by a considerable margin of reach and muscle. I saw Benn's eyes narrow, her shoulders grow tenser.

"Do you have that in writing?" Denton demanded. The vein in his head throbbed more angrily. "And do you really think you want me reporting this to your superiors, Lieutenant?"

"Don't push me, Denton," Murphy said, her voice hot. I winced.

"Look, Murphy," I said. I put a hand on her shoulder. "Let's just go outside for a minute." I squeezed, just a little.

Murphy turned back toward me. She chanced a brief glance up at my eyes, and then relaxed a little, a flicker of uncertainty crossing her features. She started to ease down, and I let my breath out. I definitely didn't want this dissolving into violence. It wouldn't accomplish anything.

"Get them out of here," Denton said, and there was a note to his voice that I didn't like.

Benn didn't give us any warning. She just moved, fast and hard, stepping toward Murphy and flicking some sort of martial-arts blow I wasn't familiar with toward her temple. There was a quick blur of motion. Murphy's hands got there before the blow landed, and she turned, somehow levering Benn's weight off from her legs and slamming the grey-maned woman hard into a wall.

Benn's expression went from shocked and surprised to furious in the space of half a second. Her hand dipped into her jacket, hesitated for half a second, and then resumed motion. She drew her gun with an expert's precision, smooth and quick without seeming hurried. Her green eyes blazed. I threw myself at Murphy, colliding with her and driving her over and down as the gun went off, louder than a close clap of thunder in the interior of the half-finished restaurant. We landed in a heap on the dusty floor.

"Benn!" Denton shouted. He lunged for her, heedless of the gun, and got between the armed woman and us. I could hear him talking to her in a low, urgent voice.

"You crazy bitch!" I shouted. "What is the matter with you?"

The two other FBI guys and several patrol officers from outside came running. Murphy grunted and elbowed me in the gut, urgently. I grunted back and moved off of her. Both of us climbed to our feet unhurt.

"What the hell happened?" demanded one of the officers, an older man with thinning grey hair.

Denton turned to the officer, calm and cool. "Misfire. There was a misunderstanding and Agent Benn's weapon accidentally discharged."

The officer rubbed at his scalp and eyed Murphy. "Is that true, Lieutenant?"

"Like hell!" I said. I pointed a finger at Benn. "This crazy bi—"

Murphy jammed an elbow into my stomach and glared at me. "That's true," Murphy said, while I rubbed at my gut. "It happened just like Agent Denton said. An accident."

I stared at her. "Murph, give me a break. This woman—"

"Had an accident with her weapon," Murphy said, voice hard. "Could have happened to anyone." Murphy turned her glare on the aging officer, and he blinked mildly at her, then shrugged.

Denton turned back to us and studied Murphy intently for a second. Then he nodded. "Roj, George. Why don't you two make sure the Lieutenant is all right and help her to her car?"

"Sure, sure, Phil," said a skinny kid with red hair, big ears, and freckles. "Uh, Mr. Dresden, Lieutenant Murphy. Why don't we go outside and get some air? I'm Roger Harris, and this is Agent Wilson."

The other FBI guy, a bulky, overweight man in his late forties, his hair receding and his gut overhanging his belt, just beckoned us to follow him and walked toward the door. Murphy glared at Denton for a moment, then spun on her heel and stalked after the bulky Wilson. I followed her.

"I can't believe that. You all right? Why the hell didn't you tell them what she did?" I asked Murphy, sotto voce.

"That bitch," Murphy said back, not nearly as quiet. "She tried to sucker punch me."

"She tried to *ventilate* you, Murph," I countered.

Murphy let out a breath between her teeth, but kept walking. I glanced back at the room behind us and saw Spike's torn and mangled body being surrounded by more police tape. Forensics had arrived, and the team was getting set to sweep the room. Denton was kneeling down beside Benn, who had her face in her hands, and looked as though she were weeping. Denton was watching me, his grey eyes calculating and expressionless, filing me away under "tall, slender, dark hair, dark eyes, hawkish features, no visible scars."

I stared at him for a minute and got a hunch, a solid intuition of which I was completely sure. Denton was hiding something. He knew something, and he wasn't talking. Don't ask me how I knew it, but something about him, about the way the veins bulged in his forehead, or the way he held his neck so stiffly, made me think so.

"Um," the kid, Harris, said. I blinked and turned to him. He opened the door for Murphy and me, and we walked outside. "Maybe give Deborah some slack. She's really stressed out about these Lobo killings. She hasn't slept much the past month. She knew one of the guys who got killed. She's been tense ever since."

"Shut up, Harris," the overweight Agent Wilson said, his tone disgusted. "Just shut up." He turned to the two of us and said in a calm voice, "Get the hell out of here. I don't want to see either of you around a scene that isn't on your turf, Lieutenant Murphy. Internal Affairs has enough to do, don't you think?"

He turned and went back into the building. The redheaded kid gave us an apologetic, awkward smile, and then hurried to catch up with the overweight agent. I saw him shoot a glance back at me, his expression thoughtful. Then he was gone. The door shut, leaving Murphy and me on the outside, away from the investigation and the evidence at the crime scene.

I looked up through the clear night at the almost-full moon. Werewolves jumping through windows at gangster's lackeys in unfinished restaurants. A mangled corpse in the middle of a blood-drenched floor. Berserk FBI field agents drawing guns and shooting to kill. A little kung fu, a little John Wayne, and a few casual threats.

So far, I thought, my nerves jangling, just one more night on the job.

Chapter
Three

My stomach roiled around with disgust at the macabre sights inside the building, and with tension at what had nearly happened. One of my ears was still ringing from the sound of the gunshot. I was starting to shake all over now, the adrenaline rush fading and leaving me jumpy and wired. I stuck my hands in my duster's pockets, careful of the bloodstained shard of glass wrapped in my handkerchief, and turned my face into the wind, closing my eyes.

Relax, Harry, I told myself. Calm down. Breathe in and out, and just keep doing it. See? You aren't dead. Dead people don't breathe like that. You aren't Spike, all torn to pieces on the floor. You don't have any bullet holes in you, either. You're alive, and Murphy's all right, and you don't have to look at that eyeless face anymore.

But I could see the torn body, still, behind my eyelids. I could smell the ghastly stench of his opened innards. I could remember the blood, sticky on the dusty floor, congealing, thick with tiny flecks of drywall. I tasted bile in my throat, and fought to keep from throwing up.

I wanted to scream, to run, to wave my arms and kick something until I felt better. I could understand Agent Benn's reaction, almost, if she had been working a string of killings like the one I'd just seen. You can't stare at that much blood for very long without starting to see more of it everywhere else.

I just kept taking deep breaths, in and out. The wind was cool and fresh in my face, sharp with the smells of the coming autumn. October evenings in Chicago are chilly, breezy, but I love them anyway. It's my favorite time of year to be outside. I eventually calmed down. Murphy must have been doing the same thing beside me, making herself relax. We both started walking back toward the car at the same time, no words needing to be passed between us.

"I . . ." Murphy began, and fell silent again. I didn't look at her, didn't speak. "I'm sorry, Harry. I lost control. Agent Denton is an asshole, but he does his job, and he was right. Technically speaking, I didn't have any right to be on the scene. I didn't mean to drag you into all this."

She unlocked the doors and got in the car. I got in the passenger side, then reached out and plucked the keys from her hand as she began to start the engine. She quirked her head at me, narrowing her eyes.

I closed my hands around the keys. "Just sit down and relax for a while, Murph. We need to talk."

"I don't think that's a good idea, Harry," she said.

"This is the thanks I get for saving your life. Twice, now. You're going to hold out on me."

"You should know how it works," she said, scowling. But she settled back in her seat and looked out the windshield of the car. We could see the police, forensics, and the FBI suits moving back and forth inside the building. We were both quiet for a long time.

The funny thing was that the problems between Murphy and me came from the same source as the problems with Kim Delaney earlier tonight. Murphy had needed to know something to pursue an investigation. I could have given her the information—but it would have put her in danger to do so. I'd refused to say anything, and when I'd pursued the trail by myself all the way to its end, there had been some burning buildings and a corpse or two. There wasn't enough evidence to bring any charges against me, and the killer we'd been after had been dealt with. But Murphy hadn't ever really forgiven me for cutting her out of the loop.

In the intervening months, she'd called me in for work several times, and I'd given the best service I could. But it had been cool between us. Professional. Maybe it was time to try to bridge that gap again.

"Look, Murph," I said. "We've never really talked about what happened, last spring."

"We didn't talk about it while it was happening," she said, her tone crisp as autumn leaves. "Why should we start now? That was last spring. It's October."

"Give me a break, Murphy. I wanted to tell you more, but I couldn't."

"Let me guess. Cat had your tongue?" she said sweetly.

"You know I wasn't one of the bad guys. You have to know that by now. Hell's bells, I risked my neck to save you."

Murphy shook her head, staring straight forward. "That's not the point."

"No? Then what is?"

"The point, Dresden, is that you lied to me. You refused to give me information that I needed to do my job. When I bring you in on one of my investigations, I am *trusting* you. I don't just go around trusting people. Never have." She took a grip on the steering wheel, her knuckles whitening. "Less than ever, now."

I winced. That stung. What's worse, she was in the right. "Some of what I knew . . . It was dangerous, Murph. It could have gotten you killed."

Her blue eyes fixed on me with a glare that made me lean back against the car door. "I am *not* your daughter, Dresden," she said, in a very soft, calm voice. "I am not some porcelain doll on a shelf. I'm a police officer. I catch the bad guys and I put their asses away, and if it comes down to it, I take a bullet so that some poor housewife or CPA doesn't have to." She got her gun out of its shoulder holster, checked the ammo and the safety, and replaced it. "I don't need your protection."

"Murphy, wait," I said hastily. "I didn't do it to piss you off. I'm your friend. Always have been."

She looked away from me as an officer with a flashlight walked past the car, shining the light about on the ground as he looked for exterior evidence. "You were my friend, Dresden. Now . . ." Murphy shook her head once and set her jaw. "Now, I don't know."

There wasn't much I could say to that. But I couldn't just leave things there. In spite of all the time that had gone by, I hadn't tried to look at things from her point of view. Murphy wasn't a wizard. She had almost no knowledge of the world of the supernatural, the world that the great religion of Science had been failing to banish since the Renaissance. She had nothing to use against some of the things she encountered, no weapon but the knowledge that I was able to give her—and last spring I had taken that weapon away from her, left her defenseless and unprepared. It must have been hell for Murphy, to daily place herself at odds with things that didn't make any sense, things that made forensics teams just shake their heads.

That's what Special Investigations did. They were the team specially appointed by the mayor of Chicago to investigate all the "unusual crimes" that happened in the city. Public opinion, the Church, and official policy still frowned at any references to magic, the supernatural, vampires, or wizards; but the creatures of the spirit world still lurked about, trolls under bridges, cradle-robbing faeries, ghosts and spooks and boogers of every kind. They still terrorized and hurt people, and some of the statistics I'd put together indicated that things were only getting worse, not better. Someone had to try to stop it. In Chicago or any of its sprawling suburbs, that person was Karrin Murphy, and her SI team.

She had held the position longer than any of her many predecessors—because she had been open to the idea that there might be more than was dreamt of in Horatio's books. Because she used the services of the country's only wizard for hire.

I didn't know what to say, so my mouth just started acting on its own. "Karrin. I'm sorry."

Silence lay between us for a long, long time.

She gave a little shiver, finally, and shook her head. "All right," she said, "but if I bring you in on this, Harry, I want your word. No secrets, this time. Not to protect me. Not for anything." She stared out the window, her features softened in the light of the moon and distant streetlights, more gentle.

"Murphy," I said, "I can't promise that. How can you ask me to—"

Her face flashed with anger and she reached for my hand. She did something to one of my fingers that made a quick pain shoot up my arm, and I jerked my hand back by reflex, dropping the keys. She caught them, and jammed one of them in the ignition.

I winced, shaking my stinging fingers for a moment. Then I covered her hand with mine.

"Okay," I said. "All right. I promise. No secrets."

She glanced at me, at my eyes for a breath, and then looked away. She started the car and drove from the parking lot. "All right," she said. "I'll tell you. I'll tell you because I need every bit of help I can get. Because if we don't nail this thing, this werewolf, we're going to have another truckload of corpses on our hands this month. And," she sighed, "because if we don't, I'm going to be out of a job. And you'll probably end up in jail."

Chapter Four

"Jail?" I said. "*Jail?* Hell, Murphy. Were you planning on mentioning this to me anytime soon?"

She shot me an irritated scowl, headlights of cars going the opposite way on the highway flaring across her face. "Don't even start with me, Harry. I've had a long month."

A dozen questions tried to fight their way out of my mouth. The one that ended up winning was, "Why didn't you call me in on the other killings, last month?"

Murphy turned her eyes back to the road. "I wanted to. Believe me. But I couldn't. Internal Affairs started riding me about what happened with Marcone and Victor Sells last spring. Someone got the idea that I was in cahoots with Marcone. That I helped to murder one of his competitors and took out the ThreeEye drug ring. And so they were poking around pretty hard."

I felt an abrupt twinge of guilt. "Because I was on the scene. You had that warrant out for me and then had it rescinded. And then there were all those rumors about me and Marcone, after the whole thing was over . . ."

Murphy's lips compressed, and she nodded. "Yeah."

"And if you'd have tried to tell me about it, it would have been throwing gasoline on the fire." I rubbed at my forehead. And it would have gotten me looked at harder, too, by whoever was investigating Murphy. She had been protecting me. I hadn't even considered what those rumors Marcone had spread might do to anyone besides myself. Way to go, Harry.

"One thing you're not is stupid, Dresden," she confirmed.

"A little naive, sometimes, but never stupid. IA couldn't turn anything up, but there are enough people who are certain I'm dirty that, along with the people who already don't like me, they can screw me over pretty hard, given the chance."

"That's why you didn't make an issue out of what Agent Benn did," I guessed. "You're trying to keep everything quiet."

"Right," Murphy said. "I'd get ripped open from ass to ears if IA got word of me so much as bending the rules, much less tussling with one of the bureau's agents. Believe me, Denton might look like a jerk, but at least he isn't convinced that I'm dirty. He'll play fair."

"And this is where the killings come in. Right?"

Instead of answering, she cut into the slow lane and slowed to a leisurely pace. I half turned toward her in my seat, to watch her. It was while I did this that I noticed the headlights of another car drift across a couple lanes of traffic to drop into the slow lane behind us. I didn't say anything about it to Murphy, but kept a corner of my eye on the car.

"Right," Murphy said. "The Lobo killings. They started last month, one night before the full moon. We had a couple of gangbangers torn to pieces down at Rainbow Beach. At first, everyone figured it for an animal attack. Bizarre, but who knew, right? Anyway, it was weird, so they handed the investigation to me."

"All right," I said. "What happened then?"

"The next night, it was a little old lady walking past Washington Park. Killed the same way. And it just wasn't *right*, you know? Our forensics guys hadn't turned up anything useful, so I asked in the FBI. They've got access to resources I can't always get to. High-tech forensics labs, that kind of thing."

"And you let the djinni out of the bottle," I guessed.

"Something like that. FBI forensics, that redheaded kid with them, turned up some irregularities in the apparent dentition of the attackers. Said that the tooth marks didn't match genuine wolves or dogs. Said that the paw prints we found were off, too.

Didn't match real wolves." She gave a little shudder and said, "That's when I started thinking it might be something else. You know? They figured that someone was trying to make it *look* like a wolf attack. With this whole wolf motif, someone started calling the perpetrator the Lobo killer."

I nodded, frowning. The headlights were still behind us. "Just a crazy thought: Have you considered telling them the truth? That we might be dealing with a werewolf here?"

Murphy sneered. "Not a chance. They hire conservatives for jobs at the bureau. People who don't believe in ghosts and goblins and all that crap out there that I come to you about. They said that the murders must have been done by some sort of cult or pack of psychos. That they must have furnished themselves with weapons made out of wolf teeth and nails. Left symbolic paw prints around. That's why all the marks and tracks were off. I got Carmichael to check up on you, but your answering service said you were in Minnesota on a call."

"Yeah. Someone saw something in a lake," I confirmed. "What happened after that?"

"All hell broke loose. Three bums in Burnham Park, the next night, and they weren't just dead, they were *shredded*. Worse than that guy tonight. And on the last night of the full moon, an old man outside a liquor store. Then the night after that, we had a businessman and his driver torn up in a parking garage. IA was right there breathing down my neck the whole time, too. Observing everything." She shook her head with a grimace.

"That last victim. All the others were outside, and in a bad part of town. Businessman in a parking garage doesn't fit that pattern."

"Yeah," Murphy said. "James Harding III. One of the last of the red-hot industrialists. He and John Marcone are business partners in some development projects up in the Northwest."

"And tonight, we have another victim linked to Marcone."

"Yeah." Murphy nodded. "I'm not sure what's scarier. Thinking that these are just regular animal attacks, that they're being done by a bunch of psychos with knives edged with wolf teeth, or that they're organized werewolves." She let out a strained little laugh. "That still sounds crazy, even to me. Yes, Your Honor, the victim was killed by a werewolf."

"Let me guess. After the full moon it got quiet."

Murphy nodded. "IA wrapped up with inconclusive findings, and nothing much else happened. No one else died. Until tonight. And we've got four more nights of bright moonlight left, if whoever they are sticks to their pattern."

"You sure there's more than one?" I asked.

"Yeah," Murphy said. "There's bite marks, or bitelike marks, according to Agent Denton, from at least three different weapons. As far as all the lab guys are concerned, it could be multiple perpetrators, but there's no way for forensics to be sure."

"Unless it's real werewolves we're dealing with. In which case each set of marks goes with a different set of teeth, and we're looking at a pack."

Murphy nodded. "But there's no way I'm going to just come out and tell them that. That would put the nails in my career's coffin."

"Uh-huh," I said. "This is the part where you tell me about your job being in danger."

She grimaced. "They only need a good reason to get rid of me, now. If I don't catch these guys, whoever they are, politics will hang me out to dry. After that, it'll be simple for them to get some charges going on me for complicity or obstruction. And they'll probably try to get to you, too. Harry, we've got to catch the killer, or killers. Or I'm history."

"You ever get any blood or hair from the scenes?" I asked.

"Yeah, some," Murphy said.

"What about saliva?"

Murph frowned at me.

"Saliva. It would be in the bite wounds."

She shook her head. "If they've found it, no one has said anything. Besides, all the samples won't do us a lot of good without a suspect to match them against."

"It won't do *you* a lot of good," I corrected her. "Something left blood on the window when it came through. Maybe that'll turn something up."

Murphy nodded. "That would be great. Okay, Harry. So you know what's going on now. What can you tell me about werewolves?"

I pursed my lips for a minute. "Not much. They weren't ever anything I studied too hard. I can tell you what they're not, mostly. Give me until morning, though, and I'll put together a full report on them." I glanced out the back window as Murphy pulled off the JFK Expressway. The car that I thought had been following us exited as we did.

Murphy frowned. "Morning? Can you do it any sooner?"

"I can have it on your desk by eight. Earlier, if you tell the night sergeant to let me in."

Murphy sighed and rubbed at her eyes. "Okay. Fine." We got back to McAnally's, and she pulled in next to the Blue Beetle. Behind us, the car that had been following us also came into the parking lot. "Jesus, Harry. I can't believe I'm sitting here talking to you about werewolves killing people in downtown Chicago." She turned her face to me, her eyes anxious. "Tell me I'm not going nuts."

I got out of the car, but leaned down to the window. "I don't think you're going nuts, Murph. I don't know. Maybe the FBI is right. Maybe it's not werewolves. Crazy things happen sometimes." I gave her half of a smile, which she answered with a faint snort.

"I'll probably be in my office, Dresden," she said. "Have that report on my desk by morning."

And then she pulled out of the parking lot, turning quickly out onto the street. I didn't get into the Beetle. Instead, I watched the car that had followed us into the parking lot. It cruised around the far side of the lot, then started down the row, toward me, and kept on going.

The driver, a striking woman with shaggy, dark brown hair, peppered with grey, did not turn to look at me as she went past.

I watched the car go, frowning. It left the lot, turning the opposite way Murphy had, and vanished from sight. Had that been the same vehicle that had followed us down the JFK? Or had it only been my imagination? My gut told me that the woman in the car had been following me, but then again, my instincts had cried wolf before.

I got into the Blue Beetle and thought for a minute. I was feeling guilty and a little queasy still. It was my fault Murphy had gotten in trouble. I had put her in the middle of extremely questionable circumstances by not telling her what was going on last spring. The pressure she was under now was my responsibility.

I have what might be considered a very out-of-date and chauvinist attitude about women. I like to treat women like ladies. I like to open doors for them, pay for the meal when I'm on a date, bring flowers, draw out their seat for them—all that sort of thing. I guess I could call it an attitude of chivalry, if I thought more of myself. Whatever you called it, Murphy was a lady in distress. And since I had put her there, it only seemed right that I should get her out of trouble, too.

That wasn't the only reason I wanted to stop the killings. Seeing Spike torn up like that had scared the hell out of me. I was still shaking a little, a pure and primitive reaction to a very primal fear. I did not want to get eaten by an animal, chewed up by something with a lot of sharp teeth. The very thought of that made me curl up on my car's seat and hug my knees to my chest, an awkward position considering my height and the comparatively cramped confines of the Beetle.

What had happened to Spike was as brutal and violent a death as anyone could possibly have. Maybe the thug had deserved it. Maybe not. Either way, he was only one victim of many that had been torn apart by something that regular people shouldn't have to face. I couldn't just stand aside and do nothing.

I'm a wizard. That means I have power, and power and responsibility go hand in hand. I have a responsibility to use the power I've been given, when there is a need for it. The FBI was not in any sense prepared to deal with a pack of ravening werewolves stalking down victims in the midst of a Chicago autumn. That was more my department.

I let out a long breath and sat up again. I reached into my duster's pocket for car keys, and found the shard of glass wrapped up in my white handkerchief.

I unwrapped it slowly and found the blood-smeared glass still there.

Blood has a kind of power. I could use the blood, cast a spell that would let me follow the blood back to the person who had spilled it. I could find the killer tonight, simply let my magic lead me to him, or them. But it would have to be now. The blood was almost dry, and once it was, I would have a hell of a lot more trouble using it.

Murphy would be royally pissed if I took off without her. She would probably assume that I had intended to follow the trail tonight, purposely leaving her out of the loop. But if I didn't follow the trail, I'd lose the chance to stop the killer before another night fell.

It didn't take me long to make up my mind. In the end, saving lives was more important than keeping Murphy from being pissed off at me.

So I got out of the Beetle and opened the storage trunk at the front of the VW. I took out a few wizardly implements: my blasting rod, the replacement for my shield bracelet, and one other thing that no wizard should be without. A Smith & Wesson .38 Chief's Special.

I carried all of these back to the front of the car with me and got out the shard of glass with smeared blood.

Then I made with the magic.

Chapter
Five

I got out the lump of chalk I always keep in my duster pocket, and the circular plastic dome compass that rides a strip of velcro on my dashboard, then squatted down, my voluminous coat spreading out over my legs and ankles. I drew a rough circle upon the asphalt around me with the chalk. The markings were bright against the dark surface and almost glowed beneath the light of the nearly full moon.

I added an effort of will, a tiny investment of energy, to close the circle, and immediately felt the ambient magic in the air around me crowd inward, trapped within the confines of the design. The hairs at the nape of my neck prickled and stood on end. I shivered, and took the shard of glass with its swiftly drying bloodstain and laid it down in the circle between the toes of my boots.

I began a low little chant of nonsense syllables, relaxing, focusing my mind on the effect I wanted. *"Interessari, interressarium,"* I murmured, and touched the plastic dome of the compass to the damp blood. Energy rushed out of me, swirled within the focusing confines of the circle I had drawn, and then rushed downward into the compass with a visible shimmer of silver, dustlike motes.

The compass needle shuddered, spun wildly, and then swung to the bloodstain on the dome like a hound picking up a scent. Then it whirled about and pointed to the southeast, whipping around the circle to hover steadily in that direction.

I grinned in anticipation and smudged the chalk with my boot, releasing the remaining stray energy back into the air, then took up the compass and returned to the Blue Beetle.

The problem with this particular spell was that the compass needle would point unerringly at whomever the blood had come from until the sun rose the next morning and disrupted the simple magical energies I had used to make the spell; but it didn't point out the swiftest way to get to the target, only the direct direction in which he, she, or it lay.

Traffic in Chicago isn't ever what any sane person would call friendly or simple, but I had lived there for a while and had learned to survive. I drove past Cook County Hospital, a virtual city of its own inside Chicago, and down past Douglas Park, then turned south on Kedzie. The compass needle slowly aligned to point hard to the east as I traveled south, and I wound up turning east on Fifty-fifth, toward the University of Chicago and Lake Michigan.

It wasn't exactly a good part of town. In fact, as far as neighborhoods go in Chicago, it was pretty bad. There was a high crime rate, and a lot of the buildings were run-down, abandoned, or only infrequently used. Streetlights were out in a lot of places, so when night closed in, it was darker than most areas. It's always been a favorite haunt for some of the darker things that come crawling out of the Nevernever for a night on the town. Trolls lurked about like muggers some nights, and any new vampire that came through the city always ended up in this neighborhood or one like it, searching for prey until he could make contact with Bianca or one of the lesser vampire figures of the city.

I pulled over as the compass swung to point at what looked like an abandoned department store, and I killed the engine. The faithful Beetle rattled to a grateful halt. I got the map of the city out of the glove box and squinted at it for a moment. Washington Park and Burnham Park, where four of last month's deaths had taken place, were less than a mile away on either side of me.

I felt a little shiver run through me. This sure as hell looked like the place to find Murphy's Lobo killer.

I got out of the car. I kept the blasting rod in my right hand, the dashboard compass in my left. My shield bracelet dangled on my left wrist. My gun was in the left pocket of my duster, within easy reach. I took a moment to take a deep breath, to clear my mind, and to clarify what I wanted to do.

I wasn't here to bring the killer down, whoever he was. I was just locating him for Murphy. Murphy could put the guy under surveillance and nail him the next time he tried to move. Even if I did capture him, Murphy couldn't exactly bring him up on charges, based on the word of a professional *wizard*. Municipal judges would love having a cop appear before them and start spouting such crazy talk.

I spun my blasting rod around in my fingers, grinned, and started forward. That was all right. I didn't need the justice system to recognize my power to be able to use it.

There were boards over the front windows of the once department store. I tested each one as I went past and found one that swung in easily. I stopped and examined it carefully, wary of any alarms that might be attached to it.

Such as the string tied across the bottom, lined with little jingle bells. If I had pushed the wooden sheet any farther inward, I would have set it to jangling. Instead, I slipped the string off the head of one of the nails it hung by, lowered the bells carefully, and slipped inside the dim confines of the abandoned store.

It was a skeletal place. There were still the bones of shelves, forming long aisles, but now barren of merchandise. Empty fluorescent light fixtures dangled in forlorn rows from the ceiling, and the powdered glass of shattered, tubular bulbs dusted the floor beneath them. Light seeped in from the street, mostly moonlight, but more light came from the back of the store. I checked my bloodstained compass. The needle was pointing firmly toward the light. I closed my eyes, and Listened, a skill that isn't hard to pick up, but that most people don't know how to do anymore. I heard voices, at least a pair of them, talking in hushed, urgent tones.

I crept toward the back of the store, using the barren shelves to keep myself from being seen. Then I held my breath and peeked up over the top of the last row of shelves.

Gathered around an old Coleman lantern were several people, all young, of various shapes and sizes and both genders. They were dressed in all shades of black, and most wore jackets and bracelets and collars of dark leather. Some had earrings and nose rings; one had a tattoo showing on his throat. If they had been tall, muscular folk, they would have looked intimidating, but they weren't. They looked like college students, or younger, some still with acne, or too-oily hair, beards that wouldn't quite grow all the way in, and the thinness of youth. They looked awkward and out of place.

Four or five of them were gathered behind and around a stout young man less than five and a half feet tall. He had thick glasses and pudgy fingers, and would have looked more at home with a pocket protector than with the spiked leather gloves on his fingers. He stood with his hands on his hips, glaring up at a rail-thin blond girl at least a head taller than he, the lines of her willowy body all awkward, her long, sad face set in an expression of anger. Her hair fell about her face and head in a ragged mane, but her eyes sparkled with contained wrath. Another five or six of the young people were gathered behind her, and everyone seemed tense.

"And I'm telling you," the young man snarled in a muted voice, "that we should be out there right now. We can't allow ourselves to rest until we've found them all and torn them apart." There was a murmur of agreement from the people behind him.

"I swear, Billy," the blonde said. "You're such a testosterone-laden idiot. If we were out there right now, they might catch on to us."

"Use your head, Georgia," Billy snapped back. "You think they haven't figured it out by now? They could take all of us out right this minute if they hit us."

"They haven't," Georgia pointed out. "*She* told us not to move again tonight, and I'm not moving. And if you try it, so help me, I'm going to tie your ankles to your ears."

Billy growled, actually growled, though it sounded posed and forced, and stepped forward. "You think you can handle me, bitch?" he said. "Bring it on."

Georgia's eyes narrowed. "I didn't sign on to this wolf thing to fight hapless losers like you, Billy. Don't make me start now." She glared at the young people standing behind Billy. "You know what *she* told us. Are you going to start going up against her word?"

"Listen, Alphas," Billy said, turning to look at those behind him, and then at those backing his opponent. "I've led you for all this time. I've done what I've promised to do. Are you going to stop trusting *me*?"

I peered at the discussion and then lowered my head again, back into the shadows. Holy I-Was-a-Teenage-Werewolf, Batman. I checked my compass, and it pointed firmly at the lit room, the group gathered around the lantern. Were these the killers? They looked more like a group of computer nerds geared up for Leather Night.

This was a start at least. I could clear out now, and let Murphy know what I had seen. I'd need to check around the building outside first, see if any of the group had any cars parked nearby, to be able to give Murphy the license plate numbers. Hell, we weren't far from the university. Maybe some of them would have parking passes.

"What is the meaning of this?" came a clear, strident woman's voice.

I craned my neck up to the edge of the shelf again. A dark-complected woman, as tall as the long-faced blonde, but older, solid with muscle and moving with an animal surety, had come into the room from a back door. Her brown hair was peppered with grey, and it took me only a second to recognize the woman from the car in the parking lot outside of McAnally's. My heart started to pound a little more quickly with excitement. She had been following Murphy and me, after all. She glared at the two groups of young people, her eyes an almost eerie shade of amber that could barely be construed as brown. "Have I taught you no better?" the woman demanded.

Billy and Georgia were both looking down at the floor uncomfortably. The other young people had assumed similar postures, like a group of children caught planning to go out after curfew.

"This isn't a game. Someone followed me here. They're on to us. If you start making mistakes now, you'll pay for them with your life," the woman said, stalking back and forth around the group. I checked my compass.

The needle swung back and forth as she walked, pointing solidly at her. My heart leapt into my throat. I considered this woman, with her almost animal vitality, her commanding presence and force of will. This woman, I thought, might be a killer. And she knew she had been followed. How? How in the hell had she known I was after her?

I looked up at her again, excited, only to find her staring intently at the thick patch of shadows around the shelves I hid behind. One of the young people started to say something, and the woman raised her hand for silence. I saw her nostrils flare as she breathed in through her nose, and she took a step in my direction. I held my breath, not daring to duck back down behind the shelves, lest the motion give me away.

"Join hands," snapped the woman. "Now." And then she turned to the Coleman lantern on the floor and snuffed it out, plunging the room into blackness.

There was a moment of confused murmuring, a commanding hiss from the woman, and then there was nothing but silence and the sound of shoes and boots moving over the tiles, toward the back of the store. They were getting away. I rose, blind, and headed around the shelves toward them as quickly as I could, trying to follow.

In retrospect, it wasn't the smartest decision, but I knew that I couldn't afford to let them get away. The spell I'd wrought on my compass wouldn't last long, not long enough to find the woman again, much less any of her pack of young people. I wanted to follow them out, to get the license plates on their cars, anything that would let me help Murphy locate them after they'd run.

I miscalculated the length of my stride and bounced into the wall at the end of the aisle. I sucked in a hiss of pain and reoriented myself, following them, using the darkness to conceal me as much as they did. I could have made some light for myself—but as long as no one could see, no one would start shooting, either, I reasoned. I moved out carefully, Listening, and following the sounds.

I had only a second's warning, the sound of claws sliding on the old tile, and then something large and furry slammed into my legs below the knee, taking them out from under me and sending me heavily to the floor. I let out a shout and swung my blasting rod like a baseball bat, feeling it crack down solidly on something hard and bony. There was a snarl, a deep, animal sound, and something tore the rod from my hand and sent it flying away. It clattered hollowly on the tile floor. I dropped my compass, scrabbled for my gun, and got my feet underneath me, backpedaling, yelling my fear out into a wordless challenge.

I stood still for a moment, staring at nothing, breathing hard, my gun heavy in my hand. Fear made my heart pound, and as always, anger followed hard on the heels of fear. I was furious that I had been attacked. I'd half expected something to try to stop me, but in the dark whatever had been snarling had scared me a lot more than I'd thought it would.

Nothing happened after a minute, and I couldn't hear anything. I reached into my shirt and drew out the silver pentacle that had been my mother's, the five-pointed star upright within a circle, the symbol of order, symmetry, balance of power. I focused my will on it, concentrating, and the pentacle began to glow with a faint, gentle light—hardly the blinding luminescence that came as the result of focusing power against a being of the Nevernever, but adequate enough to navigate by, at least. I moved toward the back room, blue-white light like moonlight pooled around me.

It was definitely stupid to keep going forward, but I was angry, furious enough to bumble my way through the back room of the department store, until I saw the dark blue outline of an open doorway. I headed for it, tripping over a few more things along the way that I couldn't quite make out in the werelight of my amulet, angrily kicking a few things from the path of my feet, until I emerged into an alley behind the old building, breathing open air, able to see again in dim shapes and colors.

Something hit me heavily from behind, driving me to the ground, gravel digging into my ribs through my shirt. My concentration vanished, and with it the light of my amulet. I felt something hard and metallic shoved against the back of my skull, a knee pressed into the small of my back, and a woman's voice snarled, "Drop the gun, or I blow your head off."

Chapter
Six

Call me crazy, but I'm not big on defiance when I've got a gun rammed against my skull. I carefully set the .38 in my left hand down and moved my fingers away from it.

"Hands behind your back. Do it," snarled the woman. I did it. I felt the cold metal of the handcuffs around my wrists, heard the ratcheting sound of the cuffs closing around them. The knee lifted off of my back, and my attacker shoved me over with one leg, snapped on a flashlight, and shone it in my eyes.

"Harry?" she said.

I blinked and squinted against the light. I recognized the voice now. "Hi, Murphy. This is going to be one of those conversations, isn't it?"

"You jerk," Murphy said, her voice harsh. She was still only a shadow behind the flashlight, but I recognized the contours now. "You found a lead and followed it, and you didn't contact me."

"Those who live in glass houses, Lieutenant," I said, and sat up, my hands still held tightly behind my back. "There wasn't time. It was hot and I couldn't afford to wait or I might have lost it."

Murphy grunted. "How did you find this place?"

"I'm a wizard," I told her, and waggled my arms as best I could. "Magic. What else?" Murphy growled, but hunkered down behind me and unlocked the cuffs. I rubbed at my wrists after they were freed. "How about you?"

"I'm a cop," she said. "A car tailed us back to McAnally's from the murder scene. I waited until it was gone and followed it back here." She stood up again. "You were inside. Did anyone go out the front?"

"No. I don't think so. But I couldn't see."

"Dammit," Murphy said. She put her gun away in her coat. "They didn't come out the back. There must be some way up to the roof." She stood up and peered around at the closely packed buildings, shining her flashlight around the roof's edge. "They're long gone by now."

"Win some, lose some." I got to my feet.

"Like hell," she said and turned and started into the building.

I hurried to catch up with her. "Where are you going?"

"Inside. To look for stairs, a ladder, whatever."

"You can't follow them," I said, falling into step beside her as she went into the darkened building. "You can't take them on, not with just you and me."

"Them?" Murphy said. "I only saw one." She stopped and looked at me, and I explained to her in terse terms what had happened since we parted in the parking lot. Murphy listened, the lines at the corners of her blue eyes serious.

"What do you think happened?" she asked when I was finished.

"We found werewolves," I said. "The woman, the dark one with the grey in her hair, was their leader."

"Group killers?" Murphy said.

"Pack," I corrected her. "But I'm not so sure that they were the killers. They didn't seem . . . I don't know. Cold enough. Mean enough."

Murphy shook her head and turned to walk outside. "Can you give me a good description?"

I kept up with her. "Good enough, I guess. But what do you want it for?"

"I'm going to put out an APB for the woman we saw, and I want you to describe the kids you heard talking."

"What do you need that for? Don't you have the plates off the car she was driving?"

"I already called them in," Murphy said. "Rental. Probably taken out under a false ID."

"I think you've got the wrong people, Murph," I said. "Don't put out that APB."

"Why shouldn't I?" Murphy asked. "Someone follows me back to town from the scene of a murder. Not only that, but you can confirm to me that they were the killer from the scene. Not in a court of law, I know, but you can give it to me, and that's enough. Standard investigation will turn up the rest if we know where to look."

I held up my hand. "Hold on, hold on. My spell didn't tell me that the woman was the killer. Only that it was her blood at the scene."

Murphy folded her arms and glared up at me. "Whose side are you on, anyway?"

"You still don't get it, Murphy," I said, my own temper rising a little. "You don't start something with the kind of people who live in boogety-land unless you're willing to take it all the way, right there, right then. If you start harassing a pack of were-wolves, setting the police after them, you've just declared war. You'd better be ready to fight it."

Murphy thrust her jaw out. "Don't worry about me. I can handle it."

"I'm not saying you can't," I said. "But whatever it was that tore apart Spike back at Marcone's club wasn't the same thing that was with me in the dark back there." I jerked my head at the main room of the department store.

"Oh yeah?" Murphy said. "Why not?"

"Because it could have killed me and it didn't."

"You don't think you could have taken care of yourself against a wolf, Harry?"

"In the dark?" I said. "Murphy, it's been nearly a hundred years since the wolf went extinct in most of the United States. You've got no idea, none at all, of how dangerous they can be. A wolf can run faster than you can drive a car through most of Chicago. His jaws can snap your thighbones with one jerk. A wolf can see the heat of your body in the complete dark, and can count the hairs on your head from a hundred yards off by starlight. He can hear your heart beating thirty or forty yards away. The wolf that was there in the dark with me could have killed me, easy. It didn't. It disarmed me, even after I'd hit it, and then it left."

"That doesn't mean anything," Murphy said—but she folded her arms over her stomach and glanced at the shadows around us with a little shiver. "Maybe the killer knows you. Maybe it didn't want to risk killing a wizard. Maybe, just maybe, the wolf did it to throw you off. Maybe it spared you just so you would react in this way, just to avoid suspicion."

"Maybe," I admitted. "But I don't think so. The kids I saw . . ." I shook my head. "Don't put out the APB, yet. Hold off on it, until I can get you some more information. Look, you pay me to give you my advice, to be your consultant on the supernatural. I'm your expert, right? Listen to me. Trust me."

She stared up at my face, her expression intent, looking away quickly when her eyes met mine. Murphy had known me for a while. You don't go looking into a wizard's eyes without a darned good reason. Wizards see too much.

"All right," she said finally. "I'll hold off on it—but only until tomorrow morning, when I have that report. If you can't show me anything by then, I'm going ahead after the people we saw tonight." Her mouth quirked in a fierce little grin. "I'd have a hell of a time explaining what I was doing out at the crime scene in Rosemont, anyway." The grin vanished, leaving only ferocity. "But you *will* have that information for me, Dresden, bright and early. Make no mistake. I will catch the killer before anyone else dies."

I nodded to Murphy. "In the morning," I said. "You got it."

Murphy's flashlight flickered and then went out as the filament burst with an audible pop.

Murphy sighed in the darkness. "Nothing ever works right when you're here. Sometimes, Harry," she said, "I really hate hanging out with you."

Chapter
Seven

I entered my apartment, tossed my blasting rod, which I had recovered from the abandoned department store, into the corner next to my wizard's staff and my sword cane, and locked the door behind me. It was one of those steel-frame doors, the antiburglar kind. I bought it after a demon had come stomping into my apartment six months ago and wrecked my place.

My apartment is in the basement of a huge old rooming house that somehow managed to survive all the Chicago fires. It's made almost entirely of wood, and it creaks and groans when the wind blows, which is all the time in this city, and makes gentle, soothing music. It's a place with a history, the neighbors are quiet, and my rent is cheap—though less so than it was before the demon trashed my place.

The apartment itself is devoid of electrical devices, for reasons that should be evident by now. There is a fireplace, and a kitchenette off the main room, a little bedroom adjacent to that, and a bathroom inside the bedroom. Sunken windows are high on each of the four walls, and one is on the wall of the bathroom.

I decorate in textures more than I do in colors; there were thick rugs all over the bare stone floors, layered on top of one another in most places. Demon acid had burned away most of my furniture, and I had been obliged to scavenge secondhand stores for replacements. I like furniture with a lot of old wood and soft cloth, and I had made my purchases accordingly. Tapestries hung from my walls, the oldest tapestries that I could find, covering the bare stone. In the ruddy firelight, the oranges and browns and reds that constituted the primary colors of the decor didn't look half bad.

I went over to the fireplace and built up the fire. October in Chicago is a cold, breezy month, and my dank little haven is usually chilly until I get a fire going. I dropped a few logs on the fire, and Mister made an appearance, rubbing up against my leg and purring fondly, staggering my balance off to one side.

"Been getting into the steaks again, eh, Mister?" I said, and rubbed the big, grey cat's ears. Mister is larger than a lot of dogs. Maybe one of his parents was part wildcat. I found him in a Dumpster one day when he was a kitten and he promptly adopted me. Despite my struggles, Mister had been an understanding soul, and I eventually came to realize that I was a part of his little family, and by his gracious consent was allowed to remain in his apartment. Cats. Go figure.

I fired up the wood-burning stove and prepared a quick meal of Spaghettios, grilled chicken, and toast. Mister shared in my meal, and split a can of Coke with me, as usual, and I tossed the dishes in the sink to soak before I went to my bedroom and put on my robe.

Let the wizardry commence.

I went to a spot in the far corner and moved the rug there, then lifted up the door in the floor beneath it, revealing the steep stepladder that led down to the subbasement, where I kept my lab.

I teetered down the stairs, holding a lit candle that cast a golden glow on the cheerful havoc that is my laboratory. Tables lined the walls, and the longest table filled most of the center of the room, leaving a cramped walk space around it, except for an area at the far side of the lab that I kept completely clear for my summoning circle, a ring of bright copper set into the floor. Books, notebooks, defunct ballpoint pens, broken pencils, boxes, plastic containers, old butter bowls, empty jelly jars, and plastic Baggies lay next to other containers of every size and shape that held the spices, rare stones, bones, fur, blood, oddments, jewelry, and other ingredients useful to wizardly pursuits and studies.

I reached the bottom of the ladder, stepped over a precariously balanced stack of comic books (don't ask), and started lighting the other candles that lay on dishes around the chilly room, finally bending to light up the kerosene heater that I keep down in the lab in an effort to at least blunt the cold. "Bob," I said then. "Wake up, sleepyhead."

Up on one of the shelves, huddled in the midst of a thick stack of hardbacks, was the bleached, smooth form of a human skull, its empty eye sockets gaping. Deep in those eye sockets, there was a flickering of orange light, which grew and solidified into twin points of lambent illumination. "Sleepyhead. Oh, that's rich, Harry. With a sense of humor like that, you could make a living as a garbage man anywhere in the country." The skull's mouth gaped open in the parody of a yawn, though I knew the spirit within, Bob, didn't feel fatigue in the same way that living beings did. I put up with his lip, so to speak—Bob had worked for several wizards over the course of a dozen mortal lifetimes, and he knew more about the nuts and bolts of magic than I ever would.

"What are we doing, now?" Bob sniggered. "More weight-loss potions?"

"Look, Bob," I said. "That was only to get me through a rough month. Someone's got to pay the rent around here."

"All right," Bob said smugly. "You going to get into breast enhancement, then? I'm telling you, that's where the money is."

"That isn't what magic is for, Bob. How petty can you get?"

"Ah," Bob said, his eye lights flickering. "The question is, how *pretty* can you get *them*? You aren't a half-bad wizard, Dresden. You should think about how grateful all those beautiful women will be."

I snorted and started cleaning off a space on the center table, stacking things up to one side. "You know, Bob, some of us aren't obsessed with sex."

Bob snorted, no easy feat for a guy with no nose or lips. "Some of us don't take a real, working body and all five senses for granted, either, Harry. When's the last time you saw Susan?"

"I don't know," I responded. "Couple weeks ago. We're both pretty busy with work."

Bob heaved a sigh. "A gorgeous woman like that, and here you are, down in your musty old lab, getting ready to do more ridiculous nonsense."

"Precisely," I said. "Now, shut up and let's get to work."

Bob grumbled something in Latin, but rattled a few times to shake the dust off of the skull. "Sure, what do I know? I'm just a pathetic little spirit, right?"

"With a photographic memory, three or four hundred years' worth of research experience, and more deduction capacity than a computer, Bob, yeah."

Bob almost seemed to smile. "Just for that, you get my best effort tonight, Harry. Maybe you're not such an idiot after all."

"Great," I said. "I want to work up a couple of potions, and I want to know everything you know about werewolves."

"What kind of potions, and what kind of werewolves?" Bob said promptly.

I blinked. "There's more than one?"

"Hell, Harry. We've made at least three dozen different kinds of potions down here ourselves, and I don't see why you wouldn't—"

"No, no, no," I growled at Bob. "Werewolves. There's more than one kind of werewolf?"

"Eh? More than one kind of what?" Bob tilted his skull over to one side, as though cocking an invisible hand to his ear bones.

"Werewolf, werewolf."

"*There* wolf," Bob replied solemnly, his voice seething with a hokey accent. "*There* castle."

I blinked at him. "Uh. What the heck are you talking about?"

"It's a *joke*, Harry. Stars almighty, you *never* get out, do you?"

I eyed the grinning skull and growled in frustration. "Don't make me come up there."

"Okay, okay. Sheesh. Aren't we grumpy tonight?" Bob's jaws stretched in a yawn again.

"I'm working another murder case, Bob, and I don't have time to goof around."

"Murder. Mortal business is so complicated. You never hear about murder charges in the Nevernever."

"That's because everything there is immortal. Bob, just shut up and tell me what you know about werewolves. If there's a bunch of different flavors, tell me what they are." I got out a notebook and a fresh pencil, then a couple of clean beakers with alcohol-flame burners to heat whatever liquid I put in them.

"All right," Bob said. "How much do you know?"

"Exactly nothing about werewolves. My teacher never covered that with me."

Bob barked out a harsh little laugh. "Old Justin had a lousy sense of just about everything. He got what was coming to him, Harry, and don't let anyone on the White Council tell you any different."

I stopped for a moment. A sudden rush of mixed feelings, anger and fear and mostly regret, washed through me. I closed my eyes. I could still see him, my teacher, dying in flames born of my will and anger. "I don't want to talk about it."

"Hell, the Council even suspended the sentence on you. You were vindicated. Say, I wonder what ever happened to Elaine. Now *there* was a sweet piece of—"

"Werewolves, Bob," I said, in a very quiet, very angry voice. One hand started to hurt, and I saw that my fingers had clenched into a fist, the knuckles turning white. I turned my eyes to him, glaring.

I heard the skull make a gulping sound. And then he said, "Right. Okay. Werewolves. And, uh, which potions did you want?"

"I want a pick-me-up potion. A night's rest in a bottle. And I want something that will make me imperceptible to a werewolf." I reached for the notebook and my pencil.

"First one's tough to do. There's nothing quite like a decent night's sleep. But we can make some super-coffee, no problem." He spouted out the formula to me, and I noted it down as he went, my handwriting too dark and angular. I was still angry from the mere mention of my old master's name. And the welter of emotions that rushed up with my memories of Elaine wouldn't subside for an hour.

We all have our demons.

"What about the second one?" I asked the skull.

"Can't really be done," Bob said. "Wolves have just got way too much on the ball to hide from every one of their senses without doing some major work. I'm talking, like, a greater Ring of Invisibility, not just a Shadowcape or something."

"Do I look like I'm made of money? I can't afford that. What about a partial-hiding potion, then?"

"Oh, like a blending brew? Look like an unobtrusive part of the background, something like that? I would think that would be the most useful, really. Keep you from being noticed to begin with."

"Sure," I said. "I'll take what I can get."

"No problem," Bob assured me, and rattled off another formula, which I jotted down. I checked the ingredients list, and thought that I had them all in stock among the countless containers on my shelves.

"Fine. I can get started on these. How much do you know about werewolves, Bob?"

"Plenty. I was in France during the Inquisition." Bob's voice was dry (but that is to be expected, considering).

I started on the first potion, the stimulant. Every potion has eight parts. One part is a base liquid to hold the others and provide a medium for mixing. Five parts are symbolically linked to each of the five senses. One is similarly linked to the mind, and another to the spirit. The basic ingredient to the stimulant potion was coffee, while the base for the scent-masking potion was water. I got them both to boiling. "Lot of werewolfery going on then?"

"Are you kidding?" Bob said. "It was werewolf central. We had every kind of werewolf you could think of. Hexenwolves, werewolves, lycanthropes, and loup-garou to boot. Every kind of lupine theriomorph you could think of."

"Therro-what?" I said.

"Theriomorph," Bob said. "Anything that shape-shifts from a human being into an animal form. Werewolves are theriomorphs. So are werebears, weretigers, werebuffalo . . ."

"*Buffalo?*" I asked.

"Sure. Some Native American shamans could do a buffalo. But almost everyone does predators, and until pretty recently, wolves were the scariest predator anyone around Europe could think of."

"Uh, okay," I said. "And there's a difference between types of werewolves?"

"Right," Bob confirmed. "Mostly it depends on how you go from human form to wolf form, and how much of your humanity you retain. Don't burn the coffee."

I turned down the flame beneath the beaker of coffee, annoyed. "I know, I know. Okay, then. How do you get to be a wolf?"

"The classic werewolf," Bob said, "is simply a human being who uses magic to shift himself into a wolf."

"Magic? Like a wizard?"

"No," Bob said. "Well. Sort of. He's like a wizard who only knows how to cast the one spell, the one to turn him into a wolf, and knows how to get back out of it again. Most people who learn to be werewolves aren't very good at it for a while, because they keep all of their own humanity."

"What do you mean?"

"Well," Bob said, "they can reshape themselves into the form of a wolf, but it's pretty much just topology. They rearrange their physical body, but their mind remains the same. They can think and reason, and their personality doesn't change—but they don't have a wolf's instincts or reflexes. They're used to being sight-oriented bipeds, not smell-oriented quadrupeds. They would have to learn everything from scratch."

"Why would someone do something like that?" I said. "Just learn to turn into a wolf, I mean."

"You've never been a peasant in medieval France, Harry," Bob said. "Life was hard for those people. Never enough food, shelter, medicine. If you could give yourself a fur coat and the ability to go out and hunt your own meat, you would have jumped at the chance, too."

"Okay, I think I've got it," I said. "Do you need silver bullets or anything? Do you turn into a werewolf if you get bitten?"

"Bah," Bob said. "No. Hollywood stole that from vampires. And the silver-bullet thing is only in special cases. Werewolves are just like regular wolves. You can hurt them with weapons just like you can a real wolf."

"That's good news," I said, stirring the potion. "What other kinds are there?"

"There's another version of a werewolf—when someone *else* uses magic to change you into a wolf."

I glanced up at him. "Transmogrification? That's illegal, Bob. It's one of the Laws of Magic. If you transform someone into an animal, it destroys their personality. You *can't* transform someone else without wiping out their mind. It's practically murder."

"Yeah. Neat, huh? But actually, most personalities can survive the transformation. For a little while at least. Really strong wills might manage to keep their human memories and personality locked away for several years. But sooner or later, they're irretrievably gone, and you're left with nothing but a wolf."

I turned from the potions to scribble in my notebook. "Okay. What else makes a werewolf?"

"The most common way, back in France, was to make a deal with a demon or a devil or a powerful sorcerer. You get a wolf-hide belt, put it on, say the magic words, and whammy, you're a wolf. A *Hexenwolf*."

"Isn't that just like the first kind?"

"No, not at all. You don't use your own magic to become a wolf. You use someone else's."

I frowned. "Isn't that the second kind, then?"

"Stop being obtuse," Bob chided me. "It's different because you're employing a talisman. Sometimes it's a ring or amulet, but usually it's a belt. The talisman provides an anchor for a spirit of bestial rage. Nasty thing from the bad side of the Nevernever. That spirit wraps around a human personality to keep it from being destroyed."

"A kind of insulation," I said.

"Exactly. It leaves you with your own intellect and reason, but the spirit handles everything else."

I frowned. "Sounds a little easy."

"Oh, sure," Bob said. "It's really easy. And when you use a talisman to turn into a wolf, you lose all of your human inhibitions and so on, and just run on your unconscious desires, with the talisman-spirit in charge of the way the body moves. It's really efficient. A huge wolf with human-level intelligence and animal-level ferocity."

I eyed Bob, and gathered up the other ingredients for the stimulant potion: a morning doughnut, for taste; a cock's crow, for hearing; fresh soap, for smell; bits of a washcloth, for touch; and a beam of dawn sunshine for sight; a to-do list, for the mind; and a bit of bright, cheerful music, for the spirit; and the potion was simmering along nicely.

Bob said nothing while I added the ingredients, and when I was finished I said, "Most people don't have the strength to control a spirit like that, I'd think. It would influence their actions. Maybe even control them. Suppress their conscience."

"Yeah. So?"

"So it sounds more like you'd be creating a monster."

"It's effective," Bob said. "I don't know about the good or the evil of the thing. That's something that only you mortals worry about."

"What did you call this flavor again?"

"Hexenwolf," Bob said, with a strong Germanic accent. "Spell wolf. The Church declared war on anyone who chose to become a Hexenwolf, and burned a huge number of people at the stake."

"Silver bullets?" I asked. "Bitten and turn into a werewolf?"

"Would you get off this 'bitten and turn into a werewolf' kick, Harry?" Bob said. "It doesn't work that way. Not ever. Or you'd have werewolves overrunning the entire planet in a couple of years."

"Fine, fine," I sighed. "What about the silver bullets?"

"Don't need them."

"All right," I said, and continued jotting down information to put together for Murphy in a report. "*Hexenwolf*. Got it. What else?"

"Lycanthropes," Bob said.

"Isn't that a psychological condition?"

"It might *also* be a psychological condition," Bob said. "But it was a reality first. A lycanthrope is a natural channel for a spirit of rage. A lycanthrope turns into a beast, but only inside his head. The spirit takes over. It affects the way he acts and thinks, makes him more aggressive, stronger. They also tend to be very resistant to pain or injury, sickness; they heal rapidly—all sorts of things."

"But they don't actually shape-shift into a wolf?"

"Give that boy a Kewpie," Bob said. "They're just people,

too, but they're awfully fierce. Ever heard of the Norse berserkers? Those guys were lycanthropes, I think. And they're born, not made."

I stirred the stimulant potion, and made sure it was at an even simmer. "And what was the last one? Loop what?"

"Loup-garou," Bob said. "Or that was the name Etienne the Enchanter used for them, before he got burned at the stake. The loup-garou are the major monsters, Harry. Someone has cursed them to become a wolflike demon, and usually at the full moon. That someone's got to be really powerful, too, like a major heavyweight sorcerer or a demon lord or one of the Faerie Queens. When the full moon comes, they transform into a monster, go on a killing spree, and slaughter everything they come across until the moon sets or the sun rises."

A sudden little chill went over me, and I shivered. "What else?"

"Supernatural speed and power. Supernatural ferocity. They recover from injuries almost instantly, if they become hurt at all. They're immune to poison and to any kind of sorcery that goes for their brain. Killing machines."

"Sounds great. I guess this hasn't happened all that often? I'd have heard something by now."

"Right," Bob said. "Not often. Usually, the poor cursed bastard knows enough to shut himself away somewhere, or to head out into the wilderness. The last major loup-garou rampage happened around Gevaudan, France, back in the sixteenth century. More than two hundred people were killed in a little more than a year."

"Holy shit," I said. "How did they stop it?"

"They killed it," Bob said. "Here's where the silver bullets finally come in, Harry. Only a silver weapon can hurt a loup-garou, and not only that, the silver has to be inherited from a family member. Inherited silver bullets."

"Really? Why would that work and not regular silver?"

"I don't make the laws of magic, Harry. I just know what they are and have an idea of when they're changing. That one hasn't changed. I think maybe it has something to do with the element of sacrifice."

"Inherited silver," I mumbled. "Well. We'll just have to hope that this wasn't a loup-garou, I guess."

"If it was a louper, you'd know," Bob said wisely. "In the middle of this town, you'd have a dozen people dead every time the full moon came around. What's going on?"

"A dozen people are dying every time the full moon comes around." I filled Bob in on the Lobo killings, giving him all the information Murphy had given to me, and started on the next potion. Into the water went the ingredients: plastic wrap for sight; a bit of plain white cotton, for touch; a little deodorant for smell; a rustle of wind for hearing; a leaf of plain old lettuce, for taste; and finally I threw in a blank piece of paper, for the mind, and some elevator music for the spirit. The ingredients were boring. The potion looked and smelled boring. Perfect.

"Lot of dead people," Bob commented. "I'll let you know if I think of anything good. I wish I knew something else."

"I want you to learn more," I told him. "Go out and see what else you can round up on werewolves."

Bob snorted. "Fat chance, Harry. I'm a spirit of intellect, not an errand boy." But when I said the word "out," Bob's eyes glittered.

"I'll pick you up some new romance novels, Bob," I offered.

Bob's teeth clicked a couple of times. "Give me a twenty-four-hour pass," he said.

I shook my head. "Forget it. The last time I let you out, you invaded a party over at Loyola and set off an orgy."

Bob sniffed. "I didn't do anything to anyone that a keg wouldn't have done."

"But those people didn't *ask* for you to get into their systems, Bob. No way. You had your fun, and I'm not letting you out again for a while."

"Oh, come on, Harry."

"No," I said flatly.

"It would only be one little night o—"

"No," I said again.

Bob glowered at me and demanded, "New romances. None of those tatty used ones. I want something off the bestseller list."

"I want you back by sunrise," I countered.

"Fine," Bob snapped. "I can't believe how ungrateful you are, after everything I've done for you. I'll see if I can get someone's name. There might be a spirit or two who could get you some juicy information." The orange lights that were his eyes glittered and then flowed out of the skull in a misty cloud of lambent illumination. The cloud flowed up the ladder and out of my laboratory.

I sighed and set the second potion to simmering. It would take another hour or two to cook the potions, and then to shove the magic into them, so I sat down with my notebook and started writing up my report. I tried to ignore the headache that was creeping up the back of my neck toward the crown of my head, but it did little good.

I had to help Murphy nail the killer, whoever it was, while avoiding any trouble with the FBI. Otherwise, she was out of a job, and even if I didn't end up in jail, I would be out of a living myself. Johnny Marcone's man had been killed, and I would be a fool to think he would stand idly by and do nothing in response. I was sure the gangster would rear his head sooner or later.

Aside from all of that, there was a monster of one kind or another lurking in the dark, and the police and the FBI had been helpless to stop it. That left only me, Harry Dresden, your friendly neighborhood wizard, to step in and do something about it. And, if the killer figured out that I was getting involved, he would doubtless start gunning for me next. My troubles were multiplying.

Hexenwolves. Werewolves. Lycanthropes. Loup-garou.

What will they think of next?

Chapter
Eight

The police headquarters downtown consists of a sprawling collection of buildings that have sprung up over the years as the need for law enforcement has increased. They don't match, and they come from a wildly varying selection of styles and designs, but they have somehow adapted themselves into a cohesive whole—much like the force itself. Special Investigations operates out of a big, run-down old building, a huge cube that has managed to hold up solidly in spite of the years, the grime, the smog, and the graffiti sprayed on its walls. It has bars over the windows and the doors and sits hunkered amidst buildings much taller than it, like a faithful old bulldog amidst a crowd of unruly children, struggling to maintain peace and order.

The inside of the building is plain, even dingy, but they keep it clean. The old warhorse of a desk sergeant eyed me as I entered the station, his grey mustache bristling over an impressive jaw. "Hiya, Bill," I told him, and held up the manila envelope I had under one arm. "Bringing something up to Murphy in SI."

"Dresden," he said warily and jerked a thumb toward the stairs behind him, giving me permission to go.

I hadn't gotten much sleep the night before, but I had showered and dressed nicely before I left the house, in neat business clothes, for once, instead of my usual western shirt and blue jeans. I kept the battered old duster, though, with my blasting rod dangling from a thong inside of it. I took the stairs two at a time and passed a few cops along the way. Several recognized me, and one or two even nodded, but I thought I could detect a sense of uneasiness from each of them. Apparently, I was carrying a distinct odor with the law at the moment.

I wrinkled up my nose. The police had always known me as something of a nut, the crazy guy who claimed to be a wizard, but a useful nut, who could provide good information and whose apparent "psychic abilities" had helped them on a number of occasions. I was used to being seen as one of the good guys, but now the cops were giving me the neutral, professional glances that they would give to a potential criminal, rather than the casual greetings one would give to a comrade in arms. It was to be expected, maybe, since rumor had associated my name with Johnny Marcone's, but it was still disturbing.

I was muttering to myself and deep in my own sleep-deprived thoughts when I bumped into a tall, lovely woman, dark of hair and eye, full of mouth, long of leg. She was wearing a tan skirt and jacket with a crisp white blouse. Her raven brows furrowed in consternation until she looked up at me, and then her eyes glowed with a sort of friendly avarice. "Harry," she said, her lips curving into a smile. She stood up on her tiptoes and kissed my cheek. "Fancy seeing you here."

I cleared my throat. "Hi, Susan," I said. "Did that syndication deal go through?"

She shook her head. "Not yet, but I'm hoping. After those stories you gave me last spring, people started taking me a little more seriously." She paused, drawing in a little breath. It made her chest rise and fall most attractively. "You know, Harry. If you're working with the police again, and if you should happen to be able to let me in on whatever is going on . . ."

I shook my head and tried to scowl at her. "I thought we agreed. I won't poke into your business deals and you won't poke into mine."

She smiled up at me and touched a finger to my chest. "That was whenever we were out on a date, Harry." She let her eyes wander down the length of my body, and then back up. "Or staying in on one."

"Susan Rodriguez, I never knew you were a lawyer as well as a journalist."

"Now you're getting nasty," she said, grinning. "Seriously, Harry. Another exposé like last spring could make my career."

"Yeah, well after last spring, the city made me sign about two tons of nondisclosure agreements. I can't tell you anything about the case."

"So don't tell me about the case, Harry—but if you could mention, say, a nice spot in the street where I might stand and get some good pictures, I would be very," she leaned up and kissed my neck. "Very"—the kiss traveled to my earlobe—"grateful."

I swallowed and cleared my throat. Then took a step back down the stairs, away from her. I closed my eyes for a second and listened to the thunder of my suddenly pounding heart. "I'm sorry. I can't do that."

"Oh, Harry. You're no fun." She reached out and ran a hand over my hair, then smiled to let me know that there were no hard feelings. "But let's get together soon, all right? Dinner?"

"Sure," I said. "Hey. What are you doing down here this early?"

She tilted her head, considering me. "Trade me? I'll show you mine if you'll show me yours. Off the record, even."

I snorted. "Susan, give me a break."

She let out a little sigh and shook her head. "I'll call you about dinner, all right?" She started down the stairs past me.

"All right," I said. "All right. I'm bringing a report on werewolves to Murphy."

"*Werewolves,*" she said, her eyes lighting. "Is that who's behind the Lobo murders?"

I frowned. "No comment. I thought the FBI was keeping that under wraps."

"You can't kill a dozen people and expect no one to notice," Susan said, her voice sly. "I keep track of the city morgues."

"God, you're so romantic. All right, your turn. Give."

"I was trying to talk to the investigator from the department's

Internal Affairs. Word is that they're putting pressure on Murphy, trying to clear her out of Special Investigations."

I grimaced. "Yeah. I heard that, too. Why does it concern you and the *Arcane*?"

"The most successful preternatural investigator the police department has gets hung out to dry? Even if people don't believe it, Murphy does a lot of good. If Murphy gets fired, and I can show how the numbers of mysterious crimes and unexplained deaths go up after she leaves, maybe I can get people to listen to papers like the *Arcane*. And to people like you."

I shook my head. "People don't want to believe in magic anymore. Or things that go bump in the dark. For the most part, they're happier not knowing."

"And when not knowing gets someone killed?"

I shrugged. "That's where people like me and Murphy come in."

Susan eyed me doubtfully. "All I need is something solid, Harry. An eyewitness account, a photograph, something."

"You can't photograph anything really supernatural," I pointed out. "The energies around things like that will mess up cameras. Besides, the stuff I'm dealing with right now is too dangerous. You could get hurt."

"What if I shot from a long way off?" she pressed. "Used a telephoto lens?"

I shook my head. "No, Susan. I'm not going to tell you anything. It's for your own good as much as for mine."

She pressed her lips together. "Fine," she said, her tone crisp, and went on down the stairs. I watched her go, dismayed. It seemed I was making a habit of excluding people from certain brands of information. Not only were my job and my freedom on the line, and Murphy's job, too—now it seemed that my love life, or what passed for it, was in danger as well.

I took a moment to try to sort through my thoughts and feelings on Susan, and gave it up as hopeless. Susan was a reporter for the Midwestern *Arcane*, a tabloid circulated widely from

Chicago. It usually ran headlines about Elvis and JFK singing duets in Atlantic City, or on similar topics, but once in a while Susan managed to slip in something about the real world of the supernatural, the one that people had forgotten about in favor of science. She was damned good at her job, absolutely relentless.

She was also charming, gorgeous, funny, and sexy as hell. Our dates often ended in long, passionate evenings at my place or hers. It was an odd relationship, and neither one of us had tried to define it. I think maybe we were worried that if we did, we would change our minds and write it off as a bad idea.

I continued up the stairs, my mind a tired muddle of blood-spattered corpses, savage beasts, angry ex-apprentices, and sultry, dark eyes. There are times when my work is hard on my love life. But one thing I'm not is a boring date.

The doors to the SI office swung open just before I reached for them, and I drew up short. Agent Denton of the FBI was there, tall and immaculate in his gray suit. He stopped, too, and looked at me, holding open the door with one arm. There were bags under his grey eyes, but they were still calculating, assessing, and the veins in his forehead bulged with hypertension.

"Mr. Dresden," he said, and nodded to me.

"Agent Denton," I replied, keeping my tone polite, even friendly. "Excuse me. I need to get something to Lieutenant Murphy."

Denton frowned a little, and then glanced at the room behind him, before coming all the way out into the hall and letting the door swing shut. "Maybe now isn't the best time for you to see her, Mr. Dresden."

I glanced up at the clock on the wall. It was five minutes before eight. "She wanted it early." I stepped to one side, to go around him.

Denton put a hand on my chest—just that. But he was strong. He might have been shorter than me, but he was carrying a lot more muscle. He didn't look at my eyes, and when he spoke, his voice was very quiet. "Look, Dresden. I know what happened last night didn't look good, but believe me when I say that I've got nothing against Lieutenant Murphy. She's a good cop, and she does her job. But she's got to follow the rules, just like everyone else."

"I'll keep that in mind," I told him and started to move again.

He kept up the pressure against my chest. "There's an agent from Internal Affairs in there with her right now. He's already in a bad mood from being hassled by some reporter. Do you really want to go in there and make him start asking all sorts of questions?"

I glanced at him, frowning. He lowered his hand from my chest. I didn't go around him, yet. "You know about the investigation she's under?"

Denton shrugged a shoulder. "It's to be expected, all things considered. Too much of what has happened in the past looks suspicious."

"You really don't believe, do you?" I asked him. "You don't believe that I'm a real wizard. You don't believe in the supernatural."

Denton straightened his tie. "What I believe doesn't matter, Mr. Dresden. What is important is that a lot of the scum out there believe in it. It affects the way they think and operate. If I could make use of your advice to solve this case, I would, the same as any other law officer." He glanced at me and added, "Personally, I think you are either slightly unstable or a very intelligent charlatan. No offense."

"None taken," I said, my voice wry. I nodded to the door. "How long will Murphy be busy?"

Denton shrugged. "If you like, I'll take the report in to her, drop it on her desk. You can go down the hall and call her. It doesn't matter to me, but I don't mind helping out a straight cop."

I thought it over for a second, and then passed the folder to him. "I appreciate it, Agent Denton."

"Phil," he said. For a second, he almost smiled, but then his face resumed its usual tense expression. "Do you mind if I take a look at it?"

I shook my head. "But I hope you like fiction, Phil."

He flicked the folder open and studied the first page for a moment, expressionless. He looked up at me. "You can't possibly be serious."

It was my turn to shrug. "Don't knock it. I've helped Murphy out before."

He glanced over the rest of the report, the look of skepticism on his face growing more secure. "I'll . . . give this to Murphy for you, Mr. Dresden," he said, then nodded to me and turned to walk toward the SI office.

"Oh, hey," I said casually. "Phil."

He turned to me and lifted his eyebrows.

"We're both on the same team here, right? Both of us looking for the killer?"

He nodded.

I nodded back. "What is it that you're not telling me?"

He stared for a long moment, and then blinked slowly. The lack of reaction gave him away. "I don't know what you're talking about, Mr. Dresden," he said.

"Sure you do," I told him. "You know something you can't or won't tell me, right? So why not just put it out on the table, now?"

Denton glanced up and down the hall and repeated, in precisely the same tone of voice, "I don't know what you're talking about, Mr. Dresden. Do you understand?"

I didn't understand, but I didn't want him to know that. So I just nodded again. Denton nodded back, turned, and went into the SI office.

I frowned, puzzling over Denton's behavior. His expression and reaction had conveyed more than his words, but I wasn't sure exactly what. Except for that one flash of insight the night before, I was having trouble reading him. Some people were just like that, very good at keeping secrets with their bodies and motions as well as with their mouths.

I shook my head, went to the pay phone down the hall, dropped in my quarter, and dialed Murphy's number.

"Murphy," she said.

"Denton's dropping off my report. I didn't want to wander in on you with Internal Affairs hanging around."

There was a note of relief in Murphy's voice, subtle but there. "Thank you. I understand."

"The investigator is in your office now, isn't he?"

"Right," Murphy said, her tone neutral, polite, professional, and disinterested. Murphy keeps a great poker face when it's necessary, too.

"If you have any questions, I should be at my office," I said. "Hang in there, Murph. We'll nail this guy." There was the sound of a deeper voice, Denton's, and then the slap of a folder hitting the surface of Murphy's desk. Murphy thanked Denton, and then spoke to me again.

"Thank you very much. I'll be right on it." Then she hung up on me.

I hung up the phone myself, and realized that I was vaguely disappointed that I hadn't gotten to really speak to Murphy, that we hadn't had the chance to exchange our usual banter. It bothered me that I couldn't just walk into her office anymore, made me feel a little queasy and tense inside. I hate politics, but it was there, and as long as I was being held in any amount of suspicion, I could get Murphy in trouble just by being around.

Brooding all the while, I stomped down the stairs and out the front door of the station, toward the visitor parking, where the Blue Beetle waited for me.

I had gotten in and was preparing to coax it to life when I heard footsteps. I squinted up into the morning sunshine at the skinny form and big ears of the redheaded young FBI agent from the scene in Rosemont last night. I rolled down the window as he stepped up to my car. He glanced around, his face anxious, and then knelt down beside the window so that he could not be easily observed.

"Hi there, Agent . . ."

"Harris," he said. "Roger Harris."

"Right," I said. "Can I help you, Agent Harris?"

"I need to know, Mr. Dresden. I mean, I wanted to ask you last night, but I couldn't. But I need to ask you now." He glanced around again, restless as a rabbit when a fox goes by, and said, "Are you for real?"

"A lot of people ask me that, Agent Harris," I said. "I'll tell you what I tell them. Try me and see."

He chewed on his lip and looked at me for a minute. Then nodded a jerky little nod, his head bobbing. "All right," he said. "All right. Can I hire you?"

My eyebrows went up in surprise. "Hire me? What for?"

"I think . . . I think I know something. About the Lobo killings. I tried to get Denton to let us check it out, but he said that there wasn't enough evidence. We'd never be able to get a surveillance put on them."

"On who?" I asked, wary. The last thing I needed was to be getting involved in any more shady goings-on. On the other hand, as an independent operator, I could sometimes go poking my nose where the police couldn't. If there was a chance that I could turn up something for Murphy, or find the killer and stop him outside of legal channels entirely, I couldn't afford to pass it up.

"There's a gang in Chicago," Harris began.

"No kidding?" I asked, affecting puzzlement.

It was lost on the kid. "Yeah. They call themselves the Street-wolves. They've got a really rough reputation, even for this town. A spooky reputation. Even the criminals won't go near them. They say that the gang has strange powers. Streetwolf territory is down by the Forty-ninth Street Beach." He stared at me intently.

"Down by the university," I filled in. "And by the parks where last month's murders took place."

He nodded, eager as a puppy. "Yeah, right, down there. You see what I'm getting at?"

"I see, kid, I see," I told him and rubbed at my eye. "Denton couldn't go there and look around, so he sent you down here to get me to do it."

The kid flushed, his skin turning bright red, until his freckles vanished. "I . . . Uh . . ."

"Don't worry about it," I told him. "You didn't do a bad job with the act, but you've got to get up pretty early in the morning, et cetera."

Harris chewed on his lip and nodded. "Yeah, well. Will you do it?"

I sighed. "I guess you can't go on record as paying my fee, can you?" It wasn't really a question.

"Well. No. Officially, you are a suspect source, as a consultant."

I nodded. "I thought so."

"Can you do it, Mr. Dresden? Will you?"

I was regretting it even before I spoke. "All right," I said. "I'll check it out. But in exchange, tell Denton I want any of the information that the FBI or the Chicago police has on me."

Harris paled. "You want us to copy your files?"

"Yeah," I said. "I could get them through the Freedom of Information Act, anyway. I just don't want to spend the time and postage. Do we have a deal or not?"

"Oh, God. Denton would *kill* me if he found out. He doesn't like it when someone bends the rules." He chewed his lip until I thought it would fall off.

"You mean like he's doing by sending you here to me?" I shrugged. "Suit yourself, kid. That's my price. You can find my number if you change your mind." I coaxed the Beetle to life, and it rattled and coughed and started running.

"All right," he said. "All right. Deal." He offered me his hand.

I shook it, sealing the bargain, and got an uneasy feeling as I did. Harris walked away from the Beetle as quickly as he could, still looking around nervously.

"That was stupid, Harry," I told myself. "You shouldn't be getting yourself into anything more complicated than you already have."

I was right. But the potential gains made the risk worth it. I could possibly find the killers, stop them, and additionally find out why the cops had a bug up their collective ass about me. It might help me to work things out with Murphy. It might even help me get her out of the trouble she was having.

"Cheer up, Harry," I told myself. "You're just going to go poke around a biker gang's lair. Ask them if they happen to have killed some people lately. What could possibly go wrong?"

Chapter Nine

A block from the Forty-ninth Street Beach there was a run-down garage, the sort of place you only find in the worst sections of big cities. The building consisted of corrugated metal on a steel frame, oxidating in the rain and the mist rising off the lake so that gobbets of rust ran down the walls in streaks and pooled on the sidewalks in uneven puddles. On one side of the garage was a vacant lot; on the other, what looked like the sort of pawn shop where crooks traded in their spare guns and knives for a few extra dollars when things were tight. A faded sign hung askew over one of the garage doors, reading FULL MOON GARAGE. I pulled the Beetle into the gravel parking lot, and parked a few feet from the building.

"Thank God it's not too obvious or anything," I muttered, and killed the engine. It died with a new, moaning note to its usual rattle. I got out of the car, squinted at the building, and headed toward it. I didn't have my gun with me, but I did have my blasting rod, my shield bracelet, and a ring on my right hand in which I had stored up about as much energy as someone twice my size could put into a solid punch. Gravel crunched under my shoes as I walked, and rare autumn sunshine glared in my eyes and cast a long shadow behind me.

I wasn't sure who to expect inside, if anyone. The people I'd seen with the dark-haired woman the night before, the rather nerdy bunch of young people clad in imitation biker-leathers, didn't seem to be the sort of folk to inspire fear in other criminal toughs as the Streetwolves apparently had. But maybe there was a connection. Maybe the dark-haired woman from last night was linked with the Streetwolves, somehow, as well as with the young people I had seen. What had the stout young man, Billy, called them? The Alphas.

What, then, had the Alphas been? Biker thugs in training? That sounded ridiculous, even to me. But what if those young people had been lycanthropes, like the ones Bob had told me about? What if they were being trained, somehow, as junior members of the Streetwolves until they could be brought in as full werewolves? Presuming the Streetwolves themselves were lycanthropes or werewolves, that is. Sometimes, a biker gang is just a biker gang. There might be no connection to the Alphas at all. My head spun a little, trying to sort out the possibilities.

All in all, it was far better to hope that the building was empty, and that I wouldn't have to deal with anyone, werewolves or otherwise. I would much rather just poke around and find something incriminating inside, something that I could bring back to Murphy and Denton that would point them in the correct direction.

There was a regular door beside the pair of big, roll-up garage doors. Both of them were closed. I tried the regular door, and it opened easily enough, so I went on inside. There were no windows, and the only light in the garage fell into it from the open door behind me.

"Hello?" I called into the darkness. I tried to peer around, but saw nothing other than dim shapes and outlines, what might have been a car with the hood up, a couple of those rolling tool-cabinets. There was a dull reflection of glass windows off to one side, where there might have been an office. I stepped to one side of the doorway, squinting, and waited for my eyes to adjust.

There was a quiet sound, a dull rustle of clothing.

Dammit. I reached a hand into my duster, wrapping my fingers around my blasting rod, and Listened. I could hear the sound of breathing in the room, from multiple sources in a variety of directions. There was a scuffling sound, shoes on the concrete floor.

"I'm not a cop," I said into the darkness. I had the feeling that might be important for them to know. "My name is Harry Dresden. I just want to speak to the Streetwolves."

The room dropped into dead silence. No moving. No breathing. Nothing.

I waited, tense and ready to run.

"Take your hand out of your jacket," a male voice said. "And keep your hands where I can see them. We've heard of your kind, wizard. We've heard of you. You're with the cops."

"You're late on the gossip," I said wryly. "I'm playing doubles with Johnny Marcone now. Didn't you know?"

There was a snort from the dark. "Like hell. That's just Marcone's story. We know the real deal with you, wizard."

Christ. I wished the police were as savvy as these ne'er-do-wells. "I've heard a few things about you all, too," I said. "Not much of it is too friendly. Some of it might even be considered a little weird."

There was a rough laugh. "What do you think they say about you, Dresden? Get your hands where I can see them. Now." There was the click-clack of a pump shotgun's action.

I swallowed and took my hand slowly off my blasting rod, then held both of my hands innocuously out in front of me, palms up. I willed strength through my shield bracelet as I did, drawing its protective energies about me. "All right," I said. "Come up where I can see you."

"You don't give the orders here," the male voice snarled. "I do."

I pressed my lips together and drew in a breath through my nose. "I just want to talk to you."

"About what?" said the voice.

I tried to come up with something, something believable— but I'm not much of a liar. So I told them the truth. "Some dead people last month. More dead last night."

The voice didn't answer me for a moment. I licked my lips and kept going.

"There were fake wolf tracks around the murder scenes. And the feds think someone used a weapon lined with wolf teeth to tear the victims up. You wouldn't know anything about that, would you?"

There was a flurry of mutters around the room, low voices in hushed tones all around me. A dozen, maybe. More. I got a sudden, sinking feeling in the pit of my stomach. If these people were the murderers, if they were responsible for last month's deaths, I was in big trouble.

And if they were real werewolves, if they could shape-shift and come after me before I could clear out of there, I was as good as dead, shield bracelet or no. I choked down a surge of panic and forced myself not to turn and run for the door.

"Kill him," someone said from the darkness, off to my left, a female voice with a deep, growling tone to it. There was an answering chorus of mewling sounds from the dark around me, repetitions of "Kill him, kill him, kill him."

My eyes were starting to adjust to the lack of light. I could see them now, the shapes of people restlessly pacing. Their eyes glowed like dogs' eyes in the glare of headlights. Both men and women moved around me, though I couldn't tell their ages. There were blankets and pillows made into pallets on the floor, thrown aside while their occupants had risen. The female voice I had heard continued to chant, "Kill him, kill him, kill him," while the others followed her lead. The air grew tight and heavy with a kind of energy I had never sensed before, a power that was gaining momentum as they chanted, a feral, raging current.

Directly in front of me, not fifteen feet away, stood the large shape of a man holding a shotgun. "Stop it," he snarled, turning his head toward the others in the room. I could see his body responding as the energy grew, growing tenser, more ready. "Fight it. Hold it in, dammit. You can't let it loose here. There will be cops all over us."

When his head turned, I darted toward the doorway. I kept my left palm up and turned out toward the leader, the one with the shotgun, and held on to my shield as hard as I could.

My motion triggered a frenzied howl from the others in the room and they came surging toward me like a dozen creatures with one controlling mind. The shotgun roared and threw a flash of white light over the room, showing me a frieze of half-dressed or naked men and women hurtling toward me, their faces twisted with grimaces of berserk anger. The force of the blast slammed into my shield. It wasn't quite enough to shatter the protective field, but it made my bracelet grow warm and shoved my opposite shoulder hard against the wall.

I stumbled, thrown off balance. One of the men, a heavyset fellow with his shoulders covered in tattoos, got between me and the door. I ran at him, and he spread his arms to grab me, assuming I would try to go past him.

Instead, I drove my fist at his nose as hard as I could. I don't carry a lot of power on my own when I punch. But when I added in the kinetic energy stored in the ring, my fist became a battering ram of bone and flesh, flattening the man's nose in a gout of blood, and sending him sprawling to the ground six feet away.

I was through the door in a flash and felt the sun's welcome heat on my back. I pelted toward the Beetle, my long legs covering the ground quickly.

"Stop! Stop!" the leader shouted, and I cast a glance over my shoulder to see him, an older man with greasy hair beginning to go grey. He planted his feet in the doorway, facing inside, holding the shotgun across his body and shoving at the people trying to get past him.

I threw myself into the Beetle and jammed my key in the ignition.

The car wheezed and rattled, but didn't start. Dammit.

My hands were trembling, but I kept trying to get the car going, using every trick I knew to coax the engine to life, while watching the door. The leader of the Streetwolves was still there,

fighting to hold the frenzied group inside. They were screaming and howling, but he shoved them away, clubbed them down
with the shotgun like wild dogs, the muscles in his shoulders
and back straining. "Parker!" screamed one of them, the woman
who had begun the killing chant, "Let me through!" He swatted
her down with the butt of the shotgun without hesitation.

Then Parker turned his head toward me, and I met his eyes.
There was a swimming moment, and then I was past his eyes, to
what lay behind them.

Fury overwhelmed me, naked lust for meat, for the hunt. I
needed to run, to kill. I was invincible, unstoppable. I could feel
the power in my arms and hands, feel the raw energy of the wild
coursing through me, sharpening my senses to animal keenness.

I felt his emotions like they were my own. Fury beneath rigid
control, the ocean beating at a tide wall. The fury was directed
at me, Dresden, at the man who had invaded his territory, challenged his authority, and driven his people out of control, en-
dangering them. I saw that he was the leader of the lycanthropes
called the Streetwolves, men and women with the minds and
souls of beasts, and that he was aging, was not as strong as he
once had been. Others, like the woman earlier, were beginning
to challenge his authority. Today's events might tear him from
leadership, and he would never live through it.

If Parker was to live, I had to die. He had to kill me, pure and
simple, and he had to do it alone to prove his strength to the
pack. That was the only thing that kept him from coming at my
throat that very second.

Worse, he didn't know a damned thing about the last month's
killings.

And then the moment was past, the soulgaze over. Parker's
face was stunned. He had seen me in much the same way I had
seen him. I don't know what he saw when he looked upon my
soul. I didn't want to know what was down there.

I recovered from it before he did and fumbled at the keys
again. The Beetle coughed to life, and I pulled out and onto the

street, swerving wildly before gathering speed and heading back uptown as quickly as I could.

I shook the entire way, my shoulders so tight with fear and reaction that I could hear my collarbones creaking with strain. I could still hear the mewling chants of "Kill him, kill him," in my head. Those things in that garage had not been people. They had looked like people, but they weren't. And they scared the hell out of me.

While sitting at an intersection, I slammed my hand on the steering wheel, abruptly angry. "Stupid, Harry," I said. "How could you have been so stupid? Why in the hell did you go wandering in there like that? Do you realize how close those Neanderthal freaks came to tearing you apart?" I glared ferociously out my side window, at an old lady in a business suit who was staring at me as though I were a ranting madman. Which, I suppose, was what I looked like.

I stopped myself from glaring at her, took a deep breath, and tried to calm down. A couple of blocks later, I was able to start thinking straight again.

Parker and the Streetwolves were not responsible for the murders last month. That didn't make them any less dangerous. They were lycanthropes, the kind Bob had told me about, and I could see now why they had been feared. People with the souls of beasts, possessed of a ferocity so great that it could transform them into something inhuman without altering a single cell of their bodies.

They lived in a pack, and Parker was their leader. I had challenged his dominance in my clueless, bumbling way, and now he couldn't afford to let me live, or he would be killed himself. So now I had to worry about someone else coming after me, trying to kill me. Not only that, all of this trouble had come gratis, without giving me any lead on the true culprit of the Lobo killings.

Maybe it was a good time to leave town for a while.

I brooded over that for a block or so, and then shook my

head. I wouldn't run. I had made this trouble for myself, and I would get out of it myself. I had to stay, to help Murphy find the killer, and to help save lives before the full moon rose again. And if Parker wanted to kill me, well—he'd find that doing in a full-fledged wizard is no easy task.

I gripped the steering wheel grimly. If it came to it, I would kill him. I knew I could do that. Technically, I suppose, Parker and his lycanthropes weren't human. The First Law of Magic, Thou Shalt Not Kill, wouldn't necessarily apply to them. Legally, I might be able to make a case for the use of lethal magic to the White Council.

I just wouldn't be safe from myself. I wouldn't be safe from the loathing I would feel, using a tool made of life's essence, its energy, to bring an end to life. Magic was more than just an energy source, like electricity or petroleum. It was power, true, but it was a lot of other things as well. It was all that was deepest and most powerful in nature, in the human heart and soul. The ways in which I applied it were crude and clumsy in comparison to magic in its pure form. There's more magic in a baby's first giggle than in any firestorm a wizard can conjure up, and don't let anyone tell you any different.

Magic comes from what is inside you. It is a part of you. You can't weave together a spell that you don't believe in.

I didn't want to believe that killing was deep inside of me. I didn't want to think about the part of me that took a dark joy in gathering all the power it could and using it as I saw fit, everything else be damned. There was power to be had in hatred, too, in anger and in lust, in selfishness and in pride. And I knew that there was some dark corner of me that would enjoy using magic for killing—and then long for more. That was black magic, and it was easy to use. Easy and fun. Like Legos.

I parked the Beetle in the lot of my office building and rubbed at my eyes. I didn't want to kill anybody, but Parker and his gang might not give me any choice. I might have to do a lot of killing, if I was going to live.

I tried not to think too much about what sort of person it might be who survived. I would burn that bridge when I came to it.

I would go up to my office and hold business hours for the rest of the day. I would wait for Murphy to call me, and give her any aid that I could. I would keep my eyes and ears open in case Parker or any of his gang came after me. There wasn't much more I could do, and it was frustrating as hell.

I went up to my office, unlocked it, and flipped on the lights. Gentleman Johnny Marcone was seated at my desk in a dark blue business suit, and his hulking bodyguard, Mr. Hendricks, was standing behind him.

Marcone smiled at me, but it didn't touch the corners of his eyes. "Ah, Mr. Dresden. Good. We need to talk."

Chapter Ten

Marcone had eyes the color of old, faded dollar bills. His skin was weatherworn, with an outdoorsman's deep tan. Creases showed at the corners of his eyes and mouth, as though from smiling, but those smiles were rarely sincere. His suit must have cost him at least a thousand dollars. He sat at ease in my chair, *my* chair, mind you, and regarded me with professional calm.

From behind him, Mr. Hendricks looked like an all-star collegiate lineman who hadn't been smart enough to go into the pros. Hendricks's neck was as big around as my waist, and his hands were big enough to cover my face—and strong enough to crush it. His red hair was buzz cut, and he wore his ill-fitting suit like something that he planned to rip his way out of when he turned into the Hulk. I couldn't see his gun, but I knew he was carrying one.

I stood in the doorway and stared at Marcone for a minute, but my gaze did nothing to stir him. Marcone had met it already, and taken my measure more than I had taken his. My eyes held no more fear for him.

"Get out of my office," I said. I stepped inside and closed the door.

"Now, now, Mr. Dresden," Marcone said, a father's reproof in his tone. "Is that any way to talk to a business partner?"

I scowled. "I'm not your partner. I think you're scum. The worst criminal this city has. One of these days the cops will nail you, but until then, I don't have to put up with you here in my own office. Get out."

"The police," Marcone said, a hint of correction in his voice, "would be best off run by private agencies, rather than public institutions. Better pay, better benefits—"

"Easier to bribe, corrupt, manipulate," I injected.

Marcone smiled.

I took off my duster and dropped it over the table in front of the door, the one covered in pamphlets with titles like "Witches and You," and "Want to Do Magic? Ask Me How!" I untied my blasting rod from its thong and set it calmly on the table in front of me. I had the satisfaction of seeing Hendricks tense up when he saw the rod. He remembered what I had done to the Varsity last spring.

I glanced up. "Are you still here?"

Marcone folded his hands in front of him. "I have an offer to make you, Mr. Dresden."

"No," I said.

Marcone chuckled. "I think you should hear me out."

I looked him in the eyes and smiled faintly. "No. Get out."

His fatherly manner vanished, and his eyes became cold. "I have neither the time nor the tolerance for your childishness, Mr. Dresden. People are dying. You are now working on the case. I have information for you, and I will give it to you. For a price."

I felt my back stiffen. I stared at him for a long minute, and then said, "All right. Let's hear your price."

Marcone held out his hand and Hendricks handed him a folder. Marcone put the folder down on the battered surface of my old wooden desk and flipped it open. "This is a contract, Mr. Dresden. It hires you as a consultant for my firm, in personal security. The terms are quite generous. You get to name your own hours, with a minimum of five per month. You can fill in your salary right now. I simply want to formalize our working relationship."

I walked over to my desk. I saw Hendricks's weight shift, as though he were about to jump over the desk at me, but I ignored him. I picked up the folder and looked over the contract. I'm not a legal expert, but I was familiar with the forms for this kind of deal. Marcone was on the up and up. He was offering me a dream job, with virtually no commitment, and as much money as I could want. There was even a clause that specified that I would not be asked or expected to perform any unlawful acts.

With that kind of money, I could live the life I wanted. I could stop scraping for every dollar, running my legs off working for every paranoid looney who wanted to hire me to investigate his great-aunt's possessed cow. I could catch up on reading, finally, do the magical research I'd been itching to do for the past few years. I wouldn't live forever, and every hour that I wasted looking for UFOs in Joliet was one more hour I couldn't spend doing something I wanted to do.

It was a pretty damned tempting deal.

It was a very comfortable collar.

"Do you think I'm an idiot?" I said, and tossed the folder down on my desk.

Marcone's eyebrows went up, his mouth opening a little. "Is it the hours? Shall I lower the minimum to one hour per week? Per month?"

"It isn't the hours," I said.

He spread his hands. "What, then?"

"It's the company. It's the thought of a drug-dealing murderer having a claim on my loyalty. I don't like where your money comes from. It's got blood on it."

Marcone's cold eyes narrowed again. "Think carefully, Mr. Dresden. I won't make this offer twice."

"Let me make you an offer, John," I said. I saw the corner of his cheek twitch when I used his first name. "Tell me what you know, and I'll do my best to nail the killer before he comes for you."

"What makes you think I'm worried, Mr. Dresden?" Marcone said. He let a fine sneer color his words.

I shrugged. "Your business partner and his pet bodyguard get gutted last month. Spike gets torn to bits last night. And then you crawl out from under your rock to dangle information in my face to help me catch the killer and try to strong-arm me into becoming your bodyguard." I bent down and rested my elbows on the surface of the desk, then lowered my head until my eyes were a few inches from his. "Worried, John?"

His face twitched again, and I could smell him lying. "Of course not, Mr. Dresden. But you don't get where I have in life by being reckless."

"Just by being soulless, right?"

Marcone slammed his palms down on the desktop and stood. I rose with him, enough to stand over him, and to keep my eyes on his. "I am a man of business, Mr. Dresden. Would you prefer anarchy in the streets? Wars between rival crime lords? I bring *order* to that chaos."

"No. You just make the chaos more efficient and organized," I shot back. "Stick whatever pretty words you want onto it, but that doesn't change the fact that you're a thug, a fucking animal that should be in a cage. Nothing more."

Marcone's normally passionless face went white. His jaw clenched over words of rage. I pressed him, hard, my own anger spilling out with a passion gone out of control. I poured all of my recent frustration and fear into venomous words and hurled them at him like a handful of scrap metal.

"What's out there, John? What could it possibly be? Did you see Spike? Did you see how they'd torn his face off? Did you see the way they'd ripped his guts open? I did. I could smell what he had for dinner. Can you just imagine it happening to you next, John?"

"Don't call me that," Marcone said, his voice so quiet and cold that it set my momentum back on its heels. "If we were in public, Mr. Dresden, I'd have you killed for speaking that way to me."

"If we were in public," I told him, "you'd try." I drew myself up and glared down my nose at him, ignoring Hendricks's looming presence. "Now. Get the hell out of my office."

Marcone straightened his jacket and his tie. "I presume, Mr. Dresden, that you are going to continue your investigation with the police department."

"Of course."

Marcone walked around my desk, past me, and toward my door. Hendricks followed in his wake, huge and quiet. "Then in my own interests, I must accept your offer and aid the investigation however I might. Look up the name Harley MacFinn. Ask about the Northwest Passage Project. See where they lead you." He opened the door.

"Why should I believe you?" I asked him.

He looked back at me. "You have seen the deepest reaches of my soul, Mr. Dresden. You know me in a way so profound and intimate that I cannot yet fathom its significance. Just as I know you. You should know that I have every reason to help you, and that the information is good." He smiled again, wintry. "Just as you should know that it was unwise to make an enemy of me. It need not have been this way."

I narrowed my eyes. "If you know me so well, you should know that there's no other way it could be."

He pursed his lips for a moment, and did not try to refute me. "Pity," he said. "A true pity." And then he left. Hendricks gave me a pig-eyed little glare, and then he was gone, too. The door shut behind them.

I let out a long, shaking breath, and slumped against my desk. I covered my face with my hands, noticing as I did that they were shaking, too. I hadn't realized the depth of the disgust in me for Marcone and what he stood for. I hadn't realized how much it had sickened me to have my name associated with his. I hadn't realized how much I wanted to launch myself at the man and smash him in the nose with my fists.

I stayed that way for a few minutes, letting my heart beat hard, catching my breath. Marcone could have killed me. He could have had Hendricks tear me apart, or put a bullet in me right there—but he hadn't. That wasn't Marcone's way. He couldn't eliminate me now, not after working so hard to spread the word throughout the underworld that he and I had some sort of alliance. He would have to be more indirect, more subtle. Having Hendricks scatter my brains out on the floor wasn't the way to do it.

I thought over what he had said, and the implications of his acceptance of the deal I'd offered. He was in danger. Something had him scared, something that he didn't understand and didn't know how to fight. That was why he had wanted to hire me. As a wizard, I take the unknown and I turn it into something that can be measured. I take that cloak of terror off of things, make people able, somehow, to deal with them. Marcone wanted me to stand by him, to help him not be afraid of those things lurking in the dark.

Hell. It was only human.

I winced. I wanted to hate the man, but disgust, maybe anger, was as far as I could go. Too much of what he said was true. Marcone was a businessman. He had reduced violence in the streets—while sending the number of dollars made by criminals in this town soaring. He had protected the city's flesh while siphoning away its blood, poisoning its soul. It changed nothing, nothing at all.

But to know that the man I knew, the tiger-souled predator, the businessman killer—to know that he was frightened of what I was about to go up against: That scared the hell out of me, and added an element of intimidation to the work I was doing that hadn't been present before.

That didn't change anything, either. It's all right to be afraid. You just don't let it stop you from doing your job.

I sat down on the desk, forced thoughts of blood and fangs and agonizing death from my mind, and started looking for the name Harley MacFinn and the Northwest Passage Project.

Chapter
Eleven

The demon trapped in the summoning circle screamed, slamming its crablike pincers against the unseen barrier, hurling its chitinous shoulders from side to side in an effort to escape the confinement. It couldn't. I kept my will on the circle, kept the demon from bursting free.

"Satisfied, Chauncy?" I asked it.

The demon straightened its hideous form and said, in a perfect Oxford accent, "Quite. You understand, I must observe the formalities." Then it took a pair of wholly incongruous wireframe spectacles from beneath a scale and perched them upon the beaklike extremity of its nose. "You have questions?"

I let out a sigh of relief, and sat down on the edge of the worktable in my lab. I had cleared away all the clutter from around the summoning ring in the floor, and I'd have to move it before I could clamber up out of my lab, but I didn't like to take chances. No matter how comfortable Chaunzaggoroth and I were with our working relationship, there was always a chance that I could have messed up the summoning. There were rules of protocol that demonic beings were obliged to follow—one of them was offering resistance to any mortal wizard who called them. Another was doing their best to end the life of the same wizard, should they be able to escape the confines of the circle.

All in all, squeezing information from faeries and spirits of the elements was a lot easier and safer—but Bob had turned up nothing in his search among the local spirits. They weren't always up on information to be had in the city, and Bob now resided in his skull again, exhausted and unable to help any further.

So I'd gone to the underworld for assistance. They know when you've been bad or good, and they make Santa Claus look like an amateur.

"I need information about a man named Harley MacFinn, Chauncy. And about something he was working on called the Northwest Passage Project."

Chauncy clacked his pincers pensively. "I see. Presuming I have this information, what is it worth to you?"

"Not my soul," I snorted. "So don't even start with that. Look, I could dig this up myself in a few days."

Chauncy tilted his head, birdlike. "Ah. But time is of the essence, yes? Come now, Harry Dresden. You do not call upon me lightly. The possible dangers, both from myself and from your own White Council, are far too great."

I scowled at him. "Technically," I said, "I'm not breaking any of the Laws of Magic. I'm not robbing you of your will, so I'm clear of the Fourth Law. And you didn't get loose, so I'm clear of the Seventh Law. The Council can bite me."

The bone ridges above Chauncy's eyes twitched. "Surely, that is merely a colorful euphemism, rather than a statement of desire."

"It is."

Chauncy pushed the glasses a bit higher up on his nose. "The moral and ethical ramifications of your attitudes are quite fascinating, Harry Dresden. I am continually amazed that you remain in the Council's good graces. Knowing full well that most of the Council would look the other way while their enforcers killed you, should they learn that you have willfully brought a demon into this world, you still summon me not once, but a half-dozen times. Your attitudes are much more contiguous with those of many of my brethren in the World Below—"

"And I should throw in with your side, accept the dark powers, et cetera, et cetera," I finished for him, with a sigh. "Hell's bells, Chauncy. Why do you keep on trying to sucker me into signing on with Downbelow, eh?"

Chauncy shrugged his bulky shoulders. "I admit that it would give me no small amount of status to gather a soul of your caliber into our legions," he said. "Additionally, it would free me from the onerous duties which make even these excruciating visits to your world seem pleasant by comparison."

"Well, you aren't getting my soul today," I told him. "So make me a counteroffer, or we can call a close to the negotiations and I can send you back."

The demon shuddered. "Yes, very well. Let us not be hasty, Harry Dresden. I have the information you need. Additionally, I have more information of which you are not aware, and which would be of great interest to you, and which I judge, additionally, may help to preserve your life and the lives of others. Given the situation, I do not think the price I will ask inappropriate: I wish another of your names."

I frowned. The demon had two of my names already. If he gained my whole name, from my own lips, he could use it in any number of magical applications against me. That didn't particularly disturb me—demons and their ilk had great difficulty in reaching out from the Nevernever, the spirit world beyond the physical one we inhabited, with sorcery.

But Chaunzaggoroth was a popular source of information among wizards who went to the underworld in need of it. What bothered me was the possibility that one of them would get it. Chauncy was correct—there were a lot of people on the White Council who would be happy to see me dead. If one of them got my name, there was the chance that they would use it against me, either to kill me or to magically force me to do something that would openly violate one of the Seven Laws and have me brought to trial and killed.

On the other hand, Chauncy never lied to me. If he said he had information that could save people's lives, he had it, and that's all there was to it. Hell, he might even know who the killer was, though a demon's grasp of individual human identity was somewhat shaky.

I decided to gamble.

"Done," I said. "All pertinent information on the subject of my inquiry in exchange for another of my names."

Chauncy nodded once. "Agreed."

"All right," I said. "Let's have the information on MacFinn and the Northwest Passage Project."

"Very well," Chauncy said. "Harley MacFinn is an heir to a considerable fortune made in coal mining and railroads at the turn of the twentieth century. He is one of the ten richest men in the country known as the United States. He served during the police action in Vietnam, and when he returned to this country he began divesting himself of business interests, merely accruing capital. His favorite color is red, his shoe size is—"

"We can skip the little details unless you think they will be really relevant," I said. "I could hear about his favorite food and his problems in middle school all day and it wouldn't help anything." I got out my notebook and started taking notes.

"As you wish," Chauncy assented. "The object of his endeavors for the past several years has been the Northwest Passage Project. The project is an effort to buy enormous tracts of land, beginning in the central Rocky Mountains of the American Southwest, and moving northwest into Canada, to provide for an enormous, migratory-sized preserve for North American wildlife."

"He wants to make his own private playground out of the Rocky Mountains?" I blurted.

"No, Harry Dresden. He wishes to acquire the lands that are not already owned by the government, then donate them, provided the government guarantees that they will be used as a part of the Northwest Passage Project. He has considerable backing from environmentalist groups throughout the country, and support in your capital, as well, provided he can get the land."

"Wow," I said, impressed. "You said he has a lot of support. Who wants to stop him?"

"Industrial interests still looking to expand into the Northwest," Chauncy said.

"Let me guess. James Harding III was one of them," I said, already writing it down.

"How did you know?" Chauncy asked.

"He was killed by a werewolf last month, along with his bodyguard. Several other people died as well."

Chauncy beamed. "You are a clever man, Harry Dresden. Yes. James Douglas Harding III was exceptionally interested in blocking MacFinn's efforts to acquire property. He came to Chicago to have negotiations with MacFinn, but died before they were complete."

I closed my eyes for a minute, thinking. "Okay. Harding comes to town to talk to MacFinn. Harding's in cahoots with Marcone, so maybe Marcone is hosting the talks. Harding and his bodyguard get et-all-up by a werewolf. So . . . MacFinn is the werewolf in question?"

Chauncy smiled, a rather intimidating expression. "MacFinn is a member of an ancient family line from an island known as Ireland. His family has a notable history. Sometime in the murky past, legend would have it, the man known as Saint Patrick cursed his ancestor to become a ravening beast at every full moon. The curse came with two addenda. First, that it would be hereditary, passing down to someone new each and every generation. And second, that the cursed line of the family would never, ever die out, lasting until the end of days."

I wrote that down as well. "A Catholic saint did that?"

Chauncy made a sound of distaste. "I am not responsible for the sorts of people the Other Side employs, wizard. Or the tactics they use."

"Considering the source, I think I'll note it as a biased opinion. Your folk have done a thousand times worse," I said.

"Well. True," Chauncy admitted. "But we tend to be quite honest about the sort of beings we are and the sorts of things we stand for, at least."

I snorted. "All right. This is making a lot more sense now. MacFinn is a loup-garou, one of the legendary monsters. He's trying to do some good in his spare time, make the big park for all the furry critters, but Harding puts himself in the way. MacFinn goes on a killing spree and wipes him out." I frowned. "Except that Harding was the last person to be murdered last month. You would have thought that if MacFinn was going to lose it, Harding would be the first to go." I peered at Chauncy. "Is MacFinn the murderer?"

"MacFinn is a murderer," Chauncy said. "But among humankind, he is one of many, and not the most monstrous."

"Is he the one who killed Marcone's bodyguard? The other people last month?"

"My information on that point is inconclusive, Harry Dresden," Chauncy said. His black eyes gleamed. "Perhaps for the price of another name, I could inquire of my brethren and give you a more precise answer."

I scowled. "Not a chance. Do you know who murdered the other people, last month?"

"I do," Chauncy said. "Murder is one of the foremost sins, and we keep close track of sins."

I leaned forward intently. "Who was it?"

Chauncy laughed, a grating sound. "Really, Harry Dresden. In the first place, our bargain was for information regarding MacFinn and the Northwest Passage Project. In the second, I could not tell you the answer to such a direct question, and you know it. There is a limit to how much I may involve myself in mortal affairs."

I let out a breath of frustration and rubbed at my eyes. "Yeah, yeah. All right, Chauncy. What else can you tell me?"

"Only that Harley MacFinn was planning to meet with John Marcone tomorrow night, to continue the talks."

"Wait a minute. Is Marcone the major opponent to the project now?"

"Correct," Chauncy said. "He assumed control of a majority of the business interests shared with Harding upon Harding's death."

"So . . . Marcone had a fantastic motive to have Harding killed. It broadened his financial empire, and put him in a position to gouge MacFinn for as much money as he possibly could."

Chauncy adjusted his wire-frame spectacles. "Your reasoning would seem to be sound."

I thumped my pencil on my notebook, staring at what I had written. "Yeah. But it doesn't explain why everyone else got killed. Or who did it. Unless Marcone's got a pack of werewolves in his pocket, that is." I chewed on my lip, and thought about my encounter at the Full Moon Garage. "Or Streetwolves."

"Is there anything else?" Chauncy asked, his manner solicitous.

"Yes," I said. "Where can I find MacFinn?"

"Eight eighty-eight Ralston Place."

I wrote it down. "But that's right here in Chicago. In the Gold Coast."

"Where did you expect a billionaire to live when he was in Chicago, Harry Dresden? Now, I seem to have lived up to all of my obligations. I expect my payment now." Chauncy took a few restless steps back and forth within the circle. His time on earth was beginning to wear on him.

I nodded. "My name," I said, "is Harry Blackstone Dresden." I carefully omitted "Copperfield" from the words, while leaving the tones and pronunciation the same.

"Harry. Blackstone. Dresden," Chauncy repeated carefully. "Harry as in Harry Houdini? Blackstone, the stage illusionist?"

I nodded. "My dad was a stage musician. When I was born, he gave me those names. They were always his heroes. I think if my mother had survived the birth, she would have slapped him for it." I made a few more notes on my page, getting ideas down on paper before they fled from memory.

"Indeed," Chauncy agreed. "Your mother was a most direct and willful woman. Her loss was a great sadness to all of us."

I blinked, startled, and the pencil fell from my fingers. I stared at the demon for a moment. "You . . . you knew my mother? You knew Margaret Gwendolyn Dresden?"

Chauncy regarded me without expression or emotion. "Many in the underworld were . . . familiar with her, Harry Blackstone Dresden, though under a different name. Her coming was awaited with great anticipation, but the Dark Prince lost her, in the end."

"What do you mean? What are you talking about?"

Chauncy's eyes gleamed with avarice. "Didn't you know about your mother's past, Mr. Dresden? A pity that we didn't have this conversation sooner. You might have added it into the bargain we made. Of course, if you would like to forfeit another name, to know all about your mother's past, her . . ." his voice twisted with distaste, "redemption, and the unnatural deaths of both mother and father, I am certain we can work something out."

I gritted my teeth in a sudden rush of childlike frustration. My heart pounded in my ears. My mother's dark past? I had expected that she was a wizardess, but I had never been able to prove anything, one way or another. Unnatural deaths? My father had perished in his sleep, of an aneurism, when I was young. My mother had died in childbirth.

Or had they?

A sudden, burning desire to know filled me, starting at my gut and rolling outward through my body—to know who my mother was, what she had known. She had left me her silver pentacle, but I knew nothing of the sort of person she was, other than what my gentle and too-generous father had told me before his death. What were my parents like? How had they perished and why? Had they been killed? Did they have enemies lurking out there, somewhere? If so, had I inherited them?

My mother's dark past. Did that explain my own fascination with the darker powers, my somewhat-less-than-sterling adherence to the rules of the White Council that I considered foolish or inconvenient?

I looked up at the demon, and felt like a sucker. I had been set up. He had intended, all along, to dangle this information in front of me as bait. He wanted to get my whole name, if he could, or more.

"I can show them to you, Harry Blackstone Dresden, as they really are," Chaunzaggoroth assured me, his voice dulcet. "You've never seen your mother's face. I can give that to you. You've never heard her voice. I can let you hear that as well. You know nothing of what sort of people your parents were—or if you have any other family out there. Family, Harry Blackstone Dresden. Blood. Every bit as tormented and alone as you are . . ."

I stared at the demon's hideous form and listened to his soothing, relaxing voice. Family. Was it possible that I had a family? Aunts? Uncles? Cousins? Others, like me, perhaps, moving through the secret societies of the wizards, hidden from the view of the mortal world?

"The price is comparatively low. What need have you for your immortal soul when your body is finished with it? What harm to pass on to me only one more name? This is not information easily gained, even by my kind. You may not have the chance to garner it again." The demon pressed his pincers against the barrier of the conjuring circle. His beaklike maw fairly trembled with eagerness.

"Forget it," I said quietly. "No deal."

Chaunzaggoroth's jaw dropped open. "But, Harry Blackstone Dresden—" he began.

I didn't realize that I was shouting until I saw him flinch. "I said forget it! You think I'm some kind of simp for you to sucker in, darkspawn? Take what you have gained and go, and feel lucky that I do not send you home with your bones torn from your body or your beak ground into dust."

Chaunzaggoroth's eyes flashed with rage and he hurled himself against the barrier again, howling with blood lust and fury. I extended my hand and snarled, "Oh no you don't, you slimy little shit head." The demon's will strained against mine, and though sweat burst out on my forehead, I came out ahead once more.

Chaunzaggoroth began to grow smaller and smaller, howling out his frustrated rage. "We are watching you, wizard!" he screamed. "You walk through shadows and one night you will slip and fall. And when you do, we will be there. We will be waiting to bring you down to us. You will be ours in the end."

He went on like that until he shrank to the size of a pinpoint and vanished with a little, imploding sound. I let my hand drop and lowered my head, breathing hard. I was shaking all over, and not only with the cold of my laboratory. I had badly misjudged Chaunzaggoroth, thought him a somewhat reliable, if dangerous, source of information, willing to do reasonable business. But the rage, the fury, the frustrated malice that had been in his final offer, those last words, had shown his true colors. He had lied to me, deceived me about his true nature, played me along like a sucker and then tried to set the hook, hard. I felt like such an idiot.

The phone began to ring upstairs. I stirred into sudden motion, shoving stacks of things out of my way, pushing past them and over them, to reach the stepladder stairs that led up to my apartment. I hurried up them, my notebook in one hand, and caught the phone on its fifth ring. My apartment was dark. Night had fallen while I had interviewed the demon.

"Dresden," I said, puffing.

"Harry," Murphy said, her voice weak. "We've got another one."

"Son of a bitch," I said. "I'm coming. Give me the address." I set down the notebook and held my pencil ready to write.

Murphy's tone was numb. "Eight eighty-eight Ralston Place. Up in the Gold Coast."

I froze, staring at the address I had written down on the notebook. The address the demon had given me.

"Harry?" Murphy said. "Did you hear me?"

"I heard," I told her. "I'm coming, Murph." I hung up the phone and headed out into the light of the full moon overhead.

Chapter

Twelve

Eight eighty-eight Ralston was a townhouse in the Gold Coast, the richest area of Chicago. It was set on its own little plot, surrounded by trees that hid the house from view almost entirely. High hedges, worked around the house in a small garden, added to the concealment as I drove up the white pebble drive, and parked the Beetle at the rear of a small fleet of police cars and emergency vehicles.

The strobing blue lights were almost comforting, by now. I'd seen them so many times that it felt, in an unsettling way, like a homecoming. Murphy had called me in early—I didn't see the forensics van yet, and only now were officers putting up yellow tape around the property.

I got out of my car, dressed in my jeans, button-down shirt, and boots again, my old black duster flapping around my calves. The wind was brisk, cold. The moon was riding high overhead, barely visible through the city's haze of pollution.

A chill ran down my neck, and I stopped, looking at the rows and rows of elegantly illuminated hedge sculptures, flower beds, and rows of shrubbery around me. I was abruptly certain that someone was out in the darkness; I could feel eyes on me.

I stared out at the night, sweeping my gaze slowly around. I could see nothing, but I would have bet money that there was someone out there. After a moment, the sense of being watched faded, and I shivered. I shoved my hands in my pockets and walked quickly toward the townhouse.

"Dresden," someone called, and I looked up to see Carmichael coming down the front stairs of the townhouse toward me. Carmichael was Murphy's right hand in Special Investigations. Shorter than average, rounder than average, slobbier than average, and with piggier eyes than average, Carmichael was a skeptic, a doubter, and a razor-sharp cop. He came down the stairs in his soup-stained old tie and shirtsleeves. "It's about fucking time. Jesus Christ, Dresden." He wiped a hand over his sweating brow.

I frowned down at Carmichael as we went up the stairs side by side. "That's the nicest greeting you've ever given me, I think," I said. "You change your mind about me being a fake?"

Carmichael shook his head. "No. I still think you're full of shit with this wizard-magic business. But Christ almighty, there are times when I wish you weren't."

"You never can tell," I said, my voice dry. "Where's Murphy?"

"Inside," Carmichael said, his mouth twisting with distaste. "You go on up the stairs. The whole place belongs to this guy. Murphy figures you might know something. I'm going to stay here and bog down the Feds when they show."

I glanced at him. "She still worried about looking bad for Internal Affairs?"

Carmichael grimaced. "Those assholes in IA would be all over her if she kicked the Feds out. Christ almighty, I get sick of city politics sometimes."

I nodded agreement and started up the stairs.

"Hey, Dresden," Carmichael said.

I looked over my shoulder at him, expecting the familiar jeers and insults. He was studying me with bright, narrow eyes. "I hear things about you and John Marcone. What's the deal?"

I shook my head. "No deal. He's lying scum."

Carmichael studied me intently, and then nodded. "You ain't much of a liar, Dresden. I don't think you could keep a straight face about something like this. I believe you."

"But you don't believe me when I say I'm a wizard?" I asked.

Carmichael grimaced and looked away. "Do I look like a fucking moron to you? Huh? You better get upstairs. I'll make some noise when Denton and the Stepford agents get here."

I turned to go and saw Murphy standing at the head of the stairs in a crisp grey business jacket and slacks, with sensible low heels and jewelry the color of steel. Her earrings seemed to be little more than bright beads of silver in her ears, which I had never really noticed when she had worn her golden hair long. Murphy's earlobes were cute. She'd kill me, just for thinking it.

"About time, Dresden. Get up here." Her voice was hard, angry. She vanished from the top of the stairway, and I took the rest of the stairs two at a time to catch up with her.

The apartment (though it was too big for the word to really apply) was brightly lit, and smelled, very faintly, of blood. Blood has a sweet sort of metallic odor. It makes the hairs on the back of your neck stand up, and mine snapped to attention at once. There was another smell as well, maybe incense of some kind, and the fresh scent of the wind. I turned down a short hall at the top of the stairs, and followed Murphy into what was apparently a master bedroom, where I found the source of all the scents.

There was no furniture inside the master bedroom—and it was huge, large enough to make you wince at how far you'd have to go to get to the bathroom in the middle of the night. There was no carpeting. There were no decorations on the walls. There was no glass in the huge, single-pane window, letting in the October wind. The full moon shone down through it like a picture in a frame.

What the room did have was blood. There was blood all over, scattered in droplets and splashed in spurts against one wall. The scarlet footprints of something like a large wolf led in a straight line toward the shattered window. In the center of the room were the remains of a greater circle of summoning, its three rings of symbols carefully wrought in white chalk upon the wooden floor, burning sticks of incense interspersed among the symbols of the second ring.

What was left of Kim Delaney lay naked and supine on the bloodstained floor a few feet from the circle. The expression of shock and surprise on her face wouldn't change until rigor set in. Her dark, once-glittering eyes stared up at the ceiling, and her lips were parted, as though in the middle of an apology.

A large, wheel section of flesh beneath her chin was missing, and with it Kim's larynx and trachea. Bloody red meat was showing, the ragged ends of arteries and torn sections of muscle, and pale white bones gleamed at the bottom of the wound. Long rakes down her body had opened her like a Ziploc bag, leaving her covered in scarlet.

Something went "click" in my head. Someone threw some kind of switch that just turned off my emotions entirely and immersed me in a surreal haze. I couldn't be seeing this. It simply couldn't be real. It had to be some sort of game or hoax, in which the actors would start giggling in a few moments, unable to contain the mirth of their prank.

I waited. But no one started giggling. I wiped at my forehead with my hand and found cold sweat there. My fingers began to shake.

Murphy said, her voice still tight with anger, "Apparently, the incense set off the fire alarm in the hall. When the fire department got here, no one answered, so they came on in. They found her up here, around eight o'clock. She was still warm."

Eight o'clock. When I had been talking to the demon. Moonrise?

Behind me, Murphy closed the door to the bedroom. I turned to her, away from the grisly corpse. There was anger in every inch of her, in the way she glared at me.

"Murph," I said. "I don't know if I can do this."

"What's there to figure?" Murphy said. "There's a monster in the middle of the circle. I figure it's one of those loup-garou from your report. I figure it's Harley MacFinn, the owner of this house. Someone who knows he's going to go nuts when the moon rises. The girl tries to hold the monster inside the magic circle, right? Something goes wrong when MacFinn goes furry; he gets out of the circle, wastes her, then leaves."

"Uh-huh," I said, without turning around to look at Kim's body again. "It makes sense." And I told her what I had learned from the demon about Harley MacFinn, the Northwest Passage Project, and his antagonism with Marcone's business interests. Murphy listened to me in utter silence. When I was finished, she nodded, and turned to leave the room.

"Follow," she said shortly.

I followed, almost on her heels. I didn't turn around to see the room again before I left.

She led me down the hall, into another bedroom, this one furnished and neatly kept. "Come here," she said, moving to a dresser. I did, and she handed me a photograph of a middle-aged, starkly handsome man, his skin deeply tanned, the bones of his face gaunt and sharp. He was smiling.

Beside him in the picture was the amber-eyed woman from the department store where I'd run across the Alphas. She was also smiling. Her teeth were very white, very even, and her dark skin and silver-peppered hair went well with the man beside her. I chewed on my lip for a second, trying to think.

"That's Harley MacFinn," Murphy said. "Matches the picture on his driver's license. I didn't turn up any ID on the woman next to him, though." She studied my face critically. "She matches the description of the woman you said you saw in the department store, though. The one who followed us back from the scene in Rosemont. Is that her?"

I nodded. "Yeah. That's her."

Murphy nodded, took the picture from me, and set it back on the dresser. "Follow," she said again and walked out. I stared after her. What was wrong with Murphy? Had the scene unsettled her so much? I shook my head, still stunned from what I had seen, from too many facts coming together all at once, slam-bang in my brain.

"Murph, wait," I said. "Stop a minute. What's going on?"

She didn't answer me, just shot me a glare over her shoulder and continued walking. I hurried to catch up with her.

We went down what looked like a servant's narrow spiral staircase, down into the basement. She led me to the back of a storage room and pushed open a heavy, steel door there that opened onto a small, stark chamber, all of concrete, with no other exits. In the center of the chamber was another three-ring summoning circle, but this one's symbols had been made from silver and set into the concrete of the floor. Short bars of what looked like a mixture of silver and obsidian were interspersed around the second circle, creating what would, if the circle was functional, be a very formidable barrier.

But the symbols had been marred, torn, broken. Several from the critical inner ring had been pried up from the floor and were simply missing. Some of the bars had been broken. The circle, as it was, was nonfunctional and worthless—but whole, it would have served to contain Harley MacFinn when he shifted into his beast form. The room was a prison he had created for himself, something to contain the fury of the beast inside of him.

But someone had intentionally marred the circle, made the prison useless.

And I abruptly understood Kim Delaney's request. She had to have known Harley MacFinn, maybe through her environmental activism. She must have learned of his curse, and wanted to help him. When I had refused to help her, she had attempted to re-create the greater summoning circle upstairs in the bedroom, to hold in MacFinn once the moon rose. As I had warned her would happen, she had failed. She hadn't had the knowledge necessary to understand how such a construct would function, and consequently, she hadn't been able to make it work.

MacFinn had killed her. Kim was dead because I had refused to share my knowledge with her, because I hadn't given her my help. I had been so secure in my knowledge and wisdom; withholding such secrets from her had been the action of a concerned and reasoned adult speaking to an overeager child. I couldn't believe my own arrogance, the utter confidence with which I had condemned her to death.

I started to shake, harder, too many things pressing against my head, my heart. I could feel the pressure, somewhere inside of me, that switch on the inside of my head quivering, getting ready to flick back beneath a tide of raging anger, fury, regret, self-hatred. I took deep breaths and closed my eyes, trying not to let it happen.

I opened my eyes and looked up at Murphy. God, I needed to talk to her. I needed a friend. I needed someone to listen, to tell me it would be all right whether it was the truth or not. I needed someone to let me unload on them, to keep me from flying apart.

She regarded me with cold, angry eyes.

"Karrin," I whispered.

She drew from her pocket a crumpled piece of paper. She unfolded it, and held it up to me, so that I could see Kim Delaney's graceful handwriting, the sketch of the summoning circle that she had brought to me in McAnally's. The sketch I had refused to tell Kim about. The sketch I had crumpled into a little ball and tossed on the floor, and which Murphy had picked up, absently, just to get the trash out of people's way.

And I realized why there was so much anger in Murphy's eyes.

I stared at the sketch. "Karrin," I began again. "Stars above, you've got to listen to me." I took the sketch from her hands, my fingers trembling.

"Harry," she said, in a calm tone. "You lying *bastard*," and on the word she drove her fist into my stomach, hard, doubling me over. The motion put my head within easy reach, and her fist took me across the jaw in a right cross that sent me to the floor like a lump of wet pasta, stars dancing in my vision.

I was only dimly aware of her taking the sketch back from me. She twisted my arms painfully behind my back, and snapped her handcuffs around my wrists. "You promised me," she said, her voice furious. "You *promised*. No secrets. You lied to me all along. You played me like a sucker the entire while. Goddammit, Dresden, you're involved in this and people are dying."

"Murph," I mumbled. "Wait."

She grabbed my hair, jerked my head back, and slammed me across the jaw again, near-berserk anger lending her strength. My head swam, and blackness closed over my vision for several seconds.

"No more talking. No more *lies*," I heard her say, and she dragged me to my feet, shoved my face and chest against a wall, and began searching me for weapons. "No more people torn up like meat on a block. You have the right to remain silent. Anything you say can and will be used against you in a court of law."

She took my blasting rod. My shield bracelet. The energy ring. Even my lump of chalk. Her voice went on, hard, cold, and professional, letting me know my rights.

I closed my eyes and leaned against the stone wall. Next to my head, it was the softest thing in the room. I didn't try to fight or to explain.

What was the point?

Chapter
Thirteen

Walking down stairs with your hands fastened behind your back is more difficult than you would think. You depend upon your arms for balance, whether you realize it or not. With my hands cuffed at the small of my back, and Murphy walking me up the narrow servant's staircase, and then down the front stairs of MacFinn's building in front of a gaggle of staring police officers, my balance was gone.

As we came down, I could hear arguing voices. "You want to get in my face about this?" Carmichael demanded. "Look. I'm doing my job. My boss said no one was to go up, so no one goes up. Do I need to use shorter words or what?"

I looked up to see Denton towering over Carmichael, the veins in his forehead athrob, his three associates spread out in a fan behind him. "You are interfering with a duly appointed officer executing his duties," Denton snarled. "Get out of my way, Detective Carmichael. Or do you want to get added to Internal Affairs' to-do list along with your boss?"

"It's all right, Ron," Murphy said. "I'm done with my business up there, anyway."

Carmichael looked up at me and stared, his mouth opening. Denton and his crew looked, too. I saw Denton's face twist in surprise, and then close again, hedging out any emotion from his expression. Roger, the redheaded kid who worked for Denton, was staring at me openly, his jaw dropped. Benn, the woman who had attacked Murphy last night, regarded me with an almost bored expression, and Wilson, the overweight one, let out a satisfied snort.

"Lieutenant," Carmichael said. "You sure about this?"

"He was arguing with the most recently deceased last night. I can connect him to at least one resident of the house, as well as some of the . . . decorations there. I'm taking him in for obstructing and for conspiracy to commit murder. Put him in the car, Carmichael, and then get your ass upstairs." Murphy gave me a sharp push toward Carmichael, and I stumbled. Carmichael caught me.

"So let's go, Denton," Murphy said, and turned and stalked away. Denton gave me an expressionless glance, and stepped after Murphy, beckoning his companions to follow.

Carmichael shook his head and walked me to one of the police cars. "Fuck, Dresden. And here I was getting ready to throw in on your side. Guess I'm just a sucker for the underdog."

Carmichael unlocked the back of the car and put his hand on the back of my head as I bent down to get into it. "Watch your head. Christ, what happened to your jaw?"

I sat down in the back of the car and looked straight ahead. I didn't answer him. Carmichael stared at me for a while, and then shook his head. "We'll have someone drive you downtown as soon as the scene is secure. You can get in touch with your lawyer, then."

I kept my eyes forward and still didn't answer him.

Carmichael studied me some more, then stood and shut me into the car.

I closed my eyes.

I have felt low before in my life, have experienced events that left me broken and groveling and wishing I was dead. That was pretty much how I felt now, too. It wasn't that I hadn't found the killer—I've been beaten before, taken the blow on the chin, and come out fighting the next round. I can roll with the punches as well as anyone. But I hated feeling that I had betrayed a friend.

I had promised Murphy that I would keep no secrets from her—and I hadn't. Not really. But I had been stupid. I should have been putting pieces together more quickly, more instinctively. Perhaps I had some excuse in that I had been distracted by nearly having my head blown off at the Full Moon Garage, that I had been distracted by my soulgaze upon the Street-wolves' leader, and the knowledge that he wanted to kill me. But it wasn't a good enough excuse to clear things with Murphy. I wasn't sure anything would have been. I felt alone. I felt frustrated. I felt like shit.

And I felt worse, a moment later, when I looked out the car window at the full moon and realized something that I should have put together an hour before—the real killer or killers were still out there.

MacFinn couldn't have been responsible for all of the deaths the previous month. Two of the murders had occurred on the nights before and after the full moon. If MacFinn's curse was indeed to become a ravening beast during the full moon, he could not have murdered either of last month's victims, or Spike at the Varsity last night.

Which begged the question: Who *had* done the killings?

I didn't have any answers. If the dark-haired woman who had led the Alphas was indeed connected with MacFinn, could she have been responsible? Something wolflike had attacked me in the abandoned department store when all the lights had been out—had it been her? One of the Alphas? Perhaps that would explain how the other murders happened.

But if it had been true, why hadn't the killer finished me off while I was floundering in the dark, virtually helpless?

More and more questions, and no answers.

Not that it mattered to me now. A nice, quiet jail cell didn't sound too bad, once I thought about it. At least it would keep the criminal element off of my back. Provided they didn't shut me up with a four-hundred-pound con named "Hump" or anything.

And then an odd feeling crept over me, derailing my train of thought. Once more, the hairs on my neck were standing up. Someone was watching me.

I looked around. There was no one in sight. All of the police were inside the house. I was alone in the back of the patrol car, with my hands bound. I was helpless and alone, and I suddenly became very aware of the fact that Harley MacFinn had yet to be found or apprehended. He was still lurking in the night, unable to keep from tearing apart anyone he saw.

I thought of Spike's torn corpse. Of poor Kim Delaney, covered in her own blood upstairs in the townhouse. I added imaginary (and far more horrible) images of half a dozen other victims, stacking scene upon scene of blood and death in my mind within a few seconds.

I broke out in a cold sweat and looked out the other window.

Directly into a pair of brilliant, feral, amber eyes.

I yelled and flinched away, lifting my legs to kick should something come rushing through the vehicle's window. Instead, the door opened, and the dark-haired, amber-eyed woman from the department store said, "Be quiet, Mr. Dresden, or I will not be able to rescue you."

I blinked at her, over my upraised knees. "Huh?"

"Rescue you, Mr. Dresden. Get out of the car and come with me. And quickly, before the police return." She peered past me, toward the house. "There is not much time."

"Are you crazy?" I demanded. "I don't even know who the hell you are."

"I am Harley MacFinn's fiancée, Miss West," she said. "I am called Tera."

I shook my head. "I can't leave. I'd be buying more trouble than you could imagine."

Her amber eyes glinted. "You are the only one who can stop my fiancé, Mr. Dresden. You cannot do that from a jail cell."

"I'm not the Lone Ranger," I snapped in reply. "I'm a hired consultant. And I don't think the city is going to foot the bill for this sort of thing."

Tera West's teeth showed. "If money is your concern, I assure you that it is not a problem, Mr. Dresden. Time presses. Will you come, or not?"

I studied her face. She had clean, striking features, exceptional more than attractive. There were crow's-feet at the edges of her eyes, though they were the only sign of age on her that I could see. There was, along the edge of her forehead, at the hairline, a long, slender, purpling bruise.

"You," I said. "It was you who attacked me in the department store. I hit you, and you took my rod away from me."

She glared at me. "Yes," she said.

"You're a werewolf."

"And you," she said, "are a wizard. And we have no more time." She crouched a bit lower, staring past me. I looked in that direction, and saw Denton and his cronies exiting the townhouse, engaged in an animated discussion. "Your friend," she said, "the police detective, is close to finding my fiancé. Do you really want her to be the one to face him? Is she prepared to deal with what she will find? Or will she die, as the others did?"

Dammit. The bitch (no pun intended) was right. I was the one who was capable of actually doing something about MacFinn. If Murphy was the one to catch up to him first, people would get killed. She was a fantastic cop, and was becoming more adept at dealing with the supernatural, but she wasn't able to handle a major werewolf berserker. I turned back to Tera. "If I go with you, you'll take me to MacFinn."

She stopped in the midst of turning to leave. "When I can. At dawn. If you think you can create the circle, hold him in when the moon again rises. If you can help him."

I nodded once. My decision was made. "I can. I will."

"She who was called Kim Delaney said the same thing," Tera West said, and spun on her heels to head away from me, crouched low to the ground.

I rolled out of the backseat and followed Tera West out into the shrubberies and garden shadows around the building, away from the police cars and the lights.

Someone shouted in surprise, somewhere behind me. Then there was a cry of "Stop!" I just stood and ran, as fast as I could, to get out of the lights and the line of sight of any possible shooters.

Apparently, the one shout was all the warning I was going to get. Gunfire erupted behind me as I ran. Bullets tore up the dirt next to my feet. I think I started screaming without slowing down, hunching my shoulders and ducking my head as best I could.

I was maybe five feet away from the sheltering shadows behind the hedges when something slammed into my shoulder and threw me *through* the hedge and out the other side. I landed in a roll and stumbled halfway back to my feet. There was a second of screaming, confused input from my shoulder, as though my joints could suddenly hear a welter of sound, feel a broad variety of sensation and texture beneath my skin. And then my shoulder went numb entirely, and my vision started spinning. I reached out a hand to support myself as I started to fall—and remembered that my wrists were still cuffed behind me. I went into the turf, felt the grass against my cheek.

"He's down, he's down!" came a cold, female voice—Agent Benn's, I thought. "Take him!"

There was no warning of presence, just the feeling of someone jerking me up to my feet by my duster. I felt Tera's hand slide beneath my jacket, then vanish as she pressed it to the numbed area of my arm.

"You are not bleeding badly," Tera said, her voice calm. "You were shot in the shoulder. Not the leg. Run or die." Then she turned and started making her way through the hedges.

Some encouragement—but I had a hunch I would be feeling a lot worse a few minutes from now. So I swallowed the sickly taste of fear and loped after Tera West as best I could.

We started a game of shadow-haunted hide-and-seek in the little garden, Tera and me against the agents behind us. She moved like a wraith, in utter silence, smooth and steady in the black shadows and silver light of the moon overhead. She immediately cut into the hedges, taking lefts and rights every few paces. She did not slow down for me, and I was somehow very certain that MacFinn's fiancée would not stop and wait for me should I fall. She wouldn't hesitate to leave me behind if I could not keep the pace.

I did it for a while. It wasn't even too hard. Oh, I felt a little out of breath, a little hampered by the handcuffs, but other than that, it was almost as though I hadn't been shot, aside from the trickling warmth I could feel sliding down my ribs and over my belly. Endorphins—what a rush.

Our pursuers plunged into the maze of hedges, shrubs, and statuary, but my guide seemed to have an uncanny knack for avoiding them. She kept to the darkest parts of the garden as we went, checking behind her to make sure I was keeping the pace.

I wasn't sure how much time passed that way, ghosting through the darkness while our pursuers struggled to coordinate their efforts and remain quiet at the same time, but it couldn't have been long. I've read somewhere that the initial shock of gunshot injuries always wears off after a few moments—besides, I was out of shape. I couldn't have kept up with Tera West for long. She was that fast, that good.

My shoulder began to pound double time to my laboring heart as we emerged from the last of the hedges to the street outside—and the eight-foot wrought iron fence that surrounded the property. I slid to a halt and stumbled against the fence, wheezing.

Tera looked over her shoulder, her amber eyes bright beneath the moon. She was breathing through her nose silently, the crouched run having not tired her in the least, it seemed.

"I can't climb the fence," I said. The pain from my shoulder was starting to become very real now—it felt like a runner's cramp, only higher up. "There's no way. Not with my hands cuffed."

Tera nodded once. "I will lift you," she said.

I stared at her, through a growing haze of pain. Then sighed. "You'd better hurry, then," I said. "I'm about to pass out."

She took the words in stride and said, "Lean against the fence. Keep your body stiff." Then she seized my ankles. I did my best to follow her directions, and she heaved, straining with effort.

For a second, nothing happened. And then she started, very slowly, to move me up, my good shoulder against the fence. She kept pressing my ankles higher, until I bent forward at the waist, scrabbled with my legs for a second—and then tumbled gracelessly to the ground on the far side of the fence. I hit the ground, and as I did a nuclear weapon went off in my shoulder, white fire, blinding heat.

I sucked in a breath and tried not to scream, but some sound must have escaped. There was a shout from somewhere behind me, and the sound of voices converging on our position.

Tera grimaced and turned to face the oncoming voices.

"Hurry up," I gasped. "Climb it and let's go."

She shook her head, a stirring of dark hair. "No time. They are here."

I gritted my teeth until they creaked and got my feet underneath me. She was right. The oncoming voices were close. Someone, Benn again, I thought, shouted out orders not to move. If Tera tried to clamber over the fence now, she'd be a perfect target at the top. The pursuers were too close. Tera didn't stand much chance of escaping, and if she didn't, I wouldn't make it far. I'd be caught, and in more trouble than ever—and MacFinn would be on a rampage, with no one to oppose him.

I blinked sweat out of my eyes and knelt down as my blood pattered to the sidewalk. Little curls of steam came up where it hit the cold concrete.

I took a breath and drew in every bit of will I could summon, drew in the pain and my fear and sick frustration and shoved it all into a hard little ball of energy.

"Ventas veloche," I murmured. *"Ubrium, ubrium."* I repeated the words in a breathless chant, curling my fingers in toward my palm as I did.

The curls of steam from my blood began to thicken and gather into dense tendrils of mist and fog. Back along our trail, where more of my blood had spilled, more fog arose. For a few seconds, it was nothing, just a low and slithering movement along the ground—and then it erupted forth, billows of fog rising to cover the ground as the energy rushed out of me, covering Tera from my sight and causing shouts of confusion and consternation to come from the law officials pursuing us.

I dropped to my side, overwhelmed by pain and fatigue.

There was a whisper of sound, a creak of wrought metal, and then a light thump as Tera West landed beside me, invisible in the fog though she was only a few feet away. She moved toward me, and then I saw her expression, her eyes wide with wonder, the first emotion I had seen on her face.

"Wizard," she whispered.

"Don't wear it out," I mumbled. And then everything went black.

Chapter
Fourteen

I woke up someplace dark and warm. But then I opened my eyes, and it wasn't dark anymore. Just dim.

I was in a hotel room, a cheap one, lying on my back in a double bed. Heavy curtains were drawn, but cheap curtain rods sagged in the middle and let light in from outside. I felt that I had been lying there for a while. I took a deep breath and it made my shoulder begin a dull, pounding throb. I moaned, before I could think to keep quiet. I'm not a wimp; it just hurt that bad. My throat was parched, my lips chapped.

I turned my head, which made my jaw ache where Murphy had socked me. My left shoulder was covered in thick, white bandages and wrapped firmly in tape. It looked clean and neat, except for the bruises that I could see spreading out toward my chest and down my arm from beneath the bandages. As a side note, I noticed that I was naked, and the list of candidates for who could have undressed me was awfully short.

Beyond my shoulder, on the nightstand beside the bed, was a pile of miscellany. A book entitled *SAS Survival Manual* lay open to a page with several black and white illustrations of bandaging techniques. Beside it were some empty cardboard boxes whose labels declared them to have once contained cotton gauze wrapping, medical tape, that sort of thing. A brown bottle of hydrogen peroxide lay on its side atop a hacksaw with a nicked blade. A paper sack sat on the floor beside the bed, its top folded closed.

I moved my right hand up to rub at my aching head. One bracelet of Murphy's handcuffs hung around my wrist, the chain swinging from the base of the bracelet, where it had apparently been severed by the hacksaw. The other bracelet was down on my left wrist. I could feel it as a dull, throbbing band around the lower part of my arm.

I did my best not to move too much, but the pain didn't go away. After a few minutes, I decided that my wound wasn't going to start hurting any less, so I sat up. Slowly. Rising wasn't too much more trouble, though my legs shook a little. I made it to the bathroom and made use of the facilities, then splashed water on my face with my right hand.

This time, she didn't surprise me. I heard her move out of the darkness of the back corner of the room. I glanced up into Tera West's amber-colored eyes in the mirror and said, "Tell me I didn't get lucky last night."

Her expression never blinked, as though the insinuation had flown past her. She was still dressed in the same clothes and still held herself with the same relaxed composure she had always displayed. "You were very lucky," she said. "The bullet went through the muscle and missed the bone and the artery. You will live."

I scowled. "I don't feel so lucky."

Tera shrugged. "Pain is to be endured. It ends or it does not." I saw her consider my back, and then lower portions. "You are in reasonably good condition. You should be able to withstand it."

I felt a hot rush of blood to my face, and I fumbled for a towel and awkwardly slung it around my hips. "Are you the one who bandaged me? And, uh . . ." I made a vague gesture with the fingers of the hand that was holding the towel and preserving my modesty.

She nodded. "I am. And I have procured clothing for you that is not soaked in blood. You must dress, so that we may help my fiancé."

I turned to face her, and tried out my best glower. She didn't twitch an eyebrow. "What time is it?"

She shrugged. "Late afternoon. The sun will set soon, and

the moon will rise soon after. We have no time to waste if we are to reach him before the change."

"Do you know where he is?"

She shrugged again. "I know him."

I let out a breath and slowly walked past her. I went to the paper bag on the floor next to the bed. Inside it, I found a pair of enormous purplish sweatpants and a white T-shirt with Old Glory flying on it in rippling, metallic colors, subtitled: INVEST IN AMERICA—BUY A CONGRESSMAN. I wrinkled up my nose at the sweatpants, liked the shirt, and fumbled myself into the clothing, ripping off price tags as I went.

"Where are we?" I asked.

"A hotel in East Chicago," she said.

I nodded. "How did you pay for it?"

"I used cash. MacFinn told me that the police can track the plastic cards."

I squinted at her. "Yeah. They can." I rubbed a hand over my head and went to the mirror again to study myself. I was walking more easily now—the pain wasn't any less, but I was beginning to get more used to it. "Do you have any ibuprofen, anything like that?"

"Drugs," she said. "No." She picked up a set of rental-car keys and turned toward the door.

"Stop," I told her. She turned to me, her eyes narrowed.

"We are going now," she said.

"We are not going," I replied, "until I have a few answers."

Her eyebrows furrowed, and she glared at me. Then she turned and walked out of the room, letting in a brief flood of orange-tinted sunlight before the door slammed behind her.

I considered the door for a moment. Then I sat down on the bed and waited.

Perhaps three minutes passed. Then she reappeared. "Now," she said, "we will leave."

I shook my head. "I told you *no*. Not until I get some answers."

"MacFinn will answer your questions," Tera told me. "Now, you must leave this place."

I snorted and folded my arms over my chest. My shoulder took fire and I wobbled on the bed before I lowered my left arm again. I left the right one folded across my chest, but it just didn't have the same effect. "Where is MacFinn? Why did he kill Marcone's business partner and his bodyguard? Or did he kill them at all?"

"You will leave this pl—" Tera began.

"Who are you? Why did the pair of you mess up the first circle, the one in your basement? How did you know Kim Delaney?"

Tera West snarled and seized me by the front of my shirt. "You will leave this place *now*," she said, glaring into my eyes.

"Why should I?" I snarled, and for once I didn't avert my eyes. I stared into her gleaming amber eyes and braced myself for the impact of looking into her soul, and for her to peer into mine.

Instead, nothing happened.

That, in itself, was enough to make my jaw drop incredulously. I continued the stare, and she didn't blink, didn't turn away—and didn't fall into soulgaze with me. I shuddered in reaction. What was going on? Why didn't the 'gaze begin? There were only two kinds of people whose eyes I could meet for more than a second or two: the people who had already met my eyes in a soulgaze were one kind; inhuman beings from the Nevernever were the other.

I had never looked upon Tera West's soul before. I remembered a soulgaze, every time it happened. The experience wasn't the sort of thing you could forget. That only left one conclusion.

Whoever she was—whatever she was, Tera West wasn't human.

"We will leave now," she growled.

I felt a surge of defiant grumpiness course through me. "Why *should* I?" I whispered back.

"Because I have called the police and told them that you are here, that you are acting irrational and dangerous, and that you possess a weapon. They will be here momentarily. I think that the police might be feeling threatened, given all the recent deaths. They will be likely to shoot you rather than take chances." She let go of my shirt with a little push, and stalked out of the room.

I sat on the bed for about five seconds. Then I rose and hobbled after her, taking time to snatch my duster from where it was draped over a chair. There were holes in the upper left arm, one in the front of the sleeve, one in the back, and it was crusty with dried blood that didn't much show against the black canvas. It was disgusting, but hey, it was mine. The boots and socks I had been wearing last night were next to it, and I snagged them, too.

Outside, it was late afternoon. The streets and highways would soon be crowded with commuters going home from work. Tera had rented a beat-up old car, probably from an independent rental business, rather than from one of the major chains—good move on her part. It would draw things out while the police methodically went through agency after agency, looking for someone of her description, and they always started with the big places first.

I studied her as she got in the car. She was tall and lean and pretty in a knife-edge sort of way. Her eyes moved around constantly—not nervously or randomly, but with the cool precision of someone making herself aware of everything surrounding her at all times. Her hands were scarred, long-fingered, and strong. The bruise on her head, where I had smacked her with my blasting rod the night before (no, *two* nights before; I had lost a day sleeping in the hotel room) was probably hurting like hell, but she didn't seem to notice it.

She drove us out onto the streets of East Chicago, one of the distant suburbs of the big city, down at the south end of Lake Michigan, finally turning off into a quiet drive beside a sign that read WOLF LAKE PARK.

Tera West made me nervous. She had appeared from nowhere to save me from the back of a police car, true, but what were her intentions? Was she really trying to help her fiancé keep from falling victim to his family curse again? Or were the two of them working together to remove anyone who could rebuild the magical circle that could contain MacFinn and render him harmless? That would make sense, given that once Kim Delaney was dead, they came after me.

On the other hand, that didn't fit with a lot of the other facts. MacFinn, if he was truly a loup-garou, changed into a beast only during the nights of the full moon. At least half a dozen people had been killed when the moon was waxing full, but not yet all the way there, or after it had been full for three nights already and was waning back toward half full again.

And Tera West wasn't a werewolf. A werewolf was a human being who used magic to turn into a wolf. She had looked upon my eyes and not been drawn in. Therefore, she wasn't a human being.

Could she be some kind of shape-shifter from the Nevernever? MacFinn's partner in crime, killing on the off nights to keep suspicion from falling on him? Some sort of being with which I was unfamiliar? Most of my background on the paranormal was Western European in origin. I should have been reading more books on Native American beliefs, South American spooks and haunts, African legend, East Asian folklore—but it was a little late for such regrets. If Tera West was a monster, and wanted me dead, she could have killed me already—and she surely would not have bothered to clean and dress my injury.

Of course, that begged the question: What *did* she really want?

And that question led the way to many more. Who were the

young people I had seen her with that first evening? What was she doing with them? Did she have some kind of cult of followers, like vampires sometimes built up? Or was it something else entirely?

Tera pulled over onto a little gravel lane, drove a quarter mile up it, and pulled off into the weeds. "Get out," she said. "He will be here, somewhere."

The bouncing car ride had come to an end, mercifully, and the sun was still solidly above the horizon, with moonrise not for at least an hour after sunset. So I ignored the pain and pushed my way out of the car, to follow her into the woods.

It was darker underneath the ancient oaks and sycamores, and quiet. Birdsong came to us, but from far away, as though the birds were choosing the better part of valor in remaining where the sun could still touch the tree branches. The wind sighed through the woods, sending leaves spinning down in all shades of gold and orange and russet, adding to the thick, crunchy carpeting under our feet. Our steps sounded out distinctly as we moved ahead through the leaves, and the cool wind made me grateful that I had thought to drape my duster over my shoulders.

I studied the usually quiet Tera. She was walking with exaggerated motions, planting her feet down solidly with each step, as though intentionally trying to make noise. Once or twice, she stepped out of her way to tread on a branch, snapping it with a dry popping sound. I was too tired and sore to go to any such effort. I just walked, and it made more noise than she did. Who says I can't do anything right?

We hadn't gone more than a few hundred yards when Tera abruptly tensed, crouching, her eyes scanning all around. There was a whistling sound, and then a bent sapling jerked upright, dragging a noose around Tera's ankles and hauling her across the rock- and leaf-covered floor of the woods with a yelp of surprise.

I blinked at her, and then something came up out of the

leaves, rose right up like Hamlet's dad from the stage floor. But instead of bemoaning his fate and charging me with avenging him, he slugged me across the jaw (on the same side of my face that already sported dark purple bruises) and sent me spinning to the ground, stunned.

I landed badly, but on my unwounded side, and rolled out of the way as a muddy, naked foot stomped down at my head. I grabbed on to it and jerked with more desperation than strength, and the foot's owner fell down beside me. Instead of being slowed, he slapped his arms at the ground as he hit it, in much the same way Murphy did when practicing falls. Then he rolled as I struggled to my hands and knees, and slid a hard, strong forearm beneath my throat, locking it there with the other hand and pressing back against my windpipe.

"Got you. I *got* you," snarled my attacker. I struggled against him, but he was bigger than me, stronger than me. He had me down, and he hadn't been shot or beaten up anywhere near as often as I had in the last fifteen hours or so.

I didn't stand a chance.

Chapter
Fifteen

So there I was being strangled by a ranting, half-naked madman in the middle of the woods, with a she-werewolf dangling from a rope snare somewhere nearby. My gunshot wound hurt horribly, and my jaw throbbed from where my buddy the cop had brutalized it the night before. I've had worse days. That's the great thing about being a wizard. I can always tell myself, honestly, that things could be worse.

I stopped trying to struggle against the man who was choking me. Instead, I grabbed his wrist and prepared to do something foolish.

Magic is a kind of energy. It is given shape by human thoughts and emotions, by imagination. Thoughts define that shape—and words help to define those thoughts. That's why wizards usually use words to help them with their spells. Words provide a sort of insulation as the energy of magic burns through a spell caster's mind. If you use words that you're too familiar with, words that are so close to your thoughts that you have trouble separating thought from word, that insulation is very thin. So most wizards use words from ancient languages they don't know very well, or else they make up nonsense words and mentally attach their meanings to a particular effect. That way, a wizard's mind has an extra layer of protection against magical energies coursing through it.

But you can work magic without words, without insulation for your mind. If you're not afraid of it hurting a little.

I drew in my will, my exhausted fear, and focused on what I wanted. My vision swam with dots of color. The man on my back snarled and growled incoherently, and spittle or foam dribbled onto the side of my face. Dried leaves and mud pressed against the other side of my face. Things started going black.

Then I ground my teeth together and released my will with a burst of sudden energy.

Two things happened. First, a rush of blinding thought, brilliant and wild and jangling, went through my head. My eyes swam with color, my ears with phantom sound. My senses were assaulted with a myriad of impressions: the sharp scent of the earth and dry leaves, the rippling scratch of a centipede's legs fluttering up the skin of my forearms, the sensation of warm sunlight against my scalp, dozens of others I couldn't identify— things with no basis in reality. They were a side effect of the energy rushing through my head.

The second thing that happened was a surge of electricity gathered from the air around me to my fingertips, gripped on my attacker's wrist, and surged up through his arm and into his body. He convulsed against my back, out of control, and the strength of his own reaction threw him off of me and to his back on the leaves, jerking and flopping, his face stretched in a tight-lipped expression of shock and fear.

I wheezed in a breath, stunned and shaking, then scrambled back to my feet, only to stagger against a tree. I huddled there, watching my attacker's convulsions fade into a numb paralysis. Finally, he just stared at the sky, his lips open, his chest heaving in and out.

I studied the man a little more closely. He was big. He was really big, at least as tall as me and twice as broad. He was dressed only in a pair of cutoff blue jeans, and those looked like they were ill fit. He was in a condition best described as "overwhelmingly masculine," hairy-chested and muscled like a professional wrestler. There was grey in his hair and beard, and there were lines on his face, putting his age at well into maturity. It was his eyes that showed me the most about him. They burned green, wild and haunted, fastened on the distant sky now, but heavy with the weight of too much terrible knowledge. It couldn't have been easy to live with a curse like his.

There was a scrambling sound, a muffled thump, and I looked up to see MacFinn's noose trap hanging empty, the rope swinging back and forth. My eyes tracked down to earth to find an indistinct shape stir in the leaves, and then resolve itself into Tera West's long limbs and practical clothes. She gathered her legs beneath her and crossed at once to MacFinn, her chest heaving, her eyes vague and distant.

"MacFinn," she said. "MacFinn! You've killed him," she snarled, and her eyes snapped up to mine, bright and burning with amber anger. I could have sworn I saw her face start to change, her bared teeth begin to grow into fangs. Maybe that was just the effect of the magic on my perceptions, though, or a primitive, lizard-brain sort of reaction to Tera rising to her feet and charging toward me with a howl. There was murder in her eyes.

I hadn't gotten beaten up twice, shot, and nearly strangled to get taken out by a misguided werewolf bitch. I gathered in my dizzy, spinning will and extended my good hand toward the charging woman, flicking my wrist in a circle. *"Vento giostrus!"* I trumpeted.

The winds howled down from the trees and whipped into a savage circle of moving air, lifting up dried leaves, sticks, and small stones. The miniature cyclone picked the charging Tera up off the ground and hurled her a good twenty feet through the air, into the branches of a pine tree. It also hurled out a cloud of rocks and small debris, forcing me to seek shelter behind a tree trunk.

How embarrassing. It was a little more wind than I had wanted. That's the danger of evocation, of that instantaneous, ka-blowie sort of magic. Control can be somewhat tricky. All I had wanted was something to spin Tera around and then to plop her down on her ass.

Instead, rocks hammered against the tree trunk and zipped

by, rattling against the trees all around in an almost deafening clatter. The wind shook the trees, tore branches from them, and cast half a ton of dirt and dust into the air in a choking cloud.

The wind died after about half a minute, leaving me choking and coughing on dust and dirt. I peered around the edge of my tree, to see what I could see.

The trees had been cleaned of their autumn colors in a fifty-foot-wide circle, leaving only stark branches behind. Where the bark had been brittle or dry, the cyclone had torn it from the trees, leaving pale, gleaming wood flesh visible. The leaves on the ground were gone as well, as were six or eight inches of topsoil—wind erosion gone berserk. A few stones, newly naked, could be seen in the torn earth, as could the roots of some of the trees and a number of startled worms.

MacFinn was sitting up, evidently recovered from the jolt I'd given him. His face was pasty and stunned as he looked around him. His chest rose and fell in uneven jerks.

There was a rustle, and then I caught sight of Tera West tumbling to the ground from the branches of the pine tree. She landed with a thump and sat there coughing and staring, her mouth hanging open in surprise. She blinked at me and nervously scooted a few inches backward over the ground.

"See there?" I wheezed, raising a hand and pointing at Mac-Finn. "He's breathing. He'll be all right." My mind was still spinning from my unshielded magic attack on MacFinn. I caught the strong scent of wildflowers and stagnant water, and felt what I was sure were the scales of a snake slithering across the palms of my hands, while something with wings and glittering, multifaceted eyes hovered at the edge of my vision, vanishing whenever I tried to look at it. I tried to shove everything that didn't make sense out of my way, to ignore it, but it was difficult to sort the false impressions from the ones that were in front of me.

Tera rose, and made her way toward the fallen man. She knelt down over MacFinn and wrapped her arms around him. I closed my eyes and wheezed until my head began to slow down a little. I focused on all the pain that was lurking in the midst of the confusion. Pain in my shoulder, my throat, my jaw, gave me a concrete foundation, a place that I knew was stable, if unpleasant. I fastened on it, concentrated, until I began to get less woozy. Once the pain returned in force, I wasn't sure I wanted to be less woozy, but I opened my eyes anyway.

MacFinn had his arms around Tera's shoulders, and she was kissing him as if she were trying to inhale him. I felt vaguely voyeuristic.

"Ahem," I said. "Maybe we should get somewhere out of the open?"

They disengaged, slowly, and Tera helped MacFinn to rise to his full, impressive height. He made her look like a slip of a girl, but he leaned against her a little as he stood. He studied me, and I kept my eyes away from his. I didn't want to see what was inside of him.

"Kim's dead," MacFinn said. "Isn't she?"

It wasn't a question, but I nodded. "Yeah. Last night."

The big man shuddered and closed his eyes. "Dammit," he whispered. "Dammit all."

"There was nothing you could do," Tera said, her voice low. "She knew the risks."

"And you must be Harry Dresden," MacFinn said. He glanced at the burns on his wrist, where my magic had taken him. "Sorry about that. I didn't see Tera with you. I didn't know who you were."

I shrugged. "Don't worry about it. But can we get out of the open? Last thing we need is a couple of runners or bikers to come back and report us to the police."

MacFinn nodded at me. "All right. Let's go." Tera gave me a last, wary look, and then turned with MacFinn to help him farther back into the woods. I followed them.

MacFinn's camp turned out to be hidden in the overhang of a bank of earth, heavily laced with the roots of the ancient trees above it that held it in place and kept it from simply spilling into a mound of mud. There was a small fire built at the back of the shelter the bank afforded, well shielded from sight. MacFinn made his way to the fire and settled down before it. Twilight would cast the sheltered camp into deep darkness, but for now it was only shady and out of the wind. The fire had made the place warm, comfortable. It didn't feel like we were within fifteen miles of the third largest city in the country.

Tera settled down beside MacFinn, her manner restless. I remained standing, though the throbbing in my arm made me wish I was lying down in a bed somewhere, instead of huddling in the middle of a small but genuine forest.

"All right, MacFinn," I said. "You want my help. And I want to keep more people from being hurt. But I need some things from you."

He peered up at me, his green eyes calculating. "I am hardly in a position to bargain, Mr. Dresden. What you need, I will give you."

I nodded. "Answers. I've got about a million questions."

"Dark will come in less than two hours. Moonrise is only slightly more than an hour after that. We don't have much time for questions."

"Time enough," I assured him. "Why did you come here?"

"I woke up about five miles from here this morning," MacFinn said, looking away from me as he did, staring at the fire. "I've got several stashes hidden around the city. Just in case. This is one of the older ones. The damp had gotten to the clothes, and all I had was these." He gestured at the jean shorts.

"Do you remember what you did?" The words had an edge to them, but at least I didn't say, "Do you remember murdering Kim Delaney?" Who says I can't be diplomatic?

MacFinn shuddered. "Pieces," he said. "Just pieces." He looked at me and said, "I didn't mean to hurt her. I swear to you."

"Then why is she dead?" The words came out flat, cool. Tera glared at me, but I watched MacFinn for his answer.

"The curse," he said quietly. "When it happens, when I change—have you ever been angry, Mr. Dresden? So angry that you lost control? That nothing else mattered to you but acting on your anger?"

"Once," I said.

"Maybe you can understand part of it then," MacFinn said. "It comes on me, and there's nothing left but the need to hurt something. To act on the rage. I tried to tell Kim that the circle wasn't working, that she had to get out, but she wouldn't *listen*." I heard the frustration in his voice, and his hands clenched into fists. "She wouldn't listen to me."

"It frustrated you," I said. "And when you changed . . ."

He nodded. "It's how I came back from 'Nam. Everyone else in my platoon died but me. I knew the full moon was coming. And I knew that I hated them, hated the soldiers who had killed my friends. When I changed, I started killing until there wasn't anyone left alive within maybe two miles."

I stared at MacFinn for a long moment. I believed that he was telling me the truth. That he didn't have much control, if any, over his actions when he transformed. Though it occurred to me that if he *wanted* someone dead, he could probably point his monster-self in the right direction before he lost control.

Note to self: Do not cut MacFinn off in traffic.

"All right," I said. "Why come here? Why to 'Wolf Woods'? Why not to one of the other stashes?"

He smirked at the flames. "Where else would a werewolf run, Mr. Dresden?"

"Someplace a little less freaking obvious," I shot back.

MacFinn shook his head. "The FBI doesn't believe in werewolves. They aren't going to make the connection."

"Maybe," I conceded. "But there are smarter people than the FBI looking for you now. I don't think we should stay here for long."

MacFinn glanced at me, and then around him, as though listening for pursuers. "You might be right," he admitted. "But

I'm not going anywhere until my head stops spinning. You don't look so good, either."

"I'll make it," I said. "All right, then. How did you know Kim Delaney? From her activist functions, I assume."

MacFinn's face went pale at the mention of her name, but he nodded. "Originally. We came to know of her talents about a year ago. She told us how you were helping her control her abilities. She was helping me, indirectly, with the Northwest Passage Project. Then, last month, I asked her for her help."

"Why did you do that?"

MacFinn glanced warily at Tera, and then back at me. "Someone broke my circle."

I hunkered down on my heels, resting my aching arm on my knees. "Someone broke your circle? The one in the basement?"

"Yes," MacFinn said. "I don't know who. I'm not at home a lot. We found it broken when we went downstairs before moonrise, last month."

"And you asked Kim to fix it?"

MacFinn closed his eyes and nodded. "She said she could. She told us she would be able to make a new circle—one that would keep me from . . ."

I chewed on my lip as his voice trailed off. "Last month, you were meeting with Marcone's business partner, right? Negotiations over the project?"

"I didn't kill him," MacFinn said quickly. "He died the night after the full moon. I couldn't have made the change and done it then. And the other two nights, I made sure I was well away from human beings. I didn't kill anyone the second two nights, either. I was alone."

"Your fiancée could have done those killings," I said, and flicked a glance at Tera West. She glared at my eyes for a moment, and then looked away.

"She didn't," MacFinn said, his tone cool.

"Let's go back a bit," I said. "Someone messed up your circle. To do that, they would have had to know about your curse, right? And they would have had to get into your house. So, the question is, who could do those things? And then the question is, who would have done it, and why?"

MacFinn shook his head. "I don't know," he said. "I just don't. I don't have much contact with the supernatural, Mr. Dresden. I keep my head down. I don't know anyone else who can make the change, except for her." He put his hand over that of the woman beside him.

A suspicion took root in my mind, someplace dark and sneaky. I studied Tera as I spoke to MacFinn. "You want to hear a theory?" I said. I didn't wait for him to answer. "Presuming you're telling the truth, I figure someone else did the killings the night before the full moon, last month. Some gangsters in town. Then they made sure that you would be the one going berserk the next three nights by fucking up your circle."

"Why would they do that?" MacFinn asked.

"To set you up. They kill some people, maybe just for kicks, maybe for a good reason, and then they lay the blame at your feet. Someone like me, or the White Council, comes poking around, and they go straight to you. You're notorious. Like a convicted felon. They find you over the body with a bloody knife, metaphorically speaking, and you're the one to burn at the stake. Literally."

MacFinn studied my face for a moment. "Or you think that there might be another reason."

I shrugged. "Maybe you *are* the killer. You could be trying to make it look like someone is setting you up to me and the Council. The police can't prove shit against you under the mundane justice system, and using this deception clears you with the supernatural community. So you moan and pose and say 'Woe is me, I am only the poor cursed guy,' and meanwhile a bunch of people end up dead. People who were standing in the way of your completing the Northwest Passage Project."

MacFinn showed me his teeth. "You think the world wouldn't be better off without people like Marcone and his lickspittles?"

"Good word, lickspittles," I replied, keeping my voice bland. "That doesn't really concern me right now, MacFinn. Men like Marcone know the risks and take their chances. What bothers me is that a bunch of other people are getting dead, and they don't really deserve it."

"Why would I be killing innocents?" MacFinn demanded, his voice growing tight, clipped.

"Innocents like Kim?" I said. I'm a wizard, not a saint. I'm allowed to be vindictive.

MacFinn went pale and looked down.

"Maybe you're doing it as a smoke screen. Maybe you can't help it. Or hell, maybe you really are just a poor cursed guy, and someone's using you like a puppet. There's no way for me to tell right now."

"Assuming I'm not lying," MacFinn grated, "who would have an interest in setting me up?"

I shook my head. "That's the million-dollar question. I'd say that it was Johnny Marcone—he stands to benefit if you can't oppose his business interests in the Northwest. As I understand it, the Northwest Passage would pretty much put nails in the coffin of a lot of industry up in that direction."

MacFinn nodded grimly. "It would."

"So that gives him a good motive. But how did he know about your curse? And how did he pull off ruining the circle? It doesn't sound like him. He would just have your brakes fail, or maybe arrange for you to meet a couple of big men in a dark alley. It's just his way." I shrugged. "Who else would be doing it? Can you think of anyone?"

MacFinn shook his head. "I've always been lucky. Been able to hold myself in, lock myself up. Or been able to go far away, out into the wilds where no one would find me. So that when I changed, no one would be killed."

"That's why you were backing the Northwest Passage," I guessed. "A place for you to go in safety when the full moon comes—a really big no-people zone."

MacFinn glanced aside at Tera, who was staring stoically into the distance. "That and other reasons." His jaw tightened, and he looked back to the fire. "You don't know what it's like, Mr. Dresden. To live with yourself."

I rubbed at my mouth and chin with my good hand. I needed a shave. I studied MacFinn and Tera for a moment, trying to make up my mind.

Was MacFinn telling me the truth? Was he just a victim, someone being used by a faceless villain still at large? Or was he lying to me?

If he was lying, if all of this had been his design, what purpose would he have had in luring me out here? Killing me, of course, getting rid of the only wizard who could pen up his monstrous form. That was, after all, exactly what he would have done if I hadn't have been able to shock him silly. But did that even make sense? What would he gain by removing me if I never stood in his way in the first place?

Careful, Harry. Don't get *too* paranoid. Not everyone is planning and plotting and lying. But I had to wonder about Tera West. A nasty scenario was laying itself out in my mind. What if the dear, sweet fiancée was tired of hubby? What if she had done the before- and after-moon killings, then set up her sweet-iekins to take the fall for her? She could get rid of MacFinn and Marcone's partner all in one fell swoop.

Leaving her and Marcone alive. Marcone could have found out about MacFinn from Tera, and about the weakness of his circle from Tera as well. Tera wasn't human, not even a little. She was something else, maybe a being of the Nevernever. Who knew how her mind worked?

And then there was the group of young people Tera seemed to be in charge of. How did they fit into this? What was she using them for?

I went fishing. "How are Georgia and Billy, Tera?" I asked, my tone conversational.

She blinked. Her mouth worked for a second, and then she

answered, "Fine. They are well." She pressed her lips together, clearly desiring the conversation to end.

I watched MacFinn. His face registered confusion, and then he looked between Tera and me uneasily. He didn't know who the hell I was talking about, and she didn't seem to want to let MacFinn in on what was apparently a secret.

Aha, little miss werewolf-shape-shifter-thing. What are you plotting?

I was going to press her harder, when MacFinn and Tera both looked up at exactly the same time, out toward the woods. I stared at them like a moron for a couple of seconds, my mind still running along trails of thought, tracing potential lies, possibilities. Then I shook that out of my brain and Listened.

"Both of you along that way," Murphy said from somewhere in the distance downslope. "Ron, take your three and fan out until we're even with the feds. Then we sweep west, up the hill."

"Christ, Murphy," Carmichael said. "We don't owe the feds shit. If they'd have showed up on time, we'd have been out here hours ago. If we hadn't got that report about the West woman in the hotel room, we still wouldn't be here."

"Can it, Carmichael," Murphy snapped. "Pictures of Mac-Finn and the woman have been passed out. And you all know what Dresden looks like. Spread out and nab them."

"You don't even know if they're here," Carmichael protested.

"I'll bet you sex to doughnuts that they are, Carmichael," Murphy said, her voice dripping sweet venom. "And that should tell you how certain I am."

Carmichael muttered something under his breath, and then growled orders to his men to fan out as Murphy had indicated.

"Dammit," MacFinn snarled. "How did they know I was here?"

"Where else would a werewolf go to hide?" I sniped. "Shit. How do we get out?"

"Wind," Tera said. She and MacFinn both came to their feet. "Or fog. Can you do one of those again?"

I grimaced and shook my head. "I don't think so. I'm worn out. I'd probably make a mistake and that could kill someone."

"If you don't," Tera said, "we will all be captured or killed."

"You can't solve all your problems by magic," I snapped.

"He's right," MacFinn said quietly. "We split up. The first one discovered makes a lot of noise, puts up a fight, and gives the others a chance to get away."

"No," I said. "MacFinn, you've got to stay with me. I can make the circle with some sticks and dirt, if necessary, but if I'm not there, I can't hold you in when the curse takes hold later tonight."

MacFinn's teeth showed again. "No time to argue, Mr. Dresden," he said.

"Indeed there is not," said Tera, and then she took off at a dead run. MacFinn hissed a curse and grabbed for her as she ran, but missed. Tera flew on into the woods, rushing silently down the slope on an angle that would take her past the edge of the pursuers' line. She was noticed after only a few steps, shouts going up from three or four throats.

"Bitch," MacFinn cursed, and he started after her. I seized his arm, my fingers clamping on his bicep hard enough to make him stop and stare at me, his green eyes fierce and wild.

"Split up," I said, looking back down the hill. "If we're lucky, they won't even know that we were here."

"But Tera—"

"Knows what she's doing," I said. "If the police nail us, there's no way you're going to be able to hold it in tonight. We go, now, and we meet at the nearest gas station to the park. All right?"

From down slope came the sounds of running men, a warning call, and then a gunshot. For Tera's sake, I hoped that Agent Benn wasn't down there. MacFinn clenched his jaw, and then ran up the slope, on an angle. Down below us, there were more shouts, more shots fired, and a short, sharp cry of pain.

Call me crazy, but those sounds, added to all the other things that had happened that day, were just too much for me to handle. I turned, cradling my wounded arm against me, and stumbled up the hill into a long, loping run. I kept my head down, watching my feet, only looking up often enough to make sure that I didn't run into a tree, and fled.

Chapter
Sixteen

I made it out of the park, exhausted and barely able to keep from screaming with pain. I stopped at the first gas station I could find, so I could take off my boots. Old and comfortable as they were, cowboy boots were not meant for running cross-country. I leaned against the side of the building by the pay phones, away from the street, and sat down on the sidewalk. My body throbbed with pain, slowing as my heart and breathing did.

I gave MacFinn an hour, but he didn't show up. No one did.

I got restless, fast. Could both MacFinn and Tera West have been captured? Murphy's cops may not have looked like much, but I knew they were tough and smart. It wasn't out of the realm of possibility.

I rummaged in my duster's pockets, came up with enough change to make a phone call, then made my painful way to the phone.

"Midwestern *Arcane*, this is Ms. Rodriguez," Susan said, when she picked up the phone. Her voice sounded tired, stressed.

"Hi, Susan," I said. My shoulder twinged, and I gritted my teeth, pulling my duster around me a little more tightly. The evening was bringing a cold wind and grey clouds, and the sweats and cotton T-shirt Tera West had given me weren't enough to keep out the chill.

"Harry?" she said disbelievingly. "My God. Where are you? The police are looking for you. They keep calling here. Something about a murder."

"Misunderstanding," I said and leaned against the wall.

The pain was getting worse as chills soaked in and I started to shiver.

"You sound terrible," Susan said. "Are you all right?"

"Can you help me?"

There was a pause on the other end of the line. "I don't know, Harry. I don't know what's going on. I don't want to get into any trouble."

"I could explain it," I offered, struggling to keep my words clear through the pain. "But it's sort of a long story." I dropped a subtle emphasis on that last word. Sometimes it scares me how easy it is to get people to do what you want them to do, if you know something about them.

"Story, eh?" Susan said. I could hear the sudden twinge of interest in her voice.

"Sure. Murder, violence, blood, monsters. Give you the whole scoop if you can give me a ride."

"You bastard," she breathed, but I thought she was smiling. "I would have come to get you anyway."

"Sure you would have," I said, but I felt a smile on my own lips. I told her the address of the gas station and hoped that the feds hadn't taken the time to get a wiretap for Susan's phone.

"Give me half an hour," Susan said. "Maybe more, depending on traffic."

I squinted up at the sky, which was rapidly darkening, both with oncoming dusk and heavy, brooding clouds. "Time's important. Hurry if you can."

"Just take care of yourself, Harry," she said, worry in her voice. Then she hung up the phone.

I did, too, and leaned back against the wall. I hated to draw Susan into this. It made me feel cheap, somehow. Weak. It was that whole problem with chivalry that I had. I didn't want a girl to be riding to my rescue, protecting me. It just didn't seem right. And I didn't want to endanger Susan, either. I was a murder suspect, and the police were looking for me. She could get in trouble, for aiding and abetting, or something like that.

On the other hand, I didn't have much choice. I didn't have any money for a cab, even if I could get one this far from the city. I didn't have a car. I was in no shape to walk anywhere. My contacts, in the persons of MacFinn and Tera West, were gone. I had to have help, and Susan was the only one I thought I could trust to do it. If there was a story involved, she'd go to hell itself to get it.

And I had used that against her, to lever her into helping me. I didn't like it that I had. I'd thought better of myself. I ducked my head against the cold, and shivered, and wondered if I'd done the right thing.

It was while I was leaning against the wall, waiting, that I heard a scrabbling sound around the corner of the gas station. I tensed and waited. The sound repeated itself, a definite pattern of three short movements. A signal.

Warily, I made my way to the back of the building, ready to turn and run as best I could. Tera West was there, behind the building, crouched down between several empty cardboard boxes that smelled of beer and the garbage bin. She was naked, her body a uniform shade of brown, without an ounce of excess fat on her. Her hair was mussed and had leaves and bits of twig caught in it. Her amber eyes looked even more alien and wild than usual.

She rose and came toward me, evidently unconscious of the cold. She moved with a feral sort of grace that made me all too aware of her legs, and her hips, even though I was battered, fatigued, and brooding.

"Wizard," she greeted me. "Give me your coat."

I snapped my eyes back up to hers, then slipped out of my duster, though my shoulder screamed with pain as I pulled the coat off of it, and my body sent up an entirely different round of complaints as the cold wind gleefully cut through the thin clothes I wore beneath the duster. Tera took the coat and slid into it, wrapping it around her and buttoning it closed. The sleeves were too long, and the coat dangled to her ankles, but it covered her lean, strong body well enough. I found myself faintly regretful that I'd had it with me.

"What happened?" I asked her.

She shook her head. "The police do not know how game runs, or how to chase it. One grabbed me. I made him let go." She glanced around us warily, and raked her fingers through her hair, trying to comb out leaves and sticks. "I led them away from you and MacFinn, changed, and made my way back to the camp. I followed MacFinn's trail."

"Where is he?"

She bared her teeth. "The federal people caught him. They took him away."

"Hell's bells," I breathed. "Do you know where?"

"Into a car," she responded.

"No," I said, growing frustrated. "Do you know where the car went?"

She shook her head. "But they had an argument with the one called Murphy. Murphy had more people with her, more guns. MacFinn went where Murphy wanted him to go."

"Downtown," I said. "Murphy would want him in holding down at the station. Hell, it's on the same floor as Special Investigations."

Tera shrugged, her expression hard. "As you say."

"We don't have much time," I said.

"For what? There is nothing more to be done. We cannot reach him now. MacFinn will change when the moon rises. Murphy and the police people will die."

"Like hell," I said. "I've got to get to the station before it happens."

Tera studied me with narrowed eyes. "The police are hunting for you as well, wizard. If you go there, you too will be locked in a cage. You will not be allowed to go to MacFinn."

"I wasn't planning on asking permission," I said. "But I think I can get inside. I just have to get to my apartment."

"The police will be watching it," Tera said. "They will be

waiting for you there. And in any case, we have no car and no money. How will you reach Chicago before moonrise? There is nothing more to be done, wizard."

There came the crunch of tires around the side of the gas station, and I peeked around the corner. Susan's car was just coming to a halt. Raindrops were starting to come down and to make little impact circles on her Taurus's windshield. I felt a little surge of defiant energy.

"There's our ride," I said. "Follow." I relished throwing the terse command at Tera, and she stared at me. I turned my back on her and stalked over to the car.

Susan leaned across and threw open the passenger door, then blinked at me in surprise. She blinked again when Tera slipped in front of me, threw the passenger seat forward, and slid into the backseat with a flash of long, lean legs, then regarded Susan with unreadable, distant eyes.

I pushed the seat back and settled into place. It was a real effort to shut the door, and a small sound of discomfort escaped my mouth. When I looked at Susan, she was staring at me, and at my arm. I looked down and found that the bandage, and a part of the T-shirt's sleeve were soaked through with blood. The purple bruises had spread a few inches, it seemed, and showed beneath the shirt's sleeve.

"Good Lord," Susan gasped. "What happened?"

"I got shot," I said.

"Doesn't it hurt?" Susan stammered, still stunned.

"Is this female always so stupid?" Tera asked. I winced. Susan turned in the seat and glowered at Tera, and I looked back to see Tera narrow her eyes and bare her teeth in what one could hardly say was a smile.

"It hurts," I confirmed. "Susan, take us to my place, but don't stop when you get there. Just drive past slowly. I'll tell you everything on the way."

Susan gave Tera one last, skeptical glance, particularly taking in my bullet-torn duster and Tera's bare limbs. "This better be good, Dresden," she said. Then she slapped the car into gear and started driving with irritated haste back toward the city.

I wanted to collapse into sleep, but I made myself explain most of what had happened over the past couple of days to Susan, editing out mentions of the White Council, demons, that sort of thing. Susan listened, and drove, and asked intent questions, fastening gleefully on to the information concerning the Northwest Passage Project, and Johnny Marcone's links to the businesses opposing it. Rain started coming down in a steady, murky veil, and she flicked on the windshield wipers.

"So you've got to get to MacFinn," Susan said, when I was finished, "before the moon comes up and he transforms."

"You've got it," I said.

"Why don't you call Murphy? Tell her what's going on?"

I shook my head. "Murphy isn't going to be in the mood to listen. She busted me and I fled arrest. She'd have me in a cell before I could say abracadabra."

"But it's raining," Susan protested. "We won't be able to see the moon tonight. Won't that stop MacFinn from changing?"

I blinked at the question and glanced back at Tera. She was watching the buildings pass out the side window as the streetlights started flickering on. She didn't look at me, but shook her head.

"No such luck," I told Susan. "And with these clouds, I can't even tell if the sun has gone down yet, much less how much time we have before moonrise."

Susan breathed out slowly. "How are you going to get to MacFinn, then?"

"I've got a couple things at my apartment," I said. "Drive on by. Let's see if there's anyone watching the old place."

Susan turned the car down my street, and we rolled slowly through the rain. The old boardinghouse huddled stoically beneath the downpour, its gutters gurgling and spouting streams of water. The streetlights glowed with silver halos as the rain came down. A bit down from my building, a plain brown sedan was parked, and a couple of shadowy forms could be seen inside it when Susan drove past.

"That's them," I said. "I recognize one of them from Murphy's unit."

Susan let out another breath and drew the car around the corner, parking it along the street. "Is there any way to sneak into your place? A back door?"

I shook my head. "No. There's only the one door in, and you can see the windows from here. I just need the police to not be looking for a few minutes."

"You need a distraction," Tera said. "I will do it."

I looked over my shoulder. "I don't want any violence."

She tilted her head to one side, her expression never changing. "Very well," she said. "For MacFinn's sake, I will do as you say. Open the door."

I stared at her fathomless eyes for a second, searching for any signs of deception or betrayal. What if Tera was the killer? She had known about MacFinn, and was able to transform in one fashion or another. She could have committed the murders last month, as well as the one two nights past. But if so, why had she seemingly sacrificed herself so that MacFinn and I could escape? Why had she come to find me?

Then again, MacFinn had been captured. And her words at the gas station may have been calculated to make me give up trying to help him, if one looked at them from a certain point of view. What if she was trying to take care of both MacFinn and me by throwing us to the mundane legal system?

My head spun with pain and weariness. Paranoid, Harry, I told myself. You've got to trust someone, somewhere—or else MacFinn goes furry and Murphy and a lot of other good people die tonight. There wasn't much choice.

I opened the door, and we both got out of the car. "What are you going to do?" I asked Tera.

Instead of answering, the amber-eyed woman stripped off my duster and handed it back to me, leaving herself nude and lovely under the rain. "Do you like to look at my body?" she demanded of me.

"Careful how you answer this one, buster," Susan growled from the car.

I coughed, and glanced back at Susan, keeping my eyes off of the other woman. "Yeah, Tera. That will work fine, I guess."

"Wait for twenty slow breaths," she said. There was a note of amusement in her voice. "Pick me up at the far end of this block." Then she turned on a bare heel and glided into the darkness between streetlights in a graceful lope. I frowned after her for a moment, and then drew my duster back on.

"You don't have to look quite so hard," Susan said. "Is she the human-interest angle for this story?"

I winced, holding my wounded arm close to my side, and leaned down to meet Susan's eyes. "I don't think she's human," I said. Then I stood and started walking down the street, slowing my steps so that I didn't round the corner until Tera's prescribed time limit had elapsed. Even when I did, I walked quickly, like someone hurrying home out of the rain, my hands in my pockets, keeping my head down against the grey downpour.

I crossed the street toward my apartment building, glancing at the sedan as I did.

The cops weren't watching me. They were staring at the pool of light beneath the streetlight behind them, where Tera spun gracefully through the steps of some sort of gliding dance, moving to a rhythm and a music I could not hear. There was a primal sort of intensity to her motions, raw sexuality, feminine power coursing through her movements. Her back arched as she spun and whirled, offering out her breasts to the chill rain, and her skin was slick and gleaming with water.

I tripped over the curb on the far side of the street and felt my cheeks start to flame as I hurried down the steps to my apartment. I unlocked the door and went inside, shutting it behind me. I didn't light any candles, relying upon my knowledge of the house to move around.

The two potions were in their plastic sports bottles on the counter where I had left them. I grabbed up my black nylon backpack from the floor and threw the bottles into it. Then I went into my bedroom and grabbed the blue coveralls with the little red patch over one breast pocket stenciled with MIKE in bold letters. My mechanic had accidentally left them in the trunk of the Blue Beetle the last time the Beetle was in the shop. I added a baseball cap, a first-aid kit, a roll of duct tape, a box of chalk, seven smooth stones from a collection of them I keep in my closet, a white T-shirt and a pair of blue jeans, and a huge bottle of Tylenol, zipped up the backpack, and headed back out again. At the last moment, I took up my wizard's staff from the corner by the door.

Something flashed past my legs, moving out into the night, and I almost jumped out of my skin. Mister paused at the top of the stairs to look back at me, his cat eyes enigmatic and irritated, and then vanished into the darkness. I muttered something under my breath and locked the door behind me, then headed out once more, my heart rattling along too quickly to be comfortable.

Tera was on her hands and knees in the middle of the pool of light behind the sedan, her damp hair fallen all around her face, her lips parted, facing the two plainclothes officers, who had gotten out of the car and were speaking to her from several feet away. Her chest was heaving in and out, but having seen her in action, I doubted that it was merely from the exertion of her dancing. Looked nice, though. The policemen were sure as hell staring.

I gripped my staff in hand, along with the backpack, and walked away down the street again. It didn't take long to make it back to Susan's car, and she immediately wheeled the vehicle around the block without comment. Susan hardly had begun to slow down when Tera appeared from between a couple of buildings and loped over to the car. I leaned forward, opened the door, and she got into the backseat. I threw her the extra clothes I had picked up, and she began to dress without comment.

"It worked," I said. "We did it."

"Of course it worked," Tera said. "Men are foolish. They will stare at anything female and naked."

"She's got that right," Susan said, under her breath, and jerked the car into motion again. "Oh, we are going to talk about this one, mister. Next stop, Special Investigations."

Outside the battered old police building downtown, I pulled the baseball cap a little lower over my eyes, and drank the blending potion. It didn't really have any taste to it at all, but it twitched and bubbled all the way down my gullet until it hit my stomach.

I gave the potion a few seconds to work and shifted my hands on the handle of my wizard's staff. Even though the end of it was shoved into a wheeled bucket, it still didn't look much like the handle of a mop. And even though I was dressed in the dark blue coveralls, they were ridiculously short on me. I did not look much like a janitor.

That's where the magic came in. If the potion worked, I would look like background to any casual observers, a part of the scenery that they wouldn't glance at twice. So long as they didn't give me an intense scrutiny, the potion's power should be able to keep me from being noticed, which would let me get close to MacFinn, which would let me put the containment circle around him and keep his transformed self from going on a rampage.

Of course, if it didn't work, I might just end up studying the inside of a jail cell for a few years—provided the transformed MacFinn didn't tear me apart first.

I tried to ignore the pain in my shoulder, the nervous tension in my stomach. I was rebandaged, Tylenoled, and as reasonably refreshed as I could possibly have been without drinking the potion I had brewed just for that purpose.

If I could have had both potions going in my system without them making me too ill to move, I would have downed the refresher potion the moment I got my hands on it, but without the blending potion, there was no way I could get inside to MacFinn. I could only hope that I'd find a use for it eventually. I'd hate the effort to go to waste.

I waited impatiently in the rain, sure for a moment that I had messed something up when making the potion, that it wasn't going to have any effect at all.

And then I felt it start to work.

A sort of grey feeling came over me, and I realized with a start that the colors were fading from my vision. A sort of listless feeling came over me, a lassitude that advised me to sit down somewhere and watch the world go by, but at the same time the hairs on the back of my neck prickled up as the potion's magic took effect.

I took a deep breath and walked up the stairs of the building with my bucket and my "mop," pulled open the doors, and went inside. Shadows shifted and changed oddly, all greys and blacks and whites, and for a second I felt like an extra on the set of *Casablanca* or *The Maltese Falcon*.

The solid old matron of a sergeant sat at the front desk, thumbing through a glossy magazine, a portrait done in colorless hues. She glanced up at me for a second, and tinges of color returned to her uniform, her cheeks, and her eyes. She looked me over casually, sniffed, and lowered her face to her magazine again. As her attention faded, so did the colors from her clothing and skin. My perceptions of her changed as she paid attention to me or did not.

I felt my face stretch in a victorious smile. The potion had worked. I was inside. I had to suppress an urge to break into a soft-shoe routine. Sometimes, being able to use magic was so *cool*. I almost stopped hurting for a few seconds, from sheer enjoyment of the special effects. I would have to remember to tell Bob how much I liked the way this potion worked.

I kept my head down and moved past the desk sergeant, just one more janitor coming in to clean up the police station after hours. I picked up the bucket and my "mop" and went up the stairs, toward the holding cells and the Special Investigations office on the fifth floor. One cop passed me on the stairs and didn't so much as look at me. His uniform and skin remained entirely devoid of color. I grew more confident and moved with more speed. I was effectively invisible.

Now all I had to do was find MacFinn, trick my way into seeing him, and save Murphy and all the other police from the monster MacFinn would become—before they arrested me for trying to do it.

And time was running out.

Chapter
Seventeen

Ever wish you had an almanac?

I did, that night. I had no idea what time the moon was supposed to rise, and I hadn't exactly had time to run to the library or a bookstore. I knew that it was supposed to happen an hour or so after sundown, but the way the clouds rolled in had made it uncertain exactly when sundown had happened. Did I have twenty minutes? Ten? An hour?

Or was I already too late?

As I climbed the stairs, I thought about being alone in the building with MacFinn after he had changed. For all my vaunted wizard's knowledge, I had no real idea of his capabilities; although after seeing Kim's body, I had something of an idea of what he could do. Bob had said that loup-garou were fast, strong, virtually immune to magic. What could I do against something like that?

I just had to pray that I would be able to get the circle up around MacFinn before I had to find out. I checked the bucket, to make sure I still had the chalk and the stones I would need to construct the greater circle around MacFinn. You didn't necessarily have to make them out of silver and gold and whatnot. Mostly, you just had to understand how the construct channeled the forces that were being employed. If you knew that, you could figure out how to make it out of less pure materials. The very best wizards don't need much more than chalk, table salt, and a wooden spoon to pull off some remarkable stuff.

My thoughts were rambling now, panic making them scamper around like a frightened chipmunk. That was bad. I needed focus, direction, concentration. I drove my legs a little harder, went up the stairs as fast as I dared, until I came out on the fifth floor. The door to Special Investigations was ten feet away. The holding cells were down the hall and around the corner, and I started that way at once.

"What do you mean, you can't find him?" Murphy's voice demanded as I walked past the office door.

"Just that. The men on his apartment said that they kept a real good eye on the place, but that he got in and out again without them seeing anything." Carmichael's voice was tired, frustrated.

Murphy snorted. "Christ, Carmichael. Is Dresden going to have to walk right into the office before you can find him?"

I hurried on past the door and down the hall. Tempting as it was to listen to a conversation about myself without the participants knowing, I just didn't have time. I wheeled my wobbling, squeaking bucket down the hall, half jogging in my hurry.

Holding was set up, unsurprisingly, behind bars. There was a swinging barred door that the station guard had to buzz to open, if you didn't have the key. Beyond that was a sort of antechamber with a couple of wooden chairs and not much else besides a counter with a window made of bulletproof glass. The jailer sat behind the glass at his desk, his expression baggy eyed and bored. Past the jailer's window was another door, made of steel with a tiny little window, which led into the row of cells. The jailer had the controls to that door at his desk as well.

I went to the first barred door, kept my head down, and rapped on the metal slats. I waited for a while, but nothing happened, so I rapped on the bars again. It occurred to me that it would add a nice touch of irony if the same blending potion that got me into the building also kept me from being noticed by the jailer and let inside. I rapped on the bars again, harder this time, with the shaft of my wooden "mop."

It took some determined rapping to get him to look up from his magazine, but he finally did, and peered at me through thick glasses. His colors swirled and gained a bit of tint before settling back toward grey. He frowned at me, glanced back at a calendar on the wall, and then pushed the button.

The barred door buzzed and I shoved it open with my bucket, wheeling inside with my head down. "You're early this week," the jailer said, his eyes back on the magazine.

"Out of town on Friday. Trying to get done sooner," I replied. I kept my voice in a monotone, as grey and boring as I could manage. To my surprise, it came out as I intended it. I'm usually not much of a liar or an actor, so the potion must have been helping me on some subtle and devious level. One thing I'll say for Bob: He's annoying as hell, but he knows his stuff.

"Whatever. Sign here," the jailer said in a bored tone, and shoved a clipboard and a pen at me through a slot at the base of the Plexiglas window. He turned a page in his magazine, showing me a picture of an athletic-looking young woman doing something anatomically improbable with an equally improbable young man.

I hesitated. How in the hell was I supposed to sign in and out? I mean, Bob's potion may have been good, but it wasn't going to change a signature after I'd put it on the paper. I glanced at the inner door, and then at the clock on the wall. To hell with it. I didn't have time to hang around. I went over to the counter and scribbled something unreadable on the admissions sheet.

"Have any trouble tonight?" I asked.

The jailer snorted, turning his magazine to the right by ninety degrees. "Just that rich guy they brought in earlier. He was yelling for a while, but he's shut up now. Probably coming down off of whatever he was on." He collected the clipboard, gave it a perfunctory glance, and hung it back up on its peg beside a bank of black-and-white monitors.

I leaned closer to the monitors, sweeping my eyes over them. Each was apparently receiving a signal from a security camera, because each one of them displayed a scene that was exactly the same except for the actors in it—a small cell, maybe eight feet by eight, with bars serving as one wall, smooth concrete for the other three, a bunk, a toilet, and a single door. Maybe two thirds of the monitors had a strip of masking tape stuck to the lower right-hand corner of the screen, with a name, like HANSON or WASHINGTON, written in black marker. I frantically scanned the bank of monitors until, in the lower corner, I found the one that said MACFINN. I looked at his monitor. The video was blurred, flecked with snow and static, but I could see well enough what had happened.

The cell was empty.

Concrete dust drifted in the air. The wall of bars was missing, apparently torn from the concrete and allowed to fall away. I could see the scraps of MacFinn's denim shorts lying on the floor of the cell.

"Hell's bells," I swore softly. There was a flicker of motion on another monitor, the one next to MacFinn's. The tape at the bottom of the screen read MATSON, and a starved-looking, unshaven man in a sleeveless white undershirt and blue jeans could be seen curled up on the bunk, his back pressed to the rear corner of the cell. His mouth was open and his chest straining, as though he was screaming, but I could hear nothing through the thick security door and the concrete walls. There was a flicker of motion, a huge and furry shape on the camera, out of focus, and Matson threw up his skinny arms to protect himself as something huge and quick shoved its way between the bars, like a big dog going through a rotten picket fence, and engulfed him.

There was a burst of static and violent motion, and then a spattering of black on the grey walls and floor of the cell, as though someone had shaken up a cola and sprayed the walls with it. Then the huge form was gone, and left behind was a ragged, quivering doll of torn flesh and blood-soaked clothing. Matson stared up at the security camera, his dying eyes pleading with mine—and then he jerked once and was gone.

The entire thing had taken perhaps three or four seconds.

My eyes swept over the other security monitors as a sick sort of fascination settled over me. Prisoners were straining to the front of their cells, shouting things out, trying to get enough of a look to see what was going on. I realized that they couldn't see what was happening—they could only hear. They wouldn't be able to look out and see the transformed MacFinn until he was at the bars of their cell.

Fear, sick and horrible and debilitating, swam over me and tangled up my tongue. The creature had gone through the bars of the cell as though they'd been made of cheap plastic, and it had killed without mercy. I stared at Matson's dead eyes, at the ruined mess of what had been his guts, at the detached pieces of meat and bone that had once been his right arm and leg.

Stars above, Harry, I thought to myself. *What the hell are you doing in the same building with that thing?*

On another monitor, there was a replay of what had happened seconds before, and an aging black man named CLEMENT went down beneath the creature, screaming as he died. Seeing what was happening set off some primal, ancient fear, something programmed into my head, a fear of being found in my hiding place, of being trapped in a tiny space from which there was no escape while something with killing teeth and crushing jaws came in to eat me. That same primitive, naked part of me screamed and gibbered and shouted at my rational mind to turn around right now, to turn around and run, fast and far.

But I couldn't let it go on. I had to do something.

"Look," I said and pointed at the monitor. My finger trembled, and my voice came out as a ghost of a whisper. I tried again, jabbing my finger at the monitors and half shouting, "Look!" at the jailer.

He glanced up at me, tilted his head, and frowned. I saw some colors start to bleed into his face, but that didn't matter now. I continued to point at the monitors and tried to step closer to them. "Look, look at the screens, my God, man!" By now my voice was coming out in a high, panicky tone. I pressed as close to the monitors as I could, yelling, excited.

I should have known better, of course. Wizards and technology simply do not mix—especially when the wizard's heart is pounding like the floor of a basketball court and his guts are shaking. The monitors burst into frantic displays of static and snow, flickering images sometimes visible, sometimes not.

The guard gave me a disgusted look and turned around to glance at the monitors. He blinked at them for a second, while a man named MURDOCH died in flickering, poor reception.

"What the hell is wrong with those things now?" the jailer complained, and took off his glasses to clean them. "There's always something going wrong with the damn cameras. I swear, it isn't worth the money they cost to keep on fixing them."

I frantically backed up from the monitors. "They're dying," I said. "God, you've got to let those men out of there before it kills them."

The man nodded. "Uh-huh. Tell me about it. Just goes to show you how smart the city is, right?" I stared at him for a second, and he put his glasses back on to give me a polite, bored smile. His colors had gone back to black and white, and I must have looked like a dull, humdrum old janitor to him once again. The potion had blended my words into something that the guard's brain would accept without comment, and let pass, just boring, everyday conversation like you have with people ninety percent of the time. The potion was fantastic. Way, way too good.

"Look at the monitors," I screamed in frustration and fear. "He's killing them!"

"The monitors won't stop you doing your job," the guard assured me. "I'll just buzz you in." And with that, he pressed a button somewhere behind the Plexiglas window, and the security door that led into the hallway of cells made a humming sound, clicked, and swung three or four inches open.

Screams poured out of the cells, high sounds that you wouldn't think could come from a man's throat, panicked and terrified. There was a horrible, wrenching sound, a screech of protesting metal, and one of the screams peaked at a shivering, violent point—then dissolved into a strangled mishmash of sounds, of tearing and snapping and popping, of gurgling and thudding. And when they were finished, something, something big, with a cavernous, resonating chest, snarled from not ten feet beyond the security door.

I shot a glance to the guard, who had stumbled to his feet and was grabbing for his gun. He headed out of his station, opening a door that led into the antechamber, presumably to investigate.

"No!" I shouted at him, and threw myself at the security door. I sensed, rather than saw, something else, on the other side of the wall, heading for the exit. I could hear its breath, feel its massive motion through the air, and I hurled my shoulder against the door, slamming it forward, just as something huge and strong thrust a paw through the doorway. The edge of the steel security door slammed forward onto the paw, a member that was neither wholly a paw nor a hand, but somewhere in between, tipped with huge black claws, and drenched in wet, dark, blood. I heard the creature on the far side of the door, only three inches of steel away, snarl in a fury and hatred so pure as to be painful to hear.

Then it started shoving at the door.

The first shove was tentative, but though I strained with all my strength, it still slapped me back a foot across the floor, my boots slipping on the tile. That paw-hand turned, and the talons sank into the steel door in a sudden, snapping motion as the thing took hold of it and started wrenching it back and forth in berserk anger.

"Help me!" I shouted at the guard, struggling to force the door closed. The jailer blinked at me for a second, then flooded with color.

"You!" he said. "My God. What is happening?"

"Help me close this door or we're both dead," I snarled, continuing to push forward with every ounce of strength I could summon. On the far side of the door, the loup-garou gathered its weight and hurled itself against the door again just as the guard rushed forward to help me.

The door exploded inward, throwing me back like a doll, past the guard, who stumbled back through the door that led behind the counter where he'd been sitting and fell to the ground. My upper back hit the barred door that led out into the hallway, eliciting an instant flash of hot agony from my wounded shoulder.

There was a snarl, and then the creature that had been Harley MacFinn came through the doorway. The loup-garou was a wolf, in the same way that a velociraptor is a bird—same basic design, vastly different outcome. It must have been five or five and a half feet tall at the tip of its hunched shoulders. It was wider than a wolf, as though a wolf had been squashed down with an extra five or six hundred pounds of muscle. Its pelt was shaggy, jet-black and matte, except where fresh blood was making it glisten. Its ears were ragged, upright, focused forward. It had a muzzle that was too wide to belong to anything natural, a mouthful of teeth, and MacFinn's blazing eyes done in monochrome grey, the whole stained with blood that looked black beneath the influence of the blending potion. Its limbs were disproportionate, though I couldn't say whether they looked too long or too short—just *wrong*. Everything about it was wrong, screamed with malice and hate and anger, and it carried a cloak of supernatural power with it that made my teeth hurt and my hair stand on end.

The loup-garou came through the door, swept its monochrome gaze past me, then turned to its left with unholy grace and flung itself at the jailer.

The man got lucky. He looked up and saw the creature as he was regaining his feet, then convulsed in a spastic reaction to the sight of the fanged horror. The reaction threw him a few inches out of the loup-garou's path. He scrambled back, behind the counter and out of my sight.

The loup-garou turned to pursue the jailer behind the counter, slowed because it had to shoulder its way between the counter and the wall, making the counter buckle outward into the room. The jailer got to his feet, gun in hand, took a creditable shooting stance, and emptied the pistol's clip into the loup-garou's skull in the space of maybe three seconds, filling the little antechamber with the sound of thunder and drowning out the cries of the prisoners in their cells in the hall beyond.

The monster kept coming. The bullets bothered it no more than a fly ramming the forehead of a professional wrestler. It rose up as the guard screamed, "No, no, no, nononononono!" And then it fell upon him, claws and fangs slashing. The jailer tried to turn, to run where there was no place left to go, and the thing turned its head and sank its jaws into the small of the man's back, releasing a spray of blood. The jailer screamed and grabbed frantically at the console, but the loup-garou shook its head violently from left to right, tore him from the console, and hurled him to the floor behind the counter.

I didn't see the guard die. But I saw the way the blood flew up over the hunched, gnarled shoulders of the loup-garou, to decorate the walls and the ceiling. I felt silently grateful when the bent and warping panes of Plexiglas became obscured with scarlet.

It was sometime right around then, as paralyzing agony seared through my shoulder and terrified prisoners screamed and cried out to God or Allah to save them that I noticed that a new noise had been added to the din. The guard had tipped off the alarm when he had scrambled at the console, and it was hooting enthusiastically. Cops were going to come running, and one of the first was going to be Murphy.

The loup-garou was still savaging the jailer's body, and I hoped for his sake that the man wasn't still alive. My best option would have been to slip into the cell block, close the security door behind me, and hope the creature went out into the building at large. Within the cell block, I would have time to put up a warding barrier, something that would keep the monster from coming through the door or the walls to get at me and the prisoners in there. I could fort up there, wait for morning, and live through the night, almost certainly. It was the smart thing to do. It was the survivable thing to do.

Instead, I turned to my staff, at the other side of the little room, and held forth my hand. *"Vento servitas,"* I hissed, forcing out tightly focused will, and a sudden current of air simultaneously threw my staff to me and slammed shut the door to the cells, giving the trapped prisoners what little protection it offered. I caught the staff in my outstretched hand and turned to the barred gate that held me shut in the antechamber with the loup-garou.

I thrust my staff in between the bars and leaned against it as though to pry the bars apart. Had it been only wood and muscle involved, I might have snapped the ancient ash. But a wizard's staff is a tool that helps him to apply forces, to manipulate them and maneuver them to his will. So I leaned my will and my concentration on the staff at the same time I did my body, and worked on multiplying the force I was applying to the steel bars.

"Forzare," I hissed. *"Forzare."* The metal began to strain and buckle.

Behind me, the loup-garou started thrashing around. I heard the shattering of Plexiglas and shot it a look over my shoulder. The scant protection offered by the potion collapsed, colors flooding my vision. The black of its muzzle warmed to a scarlet-smeared wash of dark brown, stained with wet scarlet. Its fangs were ivory and crimson. Its eyes became a brilliant shade of green. It cut through the blending potion with the ferocity of its stare, and focused on me with an intensity that sent every instinct in my body screaming that death was here, that it was about to jump down my throat and rip me inside out.

"Forzare!" I shouted, shoving against the staff with every ounce of strength I had. The bars bowed out in the middle, parted to an opening perhaps a foot wide and twice as long. The

counter exploded outward as the loup-garou came through it, showering me with debris and minor, painful cuts.

I dove through the opening, heedless of my shoulder, conscious only of the beast closing in behind me. My body sailed through with more grace than I could have managed under less panicked circumstances, almost as though the rush of air moving before the charging creature had helped lift me through. And then something closed on my left foot, and I simply lost all sensation in it.

I fell short, to the floor, bumping my chin hard enough to draw blood from the corner of my tongue. I looked over my shoulder to see the loup-garou with one of my boots held in its jaws, its broad head shoved through the opening in the bars and caught there. It was shaking its body back and forth, but its paws were smeared with scarlet blood, and its feet slipped left and right on the tile floor. Incredible strength or no, it couldn't get the leverage it needed to tear the bars apart like tissues.

I heard myself making desperate animal sounds, struggling in a panic, writhing. The alarm was howling all around me now, and I could hear shouts and running footsteps. Dust was falling down around the edges of the bars, and I could see that the loup-garou was slowly tearing them from their mountings in the floor and ceiling, despite its bad footing.

I twisted my foot left and right, horrid images of simply losing it at the ankle flashing in my mind, and then abruptly shot forward several feet along the floor. I glanced down at my leg and saw a bloodstained sock before I scrambled up and started running for my staff.

Behind me, the loup-garou howled in frustration and began to throw itself about. It must have scraped enough of the blood off of its paws, because it then tore through the wall of bars in two seconds flat and rushed after me.

I took up my staff and spun to face the creature, planting my feet on the floor, holding the ash wood before me. *"Tornarius!"* I thundered, thrusting my staff upward, and the thing threw itself at me in a rush of power and mass.

My aim was to reflect the loup-garou's own power and momentum back against it, force equals mass times acceleration, et cetera, but I had underestimated just how much power the thing had. It overloaded my limits and we split the difference. The creature slammed against a solid force in the air that canceled its momentum and flung it to the floor.

Approximately equal force was also applied to me—but I was probably a fifth of the mass of the loup-garou. I was flung back through the air like a piece of popcorn in a sudden wind, all the way to where the hall turned the corner to lead down to Special Investigations. I hit the floor before I hit the wall, thankfully, bounced, rolled, and slapped into the wall at last, grateful to be at a stop and aching all over. I had lost my staff in the tumble. The tile floor was cool against my cheek.

I watched the loup-garou recover itself, focus its burning eyes on me, and hurtle down the hallway. I was in so much pain that I could appreciate the pure beauty of it, the savage, unearthly grace and speed with which it moved. It was a perfect hunter, a perfect killer, fast and strong, relentless and deadly. It was no wonder that I had lost to such a magnificently dangerous being. I hated to go, but at least I hadn't gotten beaten by some scabby troll or whining, angst-ridden vampire. And I wasn't going to turn away from it, either.

I drew in what was to be my last breath, my eyes wide on the onrushing loup-garou.

So I could clearly see as Murphy looked down at me with crystal-blue eyes that saw right through the potion's remaining effects. She gave me a hard glance and placed herself between me and the onrushing monster in a shooter's stance, raising up her gun in a futile gesture of protection.

"Murphy!" I screamed.

And then the thing was on us.

Chapter

Eighteen

I tried to make my stunned body respond, to get to my feet, to unleash every ounce of magic at my command to protect Murphy, and to hell with the consequences.

I failed.

The loup-garou hurtled down the hallway, moving faster than I could have believed something so massive *could* move. Its claws gouged into the tile floor like it was soft clay. The walls shook around the beast, as though its very presence was enough to make reality shudder. Bloodstained drool spilled from its foaming jaws, and its green eyes blazed with hellish fury.

Murphy, standing at her full five-feet-and-change tall, was shorter than the loup-garou, its eyes on level with hers. She was wearing jeans again, hiking boots, a flannel shirt rolled up past the elbows, a bandanna around her throat. She was without makeup or jewelry, her earlobes curiously naked and vulnerable without earrings. Her punky little haircut fell down around her eyes, and as she raised her gun, she thrust out her lower lip and puffed out a breath, flipping her bangs up out of her vision. She started shooting when the loup-garou was about thirty feet away—useless. The thing had laughed off bullets fired into its skull at point-blank range.

I noticed three things at that point.

First, Murphy's gun was not the usual heavy-caliber Colt semiautomatic she carried. It was smaller, sleeker, with a telescopic sight mounted at its rear.

Second, the gun made a sharp little *bark, bark, bark*, rather than the more customary *wham, wham, wham*.

Third, when the first bullet hit the loup-garou's chest, blood flew, and the creature faltered and buckled, as though surprised. When the second and third shots slammed into its front leg, the limb slipped and went out from under it. The loup-garou snarled and rolled its momentum to the side, put its head down, and simply smashed its way through the wall and into the room beyond.

Murphy and I were left in the dust-clouded hallway, the escape alarm whooping plaintively in the background. Murphy dropped down next to me. "And I told Aunt Edna I'd never get any use out of those earrings," she muttered. "Christ, Dresden, you're covered in blood. How bad is it?" I felt her slip her hand inside an enormous tear in the blue jumpsuit that I hadn't seen before and run her palm over my chest and shoulders, checking the arteries there. "You're under arrest, by the way."

"I'm okay, I'm okay," I panted, when I could breathe. "What the hell happened? How did you do that?"

Murphy rose up, lifted the gun to half raised, and stalked toward the hole the loup-garou had left in the wall. We could hear crashing sounds, heavy thumps, and furious snarling somewhere on the other side. "You have the right to remain silent. What do you think happened, moron? I read your report. I make my own loads for competition shooting, so I ran off a few silver bullets last night. But they're only in twenty-two caliber, so I'm going to have to put one through his eye to take him out. If that will do it."

"Twenty-two?" I complained, still breathless. "Couldn't you have made some thirty-eights, some forty-fours?"

"Bitch and whine," Murphy snarled at me. "You have the right to an attorney. I don't make my loads for work, and I didn't have the materials for it. Be happy with what you have."

I scrambled to my feet and leaned against the wall by the ragged hole. There was the sound of running feet, moving toward us down the hall. "I can't believe you're *arresting* me. What's through that wall?"

"Records, archives," Murphy said, leveling the target pistol at the hole. "A bunch of big old file cabinets and computers. Everyone who works there went home hours ago. How's that thing react to tear gas?"

"Send some in there and I'll tell you," I muttered, and Murphy shot me a dire look.

"Just stay down, Dresden, until I can get you locked up somewhere safe and get a doctor to look at you."

"Murph. Listen to yourself. We're stuck in a building with one of the nastiest creatures around, and you're still trying to *arrest* me. Get some perspective."

"You made your bed, jerk. Now lie in it." Murphy then raised her voice, without turning her head from the hole in the wall. "Carmichael! Down here! I want four on the doors going out of Records, and the rest with me. Rudolph, get down here and get Dresden back to the office, out of the way." She glared at my wrists, where the handcuffs she'd put on me the night before still dangled. "Christ, Dresden," she added in a mutter. "What is it with you and my handcuffs?"

Police, most of them plainclothes guys from Special Investigations, came pouring into the hall. Some of them had pistols, some of them had pump-action riot guns. My vision blurred and swirled between grey tones and Technicolor, and adrenaline made my nerves jangle and jerk. The potion must have been wearing off; most potions only lasted for a couple of minutes, anyway.

I took inventory. The loup-garou's teeth had scored my foot, through the boot. It hurt, and my sock was soaked in blood. I would leave little red footprints on the floor when I started walking. I could taste the blood in my mouth, from where I had bitten into my tongue, and I either had to spit or swallow. I swallowed. No comments, please. My back was mostly numb, and what wasn't numb hurt like hell. My wounded shoulder, naturally, was pounding so hard that I could barely stand.

"Bastard chewed up my good boot," I muttered, and for some

reason, the statement struck me as incredibly funny. Maybe I had just seen too much for the evening, but whatever had caused it, I sailed into panting, wheezing gales of laughter.

Carmichael dragged me back. His round face was red with exertion and tension, and his food-stained tie was loose around his throat. He passed me into the custody of a young, good-looking detective, who I didn't recognize. He must have been the rookie at SI. I leaned against the young man and laughed helplessly.

"Take him back to the office, Rudolph," Carmichael said. "Keep him there, out of the way. As soon as this is under control, we'll get him to a doctor."

"Jesus Christ," Rudolph said, his eyes wide, his short, dark hair coated with drifting dust. He had a tense, panicky voice, and in spite of his youth, he was panting twice as heavily as the veteran Carmichael. "You saw it on the security monitors, right? What that thing did to Sergeant Hampton?"

Carmichael grabbed Rudolph by the front of his shirt and shook him. "Listen up, rook," he said, his voice harsh. "It's still there, and it can do it to us just as quick as to Hampy. Shut your hole and do what I told you."

"R-right," Rudolph said. He straightened, and started jerking me back down the hall away from the records office. "Who is this guy, anyway?"

Carmichael glared at me. "He's the guy who knows. If he comes to and says something, listen to him." Then he picked up a riot gun and stomped over to where Murphy was getting set to lead a group through the hole in the wall after the loup-garou. She was going over instructions, that if she went down one of the men was to pick up her gun and try to put out the thing's eyes with it.

The rookie half dragged and half led me around the corner and down the hall to the Special Investigations office. I stared down at my feet as he did, at the trail of bloody footprints behind me, giggling. Something was nagging at me, somewhere behind the madness of the laughter, where a diffident, rational corner of my mind was waiting patiently for my consciousness to take notice of an important thought it had isolated. Something about blood.

"This isn't happening," Rudolph chanted to himself along the way. "This isn't happening. Sweet Jesus, this is a trick for the new guy. A prank. Got to be." He stank of sour sweat and fear, and he was shaking horribly. I could feel it in my biceps, where he held me.

I think it was his terror that let me see through my own hysteria, fight it down and shove it under control again. He hauled me through the door, into the Special Investigations office, and I stumbled to the battered, sunken old couch just inside the door. I gasped for air, while the rookie slammed the door and paced back and forth, his eyes bulging, wheezing for air. "This isn't happening," he said. "My God, this isn't happening."

"Hey," I managed, after a minute, struggling to sort out all the input raging through my body—tears, bruises, maybe a sprain or two, a little bit of chill where shock was lurking, and aching sides from the laughter, of all things. The rookie didn't hear me. "Hey, Rudy," I said louder, and the kid snapped his eyes over to me as though shocked that I'd spoken. "Water," I told him. "Need some water."

"Water, right," Rudolph said, and he turned and all but ran to the water fountain. His hands were shaking so hard that he crushed the first two paper cones he took from the dispenser, but he got the third one right. "You're that guy. The fake."

"Wizard," I rasped back to him. "Harry Dresden."

"Dresden, right," the kid said, and came back over to me with the paper cone. I took it and splashed the contents all over my face. It was a cool shock, something else to draw me back from the land of giggles and throbbing nerve endings, and I clawed for all the sane ground I could get. Then I handed the cone back to him. "One more for the inside."

He stared at me as though I was mad (and who's to say, right?)

and went to get another cone cup of water. I drank the second one down and started sorting through my thoughts. "Blood, Rudy," I said. "Something about blood."

"God," the rookie panted, the whites of his eyes glaring. "It was all over Hampton. Blood all over the room, splashed on the Plexiglas and the security camera. Blood, goddamn blood everywhere. What the fuck *is* that thing?"

"Just one more tough bad guy. But it bleeds," I said. Then fastened on the idea, my brain churning to a ponderous conclusion. "It bleeds. Murphy shot it and put its blood all over the floor." I gulped down the rest of the water and stood. "It bleeds, and I can nail it." I lifted my fist to shake it defiantly over my head and strode past the stunned Rudolph.

"Hey," he said, feebly. "Maybe you should sit down. You don't look so good. And you're sort of under arrest, still."

"I can't be under arrest right now," I said back to him. "I don't have the time." I limped down the rows of desks and partitions to Murphy's office. It's a little tacked-on office, with cheap walls of wooden paneling and an old wooden door, but it was more than anyone else in the disfavored department had. There was a paper rectangle taped neatly to the door, where a name placard would be on any other office in the building, which read in neat, block letters of black ink: LT. KARRIN MURPHY, SPECIAL INVESTI-GATIONS. The powers that be refused to purchase a real name plaque for any director of SI—sort of their way of reminding the person they stuck in the position that they wouldn't be there long enough to matter. Underneath the neat paper square, at an angle, was a red and purple bumper sticker that said: TRESPASS-ERS WILL BE KILLED AND EATEN.

"I hope she didn't leave her computer on," I mumbled and went into Murphy's office. I took one look around the neatly organized little place and stepped in to pluck my blasting rod, bracelet, amulet, firearm, and other accoutrements I'd had in my possession when I'd been arrested from the table next to the computer. The computer was on. There was a cough from the monitor as my hand passed near it, and a little puff of smoke, then a bright spark from somewhere within the plastic console of the hard drive.

I winced and collected my things, putting on the shield bracelet with fumbling fingers, ducking my head into the loop of my pentacle amulet, stuffing my pistol into the jumpsuit's pocket, and taking my blasting rod firmly in my right hand, the side of the body that projects energy. "You didn't see that, Rudy. Okay?"

The rookie had a stunned look on his face as he stared at me and at the smoking computer and monitor. "What did you do?"

"Nothing, never came close, didn't do anything, that's my story and I'm sticking to it," I muttered. "You got that paper cup? Right, then. All we need is a stuffed animal."

He stared at me. "Wh-what did you say?"

"A stuffed animal, man!" I roared at him. "Don't mess with a wizard when he's wizarding!" I let out a cackle that threatened to bring the wild hysteria that still lurked inside of me back in full force, and banished it with a ferocious scowl. Poor Rudolph bore the brunt of both expressions, got a little more pale than he already was, and took a couple of steps back from me.

"Look. Carmichael still keeps a couple of toys in his desk, right? For when kids have to wait on their parents, that sort of thing?"

"Uh," said the rookie. "I, uh."

I brandished my blasting rod. "Go look!"

Maybe the kid would have taken any excuse at that point, but he seemed willing enough to follow my instructions. He spun and ran out into the main room and started frantically tearing open desks.

I limped out of Murphy's office and glanced back at the bloody footprints I left on the puke-grey carpet behind me with my soaking sock. The room was getting colder as I lost more blood. It wasn't serious, but it was all the way at the bottom of my considerably long body, and if I didn't get the bleeding stopped before too much longer it was bound to cause problems.

I was going to bend over and try to get a better look at my wounded foot, but when I started to, I swayed and wobbled dangerously, and thought it would be a better thing to wait until someone else could do it. I stood up and took a few deep breaths. Something nagged me about this entire deal, something that was missing, but I'd be damned if I could figure out what it was.

"Rudy," I called. "Get that animal yet?"

The rookie's hand thrust up from one of the partitioned cubicles with a battered stuffed Snoopy doll. "Will this work?"

"Perfect!" I cheered woozily.

And then all hell broke loose.

Chapter

Nineteen

From out in the hallway, there came a scream that no human throat could have made, a sound of such fury and insane anger that it made my stomach roil and my guts shake. Gunfire erupted, not in a rattling series of individual detonations, but in a roar of furious thunder. Bullets shot through the wall, somewhere near me, and smashed out a couple of windows in the Special Investigations office.

I was on my last legs, exhausted, and terrified half crazy. I hurt, all over. There was no way I was going to have the focus, the strength I needed to go up against that monster. Easier to run, to plan something out, to come back when I was stronger. I could win a rematch. It's tough to beat a wizard who knows his enemy, who comes prepared to deal with it. It was the smart thing to do.

But I've never been known for my rational snap judgment. I gripped the blasting rod and started sucking in all the power I could reach, scooping up my recent terror, reaching down into the giggling madness, scraping up all the courage I had left, and pouring it into the kettle with everything else. The power came rushing into me, purity of emotion, complex energies of will, and raw hardheadedness, all combining into a field, an aura of tingling, invisible energy that I could feel enveloping my skin. Shivers ran over me, overriding the pain of my injuries, the ecstasy of power gathering my sensations into its heady embrace. I was pumped. I was charged. I was more than human, and God help anyone who got in my way, because he would need it. I drew in a deep, steadying breath.

And then I simply turned to the wall, pointed my rod at it, and snarled, *"Fuego."*

Power lanced out through the rod in a flood of scarlet light that charred a six-foot circle of wall into powder and ash and sent it flying. I stepped through it, wishing for my duster, for a second, just for the cool effect it would have.

The hallway was a scene out of hell. Two officers were hauling a third down the hall toward me, while three more with shotguns fired wildly around the corner. I don't think the rescuers had taken the time to note that the body they were dragging away from the combat had no head attached to it.

One of the cops screamed as the riot gun he held ran empty, and something I could not see jerked him forward, around the corner and out of my vision. There was a horrible shriek, a splash of blood, and the two remaining shooters panicked and fled up the hall and toward me.

The loup-garou came around the corner after them, hauling one of the men down and ripping its claws across his spine with a simple, savage motion that left the man quivering on the bloody tiles and hardly made the beast miss a step. It set its eyes on the next man, one of the plainclothes SI detectives, and hamstrung him with a slash of its jaws. The beast left him howling on the tiles and hurtled toward the retreating pair, still frantically dragging their corpse away.

I stepped forward, between the fleeing men and the beast, and lifted the blasting rod. "I don't think so, bub."

The loup-garou crouched down, its massive body moving with unholy grace, its head and forequarters soaked in blood. I saw its eyes widen, and its muscles bunch beneath its dark brown pelt. Power gathered at my fist, red and brilliant, and the length of my blasting rod turned an incandescent white. Energy seethed through me as I prepared to release hell on earth at the monster. My teeth ached and my hair stood on end. I tensed every muscle I had, holding it all back until I could put every scrap of strength I had into the strike.

And then there was the *bark-bark-bark* of Murphy's little target pistol, and the loup-garou's rear flank twitched and threw out little bursts of blood. Its head whipped to one side, back down the short hallway, and its body followed suit, faster than a serpent. There was a surge of enormous muscles, a howl of rage, and then the thing was gone.

I spat a curse and ran down the hall after it. The hamstrung officer lay on the floor screaming, and the other man, the one who'd had his spine ripped out, was choking and twitching, unable to draw in a breath. Red anger flooded me, rage that I realized with some dim part of my mind was as much a part of the beast and its blood-maddened frenzy as it was of me.

I rounded the corner in time to see Murphy, standing in front of a litter of bodies, take a last shot at the loup-garou. And then it snarled and she vanished underneath its bulk.

"No!" I screamed and ran forward.

Carmichael beat me to it. His round belly had been ripped open. There was blood all over his cheap suit, though his food-stained tie had somehow remained untainted. His face was grave pale and set with the sort of intensity that only a dying man can have. He held a bent and twisted riot gun in his hands and he hurled himself onto the loup-garou's back as though he weren't sixty pounds overweight and long past his agile years. He wedged the riot gun between the loup-garou's jaws, but the beast turned and slammed Carmichael into the wall with a sickening crunch of bone and a gout of blood from the man's mouth.

Murphy slithered out from between the beast's paws on her shoulder blades and buttocks, her cute little cheerleader's face set in a berserker's fury. She jammed the end of her little gun beneath the thing's chin. I saw her hands convulse on the trigger. But instead of a flash of light and a dead loup-garou, there was only the whooping of the alarm and a look of shocked surprise on Murphy's face. The gun had run empty.

"Murphy!" I shouted. "Roll!"

She saw me with the blasting rod and her eyes flew wide. The loup-garou shook its shoulders free of Carmichael's corpse and bit completely through the riot gun, thrashing its head left and right. Murphy scuttled sideways across the tiles and through the hole in the wall the beast had made earlier.

It took one snap at her and then whipped its head around to snarl at me. I saw the crimson light reflected in its eyes as I focused every bit of fury in the world on the tip of my rod, and shouted, *"Fuego!"* I saw the reflected image in the beast's eyes brighten to nuclear-white in front of a tall, lean figure of black shadow, saw the flood of energy as big around as my hips rush down the hall like a lance of red lightning and hammer into the beast. Sound rushed along with it, a mountain's roar that made the gunshots and screams of the evening seem like a child's whispers in comparison.

The power lifted the loup-garou, hurtling it over the wounded figures moaning on the floor, down the hall, into holding, through the security door, through the cell door immediately across from it, then through the brick exterior wall of the building and out into the Chicago night. But it wasn't over yet. The lance of power carried the loup-garou across the street, through the windows of the condemned building across from the station, and through a series of walls within, each one shattering with a redbrick roar. Before the red fire died away, I could see the far side of the building across the street, and the lights of the next block over through the hole the loup-garou had made.

I stood in a blood-splattered hallway, filled with the moans of the wounded and the wail of the escape alarm. The sounds of emergency vehicles drifted into the building through the ragged hole in the wall. A slender young black man stood up from the floor of the cell the loup-garou had smashed through and gawked at the hole in the wall, then followed the destruction back down the hallway to where I stood. *"Damn,"* he said, and it had the same hushed tone to it as a holy word.

Murphy struggled out of the hole in the wall to pitch down

on the floor of the hallway, gasping. I could see the bulge of bone warping out the skin of her lower arm where it had been snapped, somehow. She lay white-faced and gasping, staring at Carmichael's crushed body.

For a moment, I couldn't do anything but stand there gawking. There was another hole in the wall, where the loup-garou must have crashed back into the hall, putting itself between the two groups of policemen, where they couldn't risk shooting at it without hitting one another. Or maybe they had. Some of the men who were down looked as though they had bullet wounds.

And from outside, over the sirens and the moans and the noise of a city night, I heard a long, furious howl.

"You've got to be kidding me," I breathed. My limbs felt like bruised jelly, but I turned to limp back around the corner and found Rudy there, staring, a paper cup in one hand and the Snoopy doll in the other. I took both from him, and stalked back into the hallway, to the second hole the loup-garou had made.

I found what I was looking for at once—blood on the inside of the hole in the wall, where the beast had plowed through it. The loup-garou's blood was thicker, darker than human fluids, and I scooped it into the paper cup before going back into the hallway.

I swept clean a place with my foot, set down my blasting rod, got out my chalk, and drew a circle on the ground. Rudolph approached me, his head jerking back and forth between grisly corpses and splashes of blood. "You. My God. What are you doing?"

I slapped the Snoopy down in the middle of the circle, then smeared the beast's blood over its eyes and mouth, over its ears and nose. "Thaumaturgy," I said.

"Wha—?"

"Magic," I clarified grimly. "Make a symbolic link between a little thing," I nodded at the Snoopy doll, "and a big thing. Make it happen on the smaller scale and it happens on the larger scale, too."

"Magic," Rudolph echoed.

I glanced up at him. "Go downstairs. Send the emergency people up here, Rudy. Go on. Send them up here to help the wounded."

The kid twitched his eyes from the bloody Snoopy back to me and jerked his head in a nod. Then he turned and fled down the hallway.

I turned my attention back to the spell I was working. I had to keep the rage and anger I felt away from the working of my magic. I couldn't afford to flood my spirit with grief, fury, and thoughts of vengeance for the dead men, for their deaths, for the pain that would be visited on their families. But God as my witness, I wanted nothing more than to try to set that thing on fire and hear it burn somewhere outside.

I tried to remind myself that it wasn't MacFinn's fault. He was under a curse, and not to blame. Killing him wouldn't bring back any of the dead men in these bloody hallways. But I could keep any more men from dying tonight.

And I could do that without killing him.

In retrospect, it was just as well that I didn't try to murder MacFinn. Magic like that takes a lot of energy—certainly more than I had. I would probably have killed myself in the effort to finish off the loup-garou. Not to mention that the Council would get their feathers ruffled by the concept—even though technically, MacFinn wasn't a human being at the moment. Killing monsters isn't nearly as much of an issue with the Council. They don't hold with equal-opportunity mercy.

Instead, as my vision started to fade, I began to chant nonsense syllables in a low, musical refrain, focusing the energy I would need inside the circle I had closed around me. It wasn't until later that I would realize that I was babbling a chant of "Ubriacha, ubrius, ubrium," to the Peanuts theme music. I tore off a strip of my own bloodied jumpsuit and bound it across the Snoopy's eyes, its ears. I bound up the ends of its fuzzy, cute little paws. Then its mouth, as though muzzling it.

I felt the spell grow and prepare itself, and when it was ready, I released the power and broke the circle, feeling it flow out into the night, following the blood back to the loup-garou, winding itself about the creature, blinding its eyes, fouling its ears, lashing around its jaws and forcing them shut, crippling its taloned paws. The spell would hamper and confuse the beast, hopefully drive it to ground where no one could disturb it, keep it from venting its rage upon the people of the city. And it would last until dawn. The energy flowed out of me, left me feeling empty, exhausted, dizzy.

And then people were all around me, emergency folk in uniforms, cops and paramedics and firemen, oh my. I stood up from my circle, grabbed my blasting rod, and shambled off blindly.

I walked past Carmichael's corpse, stunned. Murphy was rocking back and forth over it, weeping, shaking, while a man tried to slide a blanket over her shoulders. She didn't notice me. Carmichael looked relaxed in death. I wondered for a minute if he had a family, a wife who would miss him. He'd died saving Murphy from the beast. He'd died a hero.

It seemed so empty to me, at that moment. Meaningless to be a hero. I felt burned on the inside, as though the fire I had hurled at the creature had scoured away all the gentle feelings that had been there and left a fallow ground behind where only red emotions could flourish. I stumbled past Murphy and Carmichael and turned to walk out of the building, dimly realizing that in the confusion I might actually have fair odds of making it back outside where Tera and Susan would be waiting in the car. No one tried to stop me.

The stairs were tough, and for a minute I thought I might just lie down and die on the first landing, but a helpful old fireman lent me a hand down to the first floor, asking me several times if I needed a doctor. I assured him that I was fine and prayed that he didn't notice the handcuffs still dangling from either wrist. He didn't. He was as wide around the eyes as everyone else, stunned.

Outside was chaos. Police were struggling to establish some sort of order. I saw a couple of news vans rolling up the street, while other people crowded around, trying to see. I stood in the door, dismayed, trying to remember how to walk down the steps.

And then someone warm and gentle was at my side, taking some of my weight. I let her have it, and closed my eyes. I smelled Susan's hair when I inhaled, and it made me want to wail and hold on to her, to try to explain what I had seen, to try to clean the stains from inside my head. All that came out was a little choking sound.

I heard Susan speak to someone else, and another person got on the other side of me, helped me down the stairs. Tera, I thought. I dimly remember them guiding me through the hectic area in front of the police station, around ambulances and shouting men, around policemen who were trying to get the bystanders to move away. I heard Susan explain to someone that I was drunk.

Finally there was quiet, and then we were moving among cars in a parking lot, cool light gleaming on cool metal shapes, cool rain coming down on my head, my hair. I tilted my face up to feel the rain, and everything swam crazily.

"I've got you, Harry," Susan murmured against my ear. "Just relax. I've got you. Just relax."

And so I did.

Chapter Twenty

I awoke in a dark place. It was like the inside of a warehouse, or a big, underground garage, all black, with a smooth, even floor, and a pool of bleak, sterile radiance in the middle of it that came from a source I could not see or identify. I felt like hell, and looked down to see myself covered in scratches, bruises, welts, blood, bandages, and ill-fitting clothing. I wore none of my implements or devices, and there was a curious sense of distance between me and the pain of my injuries—I was more than aware of them, but they seemed to be something that was merely noted in passing, and unimportant to my life as a whole.

I stood just outside the circle of light, and it seemed to me proper that I move forward into it. I did. And as I did, there appeared in the circle opposite me . . . me. Myself. Only better groomed, dressed in a mantled duster of black leather, not the sturdy, if styleless canvas that I wore. My double's pants and boots and shirt were all black as well, and they fit him as though tailor-made, rather than off-the-rack. His eyes were set deep, overshadowed by severe brows, and glittering with dark intelligence. His hair was neatly cut, and the short beard he wore emphasized the long lines of his face, the high cheekbones, the straight slash of his mouth, and the angular strength of his jaw. He stood as tall as I, as long limbed as I, but carried with him infinitely more confidence, raw knowledge, and strength. A faint whiff of cologne drifted over to me, cutting through my own sour sweat and blood smells.

My double tilted his head to one side, looked me up and

down for a long minute, and then said, "Harry, you look like hell."

"And you look like *me*," I said, and limped toward him, peering.

My double rolled his eyes and shook his head. "Hell's bells, you make me sick with how thick skulled you are, sometimes." He took steps toward me, mirroring my own movements. "I don't look like you. I *am* you."

I blinked at him for a few seconds. "You are me. How does that work?"

"You're unconscious, moron," my double said to me. "We can finally talk to one another."

"Oh, I get it," I said. "You're Evil Harry, lurking inside Good Harry. Right? And you only come out at night?"

"Give me a break," my double said. "If you were that simple, you'd be so insufferably boring you'd probably blow your own head off. I'm not Evil Harry. I'm just Subconscious Harry. I'm your inner voice, bub. Your intuition, your instinct, your basic, animal reactions. I make your dreams, and I decide which nightmares to pop in the old psychic VCR at night. I come up with a lot of the good ideas, and pass them along to you when you wake up."

"So you're saying you're wiser than me? Smarter than me?"

"I probably am, in a lot of ways," my double said, "but that's not my job, and it's not why I'm here."

"I see. So what are you doing here, then? You're going to tell me how I'm going to meet three spirits of Harry Past, Present, and Future?" I asked.

My double snorted. "That's good. That really is, the banter thing. I can't do the banter very well. Maybe that's why you're in charge. Of course, if *I* was in charge more often, you'd get laid a lot more—but no, that's not it, either."

"Can we speed this along? I'm too tired to keep on guessing," I complained.

"No joke, jerk. That's why you're asleep. But we don't have

long to talk, and there are some issues we need to work through."
He said "issues" in the British manner, iss-ewwws.

"Issues to work through?" I said. "What, am I my own thera-
pist, now?" I turned my back on my double and started stalking
out of the lighted circle. "I've had some weird dreams, but this
has got to be the stupidest one yet."

My double slipped around me and got in my way before I
could leave the circle of light. "Hold it. You really don't want
to do this."

"I'm tired. I feel like shit. I'm hurt. And what I really don't
want is to waste any more time dreaming about you." I narrowed my eyes at my double. "Now get out of my way." I turned
to my right and started walking toward the nearest edge of the
circle.

My double slipped in front of me again, apparently without needing to cross the intervening space. "It isn't that simple,
Harry. No matter where you go, there you are."

"Look, I've had a long night."

"I know," my double said. "Believe me, I know. That's why
it's important to get some of this out now, before it settles in.
Before you blow a gasket on your sanity, man."

"I've not worried about that," I lied. "I'm as solid as a brick
wall."

My double snorted. "If you weren't getting pretty close to
crazy, would you be talking to yourself right now?"

I opened my mouth. Closed it again. Shrugged. "Okay.
You've got a point."

"I've got more than that," my double said. "Things have
been happening to you so quickly that you haven't had time
to think. You need to work through some of this, and then you
need to do some hard thinking, fast."

I sighed and rubbed at my eyes. "All right, then," I said.
"What do you want to hear?"

My double gestured, and there was Murphy as she had appeared in the hallway of the police station, the flesh of her bicep

tented out by the broken bone, her face pale, spotted with blood, and streaked with tears and hopeless anguish.

"Murph," I said, quietly, and knelt down by the image. "Stars above. What have I done to you?" The image, the memory, didn't hear me. She just wept silent, bitter tears.

My double knelt on the other side of the apparition. "Nothing, Harry," he said. "What happened at the police station wasn't your fault."

"Like hell it wasn't," I snarled. "If I'd have been faster, gotten there sooner, or if I'd told her the truth from the beginning—"

"But you didn't," my double interjected. "And you had some pretty damned compelling reasons not to. Ease up on yourself, man. You can't change the past."

"Easy for you to say," I snarled.

"No, it isn't," my double said quietly. "Concentrate on what you will do, not what you should have done. You've been trying to protect Murphy all along, instead of making her able to protect herself. She's going to be fighting these kinds of things, Harry, and you won't always be there to babysit her. Instead of trying to play shepherd, you need to play coach, and get her into shape to do what she needs to do."

"But that means—"

"Telling her everything," my double said. "The White Council, the Nevernever, all of it."

"The Council won't like it. If I tell her and they hear about it, they might consider her a security risk."

"And if you don't make her able to understand what she's fighting, something's going to eat her face some dark night. Murphy's a big girl. The Council had better be careful if they decide to go messing with her." My double considered Murphy for a moment. "You should ask her out sometime, too."

"I should *what*?" I said.

"You heard me. You're repressing big time, man."

"This is all getting way too Freudian for me," I said, and stood up, intending to walk away again. I was confronted with an image of Susan, as she had appeared on the steps to the police station, tall in her heels and dress suit, elegant and beautiful, her face stretched with worry.

"Think she's going to get a good story out of this?" my double asked.

"Oh, that's below the belt. That's not why she's seeing me."

"Maybe, maybe not. But you're asking yourself that question, aren't you?" My double gestured to himself and to me, demonstratively. "Shouldn't that make you ask a few more questions?"

"Like what?" I asked.

"Like how come you don't trust anyone," my double said. "Not even someone like Susan who has been going out on a limb for you tonight." He lifted a long-fingered hand and stroked at the short beard with his fingertips. "I'm thinking this has to do with Elaine. How about you?"

And then there she was, a girl of elegant height, perhaps eighteen or nineteen years of age—gawky and coltish, all long legs and arms, but with the promise of stunning beauty to add graceful curves to the lean lines of her body. She was dressed in a pair of my blue jeans, cut off at the tops of her muscled thighs, and my own T-shirt, tied off over her abdomen. A pentacle amulet, identical to my own, if less battered, lay over her heart, between the curves of her modest breasts. Her skin was pale, almost luminous, her hair a shade of brown-gold, like ripe wheat, her eyes a startling, storm-cloud grey in contrast. Her smile lit up her face, made her eyes dance with secret fires that still, even after all the years, made me draw in a sharp breath. Elaine. Beautiful, vital, and as poisonous as any snake.

I turned my back on the image, deliberately—before I could see it change into the Elaine that I had last seen—naked, festooned in swirling paints that lent a savage aura to her skin. Her lips had been stained brilliant, wet red, curving around twisting, rolling phrases as she chanted in the midst of her circle, its sigils meant to focus pain and fury into tangible power that had been used to hold a foolish young man helpless while his mentor offered him one last chance to sip from a chalice of fresh, hot blood.

"That's been over for a long time," I said, my voice shaking.

My double answered me quietly, "It isn't over. It isn't over yet, Harry. As long as you hold yourself responsible for Justin's death and Elaine's fall, it still colors everything you think and do."

I didn't answer myself.

"She's still alive," my double said. "You know she is."

"She died in the fire," I said. "She was unconscious. She couldn't have lived through it."

"You'd have known if she died. And they never found a second set of bones."

"She died in the fire!" I screamed. "She's dead."

"Until you stop pretending," my double said, appearing before me, "and try to face reality, you're not going to be able to heal. You're not going to be able to trust anyone. Which reminds me . . ."

My double gestured, and Tera West appeared as I had seen her crouched behind the garbage bin at the rear of the gas station, naked, her body lean, feral, leaves and bits of bracken in her hair, her amber eyes gleaming with cold, alien intelligence. "Why in the *hell* are you trusting *her*?"

"I haven't had much choice," I snapped. "In case you haven't noticed, things have been sort of desperate lately."

"You know she's not human," my double said. "You know she was at the scene of the crime, at Marcone's restaurant, where Spike was torn up. You know she has some kind of hold on a group of young people, the favorite targets of the creatures of the Nevernever. In fact, you can be pretty damn sure that she is a shape-shifter of one kind or another, who isn't telling you the whole truth, but still comes asking for your help."

"Like I can throw stones for not telling the whole truth," I said.

Hngh, my double said in answer. "But you haven't confronted her about what she isn't telling you. Those kids. Who the hell were they, and what were they doing? What is she getting them into? And why was she keeping it a secret from MacFinn? He didn't recognize the names when you dropped them."

"All right, all right," I said. "I was going to talk to her anyway. As soon as I wake up."

My double chuckled. "If things are that leisurely. These murders are still happening, and they're starting to pile up. Are you serious about doing something about them?"

"You know that I am."

My double nodded firmly. "I'm glad we agree on something. Let's look at some facts. MacFinn couldn't have committed all the murders. Most particularly, he couldn't have committed the most important murder—the industrialist, Marcone's partner. He and his bodyguard were killed the night after the full moon. And Spike was wiped out the night before the full moon. MacFinn doesn't have any control over his shape-shifting. He couldn't have been the one to pull off those murders."

"So who could have?" I asked.

"His fiancée. The men were ripped apart by an animal."

"But the FBI lab said that it wasn't a true wolf that did it."

"Werewolves are slightly different from real wolves," my double said.

"How do you know that?" I demanded.

"I'm the intuition, remember?" my double said. "Think about it. If you were going to change yourself into a wolf, do you think you could hold that image in your head, perfectly exact? Do you think you could make all the millions of subtle, tiny changes in skeletal and muscular structure? Magic doesn't just work—a mind has to direct it, shape it. Your emotions, your feelings toward wolves would color it, too—change the image and the shape. Ask Bob, next chance you get. I'm sure he'll tell you I'm right."

"Okay, okay," I said. "I'll buy that. But the FBI said that there was more than one set of tooth marks and prints, too."

"MacFinn explains some of them. During last month's full moon, he probably killed some people when his circle went ka-blooey."

"And the group Tera had—they called themselves the Alphas—could explain the rest of them, if they were shape-shifters."

"Now you're catching on," my double said, approval in his tone. "You're smarter than you look."

"Do you think they were behind spoiling MacFinn's contain-ment circle? The fancy one with all the silver and stuff?"

"They had the knowledge to do it, through Tera. Tera could have let them in, providing opportunity," my double said.

"But they didn't have a motive," I said. "Why would they have done it?"

"Because Tera told them to, maybe?"

I frowned and nodded. "She is a creature of the Nevernever. Who knows what's going through her—its head. It doesn't nec-essarily have to be understandable by human logic."

My double shook his head. "I don't buy that. I saw the way she looked at MacFinn—and how she sacrificed herself to divert the FBI and the police so that he could escape. Your instincts are telling you that she is in love with MacFinn, and that she wouldn't act against him."

"Yeah. You told me that about Elaine, too," I shot back, an-other pang of memory going through my chest.

"That was a long time ago," my double said defensively. "I've had time to get keener since then. And less easy to distract."

"All right," I sighed. "So where does that leave us?"

"I don't think we've run into the real killers yet. The ones who ruined MacFinn's circle and whacked the mob guys on the non-full-moon nights."

I squinted at my double. "You think so?"

He nodded and stroked his beard again. "Unless the Alphas are doing it without Tera knowing, and they look a little too bright eyed and bushy tailed to be doing that. I think it's someone else entirely. Someone trying to set up MacFinn and take him out of the picture."

"But why?"

"Maybe because they didn't want him putting the Northwest Passage Project through. Or, gee, maybe because he's a freaking werewolf, Harry, and someone caught on to it and wanted him dead. You know that there are organizations who would do that—some of the Venatori Umbrorum, members of the White Council, others who are in the know."

"But you don't think I've seen them, yet?"

"I don't think you've picked them out from the background," my double said. "Keep your eyes open, all right? Which brings us to the next topic of discussion."

"Does it?"

My double nodded. "Threat assessment. You've got all kinds of things staring you right in the face, and you're not noticing them. I don't want you to get killed because you're too distracted." He glanced to one side, frowned, and said, "We're almost out of time."

"We wouldn't be if you weren't such a wiseass."

"Bite me," my double said. "Don't forget Marcone. You pissed him off by not taking the deal he offered you. He thinks the killers are coming after him next, and he might be right. He's scared, and scared people do stupid things—like trying to off the only man in town who has a chance of stopping what's going on."

"Let me worry about Marcone," I said.

"I *am* you, and I'm worried. Next is the cops. Some of Murphy's people are dead. There is going to be hell to pay once she gets that arm fixed—and someone is going to remember that you were around, and with your luck, they won't remember that you kept even more people from dying. You see Murphy and the police again, you'd better be careful or you're going to get shot to death resisting arrest."

"I'll be careful," I said.

"One more thing," my double said. "You have forgotten about Parker and the Streetwolves entirely. Parker needs you dead if he's going to remain in control of his people."

"Yeah. You'd have thought he'd have been more on the ball than this."

"Exactly," my double said. "You've been hiding and away from your apartment for a while—but you show up in public again, and you can bet that Parker will be on your trail. And *think*. He knew the real deal between you and Marcone, and he's a petty thug in Chicago. There's probably a connection between them, and you've been too dumb to think of it."

"Stars above," I muttered. "It's not as if the situation is very complicated. No pressure, right?"

"At least you're willing to deal with it now, instead of just closing your eyes and pretending that they can't see you. Be careful, Harry. It's a real mess, and you're the only one who can clean it up."

"Who are you, my mother?" I asked.

My double snapped his fingers. "That reminds me, right. Your mother—" He broke off, glancing up and around him, an expression of frustration coming over his face. "Oh, hell."

And then someone was shaking my unwounded shoulder, shaking me roughly awake. I blinked open my eyes in shock, and all the pains of my body came flooding back into me with renewed energy and agony. My brain reeled for a few minutes, trying to shift gears.

I was sitting in the passenger seat of Susan's car. We were rolling down an expressway, somewhere, but rain was clouding the view of the skyline so that I couldn't orient myself to where we were. The glowing numbers of the dashboard clock said that it was only a few minutes after nine. I'd had less than half an hour's sleep. There was an old beach towel wrapped around my wounded foot, and my face felt cool, as though someone had wiped it clean.

"Is he awake?" Susan said, her voice high and panicky. "Is he awake?"

"I'm awake," I said blearily, blinking open my eyes. "Sort of. What? This better be good."

"It is not good," Tera said from the backseat. "If you have any power left, wizard, you should prepare to use it. We are being followed."

Chapter
Twenty-one

I rubbed at my eyes and mumbled some vague curse at whoever was following us. "Okay, okay. Give me a minute."

"Harry," Susan said. "I'm almost on empty. I don't know if we *have* a minute."

"It never rains," I moaned.

Tera frowned at me. "It is raining now." She turned to Susan. "I do not think he is coherent."

I snorted and looked around blearily. "It's a figure of speech. Hell's bells, you really don't know *anything* about humans, do you?

"Are you sure there's someone following us?"

Tera glanced back at the traffic behind us. "Two cars back. And three cars behind that one. Two vehicles are following us."

"How can you tell?" I asked.

Tera turned those odd amber eyes back to me. "They move like predators. They move well. And I feel them."

I narrowed my eyes. "Feel them? On an instinctual level?"

Tera shrugged. "I feel them," she repeated. "They are dangerous."

The taste of blood was still in my mouth, annoying input, like static on a phone. Of all the people who might be chasing me in cars, I could only think of a few who would trigger the supernatural senses of an inhuman being. I thought that it might be a pretty good idea to listen to what my dapper double had to say. "Susan," I said, "I want you to get off the expressway."

Her dark eyes flashed beneath the streetlights as she looked at me, then down at her fuel gauge. "I have to in the next couple of miles anyway. What do you want me to do?"

"Pull off, and get to a gas station."

She flashed me another nervous look, and I had the time to note that she was gorgeous, like some sort of Latin goddess. Of course, I might have been a little less than entirely objective. "Then what?" she said.

I checked my foot and idly took off my remaining boot, so that my hips would be parallel with the floor while I was standing. "Call the police."

"What?" Susan exclaimed and guided her car off the freeway and down an exit ramp.

I felt around in the jumpsuit's tool pouch, until I came out with the little sports bottle with my second potion in it. "Just do it," I said. "Trust me on this one."

"Wizard," Tera said, her voice still utterly calm. "There is no one but you who can help my fiancé."

I shot Tera an annoyed glance. "I'll meet you where you hold your Cub Scout meetings."

"Harry?" Susan said. "What are you talking about?" She pulled the car down the exit ramp, onto a one-way access road.

"I understand what you're doing," Tera said. "I would do the same for my mate."

"*Mate?*" Susan said indignantly. "Mate? I am most certainly *not* his—"

I didn't get to hear the rest of what Susan said, because I grabbed my blasting rod in one hand, the potion in the other, opened the door to the car, unfastened my seat belt, and rolled out onto the shoulder of the road.

I know, I know. It sounds really stupid in retrospect, even to me. But it made a sort of chivalrous, cockamamie sense at the time. I was pretty sure that Parker and his cronies in the Streetwolves were shadowing us, and I had a precise idea of how dangerous they could be. I had to assume that they were even worse during the full moon. Susan had no idea of the level of danger she was in, and if I stayed near her I would only draw her more deeply into it. And Tera—I still didn't trust Tera. I wasn't sure that I wanted her fighting at my back.

I wanted to deal with my pursuers myself, to deal with my own mistake myself, and not to make an innocent bystander like Susan pay for it.

So I, uh, sort of threw myself out of the passenger seat of a moving car.

Don't look at me like that. I'm telling you, it made sense at the time.

I held out my arms and legs in a circle, as though I were trying to hug a barrel, and then scrape, scrape, rip, bumpity-bumpity-bumpity, whip, whip, whip, and thud. Everything whirled around the whole while. I managed, somehow, to keep my sense of direction, to maintain my momentum largely in a roll, and to angle myself toward the dubious comfort of the thick weeds at the side of the access road. By the time I came to a stop, I was among freshly crushed plants, all damp and cold from the rain, the smell of mud and gas and asphalt and exhaust clogging up my nose.

There was pain, pain everywhere, spreading out from my shoulder and my foot, whirling dizziness, blackness that rode on my eyelids and tried to force them down. I struggled to remember exactly what I had planned on doing when I had thrown open the door to Susan's car.

It came to me in a moment, and I jerked the squeeze top of the sports bottle open with my teeth and then crushed the plastic bottle, forcing the potion inside it out through the narrow nozzle and into my mouth. Eight ounces of cold coffee, I thought, dimly. Yum.

It tasted like stale cardboard and too-old pizza and burned coffee beans. But as it went down my gullet, I could feel the power in the brew spreading out into me, active and alive, as though I had swallowed a huge, hyperkinetic amoeba. My fatigue quite simply vanished, and energy came rushing into me, like it sometimes does at the end of a really good concerto or overture. The pain receded down to levels that I could manage. The soreness lifted out of my muscles, and my cloudy, cloggy thought processes cleared as though someone had flushed my synapses with jalapeño. My heart rate surged, and then held steady, and I came to the abrupt conclusion that things just weren't as bad as I had thought they were.

I pushed myself up using my bad arm, just to spite the injury that Agent Benn had dealt me, and brushed myself off. My jumpsuit was torn and there was fresh blood on it, scrapes from the asphalt and darkening bruises on my arms and legs that I could already see—annoying little bastards. I held them in contempt.

I shook my shield bracelet loose around my left wrist, took my blasting rod in my right hand, and turned toward the access road. I drew in a breath, smelling the odor of the rain on the asphalt, and more distantly the crisp, clean scent of autumn, almost buried by Chicago's stink. I considered how much I loved the autumn, and composed a brief poem about it as I watched traffic force Susan's car along and out of sight. I turned my head to view a pair of cars cut frantically across traffic and cruise down the access road. The lead car was a two-ton pickup, one of the really big ones, and Parker sat behind the wheel, looking around wildly until his eyes lit upon me, standing there in the tall weeds beside the road.

I smiled at him and contemplated his shocked expression to my own satisfaction.

Then I drew in a breath, and my renewed will with it, lifted the rod in my right hand, murmured a phrase in a language I didn't know, and blew the tires off his fucking truck.

They all went at once, in one satisfying THUMP, complete blowouts resulting from a sudden heating of the air inside the tires—a pretty slick spell to pull on the fly, heating up the air inside of the tires of a moving vehicle. The truck slewed left and right, and I could see Parker frantically rolling the steering wheel in an effort to maintain control. Two people sat in the cab with him, faces I didn't recognize from here, and they evidently didn't believe in seat belts. They were tossed about the inside of the truck like toys. The truck careened off the road in a spray of gravel, went past me into the weeds, hit some sort of ditch, and went into a ponderous roll.

There was an enormous crunching sound. Car wrecks, when they happen for real and not on television, are surprisingly noisy. They sound like someone pounding empty trash cans out of shape with a sledgehammer, only louder. Parker's truck tumbled over twice, crunched into the side of a hill, and lay on its passenger side.

"Well then," I said with a certain amount of professional pride. "That should take care of that."

I spoke too soon. There was a brittle, grinding sound, and the windshield of the truck exploded into a hectic spiderweb pattern. The sound repeated itself, and the safety glass shattered outward, followed by a foot wearing a heavy black combat boot. More glass flew outward, and then people started crawling out of the pickup, battered and bloodied. Besides Parker, there was the lantern-jawed lout whose nose I had flattened a few days ago, his nose now swollen and grotesque, and the bloodthirsty woman who had led the group into their berserk fit of lust. They were all dressed in the same variants of denim and leather, and cuts and bruises from the tossing they'd had were much in evidence.

Parker led them out of the truck, looked back at it, stunned— and then he looked at me. I saw fear flicker in his eyes, and it brought out a satisfied surge within my own pounding heart. Served him right, the jerk. I spun my rod around once in my fingers, started whistling a bit from the overture to *Carmen*, and walked toward them through the grass, annoyed that I was limping and that I was dressed in a ridiculous blue jumpsuit that left inches of my arms and legs bare.

Flatnose saw me and grunted out some sort of Neanderthal noise of surprise. He drew a handgun from inside his jacket, and it looked tiny in his hands. Without preamble he started squeezing off shots at me.

I lifted my left hand, forced more of my boundless energy through the shield bracelet, and sang a few phrases in what I supposed could have been taken for Italian to verbally encase the spell. I continued walking forward as bullets bounded off the shield before my hand in cascades of sparks, and I even had enough breath left over to keep on whistling *Carmen*.

Parker snarled and slashed at Flatnose's wrist with the edge of his hand in a martial-arts-style movement. I heard a bone break, very clearly, but Flatnose only jerked his hand back toward his body and flashed Parker a scowl.

"Remember why we're here," the shorter man said. "He's mine."

"Hello there, Mr. Parker," I called cheerfully. I suppose that the image I presented as I walked toward them would have been comic—except for all the blood, and the big smile I felt spreading over my face. It seemed to have a somewhat intimidating effect on the Streetwolves at any rate. The woman snarled at me, and for a second I could feel a wild, savage energy, the same that had surrounded the frenzying lycanthropes at the Full Moon Garage, starting to build in the air around me.

I gave the bitch an annoyed look and slashed my hand at the air, drawling, *"Disperdorus."* I forced out an effort of will I might have found daunting on another night, one when I was feeling a little less all-powerful, and the woman jerked back as though I had slapped her in the mouth. The energy she had been gathering fractured and flew apart as though it had never been. She stared at me, growing tense and nervous, and reached a hand toward a knife in a case at her hip.

"Let's have none of that nonsense. As I was saying," I continued, "hello there, Mr. Parker. I know why you're here. Heard about the ruckus on a police scanner and came down by the station looking for me, right? Hate to disappoint you, but I'm not going to allow you to kill me."

Flatnose scowled and said, "How did you know th—"

Parker shoved the heel of his hand across Flatnose's mouth in a sharp blow, and the big man shut up. "Mr. Dresden," Parker growled. He eyed me up and down. "What exactly makes you think you can stop me from killing you?"

I had to smile at the man. I mean, you have to smile at idiots and children. "Oh, I don't know," I chuckled. "Maybe because the second you step out of line, I'm going to wreck you a whole hell of a lot worse than that truck. And because in just a couple of minutes, the police are going to be arriving to sort you out." There was a momentary flash of dimness, where the streetlight seemed to fade, the rain to grow very cold, and then it was gone again. I blinked a little blood out of my eyes, and renewed my smile. Mustn't let the children see weakness.

Parker snarled his thin lips into a smile. He had bad teeth. "The cops are after your ass too, Dresden," he said. "I don't believe you."

"Once they're here, I'm going to mysteriously disappear," I said. "Just like, well, gosh, magic. But you guys are . . ." I forgot what I had been going to say for a moment. There was something nagging at the back of my mind, a detail I had forgotten.

"I can smell your blood, wizard," Parker said, very quietly. "God, you got no idea what it smells like." Parker didn't move, but the woman let out a little mewling sound and pressed against Flatnose's side. Her eyes were focused intently on me.

"Get a good whiff," I managed to say. "It's the last time you'll smell it." But my smile was gone. A creeping vine of uncertainty was beginning to crack the wall of confidence I had been enjoying. The rain was getting colder, the lights dimmer. My extended left arm began to ache, starting at the wounded shoulder, and my hand shook visibly. Pain started leaking in again, from every part of my battered body.

Sanity returned in a rush. The potion. The potion was giving out on me. I had pushed myself way too hard while the first euphoria was going over me. Dispelling the intimate aura of rage and lust that the woman had begun to gather over them had been a feat I would never have considered in a stable frame of mind. There were too many unknowns. My heart was laboring along now, and I started panting. I couldn't get enough breath to slow down my rocketing heartbeat.

Parker and his two companions grew tense together, all at once, with no visible signal passing between them. I could feel that wild energy again, coursing down to the lycanthropes from beyond the rain clouds overhead. I swear to you, I could see the cuts on their body, from the crash, closing up before my eyes. Flatnose rolled the wrist that had just been broken, flexed his fingers at me, and gave me a grim smile.

Okay, Harry, I told myself. Keep calm. Do not panic. All you have to do is to hold them until the cops get here, and then you can bleed to death in peace. Or get to a doctor. Whichever hurts less.

"You know, Parker," I said, and my voice had a fluttering quaver to it, a fast, desperate quality. "I didn't really mean to show up at your garage. Hell, I wouldn't have been there at all if Denton's goon hadn't turned me on to the idea."

"That doesn't matter now," Parker said. His voice had a quiet, certain tone to it, and he had visibly relaxed. He smiled at me, and showed me more of his teeth. "That's all in the past." Then Parker took a step forward, and I panicked.

I jammed the rod at him and snarled, *"Fuego."* I funneled my will through it, and to hell with what the Council thought of me killing someone with magic.

Nothing happened.

I stared in disbelief, first at Parker, and then at the blasting rod. My fingers went numb as I looked at them, and the rune-engraved ash rod fell to the ground, though I tried a clumsy grab to catch it. Instead, my weight came down on my torn foot, and the ripped muscles went into a sudden cramp that sent fresh agony up through my leg. It buckled and pitched me forward into the weeds and the mud. The last wisps of my shield vanished as I fell. My magic had failed me altogether.

Parker laughed, a low and nasty sound. "Nice trick. Got another?"

"One more," I rasped, and fumbled at the jumpsuit's tool pouch. Parker walked slowly toward me, confident, relaxed, and moving like a man thirty years younger than he. My fingers were aching with cold, torn from the asphalt, numb from all the pain and scrapes and bruises. But the handle of my Chief's Special was easy enough to find.

I drew it out, thumbed back the hammer, and pointed it up at Parker. His eyes widened and his weight settled back on his heels—not quite retreating, but not coming any closer, either. From three feet away, even down in the mud, it would be tough to miss him, and he knew it.

"I didn't pick you for the kind to carry a gun," he said. The rain plastered his greasy hair down over his eyes.

"Only on special occasions," I said back. I had to delay him. If I could hold him in place, just for a few minutes, the cops would show up. I had to believe that they would, because if they didn't I was dead meat. Maybe literally. "Stop where you are."

He didn't. He took a step toward me.

So I shot him.

The gun roared, and the bullet smacked into his right kneecap. It exploded in a burst of blood and flying chips of bone, and the leg went out from under him, hurling him to the muddy ground. He blinked once, surprised, but the pain he must have been feeling didn't seem to register. He scooted back a couple of feet and stared at me for a second, reassessing me.

Parker then drew his legs beneath him, and ignoring his ruined knee, hunkered down on his heels and rested his elbows on his thighs as if we were old friends, keeping his hands in plain sight. "You're tougher than you look. We tried to catch you at your apartment, you know," he said, as though I hadn't just shot him. "But the cops were all over it. Police band said you'd gotten arrested, but I guess you got away. We paid the jailer to let us know when they rounded you up." He grinned his snaggle-toothed grin and looked almost friendly. "Hell, kid. We were hanging around in a bar two blocks from the station for almost two days, just hoping to be there when they brought you up the steps. Drive-by." He pointed his finger at me in a bang-bang motion, and let his thumb fall forward.

"Sorry to disappoint you," I mumbled. I was working hard not to give in to the shakes, the cold, or the darkness. I knew he was up to something, but there was too much to deal with—too much injury, too much exhaustion, too much blood on my hands. I squinted past him to see Flatnose and the woman still in the same spot, both of them watching me with the intent look of hungry animals.

Parker chuckled. "And instead, everything goes to hell at the station. Gunshots, explosions, sounds like a war inside. Which was fun to watch. And then we see you stumbling out of the middle of it, right there in front of the cop station, with a cute little piece on either side helping you down the stairs. We just rolled out right after your ass."

"I hope you're insured."

Parker shrugged. "Truck wasn't mine." He plucked up a long blade of grass and traced it over the ruin of his knee, painting it red with his blood before crushing it up in his fingers. "Most of my people are out by the lake tonight. They got to let off some steam during the full moon. Damn, but I want to take you out right there in front of all of them. You got a real badass reputation, kid."

"Can't have everything you want," I said. I blinked rain, or blood, from my eyes.

Parker's smile widened. "You know, kid. I think there's something you don't know."

In the distance, I could hear the sound of sirens speeding

down the freeway toward me. Hot damn, I thought. I finally did something right. "Oh yeah?" I asked, daring to feel a satisfied thrill of victory.

Parker nodded and looked off to one side. "There were two cars behind you."

And something smashed down on my right hand, making it go numb, and sending the gun to earth. I looked up and had time to see another of the lycanthropes from the garage lift a lead pipe wrapped in electrical tape, and bring it down hard at me. The woman screamed and rushed toward me. She had steel-toed boots. Flatnose lumbered after her, and was content to use the barrel of his pistol as a dumb club.

Parker just sat there, squatting on his heels, and watched them. I could see his eyes. My blood spattered onto his cheek.

I don't like thinking about what they did. They didn't want to kill me. They wanted to hurt me. And they were good at it. I couldn't fight. I couldn't even curl up into a ball. There wasn't that much spirit left in me. I could hear myself making choking sounds, gagging on my own blood, sobbing and retching in pathetic agony. I would have screamed if I could have. You hear stories about men who keep silent through all the torture and agony that anyone inflicts on them, but I'm just not that strong. They broke me.

At some point, the mind says "no more" and it gets the hell away from all that pain. I started going there, to that away-place, and I wasn't sorry to do it at all.

I could dimly hear Parker shoving people off of me, once I stopped moving. He broke a few more of their bones, and they backed off with snarls of rage. He was walking on the leg again already, though my shot must have torn the joint to pieces. At his orders, they picked me up and carried me to another car, just lugged me along like a sack of broken parts. Duct tape went around my wrists and ankles, knees and elbows and mouth. Then they threw me in the trunk.

Parker reached up to close the lid. I didn't have enough energy to move my eyes. I just stared out, letting them focus wherever they would.

I saw a face behind the wheel of a car going past on the access road—just a sedan, something that would blend in with all the other cars in the city. The face was young, strained, sprinkled with freckles, the hair red, the ears big.

Roger Harris, FBI. Denton's redheaded lackey.

The sedan rolled by without even slowing, and Harris didn't look over at me, didn't break his surveillance. I wasn't the only one, it seemed, who was being followed that night.

Parker slammed shut the trunk, leaving me in darkness. The car started going just as the sirens began to arrive at the access road. My captors' car bounced along and made a casual getaway, leaving me in an agony more thorough, sickening, and acute than any I had felt before.

And, behind the gag, I started laughing. I couldn't help it. I laughed, and it sounded like I was choking on raw sewage.

The pieces had all fallen into place.

Chapter
Twenty-two

There's a point after which one cannot possibly continue doing complicated things like thinking and keeping one's eyes open. Blackness ensues and everything stops until the body, or the mind, is ready to function again. The blackness came for me and I welcomed it.

When I started to wake up, I smelled motor oil.

That in itself boded ill. I was seated upright, and an upright metal beam pressed into my back. I felt something constricting my wrists and my ankles. Duct tape, still, perhaps. There was cold concrete floor beneath me. I was aching everywhere, and stiff. But there was something soft over me, a blanket, maybe. I wasn't as cold as I might have been.

My first emotion was a vague surprise that I was still alive.

The second was a cold, nasty little shiver. I was a prisoner. And as long as I was, survival was by no means certain. First things first, then. Make it certain. Find out where I was, devise a plan, and get my skinny wizard ass out of there.

After all, it would be a real pity to die when I'd finally put tabs on who had gotten me into this mess—as well as who was responsible for the recent killings that couldn't be attributed to MacFinn, and probably who had set him up as well.

To that end, I opened my eyes and tried to get a look at my surroundings.

I was in the enemy's stronghold, the Full Moon Garage. It was dim inside, and from what I could hear, it was still raining without. There was a dirty, but warm blanket over me, which came as something of a surprise. There was also a little stand with a mostly empty plastic bag of what I took to be blood, dripping down a plastic tube that vanished behind me, out of my sight, and presumably ended at my arm.

I wiggled my feet out from beneath the blanket. My legs had been duct-taped together above and below the knee, and at the ankle. My bitten foot had been wrapped in clean bandages, then covered in my bloodied sock. In fact, I found a number of clean bandages on various cuts and scrapes, and I could smell, faintly, as though my nose had been given a while to get used to it, the sharp, medicine smell of disinfectant. I couldn't feel Murphy's sawed-through handcuffs on my wrists, and found myself vaguely missing them. At least they'd been familiar, if not comfortable.

So, not only was I alive, but I was in considerably better shape, after presumably several hours of sleep and medical attention.

But that didn't explain who had done this to me. Or why.

I looked around the dimness of the garage. My eyes were now adjusted to it, but even so, there were pockets of shadows too deep to see into. An L-shaped ribbon of yellow light showed beneath the door to the manager's office, and the sound of rain on the corrugated roof was a low, soothing roar. I closed my eyes, trying to orient myself, to determine what time it was from the feel of the air and the sound of the rain. Late afternoon? Early evening? I couldn't tell for sure.

I coughed and found my throat dry, but functional. My hands were bound, and I didn't have any way of making a circle. Without a circle, I couldn't use any delicate magic to free myself—all I had access to was the kaboom sort of power, which, while great against nasty loup-garou and other monsters, isn't much good for getting rid of several layers of duct tape resting within half an inch of my own tender skin. Magic was out.

Did I ever tell you about my dad? He was a magician—not a wizard, mind you, but a magician, the kind you see at old-fashioned magic shows. He had a black top hat, a white rabbit, a basket of swords, and everything. He used to travel around the country, performing for the kids and the old folks, barely making enough to scrape by. After Mom died during childbirth, Dad had the job of raising me all by himself, and I guess he did the best he could. He meant well.

I was real young when he died (I refused to believe Chaunzaggoroth's insinuations until I had looked into them further) of a brain aneurism. But I learned a thing or three about what he did before then. He'd named me after three magicians, after all, the first of which was Houdini himself. And one of Houdini's first rules was that the means to escape was always within your grasp. Positive attitude. It's a fact that a human being can escape from just about everything, given enough time.

The only question was, how much time did I have left?

The duct tape was strong, and it was fastened tightly—but it was also cheap, easy to transport, and simple to apply. Even though it was wound about me in multiple layers, it wasn't the best thing for holding people, or else the cops would use duct tape and not handcuffs and manacles. It could be beaten.

So I started looking for ways to beat it.

A little writhing showed me that my hands weren't fastened as tightly as they could have been. I could feel a sharp pain in my forearm, and guessed that was from the IV. They had to loosen the tape on my arms to get the needle into my forearm. I wiggled my shoulders, which set the wounded one to aching fiercely. The tape put pressure on my wrists and tore the hair from my arms with an audible ripping sound, and I clenched my teeth over this particular torment.

It hurt, and it took me the best part of ten minutes, but I got my wrists and hands free. I ditched the IV needle while I was at it, imagining some deadly fluid flowing down the tube into my veins. Then I flexed my arms repeatedly and got them free.

My fingers were numb, stiff, not really responding, but I started fumbling at the tape on my legs as best I could, trying to get tears started so that I could just flex my legs and get the whole thing to go at once. It took more effort than I thought it would, but I finally flexed my legs, thankful that the jumpsuit kept me from losing stripes of hair from my thighs and calves (if not from my ankles). My legs were much stronger than my arms, so snapping the layers of duct tape on them was a lot simpler and quicker.

Just not simple or quick enough.

Before I'd gotten out of the last loop of duct tape, there was a click-clack, and the office door swung open, accompanied by a murmur of low voices and a tinny din of old-time rock-and-roll music.

I panicked. I couldn't run—my ankles were still bound. By the time I got free and struggled to my feet, they'd be on me. So I did the next best thing. I whipped the blanket up and over me, snaked my hands back behind the pole, grabbing up the IV needle as I went and concealing it in my hand, and bent my head far forward as though I were still asleep.

"I still don't get why we can't just put a bullet in him and dump him," said a harsh voice with no nasal tone at all—Flatnose.

"Stupid," Parker growled, his voice like sandpaper. "One, we don't do it without having the others here to see. And two, we don't do it until Marcone's had a chance to see him."

"Marcone," Flatnose said with a sneer in his voice. "What's he want with him?"

Good question, I thought. I kept my head down, my body relaxed, and tried to think sleepy thoughts. Marcone was coming here?

"Who cares?" Parker answered. "I made sure he'd live through the day. Either way, I wanted him here tonight. No skin off my teeth."

Flatnose grunted. "Chicago sees a lot of mobsters. Marcone's just one more. But one call from him, and this wizard character gets a reprieve. Who is this guy, huh? The freaking governor?"

"Always thinking with your balls," Parker said, his voice calm. "Marcone isn't just a mobster. Running Chicago is just his sideline, see. He's got business all over the country, and he owns people from here to the governor's mansion to Washington and back, and he's got more money than God. He can set us up, take us out, have the police on our ass anytime he wants. You don't screw with someone like that lightly."

There was a pause, and then Flatnose said, "Maybe. Or maybe Lana's right. Maybe you're getting soft. Marcone isn't one of us. He doesn't give us orders. The Parker I knew ten years ago wouldn't have thought twice of telling Marcone to fuck off."

Parker's voice became resigned. "Don't do this, man. You were never good enough, even when we were young. The Parker you knew ten years ago would have gotten all of us killed by now. I've kept you in cash, in dope, women, whatever you wanted. So settle down."

"I don't buy it," Flatnose said back. "I think Lana's right. And I say we off this skinny son of a bitch right now." I felt myself tense and prepared to make a run for it, hopeless or not. I'd rather get killed trying to get away than trying to pretend I was asleep.

"Back down," Parker said, and then there was a scuffling noise of boots on old concrete. I heard a couple of grunts and an abrupt yelp, and smelled sour sweat and stale beer as Flatnose was forced to his knees less than a foot away. He kept making small noises of pain, thick with tension, as though Parker was holding him in some kind of lock. I forced myself to relax, not to just stagger up and start running, but I felt a bead of sweat trickle down my face.

Parker snarled over Flatnose's whimpers, "I told you. You were never good enough. Challenge me again, in public or alone, it doesn't matter—and I will rip your heart out." The way he spoke the threat was eerie; not with the hissing, villainous emphasis one would expect, but in a calm, measured, almost bored tone, as though he were mentioning switching out a carburetor or changing a lightbulb. There was a rippling sort of sound, and Flatnose let out a howl of pain that dissolved into a string of doglike whimpers. I heard Parker's boots move a few steps away. "Now, get up," he said. "Call Tully's and get the others back here before the moon rises. We'll have blood tonight. And if Marcone isn't polite enough, we'll have a lot more."

I heard Flatnose make his way to his feet and shuffle off in a slow and haphazard fashion. He vanished into the office and closed the door behind him. I waited for a few moments, hoping that Parker would wander off and I could make my escape, but he didn't. Dammit.

I was running out of time. If I waited until the rest of the lycanthropes returned to the garage, I'd never be able to get away. The numbers would be stacked too high. If I was going to make a break for it, logically, the time was now.

Of course, I was still bound. By the time I got my legs free, Parker would be on me. And I had just listened to him disable a man twice his size and threaten to rip his heart out. He'd meant it, too, I could tell. When I had looked inside of him, I had seen a dark and angry place, the source of all that power and force of will. He could tear me to pieces with his bare hands, literally—and what was worse, he would. I had to have a head start if I was going to run.

I could make him mad, maybe. Antagonize him into going to get a baseball bat, or another roll of duct tape for my mouth. Then I could run, make a clean getaway. The one problem with that plan was that he might just rip my heart out on the spot— but nothing ventured, nothing gained. I didn't have time to be picky.

So I lifted up my head enough to squint at him in the semi-darkness and said, "You certainly have a way with people. You must have read a book or something."

My voice startled him, and he spun with the reflexes of a nervous cat. He stared at me for a long minute before starting to relax. "So. You're alive. It's just as well, I suppose."

"Mostly I was just tired. Thanks for the sack time."

He showed me his teeth. "No problem. Checkout is in a couple hours."

That scared me enough to make a rational man pee, but I only shrugged. "No problem. Good thing your people can't hit. They might have made me uncomfortable."

Parker laughed a rough laugh. "You got balls, kid. I'll give you that. At least, until Lana gets her teeth into them, later."

This wasn't going at all well. I had to find some way to piss him off, not make him laugh. "How's the knee?"

Parker narrowed his eyes. "A lot better. It didn't quite heal up before sunrise, but I figure it'll only take an hour or so after the moon comes up."

"I should have aimed higher," I said.

Parker's jaw clenched down a little. "Too late now, kid. Game over."

"Enjoy it while you can. I hear your people are getting a little sick of you. Do you think Lana will be the one to tear *your* balls off when they put you down?"

His boot came out of nowhere and hit me in the side of the head. It threw me hard to my right, and if I hadn't clenched my arms at the last minute, it would have thrown me to the floor and revealed my lack of bonds.

"You just don't know when to keep quiet, do you wizard?"

"What have I got to lose?" I shot back at him. "I mean, hell. It isn't as though all of the people that looked up to me have turned against me, right? It isn't as though I'm getting too old to manage wh—"

"Shut up," Parker snarled, his eyes taking on an eerie, greenish cast in the darkness, a trick of the light, and he kicked me again, this time in the stomach. My breath went out in a whoosh, and I fought to continue speaking.

"Waking up stiffer every morning. Eating less. Maybe not as strong as you used to be, right? Not as fast. Got to beat up on old dogs like Flatnose there, because if you try one of the younger ones, they'll take you down."

The plan was working beautifully. Now all that I needed was for him to stalk out of the room to calm down, or to fetch an instrument of mayhem or some more duct tape, anything. Instead, Parker just spun on his heel, picked up a tire iron, and turned back to me, lifting it high. "Fuck Marcone," he snarled. "And fuck you, wizard."

His muscles bunched beneath his old T-shirt as he raised the iron above his head. His eyes gleamed with the same sort of animalistic fury I had beheld in the other lycanthropes the night before. His mouth was stretched in a feral grin, and I could see the cords in his neck standing out as he wound up to give me the deathblow.

I hate it when a plan falls apart.

Chapter
Twenty-three

clenched my teeth and kicked my legs. The duct tape around my ankles gave way, but it was too late to do me any good. I didn't have time to get my weight beneath me, to run, but I made the gesture in any case. Just one of those things you do when you're about to die, I guess.

"Mr. Hendricks," came a very hard, very calm voice. "If Mr. Parker does not put down the tire iron in the next second or two, please shoot him dead."

"Yes sir, Mr. Marcone," Hendricks's rumbling basso answered. I looked over to my right, to see Gentleman Johnny Marcone standing at the door in a grey Italian business suit. Hendricks stood in front of him and a bit to one side, in a much cheaper suit, holding a pump-action shotgun with a short barrel, its stock worked into a pistol grip, in his meaty paws. The gaping black mouth of the barrel was leveled at Parker's head.

Parker's face snapped around to focus on Marcone at the same time as mine did. Parker's jaw clenched and his eyes narrowed to furious slits. His weight shifted from one foot to the other, as though he were preparing to throw the tire iron.

"That's a twelve-gauge riot gun, Mr. Parker," Marcone said. "I'm fully aware of your rather special endurance at this time of the month. Mr. Hendricks's weapon is loaded with solid-slug ammunition, and after several rounds have torn literal pounds of flesh from your body and ruptured the majority of your internal organs, I am reasonably certain that even you would perish." Marcone smiled, very politely, while Hendricks clicked the safety off of the weapon and settled his feet as though he expected firing the gun to knock him down. "Please," Marcone said. "Put down the tire iron."

Parker glanced back at me, and I could see the beast raging in his eyes, wanting to howl out and bathe in blood. It terrified me, made me go cold, right through my gut and down through my loins. There was more fury and rage there than any of the other members of the Streetwolves had demonstrated. Their own berserk losses of control had looked like a child's tantrum next to what I saw in Parker's eyes.

But he controlled it. He lowered his arm, slowly, and took two steps back from me, and I felt my breath whisper out in a sigh of relief. I wasn't dead. Yet. My kick hadn't quite dragged the blanket off of me, and I was still settled with my back against the steel post. They didn't know that I was loose underneath the rough wool. It wasn't much of an advantage, but it was all I had. I needed to find a way to use it, and fast.

"My people are coming," Parker growled. "If you try more of that heavy-handed shit, I'll have you torn apart."

"They are coming," Marcone agreed placidly. "But they are not yet here. Their motorcycles have all suffered flat tires, quite mysteriously. We have time to do business." I heard his shoes cross the concrete floor toward me, and I looked up at him. Marcone met my eyes without fear, a man in his mature prime, his hair immaculately greying at the temples, his custom-made suit displaying a body kept fit in spite of the advancing years. His eyes were the faded green of dollar bills and as opaque as mirrors.

"Hi, John," I said. "You've got good timing."

Marcone smiled. "And you have a way with people, Dresden," he said, glancing at the silent Parker with unveiled amusement. "You must have read a book. I'm already reasonably certain as to your reaction, but I thought I would give you another chance."

"Another chance to what?"

"I received a phone call today," Marcone said. "A Harley

MacFinn somehow discovered my personal number. He was quite irate. He said that he knew that it was me who had destroyed his circle and set him up, and that he was going to deal with me tonight."

"I'd say you've had it, then, John. Harley can be fairly destructive."

"I know. I saw the news programs from the station last night. A loup-garou, is he?"

I blinked. "How did you—"

Marcone waved a hand. "The report you gave to Lieutenant Murphy. Such things have to be paid for, and thus copied and filed and copied and filed. It wasn't hard to obtain a copy for myself."

I shook my head. "Money isn't going to buy off Harley MacFinn."

"Quite," Marcone said. "And my parents, God rest their souls, were in no position to leave me anything, much less articles of silver, or I'd deal with him myself. I have no idea who told him that I had wronged him, or why, but it seems perfectly clear that he believes it. Which brings us to you, Mr. Dresden." He reached into that expensive Italian jacket and drew out a folded sheaf of papers—the contract I'd seen before. "I want to make a deal with you."

I stared at him in silence.

"The same stipulations as before," Marcone continued. "In addition, I will promise you, give you my personal oath, that I will see to it that the pressure is taken off of Lieutenant Murphy. I do have some friends in the mayor's office, and I'm certain something could be worked out."

I started to tell him to go to hell, but bit back the words. I was trapped, at the moment. If I ran, Parker would probably lose it and tear me apart. And if he didn't, Marcone would just point his finger and the hulking Mr. Hendricks would put me down with a twelve-gauge slug.

And Murphy, in spite of recent misunderstandings, was my

friend. Or maybe it was more accurate to say that in spite of what had gone on lately, I was still Murphy's friend. Saving her job, getting the pressure from the politicians off of her—isn't that why I had gotten involved in this to begin with? Wouldn't Murphy thank me for helping her?

No, I thought. Not like that. She wouldn't want that kind of help. Magic, she could accept. Help from money generated by human suffering, graft, and deception was a different story. Marcone looked good in his grey suit and his perfect hair and his manicured hands, but he wasn't.

My own hands weren't clean—but they were free. Things were desperate, and getting worse the longer I waited. Maybe I could pull off enough magic to get myself out of this.

I drew in a breath, and focused on a pile of loose tools and metal parts on a workbench twenty feet away. I gathered to-gether threads of will, feeling the pressure build with a sort of skewed intangibility to it, something I hadn't ever felt before. I focused on my goal, on the rush of air that would lift the tools and parts and hurl them at Marcone, Parker, and Hendricks like so many bullets, and I prayed that I wouldn't catch myself in the edges of it by accident and get myself killed. I'd be breaking the First Law of Magic if one of them died, and I might have to deal with the White Council later; but hell's bells, I did not want to die on that concrete floor.

My head pounded, but I pushed the pain aside, focused, and breathed out, *"Vento servitas."*

The energy I had gathered whispered out of me. The tools jumped and rattled in place—and then fell still again.

Fire erupted behind my eyes. The pain was blinding, and I sucked in a breath and bowed my head forward, struggling not to fall to one side and reveal my lack of duct-tapedness. Oh, stars, it hurt like hell, and I clenched my teeth to keep from crying out. My chest heaved and strained to give me enough breath.

I blinked tears out of my eyes and straightened again, facing

Marcone. I didn't want him to see the weakness. I didn't want him to know that my magic had failed.

"Interesting," Marcone said, glancing at the workbench, and then back at me. "Perhaps you've been working too hard," he suggested. "But I'm still willing to make the offer, Mr. Dresden. Otherwise, you understand, I have no interest in your well-being, and I will be forced to leave you here with Mr. Parker and his associates. If you do not come to work for me, you'll die."

I glared up at Marcone and gathered in a breath to spit out a curse at him. To hell with him and his whole stinking breed of parasites. Polite and smiling bastards who didn't care about the lives they ruined, the people they destroyed, so long as business continued as usual. If I was going to die here, I was going to lay out a curse on Marcone that would make the grimmest old fairy tales you ever heard sound like pleasant daydreams.

And then I glanced at Parker, who was glaring suspiciously at Marcone, and stifled the curse as well. I lowered my head, to hide my expression from Marcone. I had an idea.

"He dies anyway," Parker growled. "He's mine. You never said anything about him leaving with you."

Marcone stood, his mouth settled in a tight smile. "Don't start with me, Parker," Marcone said. "I'll take what I want to take. Last chance, Mr. Dresden."

"This wasn't part of the deal," Parker said. "I need him. I'll kill you before I let you take him." Parker put one hand behind his back, as though scratching at an itch. I glanced over, toward the office door behind him, and saw Flatnose crouched there in the doorway, mostly shielded by the door and unnoticed. Perfect.

"You needn't worry, Parker," Marcone said, his tone satisfied. "He won't accept my offer. He'd rather die."

I lifted up my head, and kept my expression as blank as I could. "Give me a pen," I said.

Marcone's mouth dropped open, and it was an intense pleasure to see the surprise on his face. "What?" he said.

I enunciated each word carefully. "Give me a pen. I'll sign your contract." I glanced aside, at Parker, and said more loudly, "Anything to get away from these animals."

Marcone stared at me for a moment and then reached toward his pocket. I could see his eyes, see him searching my expression. The gears were spinning in his head as he tried to work out what I was doing.

Parker let out a sudden scream of rage and hurled the tire iron at Hendricks, who dodged to one side, too quickly for a man his size, and lifted his weapon. The office door exploded open, and Flatnose threw himself onto the big man. They both went down to the concrete, struggling for possession of the shotgun.

"The wizard's mine!" Parker howled, and threw himself at Marcone. Marcone moved like a snake in his zillion-dollar business suit and made a curved knife appear in his hands. He swept it in an arc that was followed by a spray of blood from Parker's wrist, and the lycanthrope howled.

I got up and ran like hell toward the door. My legs were shaky, and my balance wasn't great, but I was moving again, and I thought I had a fair chance of getting away. Over to my left, there was the roar of the shotgun going off, and a wet, red spray that went all over one wall and the ceiling. I didn't stop to see who had been killed, just jerked open the door.

Agent Phillip Denton stood five feet away from me, in the cold mist of autumn rain. The veins in his forehead were throbbing, and his short hair was frosted by the mist. He was flanked by the potbellied Agent Wilson, in his rumpled suit, his mostly bald head shining, and by the lean, savage-looking woman, Benn, her dark skin even darker in the evening's gloom and the glow of streetlights, her sensuous mouth peeling back into a startled snarl.

Denton blinked in surprise, and then narrowed his intensely grey eyes. "The wizard mustn't escape," he said, his voice calm and precise. "Kill him."

Benn's eyes gleamed, and she hissed something under her breath while reaching a hand into her jacket. Wilson did the same. I brought my forward momentum to a sudden halt, fell, and started scrambling back into the building.

But instead of drawing guns out of their jackets, they changed. It happened fast, nothing like you see in the movies. One moment, there were two human beings standing there, and the next there was a flicker of shadow and a pair of enormous, gaunt wolves, one the grey of Benn's mane, one the same brown as Wilson's receding hairline.

They were huge, six feet long not including the tail, and as high as my belly at their shoulders. Their entirely human eyes shone, as did their bared fangs. Denton stood between them, his eyes gleaming with some dark breed of joy, and then he hissed, throwing his hands toward me. As though thrown by the motion, both wolves hurtled forward.

I flung myself back through the door and slammed it closed. There were heavy thuds as the wolves hit the door behind me. I saw a motion to my right and threw myself down just before Hendricks pulled the trigger. The riot gun belched forth flame and huge sound and blew a hole the size of my face in the door behind me. I could still hear Parker's furious snarling somewhere in the dark, and I scrambled forward, behind the bulk of a car, and then ran toward the back of the cavernous garage, staying low.

Outside, there was the sudden thunder of a dozen engines, and the sharp, heavy sounds of gunfire. Evidently, the Streetwolves had returned.

I stumbled through the darkness and tried not to make enough sound to give someone a chance to shoot me. The door flew open at the front of the garage, letting in a flood of dim light that didn't help me much. I heard people screaming.

I reached the back corner and sank down into it, then grabbed at something that turned out to be a toolbox. I came out with a heavy wrench and gripped it tightly. I was alone. I'd hurt myself using too much of my magic while on the go-go potion, and I didn't have anything left to throw now. Except for the wrench in my hands, I was unarmed. All around me, in the garage, there were the sounds of gunshots and screams and thuds of flesh as the animals fought for control of the jungle, and it was only a matter of time before one of them stumbled across a weakened and exhausted wizard named Harry Dresden.

Talk about frying pans and fires.

Chapter

Twenty-four

It couldn't possibly get any worse than this, I thought. I cowered in the corner, clutching my captured wrench like a child's teddy bear, with no way out, and full of the knowledge that my magic had failed me.

Oddly, that thought troubled me more than probable death. A lot more. Death was something that happened to everyone— only the timing is different, for each of us. I knew that I would, eventually, die. Hell, I even knew that I might die horribly. But I had never thought that the magic would fail me. More accurately, I had never guessed that I might fail *it*. I had pushed too hard and my body wouldn't conduct the power I needed to utilize the forces I was accustomed to commanding. Granted, maybe I should have started with something smaller than a large and violent telekinesis, but the indication was there that I had burned out some internal circuitry. It might not ever come back.

It was a loss of identity. I was a wizard. It was more than just a job, more than just a title. Wizardry was at the core of my being. It was my relationship with my magic, the way I used it, the things it let me do that defined me, shaped me, gave me purpose.

I dwelled on these things while death danced over the concrete floor, clutching them like a sailor clinging to the wreckage of his ship, trying to ignore the storm that blasted it to pieces. I noted peripheral details from my pathetic hiding place. Marcone made a break for one of the garage doors, only to be pinned down behind a rusted truck by gunfire from some of the Streetwolves. Hendricks joined him, and a moment later, the truck roared to life and crashed out through the garage door and into the gravel parking lot. Hendricks, in the rear of the truck, fired several blasts from the big shotgun back into the building, while the Streetwolves sent rounds skewing off after the truck.

The real battle, though, took place between the Streetwolves and the FBI.

It was largely a gunfight. Denton was armed with his FBI-issue automatic and what looked like an Uzi submachine gun. He cut down three of the lycanthropes with a swath of fire from the automatic weapon as he came in through the door, and the two great wolves with him hurtled into the darkness. Screams and savage snarling erupted from the shadows, and I could hear more of the lycanthropes dying, being torn apart by the enormous wolves that had once been Agents Benn and Wilson. Parker screamed orders somewhere in the dark, half incoherent with rage. Denton reached into his jacket for a fresh clip for the Uzi, and I saw something across his belly that I noted for future reference, should I have any future.

I watched the killing, and I hid, and I prayed that there would be an opportunity to flee toward the open doors of the garage before Denton or Parker noticed me. It went on forever. Oh, I knew, in some rational part of my brain, that only seconds were going by, but it felt like days. I was terrified, and my head and my body hurt, and I couldn't use magic to protect myself.

There was a sound near my ankle, and my heart leapt up out of my throat. I flinched violently away from it. The sound repeated itself in a continuous scrabble of noise. The floor, I noticed, was rough dirt and broken concrete in this corner, where the foundation platform was flawed. The scrabbling noise came from the very base of the wall, where the dirt was stirring and moving.

Something was trying to dig its way beneath the wall and into the garage, practically right underneath my butt. I felt a chill of fear, followed swiftly by anger at the thing that had added to an already overabundant flow of adrenaline. I clutched my make-shift weapon in hand and moved to crouch over the source of the disturbance, lifting it in preparation to strike at whatever came through.

I saw it in the dimness, and there was no mistaking the shape. A paw, a huge canine paw, scrabbled at the earth, digging out a shallow hole beneath the wall, frustrated by bits of concrete that got in the way. Between shots, I could hear animal sounds out-side, panting whimpers of eagerness, it seemed. Whatever was out there wanted to dig its way inside, and wanted it bad.

"Dig this," I muttered, and swung the wrench down on the paw, hard.

There was an instant yelp of pain, and the paw jerked its way back out from beneath the corrugated-metal wall. It was followed by a snarl, and the paw appeared again, whereupon I slammed the wrench down on it once more, with similar results. I heard a furious snarling sound from the other side, and I re-leased a small surge of vindictive satisfaction by leaning down close enough to the hole to say, "Hah. Bring another one in here and I'll give you the same."

I heard sounds outside for a moment, then a crunch of gravel, and Tera West's smooth, unmistakable voice. "Wizard," she hissed. "Stop that."

I blinked, startled, and leaned down close to the hole. "Tera? Is that you? How did you know it was me?"

"You are the only man I ever met," Tera growled, "who would smash the paws that are trying to free you from certain death." I flinched at another burst of gunfire from the far side of the garage. "I am going to tell them to dig again. Do not strike at their paws."

"Them?" I demanded. "Them who?"

But she didn't answer me. Instead, the scrabbling sounds began again. I looked over my shoulder at the rest of the room. I saw Streetwolves moving swiftly out through the door and the gaping hole Marcone had left in the garage door when he escaped. In a flash of automatic muzzle-flare, I saw Denton standing over the form of a lanky woman and firing down into it, apparently making absolutely certain that she would never rise again. I had enough time to recognize Lana's face, now screwed up with pain rather than bloodlust. Her body jerked and twitched as Denton emptied the remainder of the clip into her. And then everything went dark again.

By my feet, the scrabbling sounds continued—and then broke off in a yelp. I heard a series of vicious snarls and yelps from the half-dug hole beneath the wall, and I cursed.

"Tera," I whispered, as loudly as I dared. "What's going on?"

There was only more growling for answer, and a sharp yelp that carried to the far side of the garage.

I threw myself flat behind the toolbox and a pile of junk, just before a flashlight beam swept over the corner where I had been hiding. "It's that bitch," Denton snarled. "Roger's got her outside."

There was a whispering sound, and a tingling feeling along my spine. Then a throaty, sensual female voice purred, "Parker's still in here. So is that wizard. I can smell them."

"Dammit," Denton growled. "The wizard knows too much. Wilson, go help Roger."

"What about me, lover?" the female voice said, a husky laugh added to the end. Agent Benn sounded like she'd just had too much sex, drugs, and rock and roll, and was hungry for more.

"You and I stay in here. I'll cover the doors. Flush them toward me."

There was a mewling sound of pleasure from the woman. "Come with me," she urged. "Change. You know you love it so much. You know how good it feels."

I could visualize Denton's veins throbbing. "Smarter for one of us to cover the door with a gun." But there was a sort of heavy reluctance to his tone.

"Fuck smart," Benn purred. "Come with me. Change."

"It's not why we did this. Not why we made the bargain."

Benn made another sound, utterly sexual in nature. "It doesn't matter now. Taste it," she urged him. "Taste the blood." The light wavered and dropped from the corner where I hid.

I chanced a look up. Agent Benn, spattered in gore, stood before Denton in the wash of his flashlight from the floor. She had three of her fingers pressed together, and was sliding them between his lips. Denton was shaking, and his eyes were squeezed tightly closed. He suckled at her fingers, something frighteningly erotic in the motion. One of the huge, gaunt beasts from earlier, Wilson I supposed, stood nearby, watching the pair of them with gleaming eyes.

Denton made a growling sound and grasped Benn by her mane of greying hair, jerking her chin up so that he could nuzzle and lick at the blood smeared over her throat. She laughed and arched into him, her hips undulating against him in urgent motions. "Change," she moaned. "Change. Do it."

There was a howl of rage, and flash of motion, and Parker staggered from the darkness, one arm dangling uselessly, a heavy knife in his other hand, and defiance and insane anger in his glazed eyes. Denton and Benn looked up, and then they reached to their waists, flickered, and changed into a pair of the nightmare-sized wolves, their eyes glowing in the ambient light, jaws dropping open to reveal lolling tongues and vicious fangs. Parker lurched forward, greasy hair flying, and the three wolves leapt on him.

I stared in a sort of sickened fascination. The wolves buried him under a mound of fangs and fur and blood and absolute fury. He screamed, the knife flailing, and then it was cast aside, out of his hands, to land spinning on the floor not far from me. Parker tried to fight, tried to struggle up and kick, but it was hopeless. There were flashes of blood, and he screamed again and went still.

And then the wolves started to eat him. They bit off chunks of muscle and gulped them down, ripping aside clothing to get to more meat. They snarled and snapped at one another, and one of the males mounted the female, even as she continued to tear at the body, burrowing her muzzle down through the layers of stomach muscle to get at the vitals. My gorge rose, and if I'd had anything in my stomach, I would have emptied it onto the concrete floor.

Instead, I turned back to the half-finished hole in the floor and started digging at it with my wrench, frantic. I didn't want to be the next thing on the menu.

There were more yelps from outside, more growls, and I opened the hole up enough that I thought I might be able to get out. I flattened myself down and wormed my way into the dirt, the corrugated metal scraping at my back, my wounded shoulder paining me again.

I jerked my way out into the open air, to find myself in an alley behind the garage, dimly lit by a distant streetlight.

There were wolves everywhere.

Three wolves, smaller than the ones I had seen before, were spread in a loose ring about a great russet-furred beast with bat-like ears. The great wolf's coat was spattered with blood, and two of the smaller wolves lay nearby, yelping in pain, stirring weakly, blood matting their coats. Tera was a part of the ring around the great beast as well, naked and lean, a length of pipe held in either hand. When the great wolf turned toward one of the others, the rest would begin to close in around him, and he would spin, jaws flashing, trying to pin down one of those who encircled him.

"You took your time, wizard," Tera snarled, without looking back at me.

I got to my feet, wrench in hand, and shook my head to clear it of cold sweat. "Tera," I said. "We've got to get out of here. Denton and the others will be coming."

"Go," she responded. "Help MacFinn. We will hold them." The great russet wolf lunged at her, and she skittered back, cooly staying a hair's breadth from his fangs. She fetched him a sharp blow across the nose with more speed than I could have believed and a contemptuous snort. The three smaller wolves rushed the great beast, and he spun to drive them back and away from him, drawing a yelp from one that wasn't swift enough to entirely evade his jaws.

"You can't stop them all," I said. "There's three more like this one."

"There are pack on the ground," she snarled, and jerked her head toward the wounded wolves. "We do not abandon our own."

I let out an acid curse. I needed Tera. She could confirm everything, help me sort out all my facts, make sure that I understood what was going on. She was offering to give her life for me, to stay and occupy Denton and the others for as long as she and her compatriots could, but I had seen enough people dying already tonight. I wasn't going to accept another loss on my behalf.

And I was abruptly more furious than afraid. I'd been run around and treated like a piece of baggage or a choice item on the menu for long enough. I'd flailed around in the dark and been helpless and ineffective for way too long. Too many people had been hurt, too much suffering caused by creatures of magic and the night, things that I should have been handling. It didn't matter to me, at that moment, that I couldn't work any of my spells against them. I might not have any magic available to me, but that didn't make me any less of a wizard, one of the magi, the wise. That's the true power of a wizard.

I know things.

Knowledge is power.

With power comes responsibility.

That made the entire thing pretty simple. I clutched the wrench in my hand, took a deep breath, and threw myself forward, at the great wolf's back. The huge wolf sensed me coming, spun with abrupt speed, and met me in the air. It slammed me down to the concrete and bent its jaws toward my throat. I heard

Tera cry out, and she and the other wolves moved forward—but they would never have been able to get to the thing before it killed me. That wasn't the point.

I jammed the wrench into the wolf's jaws, feeling some teeth tear at one of my fingers as I did. The wolf snarled and jerked the wrench out of my hands. It spun end over end away from me, and the great beast turned back toward me, its eyes glowing.

I had time to watch it all in great detail. The wolf's power, its speed, simply shocked me. It was huge, quick, and I didn't have a prayer against it. The distant streetlight gleamed off of its reddened fangs as its muzzle sped toward my throat.

Chapter

Twenty-five

The wolf's fur was speckled with drops of blood that had beaded on it like rain. The gravel in the alley shone in the half-light from the distant street lamps. The wolf's muzzle, a little shorter and broader than I had seen on *Wild Kingdom*, was drawn back, black lips from fangs striped white and red like peppermints. Its eyes were blue, rather than any proper lupine shade, and gleamed with a sort of demented awareness.

I had time to see all those details because I didn't need my eyes for what I wanted to do. I thrust my hands into the beast's pelt as he went for my throat, and wormed my way down between his forelegs with my buttocks, fingers digging, until I felt what I was looking for—the sharp metal edges of a belt buckle, down against the skin, almost flush to the surface. As the wolf's jaws came toward my throat, I furiously worked the buckle, feeling skin rip and tear from the wolf's hide as I jerked it open, and then threw my arm to one side, clutching hard at the trailing strap.

And abruptly, a wolf-pelt belt was sliding out from beneath the grey suit jacket of Roger Harris, the forensic specialist for the local FBI office, the kid with the red hair and the big ears. He crouched over me for a second, blinking in stunned amazement at me, blood on his mouth and lips.

"*Hexenwulf* jerk-off," I snarled and slammed my knee up into his groin. It hit home hard.

Harris gasped and rolled off me, reaching into his jacket, but I didn't let him get his gun. I stayed with him, keeping too close to him to let him move his arms freely, grabbed him by those big ears, and started slamming his head repeatedly against the gravel. He struggled against me for a few seconds, but I'd taken him by surprise. His skull banged against the rocks over and over, and after a half-dozen solid blows, he stopped struggling.

I released his ears with a little jerk and looked up at Tera and the wolves. They were closing in around him like a pack of sharks around a wounded dolphin, and I could read the blood in their eyes, in the bared fangs, and in the white-knuckled grip of Tera's hands on her lead pipes. I felt a sudden surge of frustration. Bad enough to have bloodthirsty animals roaming all over the city—I didn't need more of them on my team.

"Everyone back off," I snarled.

"He's ours," Tera answered me in kind. "He hurt those of the pack."

"Then why don't you get them some help instead of wasting your time on this guy?" I said.

"His blood is ours," Tera said, and the wolves confirmed this with a chorus of angry growls.

"He can't hurt you now. Killing him won't make your friends any better. And the lost time might finish them."

"You do not understand, wizard," Tera snarled, and the wolves echoed her in a chorus, white fangs showing. "It is our way."

I stood up slowly, to my full height. "I understand," I said in a very low and even voice, "that you do not want to make me any more angry than I already am." I met Tera's eyes and stared, hard. My jaws ached from clenching. "There's been enough killing. Take him out now, and you're no different than he is."

"Wrong," Tera said. "I would be alive, and he dead."

"Not if you cross me, you won't be."

We held the tension for a moment, glaring at one another.

I saw uncertainty waver across her face. She didn't know that I was out of gas, magically speaking, and she had seen me do too many impressive things with my powers to want to defy me lightly. She blinked first and looked away from me with a sullen sound in the back of her throat. "As you wish, wizard," she said. "We don't have the time to waste fighting one another. The rest of his pack is coming. And we have wounded to tend to."

I nodded and swept my gaze around at the three wolves around me. "Anybody else?" I challenged. They all backed away from me, and didn't meet my eyes. "All right, then," I said, and stooped to recover Harris's gun and the wolf-pelt belt. "Do you have transportation out of here?"

"Yes," Tera said. "Georgia."

One of the wolves, a leggy, lanky, pale-brown beast shuddered and paced in a circle, making small, whimpering sounds. A moment later, there was a whisper of power. The she-wolf shivered, and went still, her head bowed. And then she shook herself, and all that pale-brown hair faded from paler skin, leaving me staring at the lanky, dark-blond girl I had seen in the department store a few days ago, sans all the black leather. Georgia rose to her feet and said, "I'll have her bring the van around on the next street. Can you get them to it?" Her expression was tense, her eyes a little wide.

"Yes," Tera said. "Everyone, come back to yourselves." The other two ambulant wolves began to pace in a slow circle, gathered their own power, and their own transformations commenced, until they stood before me as a pair of naked young men—one of them the short, stout boy who had been arguing against Georgia—Billy—and the other a face I recognized but couldn't name.

Tera took charge of the situation while I held Harris's gun and kept watch down the alley. She and the two young men made a litter for one of the wolves out of Harris's jacket, and the other Tera simply picked up with a flexion of wire-tight muscle and carried, though it must have weighed a hundred and fifty pounds. The wounded wolves yelped piteously, and Tera and the two young men cast dark glances at the downed Harris while they headed down the alley, and over toward the beach, leaving me alone with the kid.

I hunkered down beside him and slapped his face until his eyes rolled open. He blinked once and then jerked, as though he was about to sit up. I stuck the barrel of the semiautomatic in the hollow of his throat and said, in a calm voice, "Hold still."

He froze, staring up at me with wide eyes.

"I'm going to ask some questions, kid. I think I've got the answers already, but you're going to talk to me, quietly and honestly. Or I demonstrate point-blank bullet impact for you right here and now. Got it?"

Harris's mouth twitched a few times before he managed to speak. "If you kill me," he said, "Denton won't stop until you're dead."

"Give me a break, Roger," I said back in a reasonable tone. "Denton wants me dead anyway. I could kill you now and it wouldn't make any difference in what he has to do."

Roger licked his lips and rolled his eyes about without moving his head, as though hoping for rescue. "How did you know? About the belt."

"I saw Denton's inside. And I saw that before you all changed, you had to reach inside your jackets for something. I figure that first night, Agent Benn was reaching into her jacket to touch the belt and tear Murphy's head off, when she got mad. But she managed to remember not to do it in time and drew her gun instead. Right?"

Harris's head twitched in a slight nod.

"The bargain," I said. "You're *Hexenwulfen*, so you've made a bargain with someone to get the power to change, to get the belts. Who is it?"

"I don't know," Harris said, and his eyes widened. "God, I don't know. Denton handled all of it."

I narrowed my eyes at him and drew back the hammer on the gun.

"Please," he squealed, breathless. "I don't know. I swear to God, Denton handled all of that. He just came to us, asked us if we wanted to back him, if we wanted to nail some of the scum that kept getting away from the law, and I told him I did. Jesus, I didn't know it was going to lead to this."

"Lead to what, Roger?" I asked, my tone frosty. "Start from the beginning, and make it quick."

"Marcone," he said, eyes on the gun. "It was all about Marcone. Denton wanted to take him down."

"You mean kill him."

His eyes flickered up to me. "He told us there was no other way to get to him. That he was doing more to poison this city than anyone alive. And he was right. Marcone's bought enough influence in this town to stay clear of city police forever, and he carries weight on the national level, too. The bureau has had more than one investigation on him called off. He's untouchable."

"So you planned to use the belts to kill him."

He nodded. "But there would be evidence. No one would believe he'd just been mauled by wild dogs. There would be a full investigation, forensics, the works."

I understood and nodded. "So you needed someone to make it a neat package. Let me guess: the Streetwolves."

Harris showed his teeth. "A gang of felons and troublemakers with a wolf motif. Murder of a criminal figure by persons with a wolf motif. No one would bother to check the figures on that one. It's obvious. And we get one more dangerous group off the street."

"Yeah, Roger, except that they'd be innocent of that particular crime. Did you think of that? Innocent like those other people who died the nights around the full moon last month. You killed them. You and the rest of Denton's team."

He closed his eyes, his face going pale, and he shuddered. "The change. When . . . when you're changed, when you're a beast, it's so incredible. So much speed, power. Your body just sings with it. I tried coke once, in college, and it was nothing compared to this. The blood . . ." His tongue flicked out again over his bloodstained lips, a thirsty motion this time, rather than a nervous one.

"I think I'm starting to see. Denton didn't tell you about that part. About how your thoughts are influenced. He probably didn't know himself. And when you've done it once . . ."

Harris nodded emphatically. "You just can't stop, man. It gets to where you're pacing the room at night. And it's better than sleep, when you get finished hunting, you feel so *alive*." He opened his eyes again, staring up at me, pleading. "I didn't mean to kill those people. We started off with criminals. Some gangsters dealing drugs. We were just going to scare them, but it was too much. They screamed and ran and we were after them, and . . . We killed them. And my God, Dresden, it was beautiful."

"And it happened again," I said. "A couple of times. Innocent people. Just poor schmucks in the wrong place at the wrong time."

Harris turned his head away from me and nodded. "Denton said that we could salvage it. He said that we could pin those killings on the Streetwolves as well. Make everyone think they had done it. And we just went along with him."

I shook my head. "That doesn't explain why you dragged MacFinn into this."

"Denton," the kid said. "It was all him. He said there was someone else we could also set up to take the blame, to be certain we'd be in the clear. That he had the man for it. We broke into MacFinn's house, and there was all this occult stuff. We messed up some of it and left. And . . . the next night, more people were dead. And more, the next night. That's when we went after that slime Marcone's business partner, and wasted the bastard and his goon."

"And then you laid low for a month."

Harris swallowed and nodded. "Denton took the belts. He hid them from us. He'd held out better than anyone. And my God, poor Benn was so far gone, it was like she wasn't even human anymore. Wilson wasn't much better. But we lasted out the month."

"And then you killed Marcone's bodyguard at the Varsity."

Harris's eyes flared. "Yes. You should see his record. The things we know he did, but that we can't get through a court. My God, Dresden, he had it coming."

"Maybe. Maybe not. Who are we to judge?"

"Who are we *not* to?" Harris demanded. "The power was in our hands. We had a responsibility to use it for the good. To do our jobs. Hell, Dresden. If you're such a do-gooder, you should be helping us, not getting in the way. These men are untouchable and you know it."

I shifted my weight uncomfortably. "I don't agree with your methods. With setting people up to take the blame for your killings."

Harris sneered. "Like MacFinn has never killed anyone. Hell, he's a murderer now, isn't he? After that scene at the police station, anyone would be convinced he was a killer."

"Except me," I said. "MacFinn would never have been there if you hadn't messed up the circle that held him."

"Yeah," Harris said, a spiteful, frustrated edge to his tone. "Except you. You got to poking around in our business. Christ, that crazy report to Murphy even talked about the belts. That was when Denton started taking you seriously. If you had any brains at all, you'd pull that trigger and get the hell out now, before Denton and the others come out of the haze and come after you. Because you know way too much."

"Why the Streetwolves?" I said, instead of shooting him. "Why send me off to check them out?"

"Denton figured they'd kill you," Harris spat. "And get you out of our hair."

I nodded. It figured, that someone else had been trying to kill me the whole while, and I hadn't really noticed. "And he knew that they were after me, after I got away from them the first time."

"Yeah. And had me tailing them, so we could find you and make sure you were dead. When I saw you in the back of that car,

I figured you were. So we planned the hit on the Streetwolves to go down tonight, before MacFinn went after Marcone."

"How'd you know about that?" I asked.

Harris snorted. "Marcone told us. The snake called asking for police protection."

I almost smiled. "Did he get it?"

"Hell, no," Harris answered me. He lifted his chin, and balled his hands into fists, and I felt him tighten up beneath me. "I'm done talking," he said. "If you aren't going to sign on with us, then get the hell out of here. Or pull the trigger. But quit wasting my time."

"I'm not done talking," I said, and I jammed the gun crosswise over the kid's throat, strangling him. "You're going to give Denton a message for me. I'm sick of dancing around. Tell him that he'll get his shot at me at moonrise, at Marcone's place."

Harris squirmed beneath me, making rasping, gagging sounds. His eyes widened at my words. "It doesn't take a genius to figure out that he'll try to be there when MacFinn shows up," I said. "That he'll want to make sure everyone there is dead so that he's the only one who can report what happened. You tell him that I'll be there. And tell him that he's not going to get away with it. Do you understand me, kid?"

I let up on the pressure, and Harris croaked out a vague affirmative. I rose away from him, keeping the gun in one hand and the belt in the other. I saw his eyes flicker to the belt, tracking its movement with a tense, strained sort of hunger.

"Why tell me?" the kid asked. "Why warn us?"

I stared down at him for long seconds before I answered him in a quiet voice. "Because I don't like what you're doing. What you are. You aren't using the power you've been given. It's using you. You're turning into animals. You're using savagery and fear to try to uphold the peace. Now it's your turn to see what it's like to be afraid."

Harris rose to his feet, his red hair askew, blood drying on his mouth, and backed several paces from me, his eyes darting around. "My belt," he said. "I want my belt."

"Forget it, kid," I told him. "The smartest thing you can do is go lock yourself in your room, and stay there until all of this is over. Because one way or another, you aren't using this belt again."

His face whitened, and he took a step toward me. I pointed the gun at him, and he froze, his hands balling into fists. "You won't get away with this," he said, his voice thick with tension.

"Moonrise," I told him, then turned on my heel and walked quickly from the alley, although my sock feet on the gravel, combined with my limp, probably spoiled the badass image.

Thirty feet down the alley, Tera appeared from the shadows and fell into step beside me, close enough to support me if I should fall. "You were wrong, wizard," she said.

I looked down at her, and she met my gaze with her soulless amber eyes. "How so?"

"They have not become animals." She looked over her shoulder, her eyes narrowed. "Animals do not do what they have done. Animals kill to eat, to defend themselves or their own, and to protect their territory. Not for the joy of it. Not for the lust of it." She looked back up at me. "Only humans do that, wizard."

I grimaced, but couldn't really refute her. "I guess you're right."

"Of course," Tera said. We walked in silence for a moment. "You will try to help my fiancé?"

"I'll try," I said. "But I can't let his curse claim any more lives."

She nodded, her eyes dark. "He would want it that way. He thinks of others before himself."

"He sounds like a good man."

She shrugged, but there was a sudden, worried weight in her shoulders. "And these others. The FBI. They will try to stop you."

"Yes."

"And when they do?"

"I can't let them go on like they have. They're out of control. I don't think they can stop themselves from killing, now."
I didn't look down at Tera, just focused on taking steps, one at a
time. "When they do . . ." I said. "When they do . . . I guess I'm
going to need to get very human."

Chapter
Twenty-six

Tera and I walked toward the shores of Lake Michigan. There, along Forty-ninth Street, idled a big old van, its engine rattling. Its headlights came on as we approached, and the driver got out to roll open the side door for us.

"Harry?" she said. "Oh, God. What did they do to you?" She hurried over to me, and then I felt Susan's warmth against me as she slid one of my arms over her shoulder and pressed up against my side. She was wearing jeans that showed off her long legs, and a dark red jacket that complemented her dark skin. Her hair was tied back into a ponytail, and it made her neck look slender and vulnerable. Susan felt soft and warm beyond belief, and smelled clean and delightfully feminine, and I found myself leaning against her. All the aches and pains that had faded into the background came throbbing back to the forefront of my awareness, in comparison to her soft warmth and gentle support. I liked the way Susan felt better than the way I did.

"They beat him," Tera explained. "But they kept him alive, as I told you they might."

"Your face looks like a sack of purple potatoes," Susan said, her dark eyes studying me, the lines in her face deepening.

"You say the sweetest things," I mumbled.

They loaded me into the van, where Georgia, Billy, and the other Alphas were crouched. Two of the young people, a boy with blinking, watery blue eyes, and a girl with mousy brown hair, lay on their backs, gasping quietly. Clean white bandages had been wrapped around their wounds. Georgia had, evidently, been the attending medic. All of the Alphas were dressed in plain, dark bathrobes, rather than in their birthday suits, and I felt an oddly grateful feeling toward them for it. Things were weird enough without needing to ride around in a van with a bunch of naked, somewhat geeky college students.

I put my seat belt on and noted the bruises on my hands and forearms—ugly, dark purple-and-brown splotches, so thickly scattered over my skin that in places I couldn't tell where one stopped and the next began. I sat down and leaned against the window, pillowing my head on my right hand.

"What are you doing here with these people?" I asked Susan when she got into the driver's seat.

"Driving," she said. "I was the only one old enough to rent the van."

I winced. "Ouch."

"Tell me about it," she said and started the engine. "After you jumped out of the car, and I finished with my heart attack, we called the police, just like you said. Tera went to look for you and told me that the police had shown up too late, and that the Streetwolves had taken you. How did that truck crash like that?"

"Bad luck. Someone made all their tires explode at the same time."

Susan gave me an arch look and started up the van. "Those bastards. Just lie still, Harry. You look like a train wreck. We'll get you to someplace quiet."

"Food," I said. "I'm starving. Tera, can you keep track of moonrise?"

"I will," she said. "The clouds are moving away. I can see the stars."

"Fantastic," I mumbled. And then I went to sleep, ignoring the jostling of the van. I didn't wake up until the smell of fried grease and charred meat made me look up at the drive-thru window of a fast-food burger joint. Susan paid for everything in cash, passing paper sacks to everyone. I snagged a golden paper crown from one of the bags and idly joined it into a circle and put it on my head. Susan blinked at me, then let out a brief laugh.

"I am," I intoned, with an imperious narrowing of my eyes, "the burger king." Susan laughed again, shaking her head, and Tera gave me a serious, level gaze. I checked the status of the young people in the back of the van, and found them, even the wounded ones, hungrily wolfing (no pun intended) down the food.

Tera caught the direction of my glance and leaned toward me. "Puppies," she said, as though the word should explain more than it did. "They were not hurt so badly as they thought. They will hardly have scars to show for it."

"That's good to know," I said and sipped at my cola and chomped down steaming-hot french fries. "But what I'm really interested in," I said, "is in knowing why your blood was in Marcone's restaurant the night before the full moon."

Tera took the hamburger patty off of the bun and started nibbling on it, holding it in her fingers. "Ask another time."

"No offense," I said, "but I'm not so sure there's going to be another time. So tell me."

Tera took another bite of meat, and then shrugged. "I knew that the pack that had harassed my fiancé was about. I deduced where they might strike, and went there to attempt to stop them."

"All by yourself?"

Tera sniffed. "Most of those who turn themselves into wolves know little about *being* wolf, wizard. But these had taken too much of the beast inside. I ran through the window glass and fought, but they outnumbered me. I left before I could be killed."

"And what about these kids?" I said, nodding toward the back of the van.

She glanced back at them, and for a moment, I saw warmth and pride gleaming in her eyes, subverting the remote, alien lines of her face. "Children. But with strong hearts. They wished to learn, and I taught. Let them tell you their tale."

"Maybe later," I said and finished off the french fries. "Where are we going?"

"To a safe place, to arm and prepare ourselves."

"Myself," I contradicted her. "To prepare myself. I'm not taking you with me."

"You are incorrect," Tera said. "I am going with you."

"No."

She fastened her amber eyes on mine. "You are strong, wizard. But you have not yet seen my beast. The men you will oppose would take my fiancé from me. I will not allow that. I will be with you, or you will kill me to stop me."

This time, it was I who looked away first. I sipped at my drink, scowling, while Tera placidly ate more of the hamburger patty. "Who are you?" I asked her finally.

"One who has lost too many of her family already," she said. And then she settled back on the seat and withdrew from the conversation, falling silent.

"One who has lost too many . . ." I grumbled, frustrated, mocking her beneath my breath. I turned back to the front of the van and hunched my shoulders over my burger. "Put some clothes on, you weird, yellow-eyed, table-dancing, werewolf-training, cryptic, stare-me-right-in-the-eyes-and-don't-even-blink wench."

There was a hissing sound from the backseat, and I flicked a scowl back over my shoulder. Tera was chewing on her meat. Her eyes were shining, her mouth was curved at the corners, and her breath was puffing out her nostrils in near-silent laughter.

The safe place we were going to turned out to be a big house up near the Gold Coast, not far from Marcone's own minipalace. The house wasn't large, by the neighborhood's standards, but that was like saying that a bale of hay isn't much to eat, by elephant standards. Susan drove the van up through a break in a high hedge, up a long driveway of white concrete, and into a six-car garage whose doors rolled majestically up before us.

I got out of the van, in the garage, and stared at the Mercedes and the Suburban also parked in it. "Where are we?" I said.

Tera opened the side door of the van, and Georgia, Billy, and the other young man emerged, assisting the two wounded werewolves. Georgia stretched, which did interesting things to the dark bathrobe, and drew her mane of tawny hair back from her lean face with one hand. "It's my parents' place. They're in Italy for another week."

I rubbed a hand over my face. "They aren't going to mind you having a party, are they?"

She flashed me an annoyed look and said, "Not as long as we clean up all the blood. Come on, Billy. Let's get these two inside and into bed."

"You go on," he said, fastening his eyes on me. "I'll be along in a minute."

Georgia looked like she wanted to give him an argument, but shook her head instead, and with the help of the other young man, took the two invalids inside. Tera, still naked and supremely unconcerned about it, followed them, glancing back over her shoulder at me before she disappeared. Susan promptly stepped in front of me, somewhat obstructing the view, and said, "Five minutes, Dresden. Come find me then."

"Uh," was my rapier reply, and then Susan went into the house, too.

I stood in the dark with Billy, the stout, short kid in thick glasses. He had his hands stuffed into his bathrobe pockets, and he was peering at me.

"Do all wizards," he said, "get the kiddie crowns and wear them around? Or is that only for special occasions?"

"Do all werewolves," I shot back, snatching the crown from my head, "wear glasses and too much Old Spice? Or is that only for full moons?"

He grinned at me, rather than taking umbrage. "You're

quick," he said. "I always wanted to be that way." He stuck out his hand toward me. "Billy Borden."

I traded grips with him wearily, and he tried to crush my hand in his. "Harry Dresden," I told him.

"You look pretty beat up, Mr. Dresden," he said. "Are you sure you can handle going out again tonight?"

"No," I answered, in a spurt of brutal honesty.

Billy nodded, and pushed his glasses up higher onto his nose. "Then you need our help."

Oh, good grief. The Mickey Mouse Club of werewolves wanted to throw in on my side. Werewolfkateer role call: Billy. Georgia. Tommy. Cindy. Sheesh.

"No way," I said. "Absolutely not."

"Why not?" he said.

"Look, kid. You don't know what these *Hexenwulfen* can be like. You don't know what Marcone can be like, and you sure as hell have never seen anything like MacFinn outside of a movie theater. And even if you had the skills to deal with it, what makes you think you have a right to be going along?"

Billy considered the question seriously. "The same thing that makes you think that you do, Mr. Dresden," he said.

I opened my mouth. And closed it again.

"I know I don't know a lot, compared to you," Billy said. "But I'm not stupid. I've got eyes. I see some things everyone else tries to pretend aren't there. This vampire craze sweeping the nation. Why the hell shouldn't there be some genuine vampires in it? Did you know that violent crimes have increased nearly forty percent in the last three years, Mr. Dresden? Murder alone has almost doubled, particularly in heavy urban areas and isolated rural areas. Abductions and disappearances have gone up nearly three hundred percent."

I blinked at the kid. I hadn't really read the numbers. I knew that Murphy and some of the other cops said that the streets were getting worse. And I knew myself, on some deep level, that the world was getting darker. Hell, it was one of the reasons I did idiotic things like I was doing tonight. My own effort to lift up a torch.

"I'm sort of a pessimist, Mr. Dresden. I think that people are almost too incompetent to hurt themselves so badly. I mean, if criminals were *trying*, they couldn't increase their production by three hundred percent. And I hear stories, read the tabloids sometimes. So what if the supernatural world is making a comeback? What if that accounts for some of what is going on?"

"What if it does?" I asked him.

Billy regarded me steadily, without looking me in the eyes. "Someone has to do something. I can. So I should. That's why we're here, the Alphas. Tera offered us the chance to do something, when she met us through the Northwest Passage Project, and we took it."

I stared at the kid. I could have argued with him, but there wouldn't be much point to it. I knew his argument, backward and forward. I'd worked it out myself. If I was ten years younger, a foot shorter, and a couple of pounds heavier, that could have been me talking. And I had to admit, the kid did have power. I mean, turning yourself into a wolf is no cheap parlor trick. But I did have one angle to play, and I took it. I didn't want this kid's blood on my hands.

"I don't think you're ready for the big leagues yet, Billy."

"Could be," he said. "But there's no one else in the bull pen."

I had to give the kid credit. He had resolve. "Maybe you should sit this one out, and live to fight another day. It could all go bad, and if it does, those *Hexenwulfen* we took on down by the beach are going to be coming for you. Someone will need to stay with your wounded people, to protect them."

"More likely, if they go through you, they're going to go through us, too. It would be smarter to pile on everything we've got in one place. With you."

I chuckled. "All your eggs in one basket?"

He shook his head. "All the money on the most likely winner."

I studied him in silence for a long minute. I was confident of his sincerity. It just oozed out of him, in a way that only the really inexperienced and idealistic can manage. It was comforting, and at the same time it was the most frightening thing about him. His ignorance. No, not ignorance, really. Innocence. He didn't know what he would be going out to face. If I let him go along, I'd be dragging him down with me. Despite what he'd seen to-night, I'd be exposing him to a whole new, violent, bloody, and dangerous world. One way or another, if I let Billy Borden and his buddies go with me, these innocent children wouldn't live to see the sunrise.

But, God help me. He was right about one thing. I needed the help.

"Everyone who's going takes orders from me," I said, and he drew in a sharp breath, his eyes gleaming. "Not Tera. You do what I say, and you do it when I say it. And if I tell you to leave, you go. No questions. You got it?"

"I got it," Billy said, and gave me a cocky grin that simply did not belong on the face of a geeky little college nerd in a black bathrobe. "You're a smart man, Mr. Dresden."

I snorted at him, and just then the automatic light on the ga-rage door opener went out, leaving us in darkness. There was a disgusted sound from the doorway, and then the lights came on again. Georgia, in all her willowy, annoyed glory, was standing in the doorway to the garage.

"Billy Borden," she said. "Don't you have any better sense than to stay here in the dark?" She stalked out toward him, scowling.

He looked up at her calmly and said, "Tell everyone we're going along. Dresden's in charge. If they can handle that, they're in, and if not, they're staying here to guard Cindy and Alex."

Georgia's eyes widened and she gave a little whoop of excite-ment. She turned to me and threw her arms around me for a moment, making my shoulder scream in pain, and then whirled to Billy and bent down to do the same thing. He winced when she did, and she stood up and jerked back his black bathrobe, clearing it off of one side of his pale chest. To give the kid credit, his stoutness was the result of what looked like quite a bit of solid muscle, and along the line of his chest there was a thickly clotted wound, still trickling blood in a few places.

"What's this?" Georgia said. "You idiot. You didn't tell me you'd gotten hurt."

Billy shrugged, and pulled his robe straight again. "It closed. And you can't bandage it and keep it on me when I change, anyway."

Georgia clucked her teeth, annoyed. "You shouldn't have gone for the hamstring on that wolf. He was too fast."

Billy flashed her a grin. "I almost got him, though."

"You almost got yourself killed," she said, but her voice had softened a few shades. I noticed that she hadn't moved her hand from the other side of Billy's chest, and he was looking up at her with an expectant expression. She fell silent, and they stared at one another for a minute. I saw her swallow.

Please, help me. Young werewolves in love. I turned to walk into the house, moving carefully.

I had never much believed in God. Well, that's not quite true. I believed that there was a God, or something close enough to it to warrant the name—if there were demons, there had to be angels, right? If there was a Devil, somewhere, there had to be a God. But He and I had never really seen things in quite the same terms.

All the same. I flashed a look up at the ceiling. I didn't say or think any words, but if God was listening, I hoped he got the message nonetheless. I didn't want any of these children getting themselves killed.

Chapter
Twenty-seven

Susan's perfume led me to her. She was waiting for me in a bedroom on the first floor. She stood in the simply furnished room, in her jeans and a white T-shirt blazoned with the words, EAT IT? I WOULDN'T SIT ON IT! It was one of mine. She lifted her chin up high when she saw me, as though trying to keep the tears in her eyes from falling.

Our gazes met, and held. We had looked into one another before, more than a year ago. She'd fainted when she saw what was inside of me through the soulgaze. I don't know what it was she saw. I don't look too hard into mirrors.

Inside of her, though, I'd seen passion, like I'd rarely known in people other than myself. The motivation to go, to do, to act. It was what drove her forward, digging up stories of the supernatural for a half-comic rag like the *Arcane*. She had a gift for it, for digging down into the muck that people tried to ignore, and coming up with facts that weren't always easily explained. She made people think. It was something personal for her—I knew that much, but not why. Susan was determined to make people see the truth.

I shut the door behind me and limped toward her.

"They'll kill you," she said. "Don't go." As I reached her, she put her hands against my chest, then her cheek.

"I've got to. Denton can't afford to let me live now. I need to finish this business, before it gets any more out of hand. Before more people die. If I don't go tonight, Denton will be able to kill Marcone and MacFinn and set MacFinn up for all the killings. He'll get away clean, and then he'll be able to focus on me. And maybe on you, too."

"We could go somewhere," she said quietly. "We could hide."

I blinked my eyes closed. She'd said "we." She hadn't really done that much, before. I hadn't really thought in those terms, either. I hadn't much thought in those terms for a lot of years. Not since the last time.

I should have said something about it. Acknowledged the implication. I knew it was there, and she knew that I had noticed it. She held still, waiting.

Instead, I said, "I'm not much good at hiding. Neither are you."

Her breath went out in a little whisper, and I felt her tighten a little against me. There would be tears on my shirt, I knew, but I didn't look down at her.

"You're right," she said a moment later. Her voice was shaking. "And I know you are. But I'm afraid, Harry. I mean, I know we haven't been really close. Friends, and lovers, but . . ."

"Work," I said. I closed my eyes.

She nodded. "Work." Her fingers tightened on my shirt, and she looked up at me, dark eyes swimming with tears, still more on the smooth lines of her cheek. "I don't want to lose you now. I don't want the work to be all that's left."

I tried to think of something smart to say. Something that would reassure her, calm her, help her to feel better, to understand what I felt for her. But I wasn't even sure what it was that I felt.

I found myself kissing her, the rough growth on my mouth and chin brushing her soft skin. She tensed at first, and then melted against me with a deliciously feminine sort of willingness, a soft abandoning of distance that left her body, in all its dark beauty, pressed against mine. The kiss deepened, slowed, became something intense and erotic and self-contained. The motion of our lips, the warmth of our bodies pressed together. The touch of my fingertips on her face, featherlight. The scratch of her nails as her fingers kneaded at my shirt. My heart was pounding, and I could feel hers, too, racing.

She broke the kiss first, and I swayed on my feet, my breath gone. Without speaking, she guided me down to the edge of the bed, and sat me there. Then she vanished into the bathroom, reappearing with a basin of warm water, some soap, and a washcloth.

She undressed me. Slowly. Delicately. She changed the bandages, murmuring softly to me when it hurt, kissing my eyes and forehead to soothe me. She bathed me with the water, its warmth washing away the dried sweat, the blood, and some of the pain. Patiently, more gentle than rain, she made me clean, while I drifted, my eyes closed. I could hear myself make a soft sound, now and then, in response to her touches.

I felt her come to me. Felt her bare skin against mine, hot and smooth. I opened my eyes and saw the silver haze of the moon on the far horizon, across the lake. I saw Susan outlined in it, all sweetly feminine curves and lines, a beautiful shadow. She kissed me again, and I returned it in kind, and it was a liquid, smooth thing, as restrained and desperate as the near-still surface of a rushing river. Her lips passed from my mouth and roamed over the skin she had just cleaned, and when I tried to touch her, she gently pressed my hands back down, telling me without words to be still.

It went on like that, all skin and light touches, soft sighs, pounding hearts, until she settled atop me, keeping her weight off me with her legs, her hands, afraid to cause any pain. We moved together, feeling the power of our need, our hunger for one another, a pure blend of desire and warmth and affection and incredible intimacy that shook us to the core. It ended in silence, the sensation all the more piercing for that, our mouths together, our breath mingling.

She lay down beside me until our pounding hearts slowed down. Then she rose, and said, "I don't know if I want to fall in love with you, Harry. I don't know if I could stand it."

I opened my eyes, and answered softly, "I've never wanted to hurt you. I don't know what's right."

"I know what feels right," she said, and kissed me again, then started touching my forehead, lifting her head up to study me with gentle, compassionate eyes. "You see so much pain. I just wanted to remind you that there was something else in the world."

I'm a pretty tough guy. I mean, look at me. I can handle some rough stuff. But some things I'm not so tough about. I started crying, hard, and Susan held me, rocked me gently, until the tears had gone away.

I wanted to stay there, where it was warm, and where I was clean, and where there wasn't anyone dying. There wasn't any blood or snarling animals, and no one was trying to kill me. I liked the idea of being there, with Susan, in her arms, a whole lot more than I liked the idea of going out into the silver light of the full moon, which was growing greater underneath the horizon, coming up in a hazy nimbus.

Instead, I drew away from her a little and sat up.

It was a fool's moon.

She rose from the bed and returned with an overnight bag and drew out a pair of my black jeans, my black sneakers, socks, a heavy, dark grey shirt, dark undies to complete the color theme, and bless her heart, ibuprofen. I rose to dress, but she pressed a hand on my shoulder and made me sit down—then dressed me herself, slowly and carefully, her attention focused on the task. Neither of us spoke.

Ever had a beautiful, naked woman dress you? Talk about girding your loins for battle. There was something indescribably soothing and at the same time, exciting, about it. I could feel my body becoming more relaxed and aware, my senses more in tune with what was around me.

I heard footsteps in the hall, and a knock at the door. Tera's voice called, "Wizard. It is time."

I stood up, but Susan grabbed my wrist. "Harry," she said. "Wait a minute." She knelt down by the bag and drew out a heavy box, flat and broad. "I was going to give it to you for your birthday. But I thought you could use it."

I tilted my head and took the box in hand. It was heavy. "What is it?" I asked her.

"Just open it, dummy," she answered, smiling up at me. I did, and inside was the smell of soft, worked leather, sensuous and thick, wrapped up in translucent paper. I tossed the lid aside, took the paper off, and found dark leather, new and matte black, hardly casting back the light. I took it out of the box, and it unfolded into a heavy, long coat, like my own duster in design, even to the mantle around the shoulders and arms, but all made of the finer material.

I blinked at the coat. "It must have cost you a fortune."

She laughed wickedly. "Yeah. But I got to wear it around naked, just to feel it on my skin." Her face sobered. "I want you to have it, Harry. Something from me. For luck." She glided to my side and helped me into the coat.

The coat settled around me with a comforting heaviness and a peculiar sort of familiarity. It just felt right. I plucked my mother's pentacle on its chain from beneath my shirt and wore it openly. And then I got Harris's confiscated side arm from my coveralls' tool pouch, and put it in the coat's pocket. I didn't have any other magical tools. And maybe not even any more magic. The gun, all things considered, seemed an uncertain weapon at best.

But I was as ready as I was going to be.

I turned to say good-bye to Susan, to find her hurriedly stepping into her clothes. "What are you doing?" I asked.

"Getting dressed," she said.

"Why?"

"Someone's got to drive the van, Dresden." She tugged on her T-shirt, slung her jacket over her shoulder, and walked past me, pausing to give me a narrow glance. "Besides. This could be the biggest paranormal event I've ever had the chance to cover.

Did you expect me to stay behind?" She pushed the door open and gave me an expectant look.

Damn, I thought. *And double damn.* One more person to worry about. One more person to protect. Susan wasn't a were-wolf. She wasn't a wizard. She didn't even have a gun. It was crazy to let her even think about going along. But I found myself wanting to make sure she was somewhere close.

"All right," I said. "But the same rules I gave the kids. I'm in charge. You do what I say, when I say, or you stay here."

Susan pursed her lips and narrowed her eyes. "I kind of like the sound of that," she said, teasing me. "I like that look on you, too. Have you ever thought about growing a beard?" Then she smiled, and vanished out into the hallway.

I scowled after her. She'd stay away from the worst of it. I'd make sure of that, if I had to tie her to the van myself. I muttered something grouchy, bent my head to one side, and inhaled, smelling the smell of new leather, of fresh clothes and soap, and of *eau de Susan* still lingering on my skin. I liked it. The jacket creaked as I started forward, and I caught sight of myself in the dresser mirror.

My double, the one from the dream, stared back out at me. Only the roughness of the three-day growth of dark whiskers, and the bruises, were at contrast with the subconscious-me's neatly trimmed beard. Everything else was precisely the same.

I turned my face away rather quickly and paced from the room, out to the van, where the others were waiting.

Showtime.

Chapter
Twenty-eight

The moon rose in silver splendor into an October sky strewn with pale clouds and brilliant stars. The clouds churned, a white-foam sea, and the moon was a vast, graceful clipper ship, its sails full of spectral light as it ran before the strength of the cold autumn winds. Pale light bleached each of the uncut stones on the nine-foot wall around Gentleman Johnny Marcone's estate, making edges sharper, shadows blacker, until it looked like a barrier made of gaping white skulls. Trees grew up thick on the other side of the wall, blocking the view of the interior, though no branches extended far enough to provide a way to climb over it.

"We've got to get over the wall," I said to the enormous, dark wolf beside me, keeping my voice low as we all crouched in the shadows of the bushes across the street from Marcone's estate. "There will be security on it. Maybe cameras, maybe infrared beams, maybe something else. I want you to find us a way past it." The wolf flickered her amber eyes toward me and made a soft, assenting growl. Then she simply turned and faded into the darkness, leaving five more furry, crouching shapes grouped around me.

The Alphas didn't exactly inspire confidence, but they had all managed to master enough rudimentary magic to transform themselves into very, very close approximations of wolves, at least. It was something.

Susan had parked the van on a hill leading up to Marcone's estate, and remained with it, in case we needed a quick getaway. When we'd arrived, a nude Tera West and five young people, three female and two male, had leapt out of the van, the Alphas hurriedly tumbling out of their robes.

"Hell's bells," I'd complained, "we're on a public street. Can you be something besides naked, here, people?"

Tera had smirked and, in a liquid shimmer, become a gaunt, dark wolf, a beast fully as large as Denton and his cronies had been, but with a narrower muzzle and cleaner proportions. Like Denton and his crew of *Hexenwulfen*, she kept the exact same shade and color of her eyes, even in wolfish form.

"Well?" I'd demanded of the others. "Let's hurry it up."

Georgia had slipped her lean body from her dark robe and melted in a few seconds into her wolf shape, then had quickly slipped past me to go to Tera. Billy had growled something under his breath as he shrugged out of his robe, catching one sleeve on his arm as he'd begun to change.

Billy-wolf had stumbled over the robe still hanging on to his forepaw, tripped, and tumbled onto the street with a whuff of expelled breath and a little whimper.

I'd rolled my eyes. Billy-the-wolf had snarled and struggled out of his robe, picked it up carefully in his teeth, like a large and particularly grumpy-looking Benji, and put it back in the van.

"Um," one of the other girls had said, a redheaded lass who filled out her robe a little too generously. "We're still a little new at this." She'd covered herself with her arms awkwardly, letting her robe fall from her shoulders as she whispered a little chant, and had become a rather round, hefty-looking she-wolf with dark auburn fur. She'd moved daintily to the edge of the cargo van and had minced, despite her weight, down to the street. The other two young people, a lanky, dark-haired boy and a scrawny girl with mouse-brown hair, had made the change and loped up the hill after Tera, and then we all had moved as quietly as we could to the rear of Marcone's estate.

Surrounded by a high stone wall, the property occupied an entire block, bounded on all four sides by individual streets. None of us had known the layout to Marcone's place, so we'd chosen to approach from the rear, on general principles of sneakiness. I hadn't thought it would be wise to walk in the front door, so I had dispatched Tera to find us a way in, while I'd remained behind with the Alphas.

I found myself tapping my fingers on my thighs as I crouched, restless. I soon realized that if I was tense, the would-be werewolves were twice as keyed up. The darkest-furred one, Billy, I thought, rose to his paws and started away, in the opposite direction from which Tera had gone. Georgia growled at him, Billy growled back, and the other male rose to follow him.

Great, I thought. I couldn't afford to let the Alphas wander off now, no matter how restless they were.

"Hey," I said quietly. "You can't go haring off now. If there's a way inside, Tera will find it."

The wolves all turned their heads, and their very human eyes, toward me.

Billy planted his paws stubbornly and growled.

"Oh, don't give me that," I snapped, glaring at him without meeting his eyes. "You promised you'd play this my way, Billy. This isn't a time to be messing around."

Billy's stance became less certain, and I beckoned all of them toward me. If I could keep them listening until Tera got back, I could at least be sure that they'd be around when I needed them. "Huddle up, everyone," I said. "I want to go over some things before we go in."

There was a brief silence, and then a crowding of furry, heavy bodies, and a snuffling of wet noses. Ten ears pricked up and rotated toward me, and ten bright, human eyes fastened upon me from lupine faces. I suppressed a sudden urge to say, "Good evening, class. I'm your teacher, Mr. Dresden," and instead put on my most serious expression.

"You all know what's at stake tonight," I said. "And that we could all get killed. We're going to be confronting a bunch of law-enforcement people who have gotten hold of some magic that's as black as anything I've ever seen, and are using it to turn themselves into wolves. They've lost control of the power they've grabbed. They're killing people, and if we don't stop them they're going kill a lot more. Especially me, because I know too much. I'm a danger to them.

"But I don't want that. I don't want anyone to get killed. Not us, and not them. Maybe they deserve it. Maybe not. The power they grabbed has turned into a drug for them, and they're not really in control of themselves anymore. I just don't think we'd be much different than them if we went in there planning to wipe them out. It isn't enough to stand up and fight darkness. You've got to stand apart from it, too. You've got to be different from it."

I cleared my throat. "Hell. I'm not good at this. Go for their belts, if you can, just like I did in the alley. Once their belts are off, they're not going to be as crazy, and maybe we'll be able to talk to them." I glanced up at the wall and back down. "Just don't get killed, guys. Do what you have to do to stay alive. That's your first priority. And if you've got to kill them to do it, then don't hesitate."

There was a chorus of growls from around me, led by the wolf Billy, but that was the great thing about being the only human being there—I was the only one who could talk. There wouldn't have been any arguments, even had they disagreed. Their enthusiasm was a little intimidating.

"If you are any louder, wizard," Tera's soft voice came from behind me, "we might as well walk through the front gate." I jumped and looked up to see Tera, naked and human, crouched down a few feet away.

"I wish you wouldn't *do* that," I hissed at her. "Did you find a way in?"

"Yes," she said. "A place where the wall has crumbled. But it is far for you to walk, around along the eastern wall, toward the front of the property. We must run if we are to get inside in time."

I grimaced. "I'm not in any shape to run anywhere."

"It would seem you have little choice. I also saw many streaks of light across the front gate. And there are black boxes with glass eyes every seventy or eighty paces. They do not see the crumbled place. It is a fortunate position."

"Cameras," I muttered. "Hell."

"Come, wizard," Tera said, crouching down on all fours. "We have no time to waste if you are to join us. The pack can cover the distance in moments, but you must hurry."

"Tera. I've had a rough couple of days. I'd fall over in about two minutes if I tried to run somewhere."

The woman blinked passionless amber eyes up at me. "Your point?"

"I'm going over the wall right here," I said.

Tera looked at the wall and shook her head. "I cannot bring the pack over that wall. They are not strong enough to keep changing back and forth, and they have no hands in their wolf form."

"Just me then. I guess you all can find me?"

Tera snorted. "Of course. But it is foolish for you to go over the wall alone. And what if the cameras see you?"

"Let me worry about the cameras," I said. "Help me up to the top. Then you and the Alphas circle around and rendezvous with me."

Tera scowled, the expression dark. "I think this foolish, wizard. If you are too wounded to run, then you are too wounded to go in alone."

"We don't have time," I said with a glance up at the moon, "to argue about this. Do you want my help or don't you?"

Tera let out a sound somewhere between a snort and a snarl, and for a moment tension in her muscles made them stand out hard against her skin. One of the Alphas let out a little whimper, and stepped away from us.

"Very well, wizard," Tera said. "I will show you the nearest camera and help you over the wall. Do not move from where you land. We do not know who is on the other side of the wall, or where."

"Don't worry about me," I said. "Worry about yourself. If there's a good way through the wall, Denton might show up there, too, to go in. Or MacFinn might."

"MacFinn," Tera said, traces of pride in her voice and fear in her eyes, "will not even notice that the wall got in his way."

I grimaced. "Just show me the camera."

Tera led me forward through the dark, silent and naked and looking as though she didn't mind the cold evening at all. The grass was damp, plush, and deep. Tera pointed out the small, silent square of the video camera settled onto the wall across the street, and almost entirely hidden by the shadows of the trees.

I licked my lips and leaned toward the camera, keeping my own form obscured by the bushes. I squinted my eyes and drew in my will, trying to focus. My head started to pound at once, and I felt sweat break out beneath my arms and across my forehead. Hexing up anything mechanical is usually fairly simple. The field of magic that surrounds practitioners of the Art plays havoc with the implements of technology. A passing thought, on the right kind of day, can blow out a cellular telephone or kill a photocopier.

This was the wrong kind of day. That field of energy around me was severely depleted from its usual levels, and the metaphysical "muscles" I would normally use to manipulate that energy were in screaming agony, reflected in pains throughout my body.

But I needed to get inside, and I really did think that I wouldn't be able to make it all the way around the property. I was running on empty already, and too much more would leave me gasping like a fish out of water and wishing I was at home in bed.

I forced calm on my thoughts and focused all the energy I had, and it hurt me, starting in my head and spreading into weary aches in my knees and elbows. But the energy built, and built, and with it the pain, until I could hold it together no longer.

"*Malivaso,*" I whispered, and pushed my hand out at the square shape, like a grade-school girl throwing a baseball wrong handed. The power I'd gathered, though it felt like it was about to split me at the seams, rushed out in an almost impotent little hiccup of magic and swirled drunkenly toward the security camera.

For a long minute, nothing happened. And then there was a flash of light, and a tiny shower of sparks from the rear of the box. Smoke drizzled up from the camera in a quavering plume, and I felt a small surge of triumph. At least I had *something* left in me, even if it was aneurism-causing labor to perform the mildest of tasks.

"All right then," I said a second later, my voice somewhat thready. "Let's go."

We looked around and made sure no cars were about, and then Tera, the Alphas, and I rushed across the road, through some decorative, leafy bushes, to the high stone wall. Tera laced her fingers together to form a stirrup. I put my good foot into it, and pushed up hard. She heaved me up, and half threw me over the wall. I caught myself at the top, saw a car's headlights coming, and swiftly rolled down the other side, falling heavily to damp, muddy earth.

It was dark. It was really dark. I was crouched at the base of the wall, underneath a spreading canopy of bare tree branches and stubborn sycamore leaves. Moonlight filtered through in random places, but it only served to make the dark spots all the more gloomy. My own black leather duster was utterly invisible, and I remembered reading somewhere that the gleam of my eyes and teeth would be the most likely to give me away—but since I didn't feel like sitting in the dark with my eyes closed, I didn't. Instead, I crouched and got my confiscated gun ready in one pocket, and took my ace in the hole out of the other, getting that ready as well.

I shivered, and worked hard to remind myself not to be afraid. Then I waited in the darkness for my allies. And waited. And waited. Time passed, and I knew that a minute would feel like an hour, so I began counting, one number for every deliberate breath.

The wind blew through the trees, brisk and cool. Leaves rustled, and droplets of rainwater fell from the trees around me, making little pattering sounds as they struck my new coat. They clung to the leather in tight beads and caught pieces of moonlight in them, brilliant against the black. The smell of rich earth and damp stone rose up with the wind, and for a moment it did almost feel as though I was in a forest rather than on a crime lord's private estate in the north end of Chicago. I took deep breaths, a little comforted by the illusion, and kept on counting.

And waited.

Nothing happened. No wolves, no sounds.

Nothing.

It wasn't until I got to one hundred that I started to get really nervous, my stomach beginning a slow twist that made weak sensations lace out through my arms and legs like slivers of ice. Where was Tera? Where were the Alphas? It shouldn't have taken them nearly so long to get inside the wall and then to cover the distance back to me. Though the estate was huge, the distance surely meant little to the flashing speed of a wolf.

The evening had obviously been moving along entirely too smoothly, I thought.

Something had gone wrong. I was alone.

Chapter

Twenty-nine

Alone.

It's one of those small words that means entirely too much. Like fear. Or trust. I'm used to working alone. It goes with the territory. Wizards of my level of skill and strength (well, my usual levels) are few and far between—maybe no more than two dozen in the United States, with a slightly higher concentration of them in Europe, Africa, and Asia. But there is a difference between working alone and finding yourself facing a hatful of foes, on a cold night, while wounded, and in the dark, and practically helpless. It took me about ten seconds to become acutely aware of that difference.

Fear settled in comfortably. Fear was something I was used to. I was able to think past it, to focus on my predicament. Yay for me. My body reacted the same old way, keying up for fight or flight, while I forced my breathing to stay even.

The smart thing to do would be to run, to turn around and go back to the van and to have Susan drive me the hell away. Granted, I probably couldn't even climb the wall on my own, but I could have tried.

But I was already committed. I was here to do battle with the forces of evil, such as they were. I had dropped the challenge to them, not the other way around. Besides, if Tera and the kids were in trouble, I was the only one who could help them.

I climbed to my feet, getting out the gun, and moved forward through the woods, in a direction that seemed perpendicular to the line of the stone wall behind me. The woods were thick, sycamores and poplars giving way to evergreens with scratchy, low branches. I slipped through them as best I could, moving as quietly as I could manage. I didn't think I made more noise than the wind did, as it rattled the branches and the fallen leaves, and stirred more droplets of water to fall. In time, maybe three or four minutes, I came to the edge of the woods, and looked out on to Gentleman Johnny Marcone's estate.

It was magnificent, something out of a home-and-garden magazine. You could have put a small golf course in Marcone's backyard. A long ways off, at the front of the property, Marcone's huge white house stood serene and flawless, artistically illuminated by dozens of lights, with a veranda or patio larger than a dance floor plotted out at its rear. Behind it, three enormous square plots, side-by-side, contained lit and lovely gardens, terraced down a gently sloping hill toward me. At the hill's base was a pretty little vale, and there lay a small pond, which I realized after a moment was an enormous, concrete-lined swimming pool, lit from beneath the surface. The pool was irregularly shaped, and one corner of the pool stirred, near the surface. Steam lay thick over the water.

Standing stately sentinel toward the center of the vale was a ring of evergreens, thick and stocky trees that concealed whatever was at their center. Two rounded hillocks decorated the left side of the vale's landscape, one of them surmounted by what looked like a replica of a small, ruined shrine or temple, all cracked marble and fallen columns.

The whole place was well lit, both by silver moonlight and by lighting placed at strategic intervals. The lawn was immaculate, and trees dotted the grounds in the sort of careless perfection that only an army of expensive gardeners could have maintained.

And they say that crime doesn't pay.

I took a position behind a screen of trees and brush and looked around the grounds with careful, stealthy caution. I didn't have long to wait.

There was a rush of motion from beneath one of the trees on

the far side of the estate, and a swift form, a dark-furred wolf, Billy, I thought, flew from beneath one tree and toward a patch of dark shadow on the grass, not twenty feet from me. I tensed, and started to rise from my hiding place in the brush, to call out to the wolf as he ran.

A bright red dot of light appeared against the wolf's fur. There was a hollow sound, something I could barely hear, like a politely covered cough. I saw the wolf jerk as a flash of blue feathered against its fur, and then the beast tumbled into a roll and fell to the ground. It struggled for a moment, back to its feet, and reached for the dart in its flanks with its jaws. Its balance wavered, and the wolf staggered to one side and fell. I could see its chest heaving, and one of its rear legs twitched spasmodically. I thought I saw the beast's eyes, Billy's eyes, focus on me for a moment, and then they glazed over and went vacant.

"Nice shot," called a deep, tense voice. In the ring of evergreens, there was motion, and then Denton appeared, walking out across the grass toward the fallen wolf. His dark, short hair was still immaculately rigid. I couldn't see the veins in his forehead, despite the bright light. It was a subtle change in him, one of several. His tie was loose. His jacket was unbuttoned. He moved with less steel in his backbone, more fire in his belly. There was an animal quality to him, a surety and savagery of purpose that had been uncertain before, and what it meant was a lot more significant than the changes that showed on his exterior.

His restraint was gone. Whatever last remnants of doubt or regret that had enabled him to maintain his own self-control, and some measure of control over the other *Hexenwulfen*, had vanished with the blood frenzy in the Full Moon Garage. It was in every line of him now, in each step and every flicker of his eyes.

The man had become a predator.

From the evergreens behind him appeared the rest of the *Hexenwulfen:* Benn, now dressed only in a white dress shirt and a grey business skirt, her legs dark and rippling with muscle in the moonlight; Harris, his ears still sticking out, his freckles dark spots against pale skin, his manner restless and hungry; and Wilson, still in his wrinkled suit, but with the shirt unbuttoned, his potbelly overlapping the belt of dark fur around his waist. He stroked and patted it with his fat fingers. His mouth was set in an odd, dangerous grin.

Denton moved across the grass to the fallen wolf, and nudged it with his toe. "Six," he said. "Did you count six?"

"Six," Benn confirmed, her voice throaty. "Can we have them now?" She reached Denton's side and pressed up against him, lifting one leg to rub against his, baring it to the top of her thigh as she did.

"Not yet," Denton said. He looked around him thoughtfully, and my gaze followed his. Scattered around a circle of perhaps fifty-yards diameter were several dark lumps I had taken to be indentations in the ground, shadows cast by the moon and the grounds lighting. I looked again and saw, with a surge of fearful understanding, that they weren't indentations. They were the wolves, my allies. The dark patch Billy had been running for gave a little whimper, and I thought I saw the moon glint off of Georgia's tawny coat. I looked around and counted the fallen.

Six. I couldn't tell them apart very well, couldn't tell which of them, if any, was Tera, but I counted six fallen wolves upon the ground. All of them, I thought, with a panicked rush of fear. All of them had been taken.

"Come *on*," Harris said, his voice tight, strained. "Fuck Mac-Finn, he isn't showing up. Let's take them out, all of them, and go find Dresden."

"We'll get to your belt soon enough, kid," Wilson snorted, his fingers stroking at the fur belt over his belly. "If you hadn't been so stupid as to lose it—"

Harris snarled, and Denton shook Benn from his side to get between the other two men. "Shut up. Now. We don't have time for this. Harris, we'll go after the wizard as soon as we can.

Wilson, keep your fat mouth shut, if you like your tongue where it is. And both of you back off." The men made low, growling noises, but they took steps away from one another.

I licked my lips. I was shaking. The gun felt heavy in my hand. There were only the four of them, I thought. They weren't more than thirty feet away. I could start shooting right now. If I got lucky, I could down them all. They were werewolves, but they weren't invincible.

I slipped the safety off of the pistol, and drew in a steadying breath. It was a damn fool thing to do, and I knew it. Life is not the movies. It wasn't likely that I would be able to shoot them all before they could draw and shoot back. But I didn't have much choice.

Denton turned toward the first hillock, with its artfully ruined temple, and waved. "All right," he called. "That's all of them."

A pair of shapes appeared in the lights that shone on the temple, and then came down the hill toward Denton and the *Hexenwulfen*. Marcone was dressed in a flannel shirt, jeans, and a hunter's vest, and he bore a gleaming rifle, an enormous scope mounted on it, in one hand. Hendricks, hulking beside him in muscle-bound silence, was dressed in what looked like black military fatigues, bearing the gun I'd seen earlier, a knife, and various other gear. Hendricks's eyes flickered over Denton and his associates warily.

I stared at Marcone in shock. It took me a moment to pick my jaw up off the ground and to piece together what was going on. Marcone didn't know. He didn't know that Denton and company were out to get him. They must have blamed the other killings on MacFinn and the Alphas.

So now Denton had Marcone and the Alphas there. Once MacFinn arrived, he would be able to kill everyone he wanted dead, everyone who knew what was going on, and be able to make up any story he damned well pleased. Everyone but me, that is. He did not, as yet, have his hands on me.

"These are all we saw on the monitors," Marcone corrected. "There was a malfunction in camera six, at the rear line of the property. Mr. Dresden and such malfunctions tend to go hand in hand."

Dammit.

"Are you sure the wizard isn't one of them?" Denton demanded. "One of these wolves?"

"I think not," Marcone answered. "But I suppose anything is possible."

Denton scowled. "Then he's not here."

"If he truly offered you a challenge, he's here," Marcone said, his tone completely confident. "I'm certain of it."

"And he just watched his werewolf friends get shot down?" Denton asked.

"Wolves run faster than men," Marcone pointed out. "Possibly, he hasn't caught up to them yet. He could even be watching us now."

"You're giving him too much credit," Denton said. But I saw his eyes shift instinctively toward the blackness of the growth of woods. If I stood up, he would be looking right at me. I froze, holding my breath.

"Am I?" Marcone smiled, and leaned down to pluck the feathered dart from Billy's furry flank. "The tranquilizers likely won't hold these beasts for very long. Decisions need to be made, gentlemen. And if you are to hold to your end of the bargain, you had best get to work producing."

I don't know if Marcone noticed Benn's sudden tension, the way she slid her hands over her stomach, but I did. "Kill these dogs now," she said in a low, heated voice. "It prevents complications later in the evening."

Marcone tsked. "Shortsighted. Let MacFinn tear them to pieces when he arrives, and any medical examiner won't bother to look for the tranquilizers. If one of you does it, it will create awkward questions once forensics takes a look at things. And I thought that was the point of you coming to me with this offer. Reducing questions."

Benn lifted her lips away from her teeth, and I saw the tips of her breasts stiffen beneath her white shirt. "I hate slimy scum like you, Marcone," she purred, sliding her hand from her thigh up over her hip and beneath the buttons of her shirt. Marcone's eyes narrowed on her, and as though connected to the crime lord by a telepathic leash, Hendricks made one simple motion, a shift of his forward arm, that chambered a round on the gun with a cold little *click-clack*.

Denton gave Marcone a sharp look and took hold of Benn's wrist with his hand. The woman tensed for a second, resisting him, but then she allowed Denton to draw her hand away from the belt that was surely beneath her shirt. Denton released her, and Benn lowered her hands, visibly relaxing. Marcone and Hendricks never so much as blinked, or broke a sweat. Fragile situations like this one were evidently second nature to them.

I let out the breath I'd been holding for a long time. Six to one and ready for a fight. If I attacked them now, I didn't have a prayer. If I tried to move, to fade back into the trees, they would be likely to notice me. Damn.

Denton glanced at the trees once more, and I held my breath again. "Don't worry, Marcone," he said. "We'll turn the wizard over to you, once we find him. No questions asked."

"That being the case," Marcone said, "I suggest you start looking, while I make preparations for Mr. MacFinn. Please remember that I want Dresden alive, if possible."

My throat constricted, and if I hadn't been holding my breath, I think I would have let out a squeak. What in the world could John Marcone want with me, after the incident in the parking garage? Nothing good, certainly. Nothing I wanted to think about. Damn, damn. This night was getting spookier all the time.

"Of course, Mr. Marcone," Denton said, his tone a little too polite. "Do you have any suggestions of where we should start looking?"

Marcone ignored the sarcasm, flicked a switch on the sight on his rifle, and pointed it negligently at the tree line. "Over there ought to do."

The red dot of the laser sight settled onto a leaf six inches to the left of my head, and the thready pulse of fear in my chest turned into an icy white streak of terror.

Damn, damn, damn.

Chapter Thirty

If I ran, I would be seen and pursued, and likely torn apart. If I remained where I was hidden, I would be found and *then* torn apart, or shot, or tranquilized and given to Johnny Marcone. A poor set of choices, but I wasn't going to get any better ones by sitting on my ass. So I got my feet underneath me and started easing back into the woods, the confiscated semiautomatic still in my hand.

"Hold it," Denton said. "Did you hear that?"

"What?" Benn asked. I could hear the sudden, eager tension in her voice, and I struggled not to make any more noise as I hurried my pace back into the shelter of the deeper trees.

"Quiet," Denton snarled, and I froze in place. Wind and rain were the only sounds for a few moments, in the chilly autumn night. "Over there," Denton said after a moment. "I think I heard it over that way."

"Could be a raccoon. Squirrel. Or a cat," Wilson suggested.

"Don't be naive," came Marcone's voice, laced with scorn. "It's *him*."

There was the immediate sound of a slide being worked on a handgun, a round being chambered into place. "Move forward," said Denton. "That way. Fan out and we'll take him. Watch yourself. We don't know all of what he can do. Don't take any chances." His voice came closer as he spoke, and I nearly bolted. There was a chorus of assenting sounds, and another couple of weapons being readied. Footsteps came toward me through the grass.

After that, I did bolt, just stood up and ran bent over as low as I could. There was a shout from behind me and a bark of a gun being fired. I pointed the semiautomatic above me, afraid to fire back at them for fear of hitting Tera or one of the Alphas by mistake, and pulled the trigger twice. The gunshots must have surprised them, because Denton and the others scattered for cover behind the nearest trees.

I ran deeper into the woods, marshaling my thoughts. I had gained a little time, but time to do what? Running would only put me up against a stone wall. I doubted I'd be able to climb it, with a bum foot and a wounded shoulder. And I could only play the rabbit in the woods for so long before I was found.

Dammit, I thought. *I'm no rabbit.*

It was about time the hunters became the hunted around here. I moved ahead, silent and intent now, and scanned around me, searching for the sort of place I would need. I found it almost at once, an inward-curving hollow at the base of a large tree, and slid into it, nestling into the wood's embrace. I put my head down, hiding the paleness of my face and the gleam of the whites of my eyes. And Listened.

They came forward quietly, and without any lights flickering around at the edges of my vision. Maybe Denton and his cronies were getting used to the darkness. They were moving forward in a ragged line, twenty or thirty paces apart, and somehow keeping mostly parallel. They were all still on two feet, by the sound of the steps, thank my lucky stars. If they'd gone to wolf form they might have had me—of course, on two legs, they still had hands free to hold guns of their own. There are pros and cons to everything, I suppose.

I held my breath when footsteps approached me. They came within ten feet. Then five. I felt the brush stir when someone walked past no more than a foot away, making leaves brush up against me. They stopped, right there, and I heard a little, whuffling sound. Sniffing. I thought of the aroma of my brand-new leather jacket, and clenched my jaws down slightly, tension thrumming through me and making my legs shake.

About ten billion years went by. And then whoever it was
began walking again, forward and past me. I would have let out
a sigh of relief, if the most dangerous part of my plan wasn't still
to come.

I got up from my hiding place, stepped forward and jammed
the barrel of the semiautomatic against the back of the neck of
the person before me. It was Denton. His back arched and he
sucked in a stunned breath.

"Quiet," I whispered. "Don't move."

Denton hissed, but froze in place. "Dresden, I should kill
you right now."

"Try it," I said, and thumbed back the hammer of the gun.
"But after the loud noise, remember to keep going down the
tunnel and toward the light."

Denton's shoulders shifted a fraction and I said, "Don't move
your arms, at all. Reach for that belt and I'll kill you before
you're halfway to furry, Denton. Drop the gun."

Denton moved his fingers enough to close the safety on his
gun and let it fall. "Not bad, Dresden," he said. "But this isn't
going to do you any good. Put the gun down, and we can talk
about this."

"Smooth, polite, nice delivery," I said. "They teach you that
at the FBI?"

"Don't make this any harder on yourself than it has to be,
Dresden," Denton said, his voice toneless. "You can't get out
of this."

"They always say that," I said and used my free hand, though
it made my shoulder twitch, to take him by the collar and hold
him steady. "My arm's feeling a little weak," I said. "Don't do
anything to make me slip."

I felt his body tense at my words. "What are you doing,
Dresden?"

"You and me, we're going to turn around," I said with a little
shove of the gun against his neck to emphasize the point. "And
then you're going to order all of your people out of the trees

and back into the light. They'll each call to you from there, so that I know they're in front of me, and then we're going to go see them."

"What do you hope to accomplish here, Dresden?" Denton said.

I let go of his neck, pressed close, and reached around him to remove the wolf-pelt belt from around his middle. I saw his jawline shift as I took the belt away, but he remained still and quiet, his hands in the air. "I was just going to ask you the same thing, Denton," I said. "Now, call your buddies out of the trees."

Denton might have been a cool customer, maybe a treacherous sneak, maybe a murderer, but one thing he wasn't was a fool. He called out to the other three agents, and told them to get out of the trees.

"Dent?" Wilson called. "Are you okay?"

"Just do it," Denton answered. "It will all be clear in a minute."

They did it. I heard them move out of the woods and call to him from the cut, level grass of Marcone's estate. "Now," I said. "Walk. Don't trip, because I swear to God I would rather blow your head off over a misunderstanding than get suckered by a trick and killed."

"Maybe you should put the safety on," Denton said. "Because if you kill me, you'll never get out of here alive."

I hate it when the bad guys have a point, but I chose to err on the side of Denton getting blown apart, and left the safety where it was. I slung the wolf belt over my shoulder, took Denton's collar again, and said, "Walk." He did. We walked out of the deep darkness of the woods and into the light.

I kept at the edge of the darkness and put a tree's trunk to my back, keeping Denton between me and the bad guys. They were spread out, the three of them, in a half circle about thirty feet away, and they all had guns. It would have been one hell of a marksman who could get at me with Denton's broad, solid form in front of me, and the shadows veiling me, but I didn't take chances. I crouched down behind him some, leaving nothing but the corner of my head and one eye showing. At least that way, I thought, if they shot me, I'd never feel it.

"Uh. Hi guys," I said a bit lamely. "I've got your boss. Put the guns down, take your belts off, and walk away from them nice and slow, or I kill him." A part of me, probably the smarter part, groaned at my course of action and started cataloguing the number of federal and state criminal codes I was breaking into tiny pieces by taking a member of the Federal Bureau of Investigation hostage and threatening to kill him and attempting to take hostage three more. I stopped counting broken laws at ten, and waited to see the *Hexenwulfen*'s response.

"To hell with you," Benn snarled. The silver-haired young woman dropped her gun, and ripped off her shirt, revealing a torso that was impressive in a number of senses—and another wolf-hide belt. "I'll tear your fucking throat out myself."

"Deborah," Denton said, his voice strained. "Don't. Please."

"Go ahead, bitch," growled Harris. His big ears created little half-moon shadows of blackness on the sides of his head. "Denton buys it and we all get promoted. Hell, the wizard will probably shoot you, while he's at it." Benn whirled toward Harris, lifting her hands as though she would strangle him, fingers clenching like talons.

"Shut up," I said. "Both of you. Put your guns down. Now."

Harris sneered at me. "You won't, Dresden. You don't have the guts."

"Roger," Denton said very quietly. "You're an idiot. The man's in a corner. Now. Put *down* your gun."

I blinked, surprised at the unexpected support. It made me instantly suspicious. That Marcone was out of sight did not mean that he was out of mind, either. Where was he? Crouched somewhere, aiming that rifle at me? I kept an eye out for bright red dots.

"That's right," I appended to Denton's statement. "You *are* an idiot. Drop the gun. You too, Wilson," I added, glancing at the overweight agent. "And you and Benn, take the belts off, too. Leave them on the ground."

"Do it," Denton confirmed, and I got a little more nervous. The man was relaxed now, not resisting me. His voice was solid, confident, unimpressed. That was bad. Denton's pack obeyed him, if reluctantly. Benn dropped the belt to the ground in the same way Scrooge might have let fall a string of diamonds, a visible ache in the motion. Wilson grunted as his belt came unfastened, and his belly flopped out a little as the catch released. He left it on the ground by his gun. Harris glared at me, but he lowered his gun, too.

"Now, step back. All of you."

"Yes," Denton said. "Harris, Wilson. Step back to the trees and bring out what we left there."

"Hey," I said. "What the hell are you talking about? Don't move, any of you." Harris and Wilson smirked at me, and began walking toward the trees. "Get your asses back here."

"Shoot at them, Mr. Dresden," Denton said, "and you will have to take your gun off me. I think I can reach it, if you do that, and turn this into a fight. You are resourceful, and intelligent, but you are also wounded. I don't think you could overcome me in hand to hand."

I glanced between the two men and Denton. "Dammit," I said. "What are you up to, Denton? You try anything funny, anything at all, and you're not going to live to regret it."

"I'm with the FBI. I don't do anything that could be construed as funny, Mr. Dresden."

I swore quietly, and could all but feel Denton's mouth stretch into a smile. "Why?" I asked him. "Why did you get involved with these belts? Why are you doing this?"

Denton began to shrug, but evidently thought better of it. "Too many years of seeing men like Marcone laugh at the law. Of seeing people hurt by him, death, misery brought on by him and people like him. I was tired of just watching. I decided to stop him. And men like him."

"By killing them," I said.

"I was given the power. I used it."

"What gives you the right to mandate their deaths?"

"What gives them the right," Denton asked, "to kill? Should I stand by and let them slaughter, Dresden, if I can stop it? I have the power, and the responsibility to use it."

I felt a little shiver run through me, as the words struck close to home. "And the other people? The innocents who have died?"

Denton hesitated. His reply was quiet. "It was unfortunate. An accident. It was never my intention."

"The belts do more than make you fuzzy, Denton. They change the way you think. The way you act."

"I can control my people," Denton began.

"Like you did last month?" I asked.

He swallowed, and said nothing.

"And you knew, didn't you? You knew that I'd find out. That's why you sent me to the Full Moon Garage."

The vein on his forehead pulsed. "After the deaths, I was warned about a governing body. A sort of magic police. The White Council. That you worked for them."

I almost laughed. "Yeah, well someone told you part of the story, anyway, Denton. That's why you messed up MacFinn's circle, isn't it? You needed a patsy and you turned MacFinn loose knowing that the Council would suspect him. The Streetwolves for the cops, and MacFinn for the Council."

Denton snarled. "Necessary sacrifices. There was work to be done, Dresden."

"Oh yeah? As one of the aforementioned sacrifices, I don't find myself agreeing with you," I said. "To hell with the law, right? That's what you're saying—that you're above the law. Like Marcone."

Denton grew tense again and turned his head a bit toward me. Like he might have been listening.

I pressed him, hard, desperate to reach him. If I could, I might get out of this situation after all. "These belts, man, the power they've given you. It's *bad*. You can't handle it. It's gotten into your head and you aren't thinking straight. Give them up. You can still walk away from all of this, do the right thing. Come on, Denton. Don't throw away everything you fought for all those years. There's a better way than this."

Denton was silent for a long time. Harris and Wilson disappeared into the thick ring of pine trees. Benn watched us, her eyes bright, her body muscled and firm in the moonlight, her breasts rather pretty and distracting as she breathed. She looked from the pair of us to the fur belt on the ground, alternately, and her breaths became ragged. "Look at her," I said. "Those belts are like a drug. Is this the kind of person she was? Is this the kind of person you want to be? Wilson, Harris, were they always like they are now? You're turning into monsters, man. You've got to get out of this. Before you're all the way gone."

Denton closed his eyes. Then shook his head once. "You're a decent man, Mr. Dresden. But you've got no idea of how the world works. I'm sorry you've gotten in the way." He opened his eyes again. "Necessary sacrifices."

"Dammit," I said. "Don't you see that this won't do you any good? Even if you do get away with wiping out everyone here tonight, Murphy is going to piece together what happened."

Denton glanced at me and said, like a mantra, "Necessary sacrifices."

I swallowed, suddenly more cold than I had been. It was eerie, the way Denton said the words—so matter-of-fact, calm, rational. There was no doubt in him, when he should have been afraid. Only fools and madmen know that kind of certainty. And I had already noted that Denton was no fool.

Harris and Wilson emerged from the trees, carrying something between them. Someone, hooded, arms and legs bound.

Harris had a knife in one hand, and it was against the base of the hood, which looked to be a pillowcase. His big ears and freckles were at sharp odds with the arrogant competence with which he held the knife.

"Damn you," I said quietly. Denton said nothing. Benn's eyes glittered in the moonlight, bright and vacant of anything but lust and hunger.

The two agents brought the prisoner over, and Wilson dropped the legs. Harris kept the knife steady, while the overweight man went to remove the hood, but I had already seen the cast on the prisoner's arm.

Murphy's face was pale, her golden hair bleached to silver by the moonlight, and falling down around her eyes. Her mouth was covered in cloth or duct tape, one of the two, and there was blood clotted at the base of one nostril, a bruise purpling over one eye. She blinked for a moment, and then kicked at Wilson. With her legs bound, it was ineffective, and when Harris snarled and pressed the knife against her throat, she stopped struggling. Her blue eyes glared in fury at Harris and then Wilson. And then they settled on me and widened.

"Kill me, Mr. Dresden," Denton said quietly, "and Harris will cut the Lieutenant's throat. Benn will go for her gun, as will Wilson. Likely, they will kill you. And then they will kill these wolves you brought with you, your allies. But even if you get all of us first, Murphy will be dead, and you will be holding the weapon that killed four agents of the FBI."

"You bastard," I said. "You cold-blooded bastard."

"Necessary sacrifices, Mr. Dresden," Denton said, but it wasn't a calm phrase anymore. It was eager, somehow, warmth curving around and through the words like a lover's hands. "Drop your gun."

"No," I said. "I won't." He wouldn't kill another cop. Would he?

"Then Murphy dies," Denton said. "Harris."

The redhead's shoulders bunched, and Murphy tried to

scream, through the gag. I cried out and swung the barrel of the gun toward Harris.

Denton's elbow came back into my gut and then his fist snapped up into my nose, casting a field of stars across my vision. The gun went off, pointed somewhere, but then Denton slapped it from my hand and drove another blow into my throat that sent me sprawling to the ground, unable to breathe or to move.

Denton stooped to recover the gun and said, "You should have shot me while you had the chance, Mr. Dresden, instead of moralizing." He pointed it at me, and I watched his lips curve into a slow, hungry smile. "Beautiful moon tonight," he said. "Sort of reminds me of a story. How did it go . . . ?"

I tried to tell him where he could stick the moon and his story, but it came out a strangled gasp. I still couldn't move. It hurt too much.

Denton thumbed back the trigger, sighted down the barrel at my left eye, and said, "Ah, yes. 'And I'll huff. And I'll puff. And I'll blow your house down.' Good-bye, wizard."

Death by nursery tale. Hell's bells.

Chapter
Thirty-one

The barrel of Denton's gun looked bigger and deeper than the national debt as it swung to bear on my face. His grey eyes glittered down the sights at me, and I saw the decision to pull the trigger flash across them. Before he could, I met his eyes hard, shoved myself out toward him with a sudden screaming pain in my temples, and locked him into a soulgaze.

There was a rushing sensation, as there usually was, a feeling of movement forward and then down, like being sucked into a whirlpool. I rode the sensation into Denton's head, a brief doubt crossing my mind. Maybe getting shot would have been better than wading heart deep into Denton's soul.

I can't describe what I found there very well. Try to imagine a place, a beautifully ordered structure, like the Parthenon or Monticello. Imagine that everything is balanced, everything is in proportion, everything is smooth and secure. Stick in blue skies overhead, green grass all around, puffy white clouds, flowers, and children running and playing.

Now, add a couple hundred years of wear and tear to it. Dull the edges. Round the corners a little. Imagine water stains, and worn spots where the wind has gotten to it. Turn the skies dirty brown with smog. Kill the grass, and replace it with tall, ugly ragweed. Ditch the flowers, and leave in their places only dried up, skeletal rose vines. Age the male children into adult winos, faces haggard with despair and self-loathing and flushed with drink, and the girls into tired, jaded strumpets, faces hard, eyes cold and calculating. Give the place of beauty an aura of rage and feral abandon, where the people who walk about watch the shadows like hungry cats, waiting to pounce.

And then, after all of that, after all the cares and trials and difficulties of the world a cop inhabits have been fairly represented, coat everything in a thick, sticky black sludge that smells like swamps and things that attract dun-colored flies. Paint it on, make it a coating that emphasizes the filth, the decay, the despair all around, that brings out that painful decline to the utmost degree. The sludge makes things stronger, and more bitter, more rotten, more putrid all at the same time.

That was Denton, inside. A good man, jaded by years and poisoned by the power that had taken control of him, until that good man had been buried and only the filth and decay remained. Until the existence of the man who had once been was only a bitter reminder that made the man who was now seem all the more downfallen by comparison.

I understood Denton's pain and his rage, and I understood how the dark power he'd taken had pushed him over the edge. There was an image of him kneeling at someone's feet as a wolf-fur belt was passed into his hands, and then it was gone. Knowing the man he had once been made clear to me the beast he had become, all violence and hunger and craving.

I felt tears on my cheeks, and violent shudders shaking down my spine. I could pity Denton, and the others with him, but now, more than ever, they scared the crap out of me. I had bought myself a few seconds, at least, with the soulgaze—but would it be enough to keep Denton from blowing my head off?

Denton stared at me as the soulgaze broke and we were released. He wasn't reacting well to whatever it was he had seen inside of me. His face had gone white, and his hand was trembling, the barrel of the gun wavering every which way. He lifted his other hand to mop beads of cold sweat away from his face.

"No," Denton said, white showing all around the grey irises of his eyes. "No, wizard." He raised his gun. "I don't believe in hell. I won't let you." He screamed then, at the top of his lungs. "I won't let you!" I tensed up, preparing for a futile attempt to throw myself out of the way of a speeding bullet.

"Yes," said a calm voice. "You will." A bright red dot appeared right on the middle of Denton's chest, cheerful as a Christmas light. I twisted my head around to see Marcone walking over the turf, his weapon pointed steadily at Denton, Hendricks looming to one side. Denton's lackeys were watching Marcone with bright, steady eyes. Murphy lay on the grass, her feet toward me, her head away. I couldn't see what condition she was in, and both fear and frustration leapt up into me, for her sake.

"Marcone," Denton said. His back straightened and his eyes narrowed. "You treacherous scum."

Marcone clucked with his teeth. "Our bargain was that you would bring him to me alive. Not execute him. Additionally, you may want to rethink the wisdom of using your own weapons. Let MacFinn kill him when he arrives."

"If he arrives," Denton snarled.

"My spotters," Marcone said, "tell me that the animals I sent out with them went mad with fear about two minutes ago, three miles west of here. I think it will not take him much longer to show up, Mr. Denton." His smile widened, but his money-colored eyes grew harder. "Now. Shall we cease antagonizing one another and finish our business?" Marcone lowered the rifle and flicked the laser sight off.

Denton looked from me to Marcone, and I saw the blackness rise up in his eyes, gather behind them, and get ready to come rolling out. "Marcone," I said. "Just shoot him now."

"I think we've both had enough of your attempts to divide and conquer, Mr. Dresden," Marcone said, his voice bored. "You're beaten. Acknowledge it with grace."

I watched a slow smile spread over Denton's face as he kept the gun pointed at my head. My voice rose by a couple notes of alarm. "I mean it, John. I really do, I shit you not. This entire thing is about them killing you."

"What a vulgar reassurance," Marcone said. "Agent Denton, we have a few details to attend to. Lower your gun and let us be about them."

"I don't think so," Denton said. And he pointed the gun at Hendricks and started pulling the trigger. The gun roared so many times, so quickly, that I couldn't tell how often Denton fired.

Hendricks snapped back onto his heels and was driven flat onto his back by the force of the bullets slamming into him. He didn't have time to twitch, much less scream, and he dropped like a felled tree. I felt it in the earth when his massive body hit the ground.

Marcone started to raise his gun, but Wilson and Harris hurtled at his back and dragged him to the ground, pounding on him with their fists. Marcone writhed like an eel and slipped away from them, but Denton stepped into his path and thrust the gun into Marcone's face.

"That's enough," he said, his voice gone hoarse. "Get them all and take them to the pit. MacFinn will be here any moment."

I took the moment to roll to my hands and knees and attempt to slip away unnoticed, but was brought up short by a pair of bare, muscular, feminine legs. My gaze followed the legs up, past the skirt, to a magnificently bare-breasted torso encircled by a wolf-pelt belt, and then to a face dominated by eyes made eerie by the lack of anything recognizably sentient in them. Benn smiled at me, set her foot against my wounded shoulder, and with a sadistic twist of her ankle and a shove of her muscled leg, sent searing pain screaming through my body, making me crumple to the ground in agony.

I remember them dragging me across the grounds. We passed into the ring of evergreens, and I remember thinking that any sounds originating in that circle of pines would be heavily muffled by their branches and needles, further muffled by the trees surrounding the property, as well as the high stone wall. Gunshots, for example, might not even be heard at all, off the property. It was the clearest thought I had while my shoulder exploded.

The next thing I remember was being shoved roughly forward. I fell, straight and hard in the dispassionate grip of gravity, and after long enough for me to start to suck in a breath, I hit water. It was only about six or eight inches deep, and beneath it was swirling, soft mud. I had a brief pang for my leather duster and then I sank down into the water, my hands slipping into the mud and getting stuck there. Cold water burbled around my face, and felt nice, for a moment, on my aching shoulder.

Someone grabbed me by the collar and hauled me out of the water, to sit on my butt. Hands steadied me, and I sat with my shoulder aching and my head whirling until I could squint up at who was there.

Murphy dropped to one knee in the water beside me and smoothed back my damp hair. "Dresden," she said. "You okay?"

I took a look around me. I was at the bottom of an enormous pit, a square maybe twenty feet deep and twice that across. Muddy water, maybe from the rain, covered the bottom of the pit, and the moon tinted its surface silvery brown. Directly above the pit's center, maybe forty feet above me, was a square made of wooden planks, maybe five by five. It was a hunter's platform, suspended by ropes leading from the circle of evergreens that surrounded the pit. I could see the tops of the trees against the moon and the clouds.

"Dresden," Murphy said again. "Are you all right?"

"I'm alive," I said. I blinked at her for a second and then said, "I thought they killed you."

Her blue eyes sparkled briefly. Her hair was a mess, and her jeans and flannel shirt were rumpled and soaked with muddy water. She was shivering from the cold. "I thought they had, too. But they stopped as soon as Denton took you out, and tossed me down here. I can't figure why they didn't do the deed themselves, instead of leaving it to MacFinn."

I grimaced. "Trying to cover their tracks from the White Council," I said. "Denton wants MacFinn to take the fall for all the deaths. I think he's lost it."

"I always wind up in the nicest places when I hang with you, Dresden."

"You were tied up," I said. "How'd you get loose?"

"She had help," someone said in a slurred, heavy voice. "For all the good it will do her." I turned my head to see a naked and dirty Tera West, sitting with her back against another wall of mud. There were five soggy, motionless forms lying around her, the Alphas in their wolf-shapes. Tera held their heads upon her lap, up out of the water. She looked bedraggled and anguished, touching each of them in turn, very gently. Her amber eyes were dull.

"I don't get it," I said. "Why did they stick us down here? Marcone just keeps a pit trap dug in his yard?"

"He was planning on trapping MacFinn down here until morning," Tera said. "When he would be vulnerable."

"Whoa, whoa," Murphy said, face pensive. "You're saying Denton was responsible for the deaths? All of them?"

"One way or another. Yeah." I gave Murphy the rundown on Denton. The way he'd gotten the belts for him and his people, lost control of the power they'd given him, and set up the Streetwolves and then MacFinn to take the blame.

Murphy broke out into acidic swearing. "That was the angle I was missing. Dammit. No wonder Denton was so hot to keep you off of the case and out of the way, and why he wanted to find you so bad after the scene at MacFinn's place. That's how he kept showing up everywhere so fast, too—he already knew that someone was dead."

There were shouts from above, and we looked up to see Marcone swing out from the edge of the pit. He hung limply from a rope. His eyes were closed. I watched as he was drawn up in a series of short jerks until his bowed head bumped the bottom of the hunter's platform above and then was left there.

"What the hell?" Murphy said, her voice soft.

"Bait," I replied. I closed my eyes for a moment. "Denton's stringing him up as bait for MacFinn. The loup-garou comes in, jumps up to get Marcone, then Denton cuts the rope and drops MacFinn down in here."

"With us," Murphy said quietly. I felt her shivers grow a little more severe. "They're going to drop that thing into this pit with us. Oh, God, Harry."

"Denton or one of his people must have gotten some silver bullets made," I said. "They'll just let MacFinn slaughter us, then shoot him from up there." I squinted up at the edge of the pit. "Pretty good plan."

"What can we do?" Murphy asked. She hugged herself, hard.

I shook my head. "I don't know."

"Nothing," Tera said quietly. Murphy and I turned to look at her. One of the Alphas was stirring, Billy maybe, and wobbled and fell when he tried to sit up. But at least he could hold his head up out of the water. "Nothing," she repeated. "We are beaten."

I closed my eyes and tried to order my thoughts, to push the pain and fatigue back down and put together some sort of plan. Murphy settled beside me, a shivering spot against my side. The cast on her arm pressed against my ribs. I opened my coat, more a polite gesture than anything else, given that it, too, was soaked, and slipped the edge of it around her shoulders with my arm. Her back stiffened and she flashed me a look of indignation, but after a second just pressed as far under the coat as she could.

After a moment, she spoke. Her voice came out quiet, uncertain—a far cry from her normal, brisk tones. "I've done some thinking, Dresden. I've decided that there's a reasonable chance you aren't involved with the killings."

I smiled a little. "That's real big of you, Murph. Doesn't what Denton did to you sort of prove I'm not involved?"

She half smiled and shook her head. "No, Harry. It just

means that he wants to kill you and me both. It doesn't mean that I trust everything you're saying."

"He wants me dead, Murph. That should mean something in my favor, shouldn't it?"

"Not really," she said, and squinted up at the top of the pit. "From what I can tell, Denton wants pretty much everybody dead. And you could still be lying to me."

"I'm not, Murph," I said, my voice soft. "Cross my heart."

"I can't just take your word on it, Harry," she whispered. "There are too many people dead. My men. My people. Civilians, the ones I'm supposed to protect. The only way to be sure is to take you all, everyone involved, and sort things out with you behind bars."

"No," I said. "There's more to it than what you can prove, Murph, more than what's going to stand up in court. Come on. You and me, we've known each other for years. You should be able to trust me by now, right?"

"I should be able to," Murphy agreed. "But after what I've seen, all the blood and death . . ." She shook her head. "No, Harry. I can't trust anyone anymore." She half smiled and said, "I still like you, Dresden. But I can't trust you."

I tried to match her smile, but my feelings were in too much turmoil. Pain, mostly. Physical pain, and a deeper heart hurt, both for Murphy's sake and for the sake of our friendship. She was so alone. I wanted to go to the rescue, somehow, to make her hurting go away.

She'd have spit in my face if I'd tried. Murphy wasn't the sort of person who wanted to be rescued, from anything. That she accepted as much comfort as my wet coat offered her came as a surprise to me.

I looked around the pit again intently. The other Alphas were recovering, enough to sit up, but apparently not enough to move. Tera just sat with her back against the wall, defeated and exhausted. Marcone swung from the platform high above me, not moving, though I thought I might have heard a moan from him at one point. I felt a pang of sympathy for him. However much of a heartless bastard he might be, no one deserved to dangle like bait from a hook.

The Alphas, Tera, Marcone, Murphy. They were all where they were because of me. It was my fault we were there, my doing that we were all about to die. Carmichael, the poor jerk, was dead, also because of me. So were other good cops. So was Hendricks.

I had to do something about it.

"I need to get out of here," I told Murphy. "Get me out of here, and maybe I can do something."

Murphy turned her head toward me. "You mean . . . ?" She waved the fingers of her unbroken arm in a vaguely mystic gesture.

I nodded. I still had my ace in the hole. "Something like that."

"Right. So how do we get you out of here?"

"You going to trust me, Murph?"

Her jaw clenched. "It doesn't look as though I have much choice, does it?"

I smiled back at her, and rose to my feet, sloshing around in the water. "Maybe we could dig into the walls a bit. Make climbing holes."

"You'll probably get shot once you get to the top," Murphy said.

"No," I said, "I don't think they'll want to hang around the pit with MacFinn coming. They're bloodthirsty, but not stupid."

"So," Murphy said. "All we need to do is get you up to the top of the pit, and then you're going to go one-on-four with a bunch of armed FBI agents-cum-werewolves and beat them in time to go up against the loup-garou that we couldn't stop before with all of your magical gizmos and a building full of police officers."

"Essentially," I answered.

Murphy looked up at me and then shrugged and let out a short, defiant laugh. She stood up too, flicked her hair back from her eyes with a toss of her head, and said, "I guess it could be worse."

There was a soft sound from above and behind me. Murphy froze, staring upward, her eyes becoming almost impossibly wide.

I turned my head very slowly.

The loup-garou crouched up at the lip of the pit, huge and gnarled and muscled and deadly. Its foaming jaws were open, showing the rows of killing teeth. Its eyes gleamed with scarlet flames in the moonlight, and they were fastened on the dangling figure of Gentleman Johnny Marcone. I quivered, and the motion made a slight sound against the water. The beast turned its head down, and when it saw me its eyes narrowed to glowing slits, and it let out a harsh, low growl. Its claws dug into the earth at the edges of the pit, tearing through it like sand.

It remembered me.

My heart started ripping a staccato rhythm in my chest. That same raw, sharp, primitive fear I'd felt before, the fear of simply being jumped on and *eaten*, returned in full force and for a moment swept away all thoughts and plans.

"You had to say that," I said to Murphy, my voice wan and pale. "Happy? It's worse."

Chapter
Thirty-two

"**O**kay," I said, fear making my voice weak. "This is bad. This is very, very bad."

"Wish I had my pistol," Murphy said, her tone resolute. "I wish we'd had some more time to talk things out, Harry."

I glanced over at Tera. One of the Alphas, the mouse-haired girl in her wolf-shape, was leaning against her and whimpering. "Close your eyes," Tera said softly and covered the little wolf's eyes with her hand. Her amber eyes met mine, without hope, without any sparkle of life.

They were going to die because of me. Dammit all, it wasn't fair. I hadn't done anything grossly stupid. It wasn't fair to have come so far, sacrificed so much, and to buy it down here in the mud, like some kind of burrowing bug. I searched the pit again desperately, but it was a fiendishly simple and complete trap. There were no options down here.

My eyes went up. Straight up.

"Marcone!" I shouted. "John Marcone! Can you hear me?"

The limp figure suspended above me stirred weakly. "What do you want, Mr. Dresden?"

"Can you move?" I asked. The loup-garou growled, low, and started pacing a circuit of the pit, glowing eyes flashing between us down at the bottom and Marcone, trying to decide who to rip apart first.

"An arm," Marcone confirmed a few seconds later.

"Do you still keep that knife on you? The one I saw at the garage?"

"Denton and his associates searched me and found it, I am afraid," came Marcone's voice.

"Dammit all. You're a miserable, stupid bastard for making a deal with Denton, Marcone. Now do you believe he wanted to kill you all along?"

The figure above me wiggled and writhed, swinging from the ropes that held him trussed up there. "Yes, do tell me that you told me so with your last breath, Mr. Dresden. I was already rather acutely aware of that," Marcone said, his voice dry. "But perhaps I'll yet have a chance to make amends."

"What are you doing?" I asked. I kept my eyes on the loup-garou, as it circled the pit, and kept myself opposite the creature, where I could see it.

"Reaching for the knife they *didn't* find," Marcone replied. He grunted, and then I saw a flicker of light on something shiny up above me.

"Forget it," Murphy said quietly, stepping close to my side as she watched Marcone. "He's just going to cut himself loose and leave us to rot here."

"We won't get the chance to rot," I pointed out. But I thought she was right.

Marcone started to spin slowly on his rope, wriggling around until his whole body was rotating on the end of it. He began to speak, his voice calm. "Ironic, isn't it? I'd planned to wait for the creature on the platform and tempt it into the pit. There are some nets ready to drop on it, after that. I would have held it until morning."

"You do know that it's right beneath you now, don't you, John?" I asked.

"Mr. Dresden," Marcone said crossly. "I've asked you not to call me that."

"Whatever," I said, but I had to admire the raw courage of the man to banter while dangling up there like a ripe peach.

"I use this place to conduct noisy business," Marcone said. "The trees muffle the sound, you see. You can barely hear even shotgun blasts on the other side of the wall." He continued to spin on the rope, slow and lazy, a shadow against the moon and the stars.

"Well. That's nice," I said, "and despicable." The loup-garou looked down at me and snarled, and I took an involuntary step back from it. The mud wall of the pit stopped me.

"Oh, quite," Marcone agreed. "But necessary."

"Is there *anything* you're not shameless about, Marcone?" I asked.

"Of course. But you don't think I'm going to tell you, do you? Now, be quiet if you please. I don't need the distraction." And then I saw Marcone's arm curl in and straighten outward. There was a flutter of metallic motion in the air, and a snapping sound from the base of one of the ropes that held the platform suspended, at its far end where it was secured to one of the pine trees.

The rope abruptly sagged, and the platform—and Marcone with it—swayed drunkenly. Marcone grunted, and bounced against his ropes a few times, making the whole affair of ropes lurch about—and then the damaged line snapped and came entirely free. It whipped out toward Marcone, lost momentum, and then fell through the evening air.

Straight down into the pit in front of me. One end was still attached to the platform above, now off center from the pit and listing to one side.

I blinked at it for a moment, and Murphy said, "Holy shit. He did it."

"I don't recommend waiting about, Mr. Dresden," Marcone said. I saw him twist his head to look at the loup-garou, and tense up as the beast trotted around the edge of the pit to the side closest to him. If it had noticed the rope that had fallen down from above, it gave no sign.

Hope lurched in my cnest like sudden thunder. I grabbed on to the rope with both hands and started shinnying up it like a monkey, pushing with my legs and using mostly my good arm to hang on with while I lifted my legs up higher for another grip.

I got up to even with the lip of the pit and started rocking the rope back and forth, getting a swinging momentum going so that I could leap off the rope and to the ground outside the pit. The ropes above creaked dangerously as I did, and Marcone swayed back and forth, still spinning about gently.

"Dresden," he shouted. "Look out!"

I had been intent on my escape, and given the loup-garou no thought. I turned my head around to see it flying through the air toward me. I could see its gleaming eyes and felt sure that I could have counted its teeth if I had waited around for it. I didn't. I let out a yelp and let go of the rope, dropping several feet straight down before clamping on to it again. The loup-garou sailed past me overhead like some huge, obscenely graceful bat, and landed on the far side of the pit with barely a sound.

My fingers felt weak, I was so shocked and terrified, but I started hauling my way up again, swinging desperately as I went. The loup-garou turned and focused its eyes on me again, but Marcone let out a sharp whistle, and the thing turned toward him, pricking its misshapen ears forward in a weirdly doggy mannerism, before it snarled and leapt upward. I bounced on the rope, and Marcone bobbed down and then back up again. The loup-garou missed him by bare inches, I think, but I didn't hang around to watch. I let out a yell and threw myself at the edge of the pit as the rope reached the apex of its swing.

I missed, my belly hitting the lip of the pit, but I started clawing at the earth and kept myself from falling. I strained and kicked, thrashing and whimpering in desperation, and managed to gain a few inches, slowly worming my way up onto the ground, until I got my feet underneath me. The loup-garou, on the far side of the pit, turned toward me and let out a sound that can best be described as a furious roar. Shouts erupted from elsewhere in the estate—Denton and his lackeys must have been watching the pit, I thought, but they were the second scariest bad guys on the field at the moment. I had bigger things on my mind.

Said thing threw itself at me, and I had a few seconds to start running, trying to arrange things so that the pit would be between me and it when it landed. I was only partly successful. The loup-garou tore up the earth where I had been standing when it came down, and turned toward me again, facing me across a scant ten feet of space, from one side of the square pit to the side adjacent to it.

The rope started bobbing again, and then with a motion full of grace and power, Tera swung up out of the pit and landed in a crouch on the ground beside me.

"Go, wizard," she snarled. "Denton and the others will kill us all if they are not stopped. I will handle MacFinn."

"No way," I said. "You can't possibly take him on."

"I know him," she responded. And then there was, in her place, the huge she-wolf, dark fur peppered with grey. She snarled and bounded at the loup-garou and it reared up like a cat about to take a mouse, plunging toward her with abrupt speed.

And that's when I saw the difference between Tera and the Alphas, Tera and Denton's *Hexenwulfen*, even Tera and the loup-garou. Where they were fast, Tera was fast *and* graceful. Where they were quick, Tera was quick *and* elegant. She made them look like amateurs. She was something more primal, more in tune with the wild than they would ever be.

As the loup-garou threw itself at her, she slipped to one side like wind, threw her shoulder beneath the beast's planted fore-paw, and shouldered it off-balance, making it stumble. It recovered and spun toward her, but she was already gone, farther away from the pit, growling defiance at the supernatural creature. It followed, impervious and snarling with rage.

I heard a gunshot, and a bullet smacked into one of the trees behind me. Benn's voice repeated a low, frantic chant, and then I heard her words turn into an animal's snarls. Denton and the others were coming. It was time to play the last option I had, the one I hadn't wanted to be forced to use. I wasn't sure what would happen if I did, but there wasn't much choice.

I slipped my hand beneath my shirt and touched the wolf belt I'd taken from Agent Harris in the alley behind the Full Moon Garage.

It was vibrating beneath my fingers, warm to the touch, alive in its own fashion, and full of the power and strength that had been channeled into it. I closed my eyes and let that dark, wild power spill into me, mingle with all the fear and pain and weariness inside of me. It was easy. It was easier than any magic I'd ever done, leaping into me with a sort of hungry eagerness, seeping into me, making pain and fatigue and fear vanish and replacing it with nothing but strength, ferocity.

Power.

"Lupus," I whispered. *"Lupus, lupara, luperoso."*

It took no more of a chant than that for the change to take me. It wasn't something that I noticed, really. But when I opened my eyes again, things were simply as they should be, *right* in a way so fundamentally profound that I wondered why I had never noticed its lack before.

My vision was sharp and clear enough to count the hairs on the head of the she-wolf orienting on me a few feet away. I could hear the pounding of her heart, the restless motion of the wind, the heavy breaths of the other agents in the trees, moving toward me like great, clumsy cows. If the sun had suddenly risen into the sky, I could not have seen any more clearly than I did, all in glorious shades of blue and green and maroon and purple, as though God had dipped his brush into a late summer twilight and replaced all the darkness with those colors.

I dropped open my mouth in a silent laugh and felt my tongue glide over the gleaming, sharp tips of my fangs. What a beautiful night. I could smell blood on the air, hear the eagerness of my enemies to kill, and I felt that same hunger rising from my own heart and surging through me. It was perfect.

Benn came through the trees first, fast and powerful, but clumsy and impatient and stupid. I could smell her excitement, pitched to an almost sexual level. She was expecting an easy kill, a sudden rush over one of the slow, graceless two-legs and then the hot, spurting blood, the frenzied writhing. I did not oblige her. As she came through the trees, I leapt forward and was at her throat before she even realized I was there. A quick rip, hot blood, and she yelped in agony and fear, throwing herself to one side.

Stupid bitch. I'd missed the heart's blood, but she was badly hurt. Two snaps severed her hamstrings as she tried to flee and left her writhing on the ground, helpless and terrified. I felt my body thrill with abrupt and vicious excitement. The bitch was mine now. She would live or die as I wished.

The surge of power and elation that flew through me at that realization could have carried me off the earth and to the silver glory of the moon and stars themselves. To the victor go the spoils. Her blood, her life, was mine to take and that was exactly how it *should* be. I stalked forward to finish her, as was only proper.

There was a puff of breath, and then Wilson, in his wolf-form, came hurtling from the woods. I slipped aside easily as he rushed by. The wounded Benn snarled and snapped blindly at him. Wilson turned on her, his fury out of control, and latched his jaws onto her throat. Blood was a black, rich, heady smell in the moonlight, and I swayed, drunk on the aroma of it. My mouth watered, jaws growing damp with saliva, as I smelled the bitch's blood, and I wanted to fling myself at her, tear her apart myself as she went screaming to her death.

"Those wolves!" screamed Harris. "They got out! They got Benn!" He came plunging out of the trees, gun at the ready, his nearly useless eyes wide and staring and panicked. He started shooting at Wilson, who released the dead Benn's throat. The first bullet smashed his left front paw to pulp. The second and third slugs hammered into his chest, and Wilson-wolf staggered to one side, yelping in sudden agony. He twisted and strained as he went down, paws scrabbling at his own stomach, until there was abruptly a balding, overweight man lying on the earth beside the dead wolf, his jacket open, his shirt unbuttoned to show the unfastened wolf belt. There was blood all over Wilson, bubbling out of his mouth.

"Holy . . ." Harris breathed, pacing closer, his gun held up, until he could see what he had done. "George? Oh, God. Oh, God, I thought you were one of them. What the hell . . ."

Agent Wilson didn't answer the redheaded kid. He simply drew his gun from his jacket and started shooting.

In their human forms, they couldn't see each other very well in the dark, I thought. They both started shooting at the muzzle flashes. More blood flooded the air, along with the sharp, acrid smell of burning gunpowder. Both men went down, bleeding out onto the earth, and I felt my jaws open in another smile, on another sense of warm satisfaction. Idiots. Who did they think they were dealing with here? They'd been making my life miserable, and the lives of others, and now they had gotten their just deserts. It would have been better had I torn out their throats myself, admittedly.

But then, I thought, there was still Denton to deal with.

That thought cheering me, I turned and made my way into the woods, hunting the last of them. My heart was pounding hard, and relaxed and steady with excitement as I melded in with the night and searched for prey.

Denton and I met as I emerged from the circle of trees. He stood in the moonlight, in the right shape, the only real shape, the moon streaking his brown coat shades paler and making his eyes glow. He was powerfully built, as in his two-leg shape, and looked quick and strong. His eyes burned with the lust of the moon, the night, with blood need and raging, wild strength, just as mine did. We faced one another and there was a mad sort of joy in it. I would have giggled if I could have.

A snarl bubbled up out of my chest like music, and I launched myself at him. We met in a tangle of scratching claws, snapping teeth, dark fur. He was the stronger, I the quicker. The fight was silent, with no breath wasted. It was a duel between us; our fangs were our swords, thick fur ruffs used as shield and armor.

I tasted his blood in my mouth from a slash to an ear and it hit me like a drug, sent a fury and power coursing through me like I had never known. I threw myself at him again, and an instant later was rewarded for my overeagerness with a hot pain on my foreleg. Scarlet-black blood stained Denton's fangs in the moonlight.

We separated and stalked one another in a slow circle, looking for weakness, our eyes never leaving one another. I laughed at him silently, and he answered me in much the same way. I understood him, then, and rejoiced with him in the power he had found. In that moment, I loved the man, felt him a brother, and longed to hold his throat in my jaws as the last of his blood flowed out of him. It was the most ancient of struggles, the deepest of conflicts: survival of the fittest. One of us would live to run again, to hunt, to kill, to taste the hot blood. And the other would be dead and cold on the grass.

It was *good*.

We came together again like partners in a dance, moving over the grass together. Dimly, of course, I was aware of Tera dancing with the loup-garou, but that didn't matter to me, really. They were far away, dozens of yards, and I took no notice of them. My joy was *here*.

We danced under the moon—and he made the first misstep. I threw myself into the opening he'd left me, knocked him to the ground with my shoulder, and as he rolled and twisted away, I took his back leg, right across the big tendon. He screamed his fury, but I heard the fear in it, too. He scrambled to his three good paws again and turned to face me, but there was terrible knowledge in his eyes, just as there was in mine. We both knew that it was all over but the bleeding.

I shuddered. Yes. The bleeding.

He could still face me, could still hurt me if I were foolish—but I wasn't. I began to wear him down, pressing him with short rushes and quick withdrawals that forced him to shift his weight awkwardly, stumble on his three working limbs, to wear him out. As his reactions became slower, I tested him with a few flashing passes of fangs. Once more, I tasted his blood.

I gave him a dozen small wounds and each taste of him made my frenzy all the more satisfying. The night, the dance, the violence, the blood—all of it was overwhelming, more than any power I had ever felt, any medicine I'd ever tasted, even in my dreams or in the wild realms of the Nevernever. It was pure beauty, pure pleasure, pure power. Victory was mine.

I grew contemptuous of him as he began to whimper, to seek escape. The fool. He should never have tested himself against me. Should never have tried his strength against mine. Had he yielded to me at once, I would have been content to lead him, to accept him as a follower, and taken him with me on the hunts. It was sad, in a way. But then, I could always find others. It would not be difficult to make the belts, I thought. To give them to a few people to try. Once they had, they'd never take them off again.

I stalked Denton as he faltered, and I thought of running with Susan, of filling our mouths with hot, sweet blood, of taking her in the ecstasy of the night and the kill and it made me shake with anticipation. I threw myself at Denton, knocked him over, and went for his throat. The fool scrambled and took his belt off, melting into the ugly two-leg form, his suit covered in blood.

"Please," he croaked. "Oh, God. Please. Don't kill me. Don't *kill* me."

I snarled in answer, and let my fangs tighten on his neck. I could feel his pulse against my tongue. Don't kill him. That he would beg at all was contemptuous. He should have known the law of the jungle before he started trying to rule it. Who did he think he was dealing with? Someone who would give him mercy, let him survive, crippled and pathetic, and feed him when he whined again? I wanted to laugh.

My jaws tightened on his throat. I wanted to feel him *die*. Something told me that everything else I'd experienced since I discovered my true self was child's candy next to the passing of a life beneath me. I shook with eagerness. Denton continued to beg, and it made me hesitate. I snarled, annoyed. No. No weakness. No mercy. I wanted his blood. I wanted his life. He had tried me and failed. Kill him. Kill him and take my rightful place.

Who did he think I was?

"Harry?" whispered a terrified voice.

Without releasing his throat, I looked up. Susan stood there in the moonlight, slender and graceful for a two-legs. Her camera was in one hand, dangling forgotten at her side. Her eyes were wide with desire, and she smelled of perfume and our mating and of fear. Something pressed at my awareness, and though part of me wanted to ignore her, to rip and rend, I focused on Susan, on her expression.

On her eyes. They weren't wide with desire.

They were terrified.

She was terrified of me.

"My God," Susan said. "Harry." She fell to her knees, staring at me. At my eyes.

I felt Denton's pulse beneath my tongue. Felt his whimpers vibrate into my mouth. So easy. One simple motion, and I would never have doubts, fears, questions. Never again.

And, something inside of me said in a calm tone, *you'll never be Harry Dresden again*.

Power. I could feel the belt's power in me, its magic, its strength. I recognized it now. That dark surety, that heady and careless delight. I recognized why there were parts of me that loved it so much.

I released Denton's throat and backed away from him. I scrambled with my paws, my stomach twisting in sudden nausea, rebelling at the very idea of what I had been about to do. I sobbed and tore the belt from my waist, ripping my shirt in the process, feeling my body grow awkward and heavy and clumsy and pained again. Injuries that had been nothing to my tru— to the *wolf* form returned in vengeance to my human frailty. I threw the belt away from me, as far as it would go. I felt hot tears on my face, at the loss of that joy, that energy, that impervious strength.

"You bastard," I said to Denton. "Damn you. You poor bastard." He lay on his side now, whimpering from his injuries, bleeding from many wounds, one leg curled limp and useless beneath him. I crawled to him and took his belt away. Threw it after the other.

Susan rushed over to me, but I caught her before she could embrace me. "Don't touch me," I told her, and I meant it with every cell in me. "Don't touch me now."

Susan flinched away from me as though the words had burned her. "Harry," she whispered. "Oh, God, Harry. We've got to get you away from all of this."

From the far side of the ring of trees, there was another furious bellow. There was motion in the trees, and then Murphy, leading a stumbling, clumsy string of naked Alphas, came out of the woods toward me, staying low. She had a gun, probably taken from one of the bodies, in her good hand.

"All right," I said, as they approached, and turned a shoulder to Susan, pressing her away. I couldn't even look at her. "Murphy, you and Susan get these kids out of here, *now*."

"No," Murphy said. "I'm staying." Her eyes flickered to Denton, narrowed in a flash of anger, and then dismissed him again as quickly. She made no move to examine his injuries. Maybe she didn't care if he bled to death, either.

"You can't hurt MacFinn," I said.

"And you can?" she asked. She leaned closer and peered at me. "Christ, Dresden. You've got blood all over your mouth."

I snarled. "Take the kids and go, Karrin. I'm handling things here."

Murphy, for answer, slipped the safety off of the gun. "I'm the cop here," she said. "Not you. This is a bust in progress. I'm staying until the end." She smiled, tight. "When I can sort out who is a good guy and who isn't."

I spat out another curse. "I don't have time to argue this with you. Susan, get the kids back to the van."

"But Harry . . ." she began.

Fury rose to the top of the rampant emotions coursing through me. "I've got enough blood on my hands," I screamed. "Get these kids out of here, damn you."

Susan's dark-toned face went pale, and she turned to the nearest of the naked, wet, shivering Alphas, Georgia as it happened. She took the young woman's hand, had the others line up in drug-hazed confusion and join hands, and then led them away. I watched them go and felt the seething anger and sorrow and fear in me twist around in confusion.

From the far side of the woods, there was another bellow of rage, a shaking of one of the evergreens, and then a sharp, sudden yelp of purest anguish. Tera. The sound of the she-wolf's pain rose to a frantic gargling sound, and then went silent. Murphy and I stared at the trees. I thought I saw a flicker of red eyes somewhere behind them, and then it was gone.

"It's coming around," Murphy said. "It will circle around to get to us."

"Yeah," I said. The loup-garou's blood was up, after the infuriating chase after Tera. It would go after whatever it saw next. My mouth twisted bitterly. I had a unique insight to its point of view now.

"What do we do?" Murphy said. Her knuckles whitened on the gun.

"We go after it and try to hold it long enough for Susan and the kids to get away," I said. "What about Marcone?"

"What about him?"

"He saved our lives," I said. Murphy's expression said she wasn't happy with that idea. "We owe him."

"You want to get him out of there?"

"I don't want to leave anyone else to that thing," I said. "How about you?"

She closed her eyes and let out a breath. "All right," she said. "But God, this smells like you're trying to set me up, Dresden. If you get me killed, there's no one left who saw what happened here, is there?"

"If you want to be safe, go after Susan," I said bluntly. "We split up. One of us attracts its attention, maybe the other one will get through."

"Fine," Murphy snarled. "Fuck you, Harry Dresden."

Famous last words, I thought, but I didn't waste any breath on voicing it.

It was time to face the loup-garou.

Chapter
Thirty-three

I circled into the trees and stepped over Harris's corpse. The kid's face had been smashed in by two bullets, though the semiautomatic was still in his dead hand. Murphy must have had Wilson's gun. Wilson lay not far from Harris, also dead. Wounds to the chest, massive bleeding. Benn lay next to him, naked but for a business skirt soaked in blood. There was a line of greenish goo around her waist, probably the remains of the wolf belt. Its magic must have died when she did. I tried not to look at the mangled meat on the back of her thighs, or the tears near her jugular. I tried not to smell her blood, or to notice the dark surge of contemptuous pride that went through me, left-overs from my experience with my own wolf belt.

I shuddered and went past the bodies. The night was silent, but for wind, and the creaking of the ropes that supported the platform in the middle of the encircling evergreens. I could still see Marcone hog-tied up there. The position must have been excruciating—it isn't every day that you get crucified and hung up as dinner for a monster, and you can't really train your muscles for it. I couldn't see Marcone's expression, but I could almost feel his agony.

I waved a hand as he spun gently toward me, and he nodded his head, silent. I pointed at my eyes, and then around at the shadowed trees, trying to ask him if he knew where the loup-garou was, but he shook his head. Either he didn't understand me or he couldn't see it, and either way it didn't do me any good.

I grimaced and moved forward through the trees, skirting

the edge of the pit. I looked for the rope that had been used to haul Marcone up to his current position. It had to have been tied off somewhere low. I peered through the near dark, followed the strand of rope back down to the tree it was tied to, and headed over toward it.

Maybe I could get out of this. Maybe Murphy and I could escape with Marcone, join Susan and the others, and get out of here.

No. That was a happy fantasy. Even if I did get everyone out, I knew I couldn't live with myself if I let the loup-garou go loose tonight, on another killing spree. I had to try to stop it.

I was already going to have a hard enough time living with myself.

The rope supporting Marcone had been secured with a hasty knot, easily undone. I started working it, rubbernecking all around, listening, trying to locate the loup-garou. It wouldn't have just run off and left us here alive. Would it?

I took a turn around the tree with the rope to give me a little leverage, and then, very carefully because of my bum arm, started lowering Marcone. If I could get him low enough, I could have him swing over to me from the pit's center, catch him, balance him, and then go back and release the rope. It would have been easier if Murphy was there, but I hadn't seen her.

A nasty thought hit me. What if Murphy had run across the loup-garou and it had killed her silently? What if it was, even now, trying to get to me?

I secured the rope and moved back over to the pit. Marcone, no dummy, was already swinging back and forth as best he could, trying to get himself over to me. I went to the edge of the pit and crouched down, keeping my weight well away from the crumbling earth at the pit's lip.

Marcone let out a sudden startled hiss and said, "Dresden! The pit!"

I looked down and saw the loup-garou's eyes glowing, down in the darkness of the pit, only a heartbeat before they surged toward me with a howl of rage. It was coming *up* the wall of the pit, simply gouging its claws into the mud and hauling itself upward, toward me. I reeled back from the thing, threw out a hand and screamed, *"Fuego!"*

Nothing happened, except a little puff of steam, like a breath exhaled on a cold night, and sudden, blinding pain in my head. The loup-garou hurtled toward me, and I threw myself down to the earth, rolling away from its claws as it came up over the edge of the pit. It raked at me, caught the edge of my leather duster, and pinned it to the earth.

I liked the coat, but I didn't like it *that* much. I slipped out of it, as the loup-garou clawed with its rear legs, much as I had only moments before, and inched up out of the pit. I was already running by the time it got out, and I heard it snarl, get its bearings, and then come after me.

I was dead. I was so dead. I had gotten the kids out, and Susan, and I had stopped Denton and his cronies, but I was about to pay the price. I slipped through the trees and out onto the grass again, panting, cold now that my jacket was off. My shoulder ached from the running, from all the motion, and my foot hurt abominably as well. I couldn't run any longer— physically *couldn't*. My steps slowed, despite the commands of my brain, and I wept with frustration, weaving around just to keep on my feet.

I was at the end of my rope. It was over. I turned to face the trees, to watch the loup-garou coming. I wanted to see it coming, at least. If I was going to be killed, I wanted to face it on my feet, head on. Go down with a little dignity.

I saw its red eyes back among the trees. It came forward, slow, low to the ground, wary of some trick. I had stung it before, if not actually hurt it. It didn't want to fall victim to another such attack, I thought. It wanted to make absolutely sure that I was dead.

I drew in a breath and straightened my back. I lifted my chin, trying to prepare myself. If I was going to go down, I'd go down as a wizard should—proud and ready to face what was beyond. I could spill out my death curse, a potent working of magic, if I had time to speak it. Maybe I could counter MacFinn's curse with it, take the horrid transformation off of him that Saint Patrick had allegedly laid on him. Or maybe I could bring down Marcone's criminal empire with it.

I debated these things, as I drew out the silver pentacle amulet I had inherited from my mother, so that it would lie bright on my chest.

My mother's amulet.

Silver.

Amulet.

Inherited from my mother.

Inherited silver.

My eyes widened and my hands started to shake. A drowning man will reach for anything that floats. The idea floated—if only I could pull it off. If only my brainlessness hadn't kept me from realizing what I had until it was too late.

I took the silver pentacle off of my neck, breaking the chain in my haste. I caught the broken ends in my fist as I fastened my eyes on the loup-garou, and started to whirl the amulet in a circle above my head with my good arm. The amulet described a circle in the night air as I spun it, and I invested that circle with a tiny spark of will, a tiny bit of power. My head pounded. I felt the circle close around me, containing magical energies, focusing them.

I hurt. I was weary. I felt as though I had betrayed myself, given myself over to the darkness I'd tried so hard to resist by donning the evilly enchanted wolf belt—because let there be no mistaking, that *is* evil. Anything with that much power and that little control, that utter lack of concern for anything but self is evil in the most effective sense of the word. There was nothing left inside of me.

But I had to find it. I had to find enough magic to stop this bloodletting, once and forever.

I searched inside of me, where everything was numb and empty and tired. Magic comes from the heart, from your feelings, your deepest expressions of desire. That's why black magic is so easy—it comes from lust, from fear and anger, from things that are easy to feed and make grow. The sort I do is harder. It comes from something deeper than that, a truer and purer source—harder to tap, harder to keep, but ultimately more elegant, more powerful.

My magic. That was at the heart of me. It was a manifestation of what I believed, what I lived. It came from my desire to see to it that someone stood between the darkness and the people it would devour. It came from my love of a good steak, from the way I would sometimes cry at a good movie or a moving symphony. From my life. From the hope that I could make things better for someone else, if not always for me.

Somewhere, in all of that, I touched on something that wasn't tapped out, in spite of how horrible the past days had been, something that hadn't gone cold and numb inside of me. I grasped it, held it in my hand like a firefly, and willed its energy out, into the circle I had created with the spinning amulet on the end of its chain.

It began to glow, azure-blue like a candle flame. The light spread down the chain and to the amulet, and when it reached it the light became incandescent, the pentacle a brilliant light at the end of the chain, spinning a circle of light around me, trailing motes of dust that fell like starlight to the grass around me.

"*Vento,*" I whispered, and then called, more loudly, "*Vento servitas. Ventas, vento servitas!*" In the bushes, the loup-garou snarled quietly, and its eyes brightened, burned with scarlet fury. It started moving toward me.

Without warning, Murphy stepped between me and the loup-garou, her gun held in both hands in a shooter's stance, though the cast made that awkward. She held her gun pointed directly at me. "Harry," she said in a very calm tone. "Get down on the ground. Right now."

My eyes widened. I could see over Murphy. I could see the loup-garou, moving rapidly toward her through the trees. I saw it focus on her, felt its malice and hunger spread toward her and envelop her.

I couldn't speak. I couldn't break the chant, or stop whirling the amulet. To do so would have released the energy I'd gathered, the very last strength I had in me. My head hammered with pain that would have had me screaming on any other night. I kept the amulet whirling, spraying motes of light, the brilliant white pentacle at the end of a leash of blue light.

"I mean it, Harry," Murphy said. "I don't know what you're doing, but *get down*." Her eyes were intense, and she lifted the gun, thumbing back the hammer.

Trust. Whatever trust she'd had in me was gone. She'd seen or thought of something that made her think I was trying to betray her. The loup-garou rushed closer, and I thought, with a sick feeling in my stomach, that Susan and the Alphas hadn't even had time to make it off the estate yet, much less all the way back to the van. If the loup-garou got through me, it would kill them, one by one, follow their trail like a hound and tear them apart.

"Harry," Murphy said, her voice pleading. Her hand was shaking. "Please, Harry. Get down."

The loup-garou came through the woods in a sudden rush, and Murphy drew in a breath, ready to fire. I kept the amulet whirling and felt the power grow, my head splitting with agony. And made my choice. I just hoped that I could finish the job before Murphy gunned me down. Everything of the past few days came down to that single instant.

It all slowed down, giving me time to view it in agonizing detail.

The loup-garou rose up behind Murphy, leaping toward her through the air. It was still huge, still powerful, and more terrifying than ever. Its jaws were open wide, aimed for her blond head, and could crush it with a single snap.

Murphy narrowed her eyes, peering down the shaking barrel of her gun. Flame blossomed from the barrel, reaching out toward me. She wasn't twenty feet away from me. I didn't think there was any way she could miss, and I thought, with a pang of sadness, that I wanted a chance to apologize to her before the end. For everything.

"Vento servitas!" I shouted and released the spell, the circle, and the amulet, as the sound of the shot hit me like a slap in the face. Power rushed out of me, everything I had left in me, focused and magnified by the circle and the time I had taken to refine it, flying forward at the leaping loup-garou. Something hot and painful hammered into my torso—almost like it had hit my back. I toppled forward, too weak and tired to care anymore. But I watched what happened to the amulet.

The pentacle flew toward the loup-garou like a comet, incandescent white, and struck the creature's breast like lightning hammering into an ancient tree. There was a flash of light, too much power unleashed in a flaring of energy as the mystic substance shattered the loup-garou's invulnerability, carved into it, coursed through it in a blinding blue-white shower of sparks. Blue fire erupted from its chest, its black heart's blood ignited into blinding flame, and the creature screamed, arching backward in agony. There was the sound of thunder, flashes of more light, someone screaming. Maybe it was me.

The loup-garou fell to earth. And changed. Muzzle melted back into human face. Fangs and claws faded. Warped muscles slithered away into globs of clear, preternatural ooze that would quickly vanish. Fur disappeared. Knotted limbs straightened into clean arms and legs—until Harley MacFinn lay before me, partly upon his side, one hand pressed to his heart.

The silver of my amulet's chain spilled out between his fingers and dangled down his chest. He stared down at the wound for a moment, and then I saw him relax. MacFinn looked up, and in his face I saw all the grief and agony and impotent rage, everything he'd felt during all those years of being unable to control himself, cursed to cause death and destruction when all he wanted was to open a park for the wildlife. And then it all flooded out of him. His eyes cleared and warmed as he looked at me, and he gave me a small, quiet smile. It was an expression of forgiveness. Something to let me know that he understood.

Then he laid down his head, and was gone.

My own blackness followed soon after.

Chapter
Thirty-four

I woke up.

That surprised me, in itself.

I woke up to see the moon still high overhead, and to feel Murphy's hand on my forehead. "Come on, Harry," she whispered. "Don't do this to me."

I blinked my eyes a few times and whispered, "You *shot* me, Murph. I can't believe you shot me."

She blinked her eyes at me, to hold back tears. "You stupid jerk," she said, her voice gentle. "You should have got down when I told you to."

"I was busy."

She glanced over her shoulder, at MacFinn's silent, still form. "Yeah. I saw, after." She turned back to me, looking a little past me, focused elsewhere.

"It's all right," I said. "I forgive you." I thought it very generous of me, appropriate to the last moments of a man's life.

Murphy blinked at me. And then stiffened. "You what?"

"Forgive you, Murph. For shooting me. Your job and all, I understand."

Murphy's eyes narrowed dangerously. "You think . . ." she said. Her face twisted with disgust and she sputtered for a moment, and then spat to one side. She began again. "You think that I thought you were one of the bad guys, still, and I shot you because you wouldn't surrender?"

I felt too weak and dizzy to argue. "Hey. It's understandable. Don't worry about it." I shivered. "I'm so cold."

"We're *all* cold, moron," Murphy snapped. "A front came

through about the same time they threw us in that freaking pit. It must be below forty, already, and we're wet besides. Sit up, El Cid."

I blinked at her. "I . . . Uh. What?"

"Sit up, dummy," Murphy said. "Look behind you."

I did sit up, and it didn't hurt much worse than it had earlier this evening, surprising me again. I looked behind me.

Denton was there. He held a fallen branch in one hand, like a club. His eyes were wide and staring and savage, his face pale with loss of blood. There was a neat hole in his forehead, right in the middle. I blinked at the body for a moment.

"But . . . How did he . . . ?"

"I shot *him*, you jerk. He came running up behind you, just as I came back from giving first aid to that naked woman. Tera West. I was shaking too hard to have a safe shot with you standing, and I didn't know the loup-garou was coming up behind *me*." Murphy stood up. "I can't believe this," she said and turned to walk away. "You thought I shot you."

"Murph," I protested. "Murph, give me a break. I mean, I thought . . ."

She snorted at me over her shoulder. She snorts well for someone with a cute little button of a nose. "You *didn't* think, Dresden," she said, flipping her hair back from her eyes. "Dramatic death scene. Noble sacrifice, right? Tragically misunderstood? Hah! I understand you, buddy. You're such a pompous, arrogant, pretentious, chauvinistic, hopelessly old-fashioned, stupidly pigheaded . . ." Murphy went on in graphic detail and at great length about me as she walked away to call the police, and an ambulance, and it was music to my ears.

I lay back on the grass, tired but smiling. Things were all right between us.

The police had one hell of a time sorting out the mess at Marcone's place. I made sure to collect all the wolf belts. Murphy helped me. We burned them, right there, in a stinking fire made of tree branches. It was too hard for me to throw them in. Murph did it for me. She understands things, sometimes, that I couldn't ever explain to her. Later, I went with Murph to Carmichael's funeral. She went with me to Kim Delaney's. Those are the kind of things friends do for each other.

Mr. Hendricks, as it turns out, had worn his Kevlar under the black fatigues. They put me next to him in the ambulance that night when I finally left the scene. They'd bared his chest, and it was a solid mass of purple bruises, so that we were a matched set. He glowered at me in silence, but he breathed steadily through the oxygen mask on his face. I felt absurdly cheered when I saw him alive. All things considered, can you blame me?

Marcone got arrested on general principles, but nothing stuck. Though everything had happened on his property, injuries on the FBI agents indicated that they had all done one another in, or been killed by an animal—except for Denton, of course. None of the peace officers there had possessed a warrant, et cetera, et cetera. I hear his lawyers had him out in less than three hours.

Marcone called me a few days later and said, "You owe me your life, Mr. Dresden. Are you sure we can't talk business?"

"The way I see it, John," I told him, "you owe me *your* life. After all, even if you'd cut yourself free, you'd have just fallen down into the pit and got eaten up with the rest of us. I figure you thought your highest chances of survival were in freeing me, the wizard who deals with this kind of thing, to handle it."

"Of course," Marcone said, with a note of disappointment in his voice. "I'd just hoped you hadn't realized it. Nonetheless, Harry—"

"Don't call me Harry," I said, and hung up on him.

Susan filmed the death of the loup-garou from less than fifty yards away with a pretty good zoom lens and special light-sensitive film. The light from my amulet illuminated the scene rather dramatically without really showing many details. You can only see my back, and it looks like I'm swinging a glow stick around, and then throwing it at the monster, which can be seen only in shadowy detail as something large and furry. At the point where I released the spell, there's a burst of static about a second long, where the magic messed up Susan's camera, even from that far away.

In the film, the static clears and you can see Murphy shoot Denton off of my back, just before he brains me with his club. Then she spins around like Rambo, jumps out of the way of the leaping furry something-or-other, and empties the rest of her clip into the thing out of reflex.

Murph and I both know the bullets didn't hurt it at all, that it was just a reflexive gesture on her part, but I don't need the attention. She was quite the hero according to the camera, and that was fine with me.

Susan's film went on the morning news and was shown for about two days afterward, exclusively on WGN Channel Nine, and it impressed Chicago a lot. The film made Murphy popular enough, with voters, that a bunch of city councilmen went to bat for her, and the internal affairs investigation got called off. She carries a little bit more clout now than she did before. The politicians down at City Hall paid for a real name tag for her office door.

The weird thing was that the film just vanished after two days. No one knew what happened to it, but the film technician in the room with the exclusive WGN Channel Nine videotape disappeared, too, leaving only a few scattered and low-quality copies. A couple of days later, some experts spoke up claiming that the tape had to be fake, and decrying it as a simple hoax perpetrated by a tabloid.

Some people just can't deal with the thought of the supernatural being real. Federal government is like that, a lot. But I'm thinking that if anyone in the government *did* believe, they would just as soon not have had proof of the existence of werewolves and the instability of a local FBI agent showing at five, six, and ten.

The film's disappearance didn't stop Susan from getting a

promotion at the *Arcane*, a big raise, and a guest slot on the Larry King show, plus a few other places. She looked good doing it, too, and made people think. She's getting her column syndicated. Maybe, in a few hundred years, people might actually be willing to consider what was real in the world with an open mind.

But I doubted it.

I didn't call Susan for a while, after she had seen me so far gone into being a monster that I might as well have been one. She didn't pressure me, but kept her presence known. She'd send me flowers, sometimes, or have a pizza delivered to my office when I was working late. Hell of a girl.

Tera was badly injured, but recovered thanks to her own reversion to human form, and Murphy's quick first aid. She asked me to meet her at Wolf Lake Park a few weeks later, and when I showed up, she was there, wearing just a long black cloak.

"I wished to tell you that what you did was necessary. And I wished to tell you good-bye," she said. And slipped the cloak off. She was naked, with a few new, wrinkled scars. "Good-bye."

"Where will you go?" I asked.

She tilted those odd amber eyes at me. "I have family," she said. "I have not seen them in a long time. I will return to them now."

"Maybe you'll call, sometime?"

Her eyes sparkled, and she smiled at me, a little sadly. "No, Harry Dresden. That is not the way of my kind. Come to the great mountains in the Northwest one winter. Perhaps I will be there." And then she shimmered into the shape of a great timber wolf, and vanished into the sunset.

All those people shape-shifting into wolves, and I had never once considered the possibility of a wolf shape-shifting into a person. I picked up Tera's cloak, musing, and took it home with me, as a reminder to keep my mind even more open to the realms of possibility.

The Alphas decided that I'm about the greatest thing since

sliced bread. Which isn't exactly the most thrilling thing in the world for me. They asked me to a campout with them, which I reluctantly attended, where all dozen-odd young people swore friendship and loyalty to me, and where I spent a lot of time blinking and trying to say nothing. They're just itching for me to lead them in some meaningful crusade against evil. Hell, I have trouble just paying the bills.

When I took some time to think about all that had happened, I couldn't help but think that the last several months had been a little too crazy for coincidence. First, a power-drunk warlock had appeared out of nowhere, and I had to duke it out with him in his own stronghold before he murdered me outright. And then, Denton and his people showed up with enchanted wolf belts and raised hell.

I never had found out who exactly was behind the warlock who showed up the previous spring. Black wizards don't just grow up like toadstools, you know. Someone has to teach them complicated things like summoning demons, ritual magic, and clichéd villain dialogue. Who had been his teacher?

And Denton and company had shown up six months later. Someone had provided them with those belts. Someone had warned Denton that I was dangerous, that I or someone like me from the Council would go after him. And by telling him that, they had pointed him at me like a gun, determined to kill me.

I'm not much of a believer in coincidence. Could it have been one of my enemies on the White Council? One of the beings of the Nevernever who had come to hate me? I was on the list of a number of nasty things, for one reason or another.

"You know what?" I told Mister one night in front of the fire. "Maybe I've finally gone around the bend, but I think someone might be trying to kill me."

Mister looked up at me, his feline features filled with a supreme lack of concern, and rolled over so that I could rub his tummy. I did, pensive and comfortable before the fire, and thought about who it might be. And then thought that I might be getting a little stir-crazy. I hadn't gone anywhere but to work and back home for a couple of weeks. Too much work and no play makes Harry a paranoid boy.

I reached for the phone and started spinning the dial to Susan's number. Mister batted at my hand approvingly.

"Or maybe I'm just too stupid to get out of trouble's way, eh?"

Mister rumbled a deep, affirmative purr in his chest. I settled back to ask Susan over, and enjoyed the warmth of the fire.